"Reminds you of... nyet?" Serov smi...

"Reminds me more of East Germany when we were thwarting the Stasi." Klykov grinned. "Look at you with your grandfather's gun. Already having to reload. You should have one of these." He shook his Beretta. "Would be better to have two."

"Is better to only have six rounds." Serov snapped the cylinder closed with a flick of his wrist. "Is not good to forget count and run out of bullets at wrong time."

"They say math keeps the mind sharp."

"Until it is blown out of your head."

Annja started to move, but Klykov restrained her. In the next moment, another wave of gunfire tore through the apartment wall.

"I wish I had grenade," Serov said in a low voice. "Grenade would make this thing so much simpler."

"Grenade would mean Annja could not question Onoprienko about the elephant," Klykov countered.

Serov nodded. "We must not let that happen. Others may get the wrong impression because we look weak."

Look weak? Annja didn't even have a response to that. The old Russian gangsters had already killed a handful of men and somehow dodged hundreds of bullets. She stayed low with both hands locked on her pistol.

It was a massacre, and Annja was in the middle of it.

Titles in this series:

Destiny
Solomon's Jar
The Spider Stone
The Chosen
Forbidden City
The Lost Scrolls
God of Thunder
Secret of the Slaves
Warrior Spirit
Serpent's Kiss
Provenance
The Soul Stealer
Gabriel's Horn
The Golden Elephant
Swordsman's Legacy
Polar Quest
Eternal Journey
Sacrifice
Seeker's Curse
Footprints
Paradox
The Spirit Banner
Sacred Ground
The Bone Conjurer
Tribal Ways
The Dragon's Mark
Phantom Prospect
Restless Soul
False Horizon
The Other Crowd
Tear of the Gods
The Oracle's Message
Cradle of Solitude
Labyrinth
Fury's Goddess
Magic Lantern
Library of Gold
The Matador's Crown
City of Swords
The Third Caliph
Staff of Judea
The Vanishing Tribe
Clockwork Doomsday
Blood Cursed
Sunken Pyramid
Treasure of Lima
River of Nightmares
Grendel's Curse
The Devil's Chord
Celtic Fire
The Pretender's Gambit

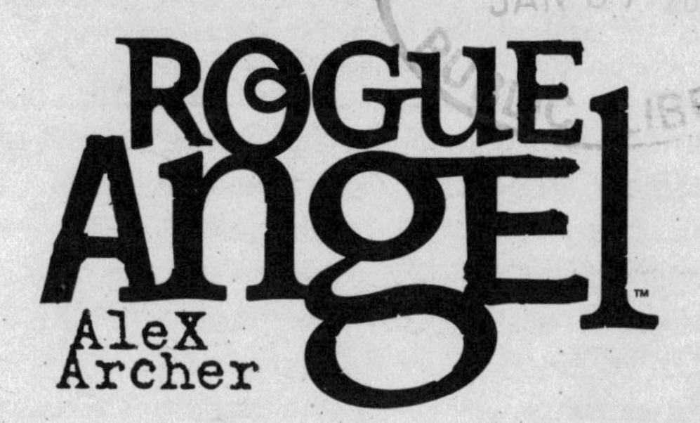

THE PRETENDER'S GAMBIT

A GOLD EAGLE BOOK FROM
WORLDWIDE®

TORONTO • NEW YORK • LONDON
AMSTERDAM • PARIS • SYDNEY • HAMBURG
STOCKHOLM • ATHENS • TOKYO • MILAN
MADRID • WARSAW • BUDAPEST • AUCKLAND

First edition November 2014

ISBN-13: 978-0-373-62171-2

The Pretender's Gambit

Special thanks and acknowledgment to
Mel Odom for his contribution to this work.

Printed in U.S.A.

THE LEGEND

...THE ENGLISH COMMANDER TOOK JOAN'S SWORD AND RAISED IT HIGH.

The broadsword, plain and unadorned, gleamed in the firelight. He put the tip against the ground and his foot at the center of the blade. The broadsword shattered, fragments falling into the mud. The crowd surged forward, peasant and soldier, and snatched the shards from the trampled mud. The commander tossed the hilt deep into the crowd.

Smoke almost obscured Joan, but she continued praying till the end, until finally the flames climbed her body and she sagged against the restraints.

Joan of Arc died that fateful day in France, but her legend and sword are reborn....

Prologue

Amchitka, Rat Islands
Aleutian Island, Russian Empire 1784

A death scream woke Hidari Kaneko in his cold bed and filled him with fear. *It's begun. They have attacked. Now we will all die.*

For a moment he clung desperately to the hope that he had only had a nightmare summoned by the ill luck that had plagued the crew of *Shinsho-maru* since the ship had sunk in the freezing water of the Bering Sea months ago. He had been the ship's pilot, charting the course until that had become impossible due to the storm and the damage done to the vessel.

Fifteen Japanese crewmen had survived the storm at Enshu and seven months of drifting helplessly till they reached the Aleutian Islands and the Russian Empire located on Amchitka. The spit of land was part of the Rat Islands that hung like a skeletal finger crooked at the Bering Sea in the freezing north of the land called Alaska.

At least, the five Russians who manned the trading post there claimed to be an empire. The Russians were all big men, noisy and loud and boastful, and the Japanese sailors did not fit in well with them. Still, the ship's crew weathered the winter at the Russian outpost, and they persevered in the hope that a trade ship would soon drop anchor there and agree to take them away from the barren landscape.

However, the fur trade in the Aleutian Islands had dropped off miserably. Ships seldom made landings at Amchitka these days, which was why there were only five Russians occupying the fort now. That decrease in trade had angered the native people, too. They had agreed to allow the foreigners to stay there in return for trade, for the tobacco, iron and other goods they so enjoyed. In the past few days, that anger had escalated to near violence, and Kaneko doubted the Russians could stand against the Aleuts. Five men against hundreds of Aleut warriors were impossible odds.

Only that morning, Nezimov, the leader of the Russians, had ordered the execution of the Aleut chief's daughter because he felt she did not try to support his position. Nezimov had earlier taken the young woman as his lover as part of the trade pact. Kaneko had only known the cruelty of sea before witnessing the callous murder, but he had been little more than a boy when he'd shipped out so there was still yet much he had not seen. He had not believed Nezimov would go through with the deed until the young woman lay dead, her life's blood pouring over the frozen ground.

Daikokuya Kodayu, captain of the Japanese vessel, had not agreed with Nezimov's course of action, but they were guests of the Russians so he could not argue for the young woman's fate. Or perhaps he, too, had not thought the Russians would go so far. In any event, all of their lots were now cast with their hosts.

Kaneko sat on his bed and peered through the darkness. He shivered against the frigid temperatures that filled every night since he'd been there. It was now May, and he had begun to believe that winter never stayed its hand in these lands. Kaneko wished only to go back to his warm home, or even the harsh existence aboard a ship. Anything to be off of this dreadful island.

Rifles barked and men screamed in pain and anger. Several objects hit the side of the small log cabin where Kaneko resided with five of his shipmates.

"What is going on?" Churyo asked in his grumbling voice. He was an older sailor, one who had been on many voyages. He had learned to enjoy the Russians' vodka and often drank far too much of it. In the soft darkness of evening that filled the cabin, he slurred his words.

"I do not know." Nakagawa pushed himself up from his bed and draped sleeping furs over his thin shoulders as he walked toward the nearest window. He, too, was an older man, a fisherman before he became a sailor. He worked with the Russians on the furs, trading his labors for drink and tobacco.

More objects thumped against the walls of the cabin and Kaneko flinched at every beat. Another volley of rifle shots cracked and echoed outside, sounding nearer this time.

"Light the lantern so that we may see what is going on." Yamashita stirred in his top bunk, rising up too quickly and banging his head on the low ceiling.

"Fool! Do not turn on the lantern," Churyo growled. "You will only invite in whatever is going on outside. We do not want those troubles. The darkness is your friend. Light the lantern and you become a target."

Nervously, Kaneko pulled his knives from under his bunk. Neither of them was long enough to be considered a sword, and he had never truly learned to defend himself, but he did not feel as vulnerable with them in his hands.

The cabin door banged open and Captain Kodayu strode inside. The chill wind followed him and banished some of the heat generated by the small fireplace. In his thirties, the captain was short and broad, rather soft in the middle. During the past months spent with the Russians, he had put weight back on that he'd lost while they'd been adrift.

"The Aleuts have attacked," Kodayu announced while gripping the hilt of the sword sheathed at his hip. "We must prepare to defend ourselves. Quickly."

"This is not our fight," Churyo objected in a surly tone. "The Russians killed that woman, not us."

"Do you believe the Aleuts will think about that when they overtake the fort?" Kodayu glared at Churyo. "Get out of that bed and dress or I will kill you myself."

Cursing softly, Churyo clambered from the bunk. All knew that Kodayu was an accomplished swordsman.

Kaneko lay his knives aside and dressed hurriedly as another volley of rifle shots pierced the night.

DRESSED IN HIS COAT, the hood pushed back so it did not interfere with his peripheral vision, Kaneko followed Captain Kodayu out into the late-evening gloom. He held his knives in his hands and hoped that he did not have to use them, and he hoped that he would not be dead before morning. He did not know if he could find his ancestors and the Celestial Heavens from this place if he were killed here.

The ground remained frozen and traces of dirty snow still gleamed white under the moonlight in some places. The breeze coming in from the Bering Sea chafed Kaneko's exposed face with burning claws. The pain would leave as soon as his face numbed, but that would take time and there could be permanent damage.

The walls of the Russian fort were low, but they were strong enough and high enough to hold back the Aleuts and provide protection for the cabins contained within. Nemizov's strong voice carried as he shouted orders and curses. Kaneko understood more of the curse words than he did of the orders, but the Russians responded at once, reloading their rifles, taking aim and firing again. None of them seemed overly distraught, obviously confident in their abilities, and Kaneko took heart in that.

Cautiously, the young pilot ducked into a position next to the rough-hewn timber of the wall where the Russian riflemen formed a line. He peered over the top while the Russians reloaded again. Aleut warriors took shelter along the timberline, but Nemizov's men proved to be capable marksmen. Or maybe it was only that there were too many natives to miss.

When the Russians fired, Aleut warriors fell, and the wounded and dying tripped others who surged behind them. Some of the Aleuts were dead before they hit the ground, but others cried out for mercy and rescue by their fellow warriors. In the darkness, seeing the warriors clearly was difficult, but Kaneko made out the long flowing fur robes and conical hats the men wore, as well as the long thin spears they hurled with incredible accuracy. Several of the spears stuck out from the side of the cabin where Kaneko had been sleeping. More had pierced the wall, and more still littered the yard beyond.

Captain Kodayu called out to his men, ordering them to take up arms. A few of the crew had rifles. Kaneko did not, nor did he care for the loud explosions the weapons made or the rough way they handled. He wished he had a rifle now, though, and that he would never get the opportunity to use his knives.

The rifles cracked again and again. The Aleuts fell and never reached the fort.

IN THE EARLY minutes of the dawn, after hours of silence, the Aleuts attacked again. With the light, Kaneko could more clearly see the warriors. During the night they had dragged away their dead, but more of them piled up now. The Russians had stayed up the whole night keeping watch, and their aim was even better in the morning light. Despite the cold, the men loaded and shot smoothly, like machines.

Gunsmoke eddied around the wall of the fort and tasted acrid to Kaneko as he stayed at his post. Finally, though, the second attack ended in retreat, as well.

Zeminov, bold and large, his weathered face almost lost in a tangle of long wild hair and his bushy beard, came to Kodayu. The brass buttons on his coat gleamed.

"We will not stay here, Captain Kodayu. I do not believe those savages will relent, and we will eventually run low on powder and shot, no matter how many graves we fill."

"I agree." Kodayu understood Russian enough to know what the fur traders talked about, but Kaneko suspected that his captain was not so confident in his speaking abilities in that language. Kodayu always kept his answers short and to the point.

"Grab what you can and we will make for the beach when the time comes."

"To do what?"

"To sail away from this place."

"There is no ship."

"Then we will make one. We can no longer stay here."

ESCAPING THE FORT was not easy, and the Russian leader proved more brutal than Kaneko had suspected. They charged into the Aleut village and took women and children as prisoners. Shortly thereafter, the Russians executed four of the Aleut leaders and there was no more talk of attacking the Russians because the indigenous people fled by boat to neighboring islands.

Sails on the horizon drew the group to the beach. Kaneko's heart leaped when he saw the Russian ship because it would, no matter where he ended up at first, take him away from this godforsaken island. He stood on the beach and gave thanks to the luck that had brought the ship to the island.

Then he noticed how low it sailed in the water, and how sluggishly it glided. Kaneko's heart stilled when the ship suddenly listed over to its starboard side.

"What is wrong?" Nakagawa asked.

"The ship is stricken," Churyo answered. "It is sinking."

As Kaneko watched with failing spirits, the ship dipped lower into the water and finally fell over onto her side. Her sails flapped in the waves instead of catching the wind.

Sailors aboard the vessel threw themselves over the side. Those that could swim struck out for the shoreline, and those that couldn't swim drowned or grabbed on to pieces of buoyant debris and kicked themselves forward.

Only twenty sailors made it ashore. The ship floated out in the water like a dead whale turned belly up to the sun.

DAYS PASSED AND the supplies rescued from the ship ran short. The threat of the Aleuts returning to continue their attacks remained. In time, Kodayu came to his men, gathering them in one of the cabins they had shared. When they had arrived on Amchitka, they had numbered fifteen. Six of them had perished of sickness over the winter and lay in lonely graves far from home.

At least their bones were at rest even if their spirits wandered, Kaneko sometimes thought.

"The Russian has a plan," Kodayu said as he looked around at the ring of faces in the room. "He does not think another ship will come soon, and we grow short on supplies since we are no longer trading with the Aleuts. We are also lacking in powder and shot. If we lose the rifles, we have no defenses."

Churyo growled a curse.

Kodayu ignored that and continued smoothly, as was his way. "The plan is to build a ship."

"From what?" Churyo demanded. "We cannot raise the one that has sunk in the harbor, and there are no trees worthy of such an endeavor."

"We make a ship from whatever we have available. It is better than dying here with a spear through our guts or of hunger."

No one argued with the captain.

THE "VESSEL," AND everyone grudgingly called it that, was constructed from driftwood and had otter skins hanging from makeshift halyards as sails. Practice voyages out in the harbor proved that the thing floated and steered easily enough, but everyone had doubts about it withstanding the sea during the journey to Russia.

Still, there was no other way. Zeminov spoke of a Russian land, a place he called Kamchatka, that was closest to their present location. They would make for that place, he said, and the Japanese sailors would be cared for there.

"We will join the Russians," Captain Kodayu said.

"We will drown in the sea," challenged Churyo.

"You may stay here if you wish," the captain replied. "Any of you that do not wish to try his luck upon the sea may stay here."

THE NEXT MORNING, they put all the supplies and water aboard the craft that they could manage and set sail for Kamchatka. No one stayed behind.

1

Now

Annja Creed walked toward the small apartment building on the other side of the police line. Yellow tape strung between police sawhorses held back the early morning neighborhood crowd that had gathered. Curious onlookers dressed in everyday clothes as well as pajamas and robes pushed through the crowd.

Two news anchors, neither of whom Annja recognized and both of whom looked young, stood in bright pools of camcorder lights and tried to be professional. One of the anchors spoke in English and the other spoke in Russian. Brighton Beach, south of Brooklyn, was nicknamed Little Odessa because so many Russian immigrants lived there.

Annja liked visiting the neighborhood to practice her Russian, and to see some of the artifacts many of the residents had brought from the "old country." Several small restaurants served meals she enjoyed.

"Excuse me." Annja made her way through the crowd, nudging gently and pushing only occasionally. She was five feet ten inches tall barefooted, and tonight she wore boots. Her chestnut hair was pulled back in a ponytail. She also wore a professional intensity that encouraged the gawkers to step aside. She'd also deliberately chosen a black duster that gave her a "cop" look. Attitude meant everything.

The crowd parted and she stopped in front of a grizzled uniformed cop who held up a hand. He was thick and broad, and seemed bored. His eyes constantly roved just like a cop's always did when in a difficult situation.

"You'll have to stop right there, miss." His Brooklyn accent was thick enough to cut.

"Would you let Detective McGilley know that Annja Creed is here? He asked me to come. I'm a consultant." Annja pulled her NYPD ID from her pocket. Bart McGilley, the police detective she was here to see, had arranged for the ID after she'd helped on a few cases involving stolen artifacts. She didn't often use it.

The cop suddenly smiled as he looked at her. "Hey, I know you." He pointed a thick forefinger at Annja. "You're on that TV show. The monster thing."

Annja smiled politely and nodded. *Chasing History's Monsters*, the cable television show she cohosted, had a big fan base. A few of the gawkers gathered around her began to talk and whisper her name, and suddenly the focus shifted from the crime scene to Annja, which made her uncomfortable.

Bart wouldn't be happy about it either. Now that Annja had been recognized, chances were good that whatever story was unfolding here would get more airplay. Of course, Doug Morrell, the show's producer, would love the free advertising.

The cop lifted the tape. "You come right ahead, Ms. Creed. Detective McGilley is waiting for you upstairs."

Annja ducked under the tape and stood waiting on the other side. An officer there took her name for the first-responder's report. One of the camcorders swung in her direction and bathed her in light. She ignored it and stared at the building ahead of her.

Seven stories tall, the apartment building looked like most of the other buildings in the area. New York was known for its towering skyline along Manhattan, but most of the buildings were seven floors or less because no elevators had to be installed. Many of the windows on the fourth floor glowed with golden light now and Annja was willing to wager that was going to be her destination.

The cold wind raced around Annja and made her put her hands in the duster pockets.

The cop squeezed the handitalker clipped to his left shoulder. "This is Sergeant Vasari outside. I got Annja Creed here for Detective McGilley." He listened for a moment, then turned his attention to Annja. "You can go on in, Ms. Creed. They're waiting for you."

Annja nodded.

"You might want to watch yourself up there." Vasari grimaced. "Heard this one was messy."

Great, Annja thought. Then she headed toward the building.

A FORENSICS GUY was waiting for Annja when she reached the fourth-floor landing. He was young and dark complexioned, hair messy in a current style and wore a lab coverall. "Annja Creed?"

"I am." Annja started to pull out the ID again.

The crime-scene tech held up a hand and grinned. "No need. I know you."

Annja put the ID away. "You've seen the show?"

"Not yet, but I've seen the ads out on Times Square. You ask me, the video doesn't do you justice."

Annja smiled. "Thank you."

"Are you flirting with my consultant, Kai?" Down the hallway, Detective Bart McGilley stood outside an apartment door. Six feet two and broad-shouldered, Bart was an imposing figure. He wore a dark blue suit coat and matching turtleneck under a charcoal gray duster. His kept his black hair cut short and his chin chiseled, but he had a five-o'clock shadow now.

"No, Detective McGilley, I am not." Kai winked at Annja. He held up a pair of pull-on pale blue disposable footies. "I'm diligently working to keep our crime scene secure while trying to maintain the public trust and present a polite demeanor."

Taking the booties, Annja quickly pulled them on, then added the disposable gloves. "Thanks."

"Sure." Kai's face turned serious and all humor left his eyes. "All kidding aside, what you're gonna see is pretty bad."

"I'll be all right. Thank you." Annja couldn't remember all the violence she'd seen since she'd inherited Joan of Arc's sword and changed her life. She didn't regret taking up the sword, though. She'd gotten to help a lot of people, but more than that she'd gotten to see a lot of things that had been lost to history forever. The deaths were going to happen, and she'd stopped more from taking place. The trade-off was worth it.

Skirting the bloody footprints and the evidence markers beside them, she walked down the hallway to join Bart. They'd been friends for years and she'd enjoyed his company. He was one of the few people who wasn't an archaeologist or a television fanboy who could listen to her for hours. She returned the favor when he needed a sounding board about a case.

"Did I get you out of bed?" Bart asked.

The smell of death lingered in the apartment behind Bart, an odor that Annja had grown far too familiar with. She breathed more shallowly.

"I was up working."

"Anything interesting?"

"Authenticating a couple of Mayan pieces for a collector."

"Sounds boring. Everybody's got a Mayan piece tucked away somewhere."

"I was also binge watching *Dr. Who* on Netflix."

A small smile twisted Bart's lips and Annja was glad to lighten his mood. He took his work seriously, and he didn't take too much time off from it. That was one of the things they had in common.

"Where are you in the Whoinverse?"

"Still missing David Tennant."

"Aren't we all." Bart's eyes narrowed as they neared the door. "I wish you didn't have to see this. The ME's office is backlogged tonight, so they couldn't make it out here to get the body, otherwise I'd have the deceased moved before I called you in. But I want to proceed with this as soon as I can because I don't want whoever did this to get away."

"It'll be okay."

Bart hesitated just a second, then turned and ushered her into apartment 4F. The door around the lock had been broken. Pieces of the locking mechanism hung shattered. Other pieces had fallen onto the floor.

THE ROOM HELD crime-scene techs and Detective Joe Broadhurst, Bart's current partner, and there was precious little room left over. Broadhurst was in his midforties, thin and fit. He had dark hair and dark eyes, a neatly trimmed goatee that—just for a moment—made Annja think of Garin Braden.

"Professor Creed." Broadhurst smiled politely and nodded at Annja.

"Detective Broadhurst."

"I would say it's good to see you. Instead, I'm just going to apologize I'm seeing you again under these circumstances."

Annja nodded and turned her attention to the room. The living area was small and neatly kept for the most part. "An older man lives here by himself?"

"Yes." Broadhurst seemed a little surprised. "Somebody told you?"

Annja pointed to the foil remains of the TV dinner sitting on the coffee table. "Single guy." She pointed to the small television in the corner. It was an older set, not a flatscreen. "Older guy who listens to the television more than he watches it." She pointed at the wall where a single black-and-white photograph of a young man and woman hung. "I'm presuming that's the guy at a much younger age. He lives alone or there would be more photographs." She touched the green easy chair that had seen better days and an equally battered, nonmatching couch. "And better furniture that wouldn't be so dusty."

Broadhurst smiled a little more. "You could be a cop."

"She's better than a cop," Bart said. "She's going to be able to help us with the elephant."

"Elephant?" Annja asked. "You've got an elephant in here somewhere? Now that would be a surprise. But if you've got an elephant in here, I'm sure that would have broken the lease. Maybe the floor."

Bart gestured to the back of the apartment. "This is where it gets bad."

"HIS NAME WAS Maurice Benyovszky," Broadhurst said. "According to a couple of the neighbors, he ran a small mail-order business out of his home. He sounds like a little old guy trying to get by. From the looks of the apartment, unless he's got a safe deposit box stuffed full of money somewhere, Benyovszky wasn't getting rich."

The dead man was in his seventies at least, and he might still have looked like the black-and-white picture in the living room if someone hadn't beaten his face into pulp. Dressed in a faded red house robe and pajamas, the old man lay crumpled on the floor in front of a large desk covered with knickknacks, a computer and a digital camera. Paper bags covered his hands, put there by the crime-scene techs to preserve evidence. He might have been five feet tall and weighed a hundred and ten pounds.

Blood stained the back wall and curtains over the room's window and the ceiling in a surprisingly straight line.

"His killer beat him to death with what was probably a hammer of some kind." Bart's voice was calm and hollow, his professional tone when he was talking about a case. "We haven't found the murder weapon yet, but that's what we're looking for. The cast-off blood tells us where the killer and his accomplice were standing."

"There were two of them?" After the initial shock of seeing the body, Annja's mind slipped into problem-solving mode.

"Yeah. The killer—" Bart pointed to large, bloody footprints that were far larger than the dead man would have made "—and the accomplice." He indicated a second set of footprints that were smaller, yet still larger than the victim's.

"Nobody saw anything?" Even though this was the metro area and early in the morning, Annja still struggled to believe no one had come to the old man's aid. He'd had time to yell for help.

"Not till one of the neighbors came through and found the lock on the apartment door shattered. Then there was the blood in the hallway. He decided not to come in or announce himself, got back to his own apartment and called us. This is what we found."

"When?"

"About twelve forty-five. When we found out about the elephant, I wanted to call you."

"Where's the elephant?" Annja asked.

Bart crossed the room over to the computer. "Here."

Walking around the dead man, Annja joined Bart at the computer. He moved the mouse and the monitor came out of hibernation, clearing to reveal a photograph of a white jade elephant. The image gave no indication of how large the piece was, but it was exquisitely rendered with a lot of careful detail.

Taken from a side view, the elephant had its trunk curled in and sharp sheaths that covered its tusks. A thick rectangle lay across its back from its neck to its tail and hung down to almost the rounded stomach. Atop its back, a pair of warriors rode in a covered basket. One of the warriors held a spear. The other held a bow with an arrow nocked. A skullcap covered the elephant's head. On the skullcap, a flowering plant stood out in worn relief.

Annja's interest flared up at once and she leaned closer to the screen. "The elephant looks Persian or Indian."

"How do you know that?" Broadhurst asked.

Bart said nothing, just took out his field notebook and started taking down information.

"The ears," Annja replied. "Indian elephants have smaller ears than African elephants."

"Maybe the guy who made this just liked small-eared elephants." Broadhurst shrugged. "Maybe large ears were harder to make."

Still amazed by the detail, certain that the piece she was looking at was really old and wishing she could examine it for real, Annja shook her head. "Whoever carved this went to a lot of trouble to get things right. Those ears are proportioned just right."

"Okay, I've heard of Indian elephants and the small-ears thing, but I haven't heard of Persian elephants."

"That's because the Persians used Indian elephants. Do you know much about war elephants?"

"No. We don't see much of them in New York."

"The Persians were the first to use elephants in wars. The first time historians know they were used was in the Battle of Gaugamela in 331 BC. King Darius II of Persia fielded fifteen elephants carrying mounted archers and spearmen at the center of his line. Seeing the elephants freaked Alexander the Great out, but it didn't stop him from defeating the Persians and claiming Darius's lands after he killed him. The Indians used war elephants a lot, too, but the possibility that this is a Persian elephant exists."

Broadhurst grimaced and looked a little frustrated. "The history lesson doesn't help us with our murder. Don't put us no closer to the creep that done this."

"Can I look through these files?" Annja asked.

"Sure. Our techs have already been through it. We'll be taking the computer back with us, but you can look through what's up there."

Annja flicked through the photographs. There were nine more images of the elephant, all of them from different angles, none of them with any reference that would tell her how big the piece was.

Before and after the images of the elephant were images of other objects—cups, pottery and toys. All of them looked old, but none of them looked as old as the elephant.

"Can I have copies of these images?" Annja asked. "It'll help me track down anything that might be out there in the archaeological communities concerning this piece."

Bart glanced at Broadhurst, who hesitated only a second before nodding.

"Keep it on the down low," Bart advised. "So far only we and the killers know about the elephant angle." He let out a breath. "And the elephant's only a clue if it wasn't deliberately left on the computer as a red herring."

Annja looked back at the computer monitor. "If this isn't a lead, I should be able to find it pretty quickly for you."

Bart's cell phone rang and he answered it, spoke briefly, then looked over at Broadhurst. "That was Palfrey. They've got the nephews downstairs. Turns out they live on the second floor."

Broadhurst nodded. "I'll stay here with the body. Why don't you question the nephews. Take Professor Creed with you. According to the old man's daughter, the nephews had something to do with our vic's business. Maybe they know something about this missing elephant she can help with."

Bart glanced at Annja. "You up for this? You're still the only antiques expert I have on hand."

"Sure." Curious, Annja followed Bart out of the room, but her mind was locked on the image of the war elephant and the mystery it represented.

2

Calmly despite the tension that ratcheted through him and the knowledge that the NYPD was across the street, Francisco Calapez knocked on the door to apartment 5E and checked the hallway again. At this late hour, no one was there, but in this city it seemed no one slept. People were always moving, always doing things. He did not like being here, and he especially did not like knocking on a stranger's door in the middle of the night.

Unfortunately, since he did not find the thing he had looked for in the old man's rooms and he did not know where it had gone, he was forced to risk this to get more information. Fernando Sequeira did not take failure well.

"Open up, please." He knocked again, dropping his knuckles heavier this time. His pulse beat at his temples as he stared at the window at the end of the hallway. The elevated heart rate wasn't the result of fear. It came from readiness. Whirling red and blue lights from the police cars parked out in the street below alternately tinted the panes.

A few feet back from him, up against the wall and out of sight of the door's fish-eye peephole, Jose Pousao stood waiting with a silenced pistol hidden under his hoodie. He was more slightly built than Calapez, and young enough to be his son, but he listened well and had a taste for killing. That was something that was hard to train into a man. Calapez had always felt that killing was in the blood, a talent a man either had or did not have. Calapez knew he was lucky to be partnered with the younger man. When things got dangerous, Pousao wouldn't hesitate to kill someone. In fact, he wouldn't hesitate to kill everyone who wasn't Calapez.

Just as Calapez was about to knock again, a man's voice answered from the other side. "Hello. Can I help you?"

"Police." Calapez spoke with an American accent, hiding his native Portuguese. Doing something like that was not hard to do after watching bootlegged American movies. He had been a good mimic since he'd been a child.

"I didn't call the police."

"We know that, sir." Calapez curbed his anger. Tonight had already been frustrating because he had not found what he had been sent for, nor did he know where he might find it. The easy thing Fernando Sequeira had asked him to do had turned out not to be so easy, and there had been only one location given. Killing a man—or a woman—was simple enough, but finding things was more difficult. If the elephant had been there, if the old man had not already been dead, the night would have gone more easily. As it was, he was stuck looking for the cursed thing. "We need to look out your window."

A moment passed and Calapez knew the man inside the apartment was studying him. Calapez wore a nondescript coat over a shirt and tie and slacks. A suit in New York City was urban camouflage, like a Hawaiian shirt in Florida around the beaches. Calapez had learned how to blend in while in many places doing Sequeira's business over the years.

"My window?"

"There was a murder next door, sir."

"No one here saw a murder. I was asleep until all the commotion started outside."

"Yes, sir. But there are security cameras on this building that might help us in the search for the killers."

"How does getting into my apartment help you with that?"

"Your apartment is close to one of the cameras. We want to see what the view would be from here before we get the necessary paperwork going."

"Can't you do that from outside?"

"Not from five stories up, sir. We haven't taken the killers into custody yet. They might still be in the neighborhood. They could be in this building. We would like to prevent anyone else from falling victim to them. Your assistance will be appreciated, and your safety may hinge on your cooperation."

The man hesitated for a moment. "Could I see your identification?"

"Of course." Calapez dug the badge and wallet out of his pocket. He'd purchased both from a street dealer who specialized in such things. The dealer had sworn no one could tell the difference.

Evidently the man in the apartment couldn't. The locks snicked back one by one. He opened the door. Of medium height and pasty, myopic behind thick lenses and his gray hair in disarray, the apartment dweller looked like an accountant or a grade-school teacher.

Calapez put away the fake identification, then took out a small notebook and flipped it open with a practiced flick of his wrist. This wasn't the first time he'd pretended to be an official and he'd encountered plenty of the real ones in his line of work.

"Could I have your name, sir?"

"Montgomery. Felix Montgomery."

Calapez swept the living area with a glance. "Are you here alone, Mr. Montgomery?"

"I am."

"Then if I can see your window, I will be only a moment."

Montgomery led the way to the window. Pousao stood nearby and kept watch over the man.

Calapez pulled the drapes to one side and peered out the window. From his vantage point he could see the windows of the apartment where the dead man had lived, but curtains blocked the view inside the rooms.

"Do you know what happened over there?" Montgomery asked.

"A man was killed."

Uneasiness made Montgomery fidget. "Was it a domestic situation?"

"No, sir. A break-in." That much would be on the news in short order. Calapez continued watching.

"That's terrible. There haven't been any break-ins that I've heard about."

"This sort of thing happens in the best neighborhoods, sir."

Calapez turned and looked at Montgomery. "Do you have a camera, sir?"

Montgomery hesitated. "I do. I teach photojournalism."

"Would you mind if I used your camera? I left mine in the squad car."

Montgomery frowned. If he was a schoolteacher, that was probably the same frown he gave students who showed up to class without a pencil or paper. "It's a digital."

"That's fine. I'll need a telephoto lens if you have one."

After another brief hesitation, Montgomery walked toward the back rooms. Pousao trailed him, silent as the man's own shadow. Only a few minutes later, while Calapez watched the group milling in front of the apartment building across the street, Montgomery returned with the camera. The telephoto lens was long and large, professional quality.

"Do you know how to use this?" Montgomery held on to the camera.

"I do."

"I still don't understand why you need to borrow—"

Calapez nodded to Pousao and the younger man drew a short, wide-bladed knife. With a practiced motion, Pousao shoved the blade into Montgomery's neck at the base of the skull. A surprised look of pain filled the man's face as life left him. Calapez snatched the camera from the dead man's hands as the body sagged to the floor.

While the man quivered, Calapez returned his attention to the apartment building across the street. "Put the body in the bedroom. Find a few more things to steal and we'll make this look like a burglary gone wrong."

Pousao grabbed the corpse and pulled it away.

Focusing on the apartment building, Calapez looked through the camera and adjusted the lens to bring the apartment into focus. He couldn't see anything, but he knew it would be a matter of time. Perhaps the police would find the elephant he had been sent there for. Then all he'd have to do would be to retrieve it. The task was more difficult, but he knew Sequeira would not accept anything less.

"Jose."

"Yes."

"I see television reporters out there. Turn on the television and find the coverage. We need to know who the chief investigator is and if they have found the elephant."

Pousao turned on the television and searched the channels till he found one reporting live from the scene. "I have discovered the woman."

"Who is she?" Calapez kept the camera aimed at the apartment building.

"Her name is Annja Creed."

"Is she police?"

"No. She is an archaeologist."

An archaeologist possibly meant the NYPD knew something about the elephant. Sequeira talked to people such as those. He had cultivated a number of resources within that circle. Calapez had visited with some of them himself, to get things Sequeira wanted. A few of those people Calapez had killed to obtain those things. Calapez didn't understand what his employer saw in antiquities, but there was no denying Sequeira's interest.

Calapez took down the archaeologist's name in his official-looking pad, then he extracted his cell phone and placed a call to his employer. Despite the lateness of the hour, or the earliness, depending on a person's point of view, the phone only rang twice before it was answered.

"Do you have it?" Sequeira sounded fully awake. His voice was deep and full-bodied, as if rumbling from a huge chest. Sequeira was a broad man in his forties and worked to stay in shape.

"There has been a complication." Calapez hated giving his employer bad news. Sequeira was not one to easily accept such a thing.

"I have been watching the news. You killed the old man?"

"Not me. He was dead when I arrived there, and the elephant was not to be found."

"Then you must locate it."

"I will. I only wanted you to know where the situation stood."

"I have faith in you, Francisco. Otherwise I would have sent another in your place."

"I will get the piece for you when I can, but there appears to be additional interest in the old man's murder. The police have summoned an archaeologist to the old man's home."

"Then they must suspect what the elephant means."

"Perhaps."

"Find out, my friend. I must know. Perhaps there will be another way to get at this thing."

"I will." Calapez heard the anticipation and frustration in Sequeira's words. Calapez did not know why the elephant piece was so important. His employer kept him in the dark about many things. "I hesitate to ask, but would it be helpful at this point if I knew more about the elephant? What makes it so interesting?"

"There is a legend about the elephant, a thing I must know from it in order to pick up a trail that vanished hundreds of years ago. For me to explain would take hours. Know only that the elephant is but the key to a mystery that has lain buried for hundreds of years as that piece wandered through the hands of queens and warriors. And there is a treasure. I want that treasure, and to find it, I must solve the mystery of the elephant."

"Then I will bring you the elephant."

"See that you do." Sequeira broke the connection.

Calapez returned the phone to his pocket and continued watching the apartment building.

NGUYEN RAO STOOD in the shadows that filled an alley across the street from the police cars and gawkers. The constant strobe of the flashing light bars had ignited a small headache deep within his skull, but that could have been the effects of the cold, as well. He wasn't used to this weather. Cambodia, where he was from, was much more temperate.

He was tall and athletic, dressed in a dark gray business suit under a long coat that was not warm enough. His eyes watered against the chill, or it may have been because he had not slept. The plane ride from Phnom Penh had drained him. He had flown a lot during the time he had been getting his education in England, but he had never learned to relax during the flights.

The arrival at JFK International Airport had been delayed in England, and then there had been confusion with New York Port Authority security that had forced a longer postponement of his assignment. As a result, he had arrived at Maurice Benyovszky's apartment too late to talk to the man regarding the sale of the elephant. Listening to the reporters and the gossiping people in the streets, Rao had learned of the old man's death and was saddened. Life was something meant to be treasured, each a treasure to be enjoyed and to further a person's education of self and that person's place in the world.

He wondered if Benyovszky's murder would in some way dim Vishnu's Eye. Actions impacted many things. Then he wondered when he had started believing in the old legend enough to even question such a thing. He wasn't given to idle fancy.

But there was something to the story. The fact that the elephant existed proved there was some validity to the myth.

A story is only a myth till it becomes part of history. At that point, myth turns into fact. Professor Beliveau had often stated that in his classes. And he would go on to state that they were in the business of separating myth from fact, yet maintaining both because sometimes it was important for a culture to have its myths and legends. Those things shaped generations and gave them a shared history.

If the elephant exists, then the way to the Lost Temple exists.

But the Eye of Vishnu? Would that truly allow a man to bridge the past and the future, to see the things that were and the things that would be?

That would be a very powerful thing. Rao felt guilty for not believing in the Eye more. His temple had discovered the legend years ago, almost lost in their records because of all the strife that had run rampant through his country for so long, but there had been nothing discovered in those ancient texts that would lead the priests to the Lost Temple. The priests had spent years looking for it. Only when the elephant was found on the internet did they find another crumb of the trail that had been left. Even that discovery had been by chance, not by deliberate research.

So much had been lost in all the years of upheaval and invaders. Even now, parts of Cambodia were not at peace, and the shadow of the Khmer Rouge continued to touch the country. A rough voice startled him from his thoughts.

"Hey! What are you doing here? Spying on people? Is that what you're doing?"

Rao chose not to answer, though he stepped sideways to look at the speaker. As a Vietnamese man in this neighborhood, especially at this time of night, he stood out. He hoped that his silence could be mistaken for not understanding the language.

The man who addressed him looked to be around thirty, about Rao's age. But the man was big through the shoulders, and powerful looking. A reddish beard covered his face under a black knit cap that fit tightly to his head. He wore fingerless gloves and a bulky coat. Three other men trailed behind him, all of them about the same age and scruffy looking. All of them held a vulpine gleam to their eyes, predators gazing upon defenseless prey.

"Did you hear me?" The man came closer. "You no speak English?"

Rao actually spoke English quite well. Better than the man standing in front of him as a matter of fact. The man confronting him spoke with a thick Slavic accent.

"I think he's just ignoring you, Vladi," one of the other men said with the same accent. The three of them circled around the bigger man like wolves preparing for a kill.

Glancing up, Rao took in the fire escapes that zig-zagged up to the roofs.

"Don't look away when I'm talking to you." Vladi thumped Rao in the chest with a thick, blunt forefinger. "If you think one of your gangs is going to muscle in on our territory, you got another think coming." The big man grinned and the expression was pure hate. "We're gonna send a message of our own back to your people." He reached for Rao.

Twisting, stepping back and giving ground before the bigger man's hand, Rao avoided his opponent's clumsy effort, caught his wrist and yanked just enough to pull the man off balance. Vladi staggered forward, fell and caught himself on his hands and knees.

Taking advantage of the big man's position, Rao leaped to Vladi's back, used it to propel himself up to catch the railing on the nearest fire escape, and clambered up the other landings as quickly as a squirrel climbing a tree. At the top of the four-story building, he leaned over the edge and looked down.

Vladi had gotten back to his feet. All of them stared at Rao in surprise, then one of them leaped up to pull down the access ladder with a loud clang that drew the attention of the police. Two of the uniformed police officers came over to the alley to investigate, turning on flashlights and holding their pistols in their holsters. Vladi and his cohorts scattered and ran back down the alley as the policemen's flashlights picked them out of the darkness.

Rao continued walking across the rooftop, intending to find a new spot to continue his surveillance. If the elephant was still attainable, he intended to have it. The priests at the temple would expect him to continue the hunt, and he was not prepared to give up on it.

3

"Hey, bro, you can't just hold us here forever. We know our rights. You can't arrest us if we didn't do anything. And this is our home anyway. You can't even be here if we don't want you here. We could make you wait in the hallway."

The speaker was the younger of the two Russian men sitting on the ratty pale green couch that looked like it had been scooped up off the street. The rest of the furniture was ill-matched and just as unkempt, spreading across three different styles and at least thirty years. None of the pieces were collector's items.

Cigarette smoke hung like a cloud in the air. European symphonic heavy-metal tracks spun through the iPod dock on top of a television, showing a futuristic military video game paused in midaction. Something was blowing up but Annja wasn't sure what it was.

She stood behind Bart with her hands in her jacket pockets and didn't say anything. Although a police investigation wasn't something she regularly took part in, she'd seen plenty on television, and she'd watched Bart in action a few times. She felt safe, and she was definitely curious.

The two Russians were obviously related and it showed in their features—the same eyes, the same facial structure. One of them was thin and lupine-faced and maybe twenty, wearing a concert T-shirt, and the other looked slightly older and was beefed up and overweight, like a martial arts fighter who'd been hitting the borscht and beer too often. The younger guy had long dark hair and a spotty beard while the older one was shaven bald and wore a dark beard with lime-green tints.

Based on the look of their apartment, and the stench, and their lackadaisical nature, both of them were delinquents and probably a total waste of time.

"You know your rights?" Bart looked impressed.

The younger brother nodded and fist bumped his brother. They waggled their fingers like the fist bump had caused an explosion. "You bet we do, bro. We know our rights back and front, and you can't just arrest us."

"What would I arrest you for?"

"Nothing, bro." The young one wiped his hands in front of him like he was cleaning a slate. "We ain't done nothing. The police chick outside—" he pointed through the door, indicating the hallway "—she said she just wanted to ask us some questions. Next thing we know, bro, here you are."

"You mean Officer Falcone said she wanted to ask you questions?" Bart asked.

"I didn't get her name, bro. Maybe that was it." His eyelids hung heavily and he moved too loosely to be completely sober. "It was that police chick out there."

"Call her Officer Falcone. She won't be happy with 'police chick.' Trust me."

"Officer Police Chick called you down here, bro? That's what you said, right? That's why you're here?"

Annja didn't know how Bart kept his composure. She was getting frustrated just listening, unable to get the memory of the murdered man out of her mind. Bart sighed in annoyed acceptance. "Yes. She did."

"Why?"

"Why do you think?"

The guy wrapped his arms around himself. "She said my uncle got killed."

"Great-uncle," the brother said quietly. "You forget, Maurice was our great-uncle on Ma's side. Her mother's brother."

"Okay, then, our *great*-uncle. Only, if you ask me, he isn't so great. He's just this old guy. Kind of bossy. Too bossy. Likes to tell people what to do." He looked at Bart. "That true, bro? Somebody killed our great-uncle?"

"I'm afraid so."

"You sure? 'Cause he was kinda old. Coulda just died."

"He didn't just die."

"Maybe he killed himself."

"No. That didn't happen."

"Then I don't know what to tell you, bro. You got me."

"I just have a few questions I'd like to ask," Bart said.

"I'm through answering questions. Through talking about my great-uncle, too. You can't arrest us, so you gotta go." He pointed to the door. "I'm revoking your apartment privileges."

Bart took out his cell phone, poked it for a second, then showed it to the younger man, revealing the mug shot there. "Demyan Koltsov. Is that you?"

The guy straightened up then, squinted and shrugged. "I don't know. Is it?"

"Well, I can arrest you on suspicion of being Demyan Koltsov, take you downtown to fingerprint you and verify that, yes, in fact, you are Demyan Koltsov, and then lock you up."

"Lock me up?" Demyan's eyes widened. "For what, bro? I didn't have nothing to do with that old man getting killed!"

"For lying to a detective in the performance of his duty, for starters. It also says here that Demyan Koltsov is wanted for FTA regarding a weed bust."

Demyan waved that off. "Those are bogus charges, bro. I was entrapped. And that failure-to-appear rap? I told the judge I couldn't be there that day, bro. I had a doctor's appointment. Had a note and everything."

"I'm not interested in an FTA. That's not my business. I want to talk about your great-uncle." Bart put his phone away. "So either you talk to me about Maurice Benyovszky here, or I cuff you and take you downtown to deal with that FTA. We can talk about your great-uncle while you're getting booked."

Demyan looked at his brother. "Can you get me out of jail, Yegor?"

The older brother frowned and shook his head. "I don't have any money. Why you come asking for money from me when you know I ain't got any? You'll just have to stay in jail until I find out if Ma has any money. And if she will bail you out." He lowered his voice into a whisper. "You didn't pay her back for bailing you out on that weed bust."

Demyan sighed like he was the most put-upon man on

the planet. "This ain't my night, bro. My girl's two-timing me with her ex. I lost my part-time job at the pizza place—"

"I don't think you can say you lost that job when you never showed up for a shift," Yegor said.

Demyan pulled his cell phone out of his pocket. "Man, they texted me and told me I was fired." He shook his head sadly. "That would have been a sweet job. I'd have been driving around, delivering pizza, everybody glad to see me."

Yegor clapped his brother on the shoulder with a big hand. "You don't have a car. The car you had was my car, and it got impounded, remember?"

"Hey." Bart's voice turned sharp, a pure cop tone that made both of the younger men focus on him instantly. "Either we talk about what I want to talk about or I'm taking you in."

Yegor shot Bart a look of sad surprise. "Me? Why you arrest me?"

Bart nodded at Demyan. "Him I got on the FTA. You I got for outstanding traffic warrants. Now, are we going to talk?"

"Sure, sure." Demyan smiled and nodded. "I hereby invite you back into our apartment. We'll talk about anything you want."

"You said you worked for your uncle?"

"We did. Me and Yegor. On account of my mom, she's Uncle Maurice's niece or something?" Demyan looked at Yegor.

Yegor thought about it and nodded. "Yeah. Her mom is sister to Uncle Maurice, so we're great-nephews. I think that's how it works."

"Anyway," Demyan said, "we got this job from the old guy on account he don't know how to do computers. Me and Yegor, we know computers. Know video games. All the tech. Uncle Maurice went into business for himself, started buying stuff from storage places. Things that people run off and leave on account they can't pay the rent on the storage no more?"

Bart nodded.

"People run off and leave some weird stuff, bro. I'm telling you. Me and Yegor, we've pulled stuff outta some of them storage units you'd think come from Mars. Had this one guy was sewing different parts of dead animals together. Saw where he'd put a bat head and wings on a cat, bro. That was messed up."

Bart started to take a note, but Annja shook her head.

"It's called rogue taxidermy," she said. "Probably not anything for you to get concerned about. People do it to create curiosity pieces for collectors of the weird."

"People don't get any weirder than a cat with a bat head and wings, bro." Demyan shook his head. "Sickest thing I ever saw. Gave me nightmares. Sometimes I still get them."

"What did your great-uncle do with the stuff he got from the storage units?" Bart asked.

"Pieced it out and sold it, bro. What else you gonna do with stuff like that? A lot of it was junk we just dumped. Never know what you're gonna get outta one of them things."

"Where did he sell it?"

"Online, wherever he could find somebody that wanted something. Me and Yegor dragged some of them things around to pawn shops and swap meets. Man is all about making a dollar. He pays me and Yegor chump change, though."

"He pays for the apartment we're living in," Yegor said quietly.

"Oh, yeah. He does that, too." Demyan looked at his brother. "Only if he's dead, he ain't gonna do that no more, is he?" He frowned. "Who's gonna pay the rent if Uncle Maurice is gone?"

Yegor shrugged and looked unhappy.

"Hey, Demyan." Bart snapped his fingers. "Focus."

Demyan looked at Bart, had to narrow his eyes a moment, then looked again. "What?"

"If you guys put the stuff up on the computer for your uncle, who managed the sales?"

"Me and Yegor. We boxed stuff up, carted it to the post office. Uncle Maurice wasn't gonna do it. Man had no skills when it came to tech and he sure wasn't gonna walk to the post office every day. Knew good stuff from the bad in storage units, though. Man could turn a dollar."

Bart pulled up a picture of the elephant on his phone. "Tell me about this."

A wide smile split Demyan's face. "Oh, yeah! The elephant! I remember the elephant!"

"Uncle Maurice said he was gonna make bank on it," Yegor added. "Said he had a bunch of different people bidding on it the first day we put it up."

"Do you know who bought it?" Bart asked.

"No." Yegor shook his head. "Uncle Maurice took care of all that. Me and Demyan just pulled stuff out of the storage units, sorted it out, boxed it when it sold, then lugged it to the post office after Uncle Maurice wrote the address on it."

"Should be information on who bought it on the website, bro," Demyan said.

"Maybe you could show me that," Bart suggested.

DESPITE BEING PARTIALLY dazed and suddenly realizing he might be homeless or moving at the end of the month, Demyan got around on the computer just fine. Annja figured it was because he played his video games night and day, a stack of them barely hid behind a giant pink plastic pig bank that had suffered a permanent appendectomy and stood open and mostly empty.

"Here, bro." Demyan waved at the laptop computer that he set up on the scarred coffee table covered in burn marks.

A website entitled Maurice's Super-Good Things showed on the screen. The site had cheap theatrics, fireworks and a slideshow showing some of the stuff that Benyovszky had featured for sale.

"Me and Yegor named the site," Demyan announced proudly.

"Yeah." Yegor nodded.

"Great," Bart said. "Now show me the elephant."

Demyan's fingers flicked across the keyboard and brought up the picture of the elephant. "Here you go."

"When did the sale close?"

Squinting at the monitor, Demyan tapped a few more keys. "A guy calls himself the Idaho Picker."

Bart frowned. “That’s not his real name.”

“No. That’s his handle on the site.”

“Can you get me his real name?”

“Sure.” Demyan tapped some more, bringing up other screens of information. “Says his name is Charles Prosch.”

“Do you have an address and phone number for Mr. Prosch?”

“Yeah.” Demyan tapped keys again.

4

Annja cycled through the items Benyovszky had up for sale on his site. He had a lot of merchandise, most of it was furniture, exercise equipment, clothing and assorted electronics, computers, video-game consoles and DVDs. She also took notes on the storage companies Benyovszky regularly bought defaulted units from, and managed to track the elephant back to a company called Illya's Storage, which appeared to cater to the Russian neighborhood. Benyovszky had kept good notes, and his nephews had entered all of the information. At least, they had evidently entered a great deal of the details in the database.

Bart was on his cell phone doing background work on Charles Prosch.

"You're pretty good on that computer, bro." Sitting on the couch, Demyan smiled at Annja as she worked the keyboard.

Bro? Annja let that pass because Demyan still referred to Officer Falcone as "police chick," too, and she didn't intend to become "computer chick." "I am."

"You could probably make somebody a good secretary."

Annja resisted the impulse to show Demyan how much fun a punch in the nose could be. Instead, she tried to ignore him.

Demyan sucked at his teeth and smoothed his mustache with his fingers. "If you want, maybe I can make some calls for you. Check around. See if there are any openings for secretaries. I know a few people. I could hook you up with a sweet job."

"Thanks. But I already have a job."

"What?" Demyan grimaced. "You got too much class. You ain't no police chick."

"No, I'm not." Annja looked at the guy, pinning him with

her gaze. "Which means I don't have to play by police rules or be nice when someone says something insulting."

Demyan broke eye contact and looked away, but only for a moment. Then he found something new to talk about. "You know who might have killed Uncle Maurice, bro?"

"Who?" Annja pulled up the bid page and looked at the other names listed there. Few of them were real names, but Bart and his digital police investigators would be able to track them down and put actual identities to online handles.

"His old cronies. Some of the other guys that were part of the Potato Bag Gang."

That caught Annja's attention and she stopped what she was doing. "The Potato Bag Gang? What's that?"

"Mafia wiseguys." Demyan touched the side of his nose and winked. "Uncle Maurice was part of the original Russian organized crime guys that came over when communism started going bust."

Bart put his phone away and crossed the room back over to Annja. "Back in the 1970s, Russian criminals, some of them, first started turning up in Brighton Beach. Those guys tended to be con artists, not hardcases. One of their main schticks was selling antique gold rubles to buyers who thought they were getting a great deal. They told the buyers that they couldn't get caught with the rubles, couldn't exchange them to a legitimate market, so they had to sell them at a loss. Only when the victims opened the bags those con artists gave them, they only found potatoes, not rubles. So those guys became known as the Potato Bag Gang." He grinned. "Don't tell me I knew something you didn't."

"You did, and it's not that hard to do. History and culture are huge. There's no way I can know it all." Some days that bummed Annja, knowing that she couldn't know everything. She usually distracted herself from that by learning something out of the ordinary. "But I also think the Potato Bag Gang is interesting. I'll have to look into it at another time. Did you get hold of Prosch?"

Bart shook his head. "Not yet. I left a message, but it's still early out in Idaho."

"Idaho? The *state* of Idaho?" Annja couldn't remember Idaho even being mentioned on the pages she'd sorted through. "You're not just saying that because of the Potato Bag Gang."

Bart grinned. "Yeah. Surprised me, too. Prosch lives in a town in the middle of nowhere named Bonner's Ferry. The town's supposed to have like ten thousand people in it. Compared to New York, it's a ghost town." He checked the time on his watch. "I'll call again in the morning." He looked at Annja. "I can have an officer take you home. Save you some cab fare."

"What are you going to do?"

"It's three o'clock. I've got a report to file and information to collect, then I need to wait for a decent hour to call Prosch. I'm going to go down to the diner at the corner and camp out. See what turns up."

"Want company?" Annja wasn't prepared to let go of the mystery that had been brought into her orbit, and Bart was a friend. It had been a long time since they'd had the excuse to hang out together.

"This isn't your thing, Annja. I feel bad about asking you to come see what you had to see earlier. I just needed answers if you had them."

"I'm thinking I could go through Benyovszky's files and get a better idea of the kind of business he was doing. If that would help."

Bart hesitated, then smiled. "It would. I don't want this to be more of an inconvenience than it already is."

Annja stood. "It won't be. An inconvenience would be me going home and not being able to sleep because I'm wondering what this is all about. Somebody killed that poor old man for a reason. I'd like to know why."

"That's the problem." Bart's eyes held a glint of bitter sadness. "Sometimes even when you know the answers, you don't understand them. People kill each other for the stupidest, most selfish reasons you can imagine."

Demyan leaned forward to insert himself into the conversation. "I'm telling you, bro, you need to listen to me. It was probably one of them old-time gangsters Uncle Maurice sometimes hung around with." He leaned back on the couch.

"Them guys, they would sit and talk about the old days, and not one of them with two nickels to rub together. They were jealous of the business Uncle Maurice, Yegor and me had going. We were making money, bro, and they wanted some of it. Uncle Maurice said that elephant was the biggest score he'd ever pulled down."

"Did he tell people about that?" Bart asked.

Demyan shrugged. "Yeah, a few people. Some of those old guys, sure. He wanted them to know when he got a fat score. Liked to rub it in and tell them they should be doing their own business when he was drinking down at The Red Bear Bar." He paused and rolled his shoulders. "Did you see how much he got for that elephant, bro?"

"I did," Bart replied.

"So…how much?"

"He didn't tell you?"

Demyan scowled. "Like I said, Uncle Maurice didn't tell me and Yegor anything except go empty out this storage unit and bring the stuff here. Put this stuff on the website. Box these things up. Go to the post office with this. That pretty much covered it. He was supposed to be training us, but he didn't." He pursed his lips. Evidently the pleasant buzz he'd had earlier was fading. "Never once did he tell me and Yegor that we were doing a good job, you know? He coulda done that. Coulda showed a little appreciation. That wouldn't have been so hard, bro."

Bart shook his head in ill-concealed disgust. "The man is dead. He put a roof over your heads and kept the two of you in enough cash to mostly keep you out of trouble. Have some respect." He headed for the door and Annja fell in behind him.

"Not all the weed we could smoke, bro," Demyan said softly. "We coulda smoked a lot more weed."

Annja put a hand on Bart's shoulder and kept him moving.

Outside in the hall, Bart walked over to Officer Falcone, a young brunette with dark hair and eyes.

"Something I can do for you, Detective?"

"I can do something for you, Officer Falcone." Bart hooked

a thumb over his shoulder. "There are warrants out on those idiots in that apartment."

"I didn't know that. We didn't background them. I was just told they were the dead man's nephews and we were supposed to hold them for you."

"Well, I'm telling you now they've got warrants out for them. Grab your partner and take those two imbeciles downtown. There's an FTA on the little one and traffic holds on the big one. That'll give you guys a couple small collars and a reason to get in out of the cold tonight."

Falcone smiled. "Thank you, Detective."

Bart waved the thanks away. "Don't mention it. Take your time booking those two clowns. I want to be able to find them if I need to for the next forty-eight hours."

CALAPEZ SPOONED THE last of the Greek yogurt from the plastic container while Pousao watched the building on the other side of the street. Finished with his meal, he glanced at his watch and discovered it was 4:14 a.m. They had been in the dead man's apartment for over four hours. The morning coming, they would have to move soon. He could already hear neighbors moving around in the other apartments. Early morning activity, footsteps and snatches of hurried conversation, sounded out in the hallway.

Pousao stood and shifted slightly, then pushed his chin toward the window. "Hey. That woman, Annja Creed, she's leaving the building with one of the cops."

Calapez crossed the room and gestured for the binoculars the younger man held. When Calapez had them, he trained his view on to the street, picking up the archaeologist instantly. She stood out in the crowd. She and the detective pushed through the reporters outside the perimeter set up by the police officers.

"Do they have the elephant?" Pousao asked.

"I don't know." Feeling more tense now because he knew Sequeira would not accept losing the object, Calapez watched as Annja Creed and the detective entered a small diner.

"They are not going far." Pousao rotated his head on his shoulders and the effort produced cracks. "What do we do?"

"What we're doing now. We wait. We watch. Going back to Sequeira without the elephant would not be good business." Calapez handed the binoculars over to his young associate, then went back to raid the dead man's refrigerator again. He opened the door and peered inside. Nothing looked good. The deceased obviously didn't dine in much. Frustrated, he closed the door again. "I will go over to the diner and bring us back something to eat. Maybe I will find out what they are talking about, or where the elephant is. While I am there, you keep watch."

Pousao nodded and returned to his vigil.

Calapez waited at the door till he heard silence, then let himself out. If the police did not have the elephant, he had to figure out where it had gone—soon.

5

Hours later, Annja stifled a yawn and looked through bleary vision at the list of storage units and buyers she had compiled. The sorting program on the software made building that list easier, but there were still a lot of names. Benyovszky had been in business for himself for eleven years.

The diner was low-key and welcoming, worn and lived-in, filled with lots of younger regulars who worked on tablets or talked on the phone while they ate their breakfast. They wore business attire and were the smallest group in the diner. Most of the clientele was older and spoke in Russian or heavily accented English. They gathered as couples or small groups. All of them looked pensive and distracted, and Annja wouldn't need a second guess to know what the topic of conversation was.

"Can I get you a refill?"

Annja looked up at the young waitress and nodded. Annja slid over her nearly empty coffee cup, did the same with Bart's, and told the young woman thanks after she'd poured the fresh-brewed coffee. Annja added cream and sugar to both coffees, turning the hot liquid the color of caramel.

Bart was talking on the phone, listening mostly, and the one-sided conversation didn't give Annja much to work with. Curiosity grew in her as she waited. Finally, Bart put the phone away and returned his attention to her.

"That was Broadhurst. He says the ME released a prelim based on the scene."

Through the large plate-glass window behind Bart, Annja could see the reflection of the apartment building across the street. The ME's long black vehicle had eased into the collection of police cars and crime-scene vans. Morning light filtered through the dregs of the night, bringing a sense of the new day. Traffic had increased, both vehicular and pedestrian. Passersby stopped only briefly to find out what was going on, then they got back to their day. Murder was nothing new in the metro area.

Even though she had seen such casual acceptance of murder and death before, in New York as well as countries around the globe, Annja still refused to think people could just keep moving without being touched by the tragedy.

She put those thoughts away and concentrated on Bart. "What does the ME say?"

"The victim had no defensive wounds. Looks like whoever killed Benyovszky hit him from behind with a hammer, or a similar weapon. The ME won't commit as to what the weapon was, but she thinks death was instantaneous. At least the old guy didn't suffer." Bart picked up his coffee, blew on it and took a sip.

"If the first blow killed Benyovszky, why keep hitting him?"

Bart shook his head. "Anger? Frustration? Maybe fear, if the murderer was afraid Benyovszky would get back up. Don't know. But whoever did it was thorough."

"You said there were no defensive wounds?"

"Yeah." Bart sipped his coffee. "Could mean that Benyovszky knew his murderer. Let the person into the apartment."

"Then why was the lock shattered?"

Bart frowned. "I don't have an answer for that one yet. You're right. If Benyovszky let his killer into the apartment, that person didn't need to break in."

"And if the killer had broken in, Benyovszky would have had defensive wounds because he wouldn't have trusted whoever came through that door."

"Yeah. That line of thinking leaves us two options." Bart counted them off on his fingers. "One, whoever killed Benyovszky panicked and left something behind, then had to break back in to get it. Or two, someone else broke into the apartment after Benyovszky was dead."

"How much time passed between the murder and the discovery of the body?"

"ME says maybe an hour. It's a tight window, but it's there."

Annja considered that, not enjoying the fact that she didn't have answers, or at least a better idea of what had gone on in that apartment. Including where the elephant statue was and what it meant.

Lying on the table, Bart's phone began to ring. He picked it up and glanced at the screen. "There's only one person I almost know in Idaho." He clicked the phone on. "This is Detective Bart McGilley of the New York City Police Department." He turned the phone outward and leaned toward Annja.

Annja leaned forward, too.

"This is Charles Prosch. You left a message on my machine, Detective McGilley. Asking me to call you?" The speaker's voice was old and hoarse, but held a quiet strength in the Western twang. "I don't usually get phone calls from New York police detectives, and I haven't been there or the East Coast in years, so you can understand how I'm curious."

"Yes, sir. I'm calling in regards to a murder that took place last night." Bart flipped open his notebook and took out his pen. "The victim was Maurice Benyovszky. I'd like to know how you knew him."

"What happened?"

"Mr. Benyovszky was attacked and killed in his apartment by unknown assailants."

"I'm sorry to hear that." Prosch cleared his throat. "I never met Mr. Benyovszky, but he seemed like a nice guy. From what I saw on his site, he did a pretty good business. Why would you single me out from all those people?"

"An auction you were involved in finished last night."

"The one with the elephant piece."

"That's right. Can you tell me about that piece?"

"I'm more of a collector than an expert, Detective. A dabbler, if you will. I buy a few things now and again, keepsakes mostly, of things I saw while I was in the Corps."

"You were in the Marines."

"I was. Thirty years. I did a lot of traveling, then I came back to Bonner's Ferry where I was born and where I buried my parents. You put down roots doing something like that. I got married, but that didn't take. She couldn't be the Marine I was, and I don't blame her for that. I've got two daughters out of it who I love, a handful of grandkids."

Annja smiled at that. Prosch's offspring sounded a lot closer than Benyovszky's hand-me-down nephews. She felt a chill as the door opened and took a sip of her coffee to warm up.

"What do you know about the elephant?" Bart frowned and looked a little frustrated.

"Like I said, not much," Prosch replied. "It's an elephant. Looks Asian, if I'm any judge, and I could be just as wrong as I am right."

"What's it made of?" Bart consulted the sheet that had been printed out regarding the piece.

"Mr. Benyovszky wasn't sure, but it looked like sandstone to me. I spent some time in Laos. As I recall, they did a lot of carving in sandstone in that area."

"You paid a lot of money for an elephant made of sandstone."

Prosch laughed good-naturedly. "Actually, I wasn't going to spend that much, but I got caught up in a bidding war."

Bart wrote that down and underlined it. "A bidding war?"

"Yeah. The other guy who wanted the elephant kept jumping my bid by a dollar. Just enough to edge me out. Kind of irritated me, and I'd talked to Mr. Benyovszky on the phone once when I called to ask him about the piece. He seemed on the up and up. So I figured I'd keep in the bidding game as long as I could, kind of drive up the price for him. Help him out. The other guy seems like he has plenty of money."

"Do you know who the other guy is?"

"Sure. I looked him up after Mr. Benyovszky mentioned him. He's a fella named Fernando Sequeira."

Glancing up, Bart cocked an eyebrow at Annja.

She shook her head and mouthed, *I don't know him.* But she turned her attention to her tablet PC and started looking the man up. She got a hit immediately. Fernando Sequeira was a successful businessman in Lisbon, Portugal. Scanning the links that turned up in her search, Annja also discovered that

Sequeira was an amateur historian, an interest he had gotten from his grandfather.

Link me, Bart mouthed.

Annja sent the page address to Bart's phone. While Bart continued talking, Annja searched for Sequeira's name linked with "elephant" but didn't pull up anything that seemed to fit with Bart's case.

"Tell you the truth," Prosch went on with a touch of chagrin, "I was surprised I won that elephant. I thought that Sequeira fella would swoop in at the last minute and take it. I musta waited twenty minutes for that to happen. When it didn't, I realized I paid a lot more for that elephant than I had counted on."

"What did you do after the sale closed?" Bart asked.

"Poured myself three fingers of whiskey, promised myself I wouldn't stick my neck out like that again and figured I'd get hold of this Sequeira fella and see if I couldn't get most of my money back. He was interested up to a point." Prosch paused and his voice turned a little harder. "Unless Mr. Benyovszky and this Sequeira fella were working together to set me up. That what happened?"

"I don't know, Mr. Prosch. For right now, I'd hang on to your money. Nobody seems to know where that elephant is."

"Is that so? Well, now that does make a body curious, don't it?"

Bart grinned. "It does indeed. Hang on to my number if you will, Mr. Prosch."

"Oh, trust me, I will, Detective."

"I'll call back if I have any more questions, and if something turns up on your end, I'd appreciate hearing from you."

"You will. Count on it."

Bart broke the connection, laid his phone on the table and glared at it. "So I got a guy out in the wilds of Idaho who hasn't been to New York in years, and I got a guy in Lisbon, Portugal, who were both interested in that elephant." He wiped a hand over his mouth and smothered a yawn, but his eyes still glowed with bright interest. "How many others were bidding on that thing?"

Annja checked the list. "Eight people."

"But they all bailed early."

"They did."

"And we still haven't found the thing." Bart knotted his hand. "I hate mysteries." He looked up at her. "I know you enjoy them, but I could live without them. Give me a case where I catch a perp red-handed and just have to fill out the paperwork. Those are the investigations I like."

Annja knew that wasn't true. Bart McGilley was clever and knowledgeable. Those were things that underpinned their friendship. They loved puzzles and mystery shows. She didn't offer to argue the point at the moment.

An Asian man entered from the street and the way he didn't fit in caught Annja's attention immediately. Bart tilted his head slightly, shifting his gaze to the man, as well.

The man wore a dark gray suit and a long jacket. On his head he had a black woolen cap. A shade under six feet tall, he looked thin for his size, but his shoulders were broad and he moved with economical grace as he strode toward their table.

Bart shifted slightly so that he could get to his service weapon more quickly, but the nonchalant look on his face never waned.

The Asian man stopped a few feet short of their table, just out of arm's reach, and smiled slightly at them. "Good morning. I do not mean to trouble you." His accent held a note of British English in it. "My name is Nguyen Rao. I have come about the elephant Mr. Benyovszky had for sale on his website. Do you have the elephant?"

6

Feeling nervous and out of place, Rao smiled at the man and woman seated at the table in front of him. Neither of them appeared to be surprised to see him, and that was good. Nervous people could sometimes make quick mistakes that would bring misfortune to all concerned.

The man broadcasted his profession in his narrowed eyes and readiness for physical confrontation. The move to access the pistol belted at his hip had not gone unnoticed. Rao had seen plenty of policemen during his journeys across Europe and throughout Asia. Criminals and policemen could be confusing, though, because both of them were similar in nature. Rao had dealt with criminals, as well. He much preferred dealing with neither and instead working on his studies.

The woman, though, was similar in some ways, but different in others. She did not seem like a policeman or a criminal because she was more open, more accepting and not shut down. Her curiosity about him showed in the glint of her eyes and the set of her lips. But she kept herself balanced and ready all the same. Composed for confrontation, yes, but she was more curious than cautious. In many, that would be a weakness. Rao was not certain that such motivation was a weakness in her.

He knew of her and of her work. Anyone who labored in the field of antiquities might possibly know her name and her face. The television show rendered her familiar to a great number of the populace, but such familiarity also took away remembrance of her work as an archaeologist.

The policeman spoke first. "What did you say your name was?"

The ploy allowed the man to think a little longer, or perhaps it was only so the microphone of the recording device he wore might pick up his name better.

"Nguyen Rao."

"I'm Detective McGilley of the New York Police Department." The detective smiled a little, and the effort was almost guileless. His face was placid as a lake in a dead calm, but his body language was tight. Rao had learned to read both while in the temple.

"It is good to meet you, Detective McGilley."

McGilley didn't offer to introduce Annja Creed. "What are you doing here?"

"I came about the elephant."

"You're not from around here."

"No." Rao made himself endure the inane questions. He knew they would be coming and he had prepared himself to deal with them.

"Where are you from?"

"Phnom Penh."

McGilley's eyes cut to Annja Creed for just a moment.

Rao spoke again to remove the confusion and lack of knowledge. "Phnom Penh is in Cambodia."

McGilley smiled a little at that. "Cambodia's a long way off, Mr. Nguyen."

"It is." Rao thought being agreeable would be best. "The trip by plane required many hours."

"I'm sure it did. When did you get to New York?"

There was almost no suspicion in the man's words to touch the ear, but Rao knew the focus that drove the question. "Too late to save Mr. Benyovszky."

"To *save* him?"

"Your inference was that I had killed him," Rao said politely. "I did not. Had I gotten to him in time last night, or this morning—I must admit to some confusion regarding the time, I might have saved him."

The cop surfaced in McGilley then, and Rao knew that the conversation was going to go badly. Still, he knew he had to try to convince the American that he was in no way responsible for Benyovszky's death.

"You knew that Benyovszky was going to be killed?"

"No. Had I known that, I would have notified authorities. I was not there. Mr. Benyovszky was. If he felt he was in no danger, then why would I have thought so?"

"You said if you had reached him earlier he might not be dead."

"I misspoke. It could just as well have been that both of us were killed. I choose to think that his death might have been prevented. But that is already in the past and we must work on the future."

"Do you know who killed Benyovszky?"

"No."

McGilley looked around, noticing then that nearby patrons were starting to pay attention. He returned his attention to Rao. "Perhaps we can talk about this somewhere else." He slid out of the booth and stood, and the woman closed her computer, tucked it away in a messenger bag and slid out of the booth, as well.

"I can save us some time," Rao offered, thinking that maybe the direct approach—though the most honest—was not working in this instance. "I only need the elephant."

"We can talk about that outside." McGilley waved toward the door and indicated Rao should precede him.

Thinking that maybe he was wasting his time, that the elephant had already been lost, probably taken by the man or men who killed Maurice Benyovszky, Rao felt disappointed and turned his thoughts to getting out of police custody, for he felt certain that was where he was headed. He turned and started for the door, then he spotted one of the Portuguese men he'd encountered weeks before.

The man stood at the counter next to the side door and nursed a coffee or a hot tea. No one else was around him.

Rao did not know the man's name, but there was no mistaking that cruel look or those dead eyes.

UNTIL THE MONK started to walk out with the police detective and Annja Creed, Calapez thought he had the situation in hand. The fact that the monk was there let Calapez know that the Asian didn't have the elephant. Evidently the piece was still in play.

However, when recognition flared in the monk's eyes, Calapez felt threatened and reacted instantly because he preferred the element of surprise to be one of his weapons rather than someone else's. He pushed away from the counter and swept his coat back, reaching for his pistol.

The detective, focusing on the Asian, was slow getting to his own weapon. Calapez had the 9mm out and started firing, aiming for the detective because he knew the American would have a weapon and the monk and the woman probably didn't.

Calapez squeezed the rounds off as quickly as he could, putting all three of them into the center of the detective's chest. The American went back and down, the pistol tumbling from his fingers. The woman dropped down beside him, concern tightening her features.

The monk came toward Calapez so quick that Calapez couldn't bring his pistol around fast enough to center his weapon on the man. It didn't matter, though, because one of the men Calapez had stationed outside stepped through the door and raised a machine pistol, spraying bullets indiscriminately.

SEEING THE MACHINE pistol in the other man's hands as he entered the diner and knowing that continuing to stay inside the building would only be endangering the rest of the patrons, Rao abandoned his forward momentum and threw himself over the counter. As he landed on fingers and toes, he swept out his left leg, caught the legs of the man tending the grill, and knocked him down as well, so the machine pistol's bullets cut the air where he'd been, instead of tearing through flesh.

The man sprawled in shock and decided to lie there, still clutching the spatula he'd been using. He mumbled, curses or prayers, Rao couldn't tell over the yammering machine pistol. Bullets hammered the stainless-steel grill vent and cored through the tile wall, spilling ceramic fragments over the floor.

Rao ran, staying low behind the counter, knowing that his

opponents would seek to find him because they had recognized him as a familiar threat even if they didn't know what he truly represented.

Hoping that his departure would draw his enemies away from the diner, Rao slid around the end of the counter and angled for the door. Bullets chased him, cutting through the air just inches behind him. Thankfully the patrons were down on the floor and out of the way.

He hit the door with both palms, spreading the impact so that the glass door shattered. He ran through the falling fragments and out into the street, thinking that the Portuguese man would have set up his cronies at that door, as well. He just managed to stay ahead of a swath of bullets from the two gunmen standing outside the wrecked door.

Traffic had been held up by a red light at the intersection. At the sound of the shots, the drivers panicked and began trying to pull around each other. Failing that, many of them got out and ran or stayed in their vehicles.

Rao ran, his head low, and knew that the gunmen pursued him.

ANNJA FELT THE shock of adrenaline hitting her system, but concentrated on examining Bart. He'd been hit by the man's bullets. That was all she knew.

She reached for him, gazing at his chest and expecting it to be a bloody ruin. It wasn't. Three bullet holes showed in his shirt, one of them piercing his coat as well, but there was no blood.

Vest, Annja thought frantically. *He's wearing a protective vest.*

Then she was aware of the swarthy man beside her. He grabbed her roughly by one elbow and shoved the hot barrel of the pistol against her neck. The barrel was so hot that her flesh seared. She almost fought back, but she knew that would only fail. All the man had to do was squeeze the trigger and the fight would end before it started.

"Move," the man ordered in a harsh voice.

Annja stood, looking down at Bart. His eyelids flickered,

but he was almost unconscious, barely aware of what was going on around him. Even with the vest, his ribs could have been cracked. One of them might have punctured a lung.

The man yanked her again, guiding her toward the back door. Annja knew she had a chance to escape then. The man wasn't paying strict attention to her. He didn't know what she was capable of.

But there were too many people around. The innocents would get hurt. She didn't want that. She held herself ready and waited.

Through the door, outside in the cold air of morning, horns blaring at the traffic jam that had taken shape in the intersection, Annja strode down the sidewalk as the man guided her. They were walking away from the building where Maurice Benyovszky had been killed, walking past the other door to the diner now.

Police would arrive quickly. She knew that. She concentrated on her breathing, keeping it smooth and regular, and she paid attention. There had been two men inside the diner, the guy who held her captive and the man who followed them that had wielded the machine pistol.

The Asian man had vanished, but the two armed men sprinting through the stalled traffic gave Annja a good idea which way Nguyen Rao had gone.

If that's even his name. Anger flared up in Annja then. She wasn't sure who to blame for Bart getting shot. From the way the guy who was holding on to her had acted, he'd chosen to shoot Bart as soon as Bart had tried to leave with the Asian man.

They definitely weren't working together. The Asian man had been asking about the elephant piece, but that didn't mean the guy holding on to her was interested in that.

"Annja Creed," the man said in that hard voice as he looked around.

She didn't respond.

Angrily, the man shook her. "You will speak when I speak to you."

"All right." Annja took note of the neighborhood. Pedestrians had been drawn to the diner, thinning out of the alley and the streets. The smart neighbors and passersby stayed in their homes and watched.

"Where is the elephant?"

Okay, so all of this is connected. Everybody has an elephant on their agenda. Annja took a breath and stepped off the curb, keeping pace with the man at her side. "I don't know."

"Does the detective have it?"

"No. The elephant wasn't in Benyovszky's apartment."

The man cursed in Portuguese. Annja understood enough of the man's invective to understand he was mad and scared.

"What is the elephant?" Annja asked.

"None of your business. If you do not know, it is better that you do not learn."

Annja kept walking, but she was aware that the man was no longer as focused on her. He was looking for a way out now, a way through the police net that would be going up even as they were speaking.

"Maybe I can help," she suggested. "Just tell me why you're looking for the elephant and maybe I'd be able to figure out where it is."

"No." The man shook her again and kept walking, glancing at the street. "Who killed Benyovszky?"

"I don't know. You didn't kill him?"

"The old man was dead when we got there." Realizing what he had just done, how he had admitted more than he'd intended, the man cursed in Portuguese again.

"There." The man carrying the machine pistol under his coat pointed to a sedan sailing swiftly down the street. He stepped toward the curb and started flagging the vehicle down.

She didn't want to get into the car with the men—escape would be harder there if not impossible. Annja lifted her right leg and drove her foot into the back of her abductor's knee, tripping him and forcing him down at the same time. She caught his gun hand in her hands and twisted. The man released the pistol with a cry of pain just before his wrist bones shattered. He fell away, dropping to the sidewalk.

The man with the machine pistol wheeled around and started bringing his weapon from under his coat.

Knowing she wouldn't reach the other man in time to prevent him from employing the machine pistol, Annja reached into the *otherwhere* and grabbed the handle of the sword that had once belonged to Joan of Arc. In less than an eyeblink, it was in this world with her, a piece of her just as surely as any of her limbs.

The sword was crude and beautiful at the same time. Over three feet in length, with an unadorned cross-guard, the handle wrapped in leather, the sword was a weapon, not a showpiece. It had been forged for battle, and Annja was intimate with its abilities. She joined her two hands together as she stepped forward and swung.

Catching the morning light, the blade sang through the air in a horizontal arc that sheared through the machine pistol a bare inch above the man's hands. Gaping in disbelief, the man stared at the useless weapon he held as the pieces tumbled to the sidewalk.

Before the man could react, Annja set herself and lashed out with a roundhouse kick that lifted the gunman from his feet and bounced him off the side of a nearby parked car. The vehicle's anti-theft alarm screamed and echoed along the street.

Annja released the sword, letting it go back into the *otherwhere* and disappear. The other man pushed himself up, but his injured wrist gave out on him and he crashed back down to his chest. Annja stomped on his hand as he reached for the dropped pistol, then picked up the weapon herself.

Backing away, Annja pointed the pistol at the second man. "Roll over onto your stomach. Lock your fingers behind your head. I'm sure you're familiar with the drill."

Without a word, the man did as he was ordered. The first man lay unconscious. Three uniformed police officers sprinted up the street toward Annja.

Out on the street, the driver of the approaching car slowed, then saw that the odds had shifted. Ducking down, the man pulled toward an alley and drove away.

The police officers pointed their weapons at Annja. One of them addressed her in a too-loud but calm voice. “Ma’am, put down the weapon.”

Annja complied, then laid on her stomach the same way the man she’d captured was. Handcuffs closed around her wrists and she kept telling herself that Bart would get her cut loose as soon as he was able.

Being handcuffed didn’t bother her so much, though. It was the thought of the elephant, lost out there, people chasing after it for some unknown reason, and she was getting behind in that pursuit.

7

"Are you sure you're okay?"

Shaking her head, Annja made an effort to stop rubbing her bruised wrists. Although the pain had subsided, they still throbbed from the constriction they'd suffered while she'd been brought down to the police station. The policeman who had put the handcuffs on had put them on tight and time had passed before Bart could get free of the paramedics and the investigators and arrive to release her. "I'm fine."

Bart squinted up at her as if taking her measure. "You don't look so good."

"Me?" She frowned at Bart, who was sitting on the other side of his desk in the detectives' bull pen. All around the station cops were fielding reports and filling out forms. Evidently Benyovszky's murder and the shoot-out at the diner hadn't been the only things going on tonight. The conversations and the constant noise distanced her from the memory of the old man lying dead in his apartment and the violence in the diner that had spilled out into the street. "You're the one who got shot."

In the uncertain glare of the fluorescent lighting, Bart looked pale and haggard. He shifted uncomfortably in his seat and breathed shallowly. His shirttails were out and his tie hung in a coat pocket. "The vest stopped the bullets."

"The vest doesn't stop the impact. That's still like getting hit in the chest with a sledgehammer."

Bart grinned at her ruefully. "How would you know something like that?"

Actually, Annja had experienced that same injury on occasion, as well as getting shot. Things hadn't been dull since the sword had come into her possession. She didn't know if the increased danger was just her lifestyle or a byproduct of having the sword.

"There was a special on the History Channel about body armor," she replied. "You should go to the emergency room and get checked out. In addition to the bruising, the hydrostatic shock caused by the impacts could have cracked your ribs or torn muscles."

"I'll be fine." Bart opened a desk drawer, took out a bottle of pain relievers and shook a couple tablets out into his hand. He swallowed them down dry and grimaced, at the taste or the pain, Annja wasn't sure which. He put the bottle back in the desk drawer. "There's a line at the hospital. There always is. If this is still hurting in a few hours, I'll go in." He took a breath gingerly and winced. "In the meantime, I've got a case I'm working on that just blew up big-time, and I still have no idea why people are shooting up the neighborhood over an elephant statue we can't find."

Annja decided not to press the issue and risk reminding Bart that she was just a civilian pushing into police business. Friendship would only carry her so far, and she knew Bart wouldn't bend regulations any further. She massaged her wrists again. "Do you have anything on the two men who were arrested at the diner?"

"I do." Bart stood with effort and picked up a file folder from the desktop. "Come with me."

"His name's Francisco Calapez." Bart peered through the one-way glass into the interview room at the man sitting alone at a desk.

Calapez sat in a straight-backed chair that was bolted to the floor. Other than the two chairs, one across from the other, and the table, the room offered nothing more in furnishings or accoutrements. Hands cuffed to the table in front of him, one of them sleeved in a temporary cast, Calapez looked uncomfortable and half-asleep.

Holding her arms across her chest because it made the bruises on her wrists throb less painfully, Annja peered through the one-way glass. "What's he saying?"

Bart shook his head. "Nothing. He started yelling *lawyer* as soon as we sat down to talk to him. We only got a name because his prints rolled up in the system. We're not even certain that's his real name yet. We're still awaiting verification on a true ID. According to the files I've seen, and there may be more hits coming in soon because this guy, whoever he turns out to be, has got a record in Europe that's coming in to us in pieces."

Annja thought about that. "What kind of history does he have?"

"Guy's a strong-arm, probably a killer, but no one's ever pinned that on him."

"He told me he didn't kill Benyovszky."

"How did you have time for a discussion in the middle of everything that was going on?"

"He brought it up. He asked me if I knew who killed Benyovszky. Calapez wants the elephant."

"Did he say why?"

"No."

"If the guy's going to shoot at you—and he did—" Bart pointed to his chest "—it's a safe bet he's going to lie to you, too."

"I don't think he killed him."

Bart sighed, but carefully. "Neither do I. If Calapez had killed Benyovszky and taken the elephant—which this all seems to focus on, he would have disappeared. We took his shoes when we brought him in because we noticed dried blood on them."

Annja glanced down at Calapez's sock-covered feet.

"The lab has the shoes now, but there were traces of blood in the tread, and I'm betting that blood at one time pumped through Maurice Benyovszky."

"No bet."

"The lab will take a while getting the results back to us, though. So for right now, I can't put Calapez in Benyovszky's apartment. Which means all I have him on is a weapons charge and intent to murder at the diner."

"Isn't that enough?"

"I hope so. Depends on the judge and how much money Calapez can get his hands on. If this guy makes bail, he could be in the wind and we might never see him again."

"Even after him blasting away inside the diner?"

"Yeah. Until we can prove he killed somebody, we can't leverage enough to guarantee he'll be held without bail. If we could prove he was a threat to national security, we could lock him down tight."

"But Calapez could walk away from this."

"He could." Bart grimaced.

On one hand, Annja couldn't believe Calapez could be released, but on the other she knew that things often happened just as Bart described. When he was feeling particularly irritated at his job, he sometimes stated that the justice system protected criminals more than it protected citizens. Of course, that took a really bad day for him to bring that up.

Annja thought about that for a moment. "Can you connect Calapez or the other man who was arrested to Fernando Sequeira?"

"No." Bart grimaced. "But I think the three of them would fit well together. Sequeira isn't a squeaky-clean television and radio mogul in Lisbon. I did a background check on him. When it comes to television and radio programming, Sequeira is something of a golden boy. However, he's got a bad habit of stealing artifacts from other countries, making illegal acquisitions. According to Interpol, Sequeira has hired people to get things for him off the books. They couldn't make a case stick against him because he took care of his hired help." Bart paused for a sip of the coffee he'd brought into the room with him. "But he's never been indicted for murder."

"So why do these guys fit together?"

"Sequeira's name came up in the bidding on Benyovszky's site. Calapez is in town asking about the elephant. Sequeira likes getting things. Calapez likes getting money for getting things for people, and he's been suspected of retrieving artifacts for Sequeira before. The math is easy."

"If Sequeira has a lot of money—"

"He does."

"—then why didn't he just outbid Charles Prosch and acquire the elephant without anyone getting hurt?"

"I'll be asking him that, if the DA's office ever gets through Sequeira's lawyers so I can get a face-to-face with him. The man's put up shields that are keeping our enquiries at bay."

"He must be hiding something." Annja knew Bart had to be thinking along the same lines.

"Maybe." Bart shrugged and winced. "Sequeira's also the kind of rich that likes to have privacy and can afford it. He's got a history of avoiding publicity except when he wants to shine the spotlight on himself. Could be he just doesn't want to deal with us."

Annja looked at the man in the interview room, watching as Calapez calmly picked at the temporary cast. "I suppose since Calapez isn't talking, neither is the other guy you have in custody."

"You'd think they were twins with a limited vocabulary from the way they shut down so quickly to lawyer up."

"What's the other guy's name?"

Bart shook his head. "We don't know. His prints aren't on file anywhere. He's young enough that he may not have been in trouble before now. After tonight, though, we'll have his prints, so he'll be in the books for anyone who needs to know."

"I don't think either one of these two guys, or any of the other guys working with them, killed Maurice Benyovszky." Annja pulled at her coat, her mind active and restless.

"Neither do I." Bart looked unhappy. "Doesn't make sense for them to kill Benyovszky, grab the elephant, then hang around to shoot me and wreak havoc in a local diner."

"That means Benyovszky's killer is still out there, and more than likely has the elephant."

"I know. We're going to be working the murder scene, the shooting at the diner, and we caught another squeal about a murder in an apartment building across the street from Benyovszky's building. One of the neighbors checked in on a guy named Felix Montgomery, found out he was dead. Other neighbors say they saw him in the building as late as eleven o'clock. So the time of death was sometime between eleven last night and this morning. Someone had rammed a blade into Montgomery's neck at the base of his skull and killed him." Bart touched the back of his neck to indicate where the blow had been delivered.

"A knife kill like that means training."

Bart glanced at her in consternation with raised eyebrows.

"Discovery Channel," Annja replied, realizing she was entirely too knowledgeable and calm about the violence. Bart wasn't privy to everything she had done since gaining possession of the sword.

"You're watching way too much television." Bart swung his focus back to the prisoner. "And one of the things Calapez did before he's been doing whatever he's been doing for the past eight years is mercenary work. He signed on with the Portuguese Army when he was eighteen, served in special forces for a few years, then mustered out. So somewhere he would have gotten that kind of training."

"What are you going to do with him?"

"Hang on to him as long as we can. Unless an attorney shows up here, I can lose Calapez in the system for seventy-two hours before I have to bring him before the judge. I will have to take him in for medical treatment, but I can finesse that, too. I don't know if we're going to be any closer to an answer by then, but we'll keep working the case. That's what we do."

Someone knocked on the door. Bart told them to enter.

A young plainclothes cop stepped into the room. "Unis caught the Asian guy who was at the diner, Detective McGilley. The guy who approached you and her." He nodded at Annja. "Sergeant Vogt wanted me to let you know."

"How did the unis find him?"

The guy smiled mirthlessly. "They *didn't* catch him. He walked up to them and turned himself in. There's nothing to arrest him on, but we're holding him as a material witness."

"Do we have a name for him?"

The detective checked the folder he was holding. "Nguyen Rao. Says here he's a professor in Cambodia."

"That's the same name he gave us at the diner," Annja said.

Bart nodded. "Did Mr. Nguyen say what he's doing in New York?"

"He's not really talkative. He asked to speak to you both."

"Where is he?"

"Got him in an interview room."

Bart headed for the door and Annja followed at his heels. This was twice the man had reached out to them.

NGUYEN RAO SAT in the interview room and looked serene. His hands rested palms-down on the desk that looked like a twin to the one in Calapez's room. His eyes were open and staring at the one-way glass, but he appeared to be asleep. Or really, really relaxed. Annja didn't know how a man could do that after nearly getting shot down just a short time ago. Then again, she was pretty calm herself, but she'd had a lot of experience at that sort of thing.

Bart thumbed through the file that he'd gotten on the man. Annja read the folder's contents over his shoulder.

There wasn't much. Nguyen Rao—that did appear to be his real name—was a professor attached to the most prestigious university in Phnom Penh. He was thirty-two years old and also worked as a curator for the national museum.

Annja took out her tablet and tapped in Rao's name, quickly locating several papers he'd written on Cambodian history ranging from the country's pre-history through the Khmer Rouge. Many of those papers included a photograph of Nguyen that matched the man in the interview room.

"Is he legit?" Bart peered over Annja's shoulder as she skimmed through the papers Rao had written.

"He is, if these papers are all truly his work and not part of a cover."

"You have a suspicious mind."

"Tonight has created a little paranoia, I suppose." Annja smiled at him.

Bart smiled back. "Paranoia's good for you. Sometimes they really are out to get you." He cut his eyes back to the tablet PC. "So he's like you? An archaeologist?"

"Not quite. He's more of a historian."

Bart returned his attention to the man on the other side of the one-way glass. "If he's a historian, then what's he doing here in New York looking for that elephant piece?"

"You'd have to ask him."

"I'm going to." Bart left Annja standing there and walked to the door down the hall.

8

Rao sat quietly at the table. The handcuffs felt cold and tight around his wrists, but the weight and the idea that he was restrained didn't bother him. He knew he could escape the handcuffs easily enough, but getting out of the building without being recaptured or shot was a different matter.

He hadn't gotten caught earlier. Once he'd seen that Annja Creed had overcome her captors, he'd allowed the police pursuing him to overtake and arrest him. He wanted to talk to the policeman again, the one who had investigated the old man's murder. Rao needed to know what had become of the elephant piece Benyovszky had listed on his site.

The door opened and Rao looked up at the arrival. The young detective, Bart McGilley, entered the room with a file in one hand and a cup of coffee in another. His expression was neutral, but Rao easily read the tension in the other man's movements.

McGilley set his coffee and the file on the table, then sat, as well. As he moved, he carried himself gingerly.

"Are you in pain?" Rao remembered the man had been shot in the diner.

"I'm fine." McGilley's answer was flat and final. "You should be worried about you."

"I have not done anything wrong, therefore I do not see anything I should be concerned about." Rao was pretty certain that fighting to defend himself was allowed in the United States. The laws here could be exasperating, but he thought he was correct about that. He had not killed anyone, and he had been attacked first. "I only turned myself in because I knew there would be questions as to my involvement in the violence at the diner."

"We'll see about that." McGilley stared him in the eye. "They said you wouldn't talk to anyone but me."

"You, or Professor Creed. Is she still here?" Actually, Rao wanted to talk to the woman more. He wanted to know how much she knew, if she could add anything to the amount of knowledge he had about the elephant.

"You're talking to me."

"Of course." Rao made himself be patient. The wheels of bureaucracy turned slowly in any country.

"Tell me about the elephant you're looking for."

"It is an object that I would like to have."

"Why?"

Rao considered that for a moment, thought that his business and that of the temple need not be discussed with the American police and decided to withhold a replay regarding those interests.

"Did you hear the question?" the detective asked.

"I did."

"Then talk to me."

"I choose not to. That has nothing to do with the events that occurred at the diner."

A flicker of anger darted through the detective's eyes. The corners of his mouth tightened in displeasure. "Things will go easier for you if you cooperate."

"I am cooperating. I turned myself in. Surely you can see that I am cooperating." Rao kept his voice calm and easygoing, offering no threat nor confrontation.

"I need to know about the elephant piece."

"I will not discuss that."

"A man was killed last night, probably for that elephant. You understand how that is important, something I should know."

"I did not kill him. I have not been inside Maurice Benyovszky's building. Your investigation will confirm that. Or, at the least, not be able to put me inside that building."

"Are you boasting?"

"I am merely stating the truth as I see it."

"Professor Nguyen—" the detective laced his fingers together on the table "—maybe you don't understand your circumstances. Potentially you're in a lot of trouble here."

"Have I broken any laws?"

"None that I'm aware of, but you're at the center of a murder, and that makes you a material witness. I can hold you on that alone for a time."

Rao had not known that. That revelation did make things more complicated.

"Tell me about you and Calapez," McGilley went on.

"I do not know anyone named Calapez." Rao guessed that must have been the name of the man inside the diner, the one who had come at him shooting. Rao was not lying. He did not know the man's name, which was what he had stated, but he had known the man was also after the elephant.

"You seemed to know him earlier."

"Calapez is the man who was in the diner." The name of the man was new to Rao. He filed it away. "He had a weapon and seemed intent on using it. I reacted."

"I saw you when you recognized him. I know you knew him then." McGilley laced his hands around his coffee and Rao knew the man was drawing warmth from the hot liquid. "He knew you, too."

"He has said this?" That would be interesting, and it would mean that the man who had sent Calapez to get the elephant knew more than Rao and his superiors had reckoned.

"I'm asking the questions."

"Of course. I meant no disrespect. I did not know the man's name until you mentioned it now."

"How do you know him?"

"Only through a chance encounter earlier. He struck me as a violent man. A killer. I am certain that if you look into his background you will discover this for yourself."

"Where did you *encounter* Calapez before this morning?"

Rao considered that quickly and thought that he would not be risking too much by telling the truth. "In Phnom Penh."

"When?"

"A few days ago."

"What was he doing there?"

"I do not know."

The detective frowned in irritation. "Where did the two of you meet?"

"We did not meet."

"Where were you when you saw Calapez?"

"In the museum where I sometimes work."

The detective checked the file. "At the national museum?"

"Yes."

"And you don't know what Calapez was doing there?"

"No."

"Between you and me, I don't think Calapez is much of a history buff or art lover."

"I do not get that impression either."

McGilley paused for a moment as if to let that sink in. "What brings you to New York?"

"I came to see Mr. Benyovszky, as I told you in the diner."

The pupils of the detective's eyes dilated, giving away his excitement even though he remained stone-faced. "Did you and Mr. Benyovszky know each other?"

"No. We had exchanged email and a few phone calls." Rao knew that would check out if the police checked Benyovszky's phone records. He did not want to get caught in a lie. That would complicate matters regarding the recovery of the elephant.

"You should really tell me about the elephant."

Rao didn't reply. He had learned what he could from the policeman. They knew nothing about the elephant. McGilley asked more questions, but Rao remained silent. Finally, in frustration, the detective got up and left the interview room.

"WHAT ARE YOU going to do with him?" Annja watched Nguyen Rao through the one-way glass.

Bart's aggravation showed in the hard lines along his jaw and the stiffness of his neck. He tossed the folder onto a nearby table. "I'm going to sit on him, hold him as long as I can. Sooner or later, someone will come looking for him, and when they do, I'll know more."

"Maybe I could talk to him. He did offer to speak to me, too."

Stubbornly, Bart shook his head. "No. That's what this guy wants, for whatever reason, and I'm not agreeing to any of his demands. I want him to sweat, let him sit in a box for a while to soften him up. I'm betting he feels more like talking then."

"What if he doesn't?"

"Then we'll discuss you talking to him. If he still wants to."

Annja knew Bart wasn't going to budge on his decision. "What are you going to do until then?"

"I'm going to go home and get some sleep. While Nguyen Rao is sitting in a cell, freaking out and realizing I'm serious about holding him, I'll be getting the rest I need. When I talk to him again, I'll have a clear head and I'll probably know more. I've got guys working on his background. We'll find whatever Nguyen is hiding. We might even have the elephant by then, too. If we do, the balance of power in our discussion will probably shift." Bart looked at her. "You need to go home, too, Annja. I appreciate all the help, and I'm sorry to have gotten you out of bed."

"And almost got me killed?" Annja raised a mocking eyebrow.

Bart nodded. "And that." He regarded her for a moment. "The guys who arrested you told me you took down Calapez and his friend. That was pretty gutsy."

"I didn't have a choice."

"I know you can defend yourself." Bart sometimes sparred with Annja in the dojo she frequented when she could. She'd taught him a lot, adding to the basic defenses he'd been trained on in the academy. "When Calapez forced you out of the diner, I was afraid something was going to happen to you."

"It didn't. We both got lucky."

"Yeah, well, Calapez ended up with a broken hand."

"I saw an opportunity and took it. I wasn't getting into the car with him."

"Why was Calapez so intent on taking you?"

"As a hostage, I suppose."

"Maybe." Bart took a deep breath and let it out. "I'm glad everything turned out okay."

Annja stepped in and gave him a hug, patting his back, thinking about how close she'd come to losing him. Bart was a friend, a really good one, and she didn't want to ever lose him. "Me, too."

OUTSIDE THE POLICE STATION, Annja turned and walked down the street, her hands in her pockets and her collar turned up against the cold wind. Bart had offered to have an officer drive her home, but she'd refused, knowing that they were busy and she wanted to be on her own.

She thought about returning to her loft, to the work she had waiting for her there, but she knew she couldn't focus on that or rest right now. Her mind was too busy, seeking out answers to the riddle of the elephant. Frustration chafed at her because she didn't know enough to ask the right questions.

Before she knew it, she'd gone down a few blocks aimlessly. Spotting a cab, she hailed it, met it at the curb and told the driver to take her to Maurice Benyovszky's building.

"ARE YOU POLICE?" The woman who asked Annja that question stood in front of a dryer in a local Laundromat two blocks down from Benyovszky's address. Annja had noted the address of the business on some receipts on Benyovszky's desk when she'd looked over his things.

Plump and in her late twenties, the woman looked Slavic and spoke with a Russian accent. Her dark hair was pulled back and frizzy from the heat inside the Laundromat. She held a three year old girl on her hip as she worked one-handed to put the wet clothes into the machine.

"No. I'm not the police." Annja helped the woman put the load of clothing into the dryer.

"I saw you with them this morning on the television." The woman pushed quarters into the machine and started it cycling. The clothing thumped as the big barrel turned, and the little girl on the woman's hip watched the contents spin.

Several other women and a few men of all ages occupied

the Laundromat, all of them dealing with their clothing. A television blared from the mount in the corner, displaying a ghost-hunting program. The whir and vibration of the machines created a soft blanket of noise that filled the building. The strong smell of detergent and bleach burned Annja's nose.

"I work for them sometimes," Annja replied. "As a consultant when they need me."

The woman was suspicious and distrustful. That was a typical reaction to anyone outside a culture. Annja wasn't of Russian heritage, wasn't from the neighborhood and her clothing separated her from everyone else in the Laundromat. The woman placed her child on the folding table in front of the dryer and fussed with her hair, combing it neatly.

"Your daughter is beautiful," Annja said.

The little girl smiled shyly and ducked her head into her mother's bosom.

"Thank you." The woman smiled, but she didn't open up anymore to Annja.

"Did you know Mr. Benyovszky?" Annja asked.

Shrugging, the woman picked up her daughter again. "I see him in the hallway sometimes. He was a good man. Very kind. His two great-nephews, though, they are a waste."

"I got that impression myself." Annja hesitated, wondering if she was pushing too hard or too sudden, and knowing there was no other route to handling the situation. "I'd like to talk to someone who knew Mr. Benyovszky."

"Why?"

"I don't want his murderer to get away."

"No one does. If anyone knew, they would tell the police." Suspicion darkened the woman's face. "They say whoever killed Mr. Benyovszky stole a fortune."

"I don't know. In fact, I don't know that anything was taken for sure. That's what I'm trying to help the police find out, but in order to know that, I need more information about Mr. Benyovszky and his business."

Another woman walked up to the first. This one was older and more plump. Her hair had turned gray and her face was weathered by years. She spoke rapidly in Russian, too fast and too low for Annja to understand.

When the first woman looked back up, she said, "My friend tells me that she sees you on television and that I should trust you because she thinks you are a nice person."

Annja smiled at the other woman. "*Spasiba.*"

The older woman nodded. "You are welcome." The words came hesitantly, but they were sincere.

"If you want to find out more about Mr. Benyovszky's business you should seek out Yelena Kustodiev," the first woman said.

"Where can I find her?" Annja asked.

"She lives in the next building." The woman hesitated, shifted her child on her hip, and looked pensive. "She is a…a very strange woman. It is best to be careful around her if you have to speak to her. I will write you the address." She accepted the pen and paper Annja handed her from her backpack. "When you go there, please do me the favor of not telling Yelena Kustodiev who told you about her." She shook her head as she wrote down the address. "She is a most intimidating woman. You will see."

9

Nguyen Rao sat in the back of the squad car and worked on the handcuffs that bound him. The locks were no problem to manipulate. The most difficult thing had been in acquiring a pick. While he had been transferred from the room where Detective McGilley had spoken with him, he'd managed to steal a ballpoint pen from the desk of another policeman on the way out without being noticed. Rao had stripped the clip from the pen, then dropped the writing utensil into a convenient trash receptacle, keeping only the slim length of metal.

Until the two policemen escorting him had placed him in the back of the squad car, he had kept the metal covered in the folds of his palm. Now he bent the metal and hooked it into the cuff on his right wrist. He didn't need both open if that wasn't possible, but managed it more easily than he'd believed. The locks had been simple, and he was dexterous, but he'd had to be patient, as well. That was made harder because he didn't know how far they planned on taking him.

The two policemen in the front seat on the other side of the metal mesh barricade separating the rear seat from the front talked about football, arguing in a good-natured way that told Rao they were friends, not just workmates. He kept that in mind, knowing he did not want to entertain any bad karma while engaged on his mission. He sought only to right an old wrong. If possible.

The first cuff clicked open, followed quickly by the second. Rao kept his hands behind him, thinking only of the elephant and of Calapez's involvement. Rao wondered who had sent the man there, and he wondered if he would have been able to entreat Maurice Benyovszky to give him the elephant in person while so many attempts over the phone had been denied.

Rao didn't know if Benyovszky was a good man or not,

but he knew that no man deserved to have his life taken from him. He wished that Benyovszky would enjoy better terms in his next life, but that was out of Rao's hands.

Not for the first time, he wished the elder monks had sent someone else. But he was the most knowledgeable about the elephant, and he spoke English easily enough. He had been the best choice for the assignment, and he had taken on the responsibility.

"I'm telling you, Frank, ain't no way the Pats are gonna squeak by this year, and if they do, the Broncos are waiting on them." The driver sipped his coffee as he pulled to a stop behind a cab at the intersection.

Glancing around, Rao tried to get his bearings. The city was an unknown area. He had managed to get around only through the map function on his phone, but he no longer had that. Still, he had confidence in himself.

He was also discomfited by the fact that he had turned himself in only to be taken into custody. He had not thought he would be placed under arrest. He still did not know how that had happened even after the police officers had explained his rights to him, then had told him he was being taken into custody as a material witness, but not as a criminal. The whole matter was highly illogical. They had said his incarceration—not their word but Rao had no other word for it—was to ensure he would provide testimony at the proper time.

He had argued, but he had quickly seen there was no other way around it, so he had given in. And he'd stolen the ballpoint pen.

Tipping over onto his right side, Rao drew back his left leg and kicked the window. The door had no handles on the inside in the rear compartment. The glass shattered and flew out to cascade against the car in the next lane.

The policemen turned around, yelling at him through the mesh separating them from him, promising dire consequences. Rao ignored them, aware of the policemen hurrying to open their doors. They were as separated from him by the mesh as he was from the front of the vehicle.

Rao spun around again, then slipped through the broken

window like an otter, hauling himself out on his arms and gaining his feet in the glass-strewn street. Fragments cracked under the thin-soled shoes the police had given him along with the orange one-piece coverall that ironically reminded Rao of his temple robes.

The driver, older and thicker, scrambled out of the car and tried to bring his pistol up. "Freeze!"

Afraid that the policeman might shoot, not that he would hit Rao, but that someone else might be injured if bullets started flying, Rao grabbed the man's gun wrist with one hand and twisted while at the same time slamming the car door closed with his other hand. The door struck the policeman with enough force to stun him. Rao pulled the weapon from the man's hand without breaking the wrist or the fingers and tossed the weapon into the backseat through the broken window.

Then he was running, throwing himself across the hood of the sedan parked beside the police car, then hurtling across the other two lanes of oncoming traffic. Horns blared and brakes screeched. He managed to slip across another car as the driver panicked and slammed on the brakes, and by the time everything calmed down, Rao was in the nearest alley, running for his life, trying to figure out how he was going to find the elephant. The only thing he knew to do was go back to where the elephant had been lost like any hunter would.

"COME, FERNANDO. YOU'RE missing your party." Joana de Campos made a moue of her lips as she walked across the length of the yacht's salon while carrying a large drink in either hand. She was a gorgeous woman, full of figure and as feisty as any of the opposite sex Sequeira had ever wanted. Long black hair tumbled down her naked shoulders, so bronzed by the sun that she looked like she'd been carved from sandalwood. The play of muscles under the skin revealed that she was alive and vibrant.

Fernando Sequeira sat on one of the white lounging sofas in the salon. No one else was there. All of his guests were out on the deck or swimming in the ocean under the careful eye of his crew. A couple inches short of six feet, broad shouldered and handsome, carefully groomed with a chin-strap beard that followed the fierce line of his chin, Sequeira sat there in aqua bathing trunks and deck shoes. His hair was black as sin and his eyes were almost amber with just a hint of green.

He smiled up at Joana, knowing that she loved looking at him. Most women found him attractive. He worked to stay that way. Deftly, he plucked one of the drinks from her.

"Thank you, Joana. For the drink and for your concern. But I am not missing my party. I enjoy watching the people I invite on these trips." He sipped the champagne, then captured her free hand in his and pulled it to his lips to briefly kiss it.

"You should be out there." Joana waved toward the yacht's stern where thirty men and women, all young, all fit, laughed and carried on. Many of them were Portuguese, but many of them were from other countries, too. Sequeira spread his business around. Communication these days was global, and it moved quickly. "You are the life of the party, you know."

Sequeira pulled her down to him, to sit next to him on the sofa. "I will go in a moment. When you get too close to business, sometimes you lose sight of the prize in all the movement. I like distance."

"You like too much distance sometimes." Joana leaned in and kissed him. She'd had a little too much to drink and the effects were showing. "You're like a lion, Fernando. You should stalk out among people and claim your space."

He laughed at her then and she thought he was laughing with her, enjoying her daring. In truth, all of that attention was what she craved. Sequeira didn't care for it so much. He leaned in and kissed her bare shoulder.

"Do you know what my father told me one day?" he asked.

"You have told me many things your father told you." She leaned against him and sipped her drink.

"I have." He nodded agreeably. "But one of the best things he told me was that a man who wanted power, to control things, that man would be content in the shadows when wielding his power. A man who wishes everyone to know him, who craves the limelight, that man is only making a target of himself."

Adrian Sequeira had been a criminal, a street thief and pickpocket when he was younger, then had built a small empire smuggling cigarettes and arms through Spain. Afterward, after getting an education, he set up straw banks and began laundering money for other criminal organizations.

During his teen years, Sequeira had fought with his father. Both of them had been prideful men and Sequeira didn't like moving slowly like his father had with his business. Nor did he want to simply inherit what his father had assembled.

Instead, Fernando Sequeira had combined his love of pop culture, movies, the Masters in Fine Arts he'd received that he'd paid for himself, and set up shop as a film and television program pirate. He'd run that business out of the back of his car for a while, then gotten more machines and employees and rented an office.

That had been fifteen years ago when he was just out of university. The profits had rolled steadily in, and his father had even laid off some of the money laundering into those businesses. Fernando hadn't been satisfied, though. By thirty, he'd bought his first television station and plowed enough money and his expertise into it to get it off the ground.

Those first few months had been hard. Communications was a tough market. He was slowly starving to death, watching his profits get soaked up trying to buy into a market share. In the end, he'd gone to his father for help.

Men who tried to stand in Sequeira's way ended up bloodied, blackmailed and financially beaten. No prisoners were taken. Slowly and surely, Sequeira had built the empire he'd dreamed of. He owned television stations, radio stations and premium movie services, including several DVD and videogame vending machines that kept the money rolling in.

These days, his father respected him as a businessman, and Sequeira understood more of what his father had been trying to teach him. There at the end little more than a year ago, when Adrian Sequeira had succumbed to a brain tumor that had taken him quickly, Fernando had gotten close to the man.

"Fernando?" Joana studied his face, her eyes narrowed and her attention fully on him.

"Yes." He smiled at her.

"Where were you?"

He squeezed her hand. "Here at your side."

"No, you weren't." Joana sighed. "Sometimes you are like that. Here with me one minute. Gone the next."

"I'm sorry. I have a lot on my mind."

"This is why I tell you that you should enjoy your guests while on this cruise. You work too hard."

"I work just enough."

Joana reached up and brushed back a lock of hair from his forehead. "You are thinking about the elephant, aren't you?"

Sequeira grinned at her, wanting to distract her from that. "No."

"Now you are lying. I saw you when you were studying that elephant on the computer."

A few days ago, in his study, where only a few people were allowed to visit and Joana was supposed to stay out of, she had seen him watching the bidding for the elephant Maurice Benyovszky had offered for sale.

He didn't bother to deny the accusation a second time.

"Honestly, my love, I don't understand what you see in those old things. Those swords and faded maps and statues of hideous things."

"I know." Sequeira sipped his champagne and felt the gentle roll of the yacht on the waves. Outside, the weather was cool enough to be enjoyable on the deck, and the water was warm enough to swim comfortably, as several of his guests were doing. Little over a mile away, Lisbon rose in the distance across the blue sea.

"I wish I did, then perhaps I would not be so jealous of the time it takes you away from me."

"A man must be allowed his diversions and passions. Otherwise he is not a true man."

"This is another thing your father taught you?"

"This is a thing I have found to be true. If I did not appreciate those things, then I would never appreciate you as I do."

"I am not an old thing."

Sequeira chuckled at her mock outrage. "No, you are not. And I am glad of it."

He was, but her beauty and attention didn't hold a candle to the treasures he'd found over the past ten years. Legends and near myths and handed-down tales still made his blood quicken. His father had done a lot of business with sailors and sea captains while smuggling, and all of those men had carried stories with them.

Sequeira had minored in history, and his fine arts degree had exposed him to a lot of the art that he cherished. Portugal was rife with tales of pirates' treasures and other artifacts left by the Romans, the Visigoths and the Moors, to name only a few. He had some items from all those cultures, and he had listened to hundreds of other stories.

Three years ago, he had found a sunken ship, a Spanish galleon, and had recovered almost two million dollars in gold coins, just a taste of what had probably been strewn across the sea floor when the ship had gone down.

"Have you ever heard of the *Neustra Senora de las Mercedes*?" he asked, knowing the answer before she gave it.

"No."

"It was a Spanish galleon, sunk in 1804 while voyaging back from South America. In addition to the many people on board, the ship also carried tons of gold and silver worth over five hundred million dollars."

Joana's eyes lit up at that. "So much?"

Sequeira nodded. "So much. The ship was found by a treasure hunter out of Florida in the United States. He had researched the maps and the records, and he had found the ship. The problem was, he told people about his find, and the Spanish took the treasure back."

"That does not sound fair."

"I don't think that it is, but it is how countries work. No one in Spain was looking for that ship, and even if they were, they were not skilled enough to find it. This man was. So, you see, Joana, these old things are worth my time."

"Will this elephant lead you to treasure like that?"

"I don't know. Perhaps."

"Do you have the elephant?"

Anger beat at Sequeira's temples and he tried to control it. "Unfortunately, not yet. I had hoped to purchase it from a man last night during an online auction. I had even sent a man to get the elephant after I won it with a bid. Instead, the internet server I was using crashed at the wrong time and I was unable to procure the piece."

"Does the person who purchased the elephant know what you know about it?"

"That is another mystery to me."

"Where do you think the elephant will lead you?"

Sequeira thought about that for a moment. "I have only rumors and superstitions about the elephant. There was a Japanese sailor who saw the elephant, a man who was rescued by Russians hundreds of years ago who saw the elephant and heard the tale about it and the fortune it would lead to."

"What fortune?"

Smiling, Sequeira shook his head. "I am sorry, but there are some things I will not share."

She feigned a disappointed look.

"In time, perhaps I will tell you." Sequeira drained his champagne glass. "I must have my passions, you know."

"I know." Joana took his glass and set it along with hers on a side table. The crew would be along soon enough to gather them up. She stood and pulled him to his feet. "Then you may pursue the elephant when we return home. Until then, you have a party to attend. The day will be over soon and you should enjoy what you can of it."

Sequeira went with her, stepping out into the bright evening sunlight. Joana quickly became lost in the crowd as music pumped from the yacht's sound system. She danced out on the deck with the other young girls, all of them laughing and showing off their slim bodies as they threw themselves to the rhythm of the music.

Alvaro, one of the ship's crew, brought Sequeira another glass. The young man was sleek and hard, a product of the streets until Sequeira had hired him seven years ago. Alvaro had tried, with considerable skill, to pick Sequeira's pocket. After Alvaro's broken arm had healed, after he'd seen Alvaro made no sound when it had been broken and did not plead for his life afterward, Sequeira had offered the boy a job.

Leaning in, Alvaro spoke into Sequeira's ear. "The tide is going out now. Captain Nogueira says we are in a good place."

"Excellent." Sequeira fell in behind Alvaro.

"Fernando!" Joana's voice cut across the din.

He turned back to her, waved and smiled. "Keep dancing! I will return in only a minute!"

Joana pouted briefly, then returned to the music.

Downstairs, Sequeira followed Alvaro to the middle of the yacht. Sequeira had spent a fortune on the craft, outfitting it for long trips, for parties and for diving. An open moon pool allowed divers to leave the yacht directly from inside the vessel.

The moon pool ran three meters square. The water lapped the sides of the opening and filled the compartment with the brine smell of the sea. Many of Sequeira's guests had enjoyed the moon pool while staying aboard the yacht.

Some of them, however, did not.

Reaching up just inside the room, Sequeira turned on the light as Alvaro closed the door behind them. The white light filled the room with bright intensity and revealed the man bound hand and foot and gagged lying on the floor.

"Hello, Jorge." Sequeira smiled down at the man, seeing the fright in Melicio's wide eyes. "You didn't think I had forgotten you, did you?"

Jorge Melicio was a member of the public security police. He worked against organized crime and terrorism. Melicio was in his sixties, gray-haired and lanky. A wide piece of surgical tape covered his mouth and bruises covered his face. He bore sailor's tattoos on both arms, and they were visible because he'd been stripped down to his underwear.

"You know, Jorge, you tried for years to put my father away." Sequeira knelt down beside the man. "My father, he could be a patient and forgiving man. You knew this and you took advantage of it. Growing up on some of the same fishing boats, perhaps he maintained a soft spot for you." He placed his hand over his heart. "Regrettably for you, I am not my father. No such soft spot exists. And I grow weary of your constant attempts to investigate me."

Melicio struggled against his bonds and worked to speak. His body writhed and his face colored and contorted.

"On another day, perhaps I would let you go. But I've had a rather disappointing night and morning." Sequeira spread his hands. "I know this is not your fault, but I have no one else to take it out on. So this will be what it will be." He paused. "Do not think you are leaving your wife a widow. She is already dead. A traffic accident a few hours ago. A tragedy."

Melicio went limp and tears leaked from his eyes.

"Do not worry so much. She will not be there alone long. You'll be seeing her in the next few minutes." Sequeira nodded at Alvaro and together they picked up the policeman and dropped him into the moon pool.

Unable to swim, Melicio sank at once, dragging at the coil of rope beside the moon pool that quickly grew taut from the bucket of lead. Sequeira heaved the heavy bucket into the water as well, then leaned over the water and watched as the old man slid to the bottom of the sea hundreds of feet below.

Perhaps, like the *Neustra Senora de las Mercedes*, Jorge Melicio would one day be found, but Sequeira didn't think so.

10

"You are not going to see the witch, are you?" The young boy peered out around a door halfway down the hallway from where Annja stood in front of an apartment with her hand raised to knock. He was about eight, thin and had narrow shoulders that bookended his head almost defensively. He wore a superheroes shirt and kept his hand on the door's edge like he was ready to bolt at any second.

"I'm here to see Yelena Kustodiev." Annja smiled, but she felt a little uneasy. She thought part of the feeling was because she hadn't had enough sleep, had been shot at only a few hours ago and still didn't have a clue about Maurice Benyovszky's elephant.

But some of the uneasiness was because the hallway was long and narrow, the building kind of on the shoddy side in a marginal neighborhood, and because the women in the Laundromat had acted the way they had. Now the boy looked afraid and had cared enough to warn a stranger about her choice of destination.

The boy lowered his voice and leaned toward Annja, but he maintained his grip on the door, ready to dart back inside. "Yelena Kustodiev. That's the *witch*."

"She's a witch?" Annja raised a skeptical eye and smiled slightly. "Seriously? Maybe she just has a bad temper now and again."

"She has that, too. She doesn't like kids. She puts the evil eye on things like Baba Yaga does."

"You know that Baba Yaga wasn't real, right?" Annja couldn't help but smile. Baba Yaga was a Russian witch who was supposed to have lived in a hut supported by chicken legs. In the evenings, Baba Yaga would lay with her feet in the fire. There were a lot of stories and legends about her.

"I know Baba Yaga isn't real. Harry Potter isn't real either, but the witch is." The boy nodded toward the door. "She'll put a hex on you and no one will ever see you again. Or maybe they'll just find you dead somewhere with your eyes and tongue gone."

Okay, somebody's been putting thoughts in his head. "I don't think that's going to happen."

"She put a hex on my cat, Petey. I never saw him again."

"Well, I'm sorry to hear that."

The boy suddenly cried out in surprise, disappeared behind the door and slammed it shut behind him. The *bang* of the door filling the frame echoed along the hallway.

A cold spot strangely took shape on the back of Annja's neck. Breath catching in her throat just a little, chiding herself for how she'd reacted, she turned back to face the door she'd been standing in front of. The hinges were well oiled because she hadn't heard a thing when it had opened.

A thin old woman with a haggard face, wild gray hair, rheumy hazel eyes the same color as the bottom of a dark beer bottle stood in the open doorway. Almost languidly, she peered out at Annja, taking her measure. The woman wore a black, shapeless dress that ran from her neck to her ankles and looked ancient. As tall as Annja was, she had to look up at the old woman, who almost had to duck under the door.

"Yes?"

Annja smiled but the effort felt stiff and false, and thought her expression probably looked like that, as well. "Good afternoon. I'm—"

The old woman raised a long-fingered hand in front of Annja's face. Startled, a bit leery, Annja stepped back.

"Do not tell me," the old woman said, staring over Annja's shoulder like she was peering into another world. "I will tell you. I have the power, you see, the power to know things and see things when the mists of the world part."

"Okay."

The old woman pierced Annja with her gaze. "You are an explorer. Someone who hunts the past. You are a world traveler, someone who has seen many things in her life. Many of those things you wish you had not seen. You often look for things that frighten other people. Perhaps some of these things are dark creatures. But you have been successful in your journeys and you have escaped with your life from these encounters."

Annja didn't quite know what to say to that.

"You seek an audience with me, *da*?" the old woman prompted.

"I was hoping to speak with Yelena Kustodiev."

Theatrically, the old woman stepped back and waved Annja into the apartment. "You already are. I am Yelena Kustodiev, seer of things in the unseen world."

Annja didn't want to enter the apartment. She tried to tell herself that reaction was because she was in a hurry, but she knew the boy's words still slithered around inside her head.

"I really didn't want to take up much of your time."

The old woman waved her into the house again, imperiously this time. "I have a few moments to answer your questions. I knew you were coming and I made an opening in my schedule. You cannot deny my generosity."

Okay, that's creepy. Cautiously, Annja stepped into the apartment.

The living room was small and looked lived-in, if the person living there was into supernatural things. Shelves filled with grotesque demon masks carved from wood, stuffed crows and ravens, two snakes coiled and kept in gallon jars of formaldehyde, a collection of still yet more stuffed and bottled dead things, and drawings of impossible creatures and places hung on the wall. Much of the items looked Slavic in origin, but a lot of them looked like fantasy stuff.

One of the odder pieces was a cat with the head and wings of a bat. The chimeric creature looked almost natural. At least, the pieces all fit together well. The black leathery membranes disappeared into the sable cat's fur as if they'd sprouted there. Seeing that, Annja relaxed—a little, but she would not put down her guard. She figured she knew what had become of the weird taxidermy project Demyan and Yegor had been talking about during the interview with Bart McGilley.

"Please sit." Yelena Kustodiev pointed to a small couch in the living room.

Annja sat, but she was ready to get out of the apartment as soon as she could. Too many odd occurrences had already happened since last night and she didn't want the trend to continue. "Thank you, but, really, I won't be but a moment."

Yelena sat on the other side of the low coffee table. "You need me, young woman. Otherwise you would not be here. *Da*?"

Not exactly true. Annja nodded, though, and sat silently as Yelena pulled an embroidered black cloth from the coffee table to reveal a crystal ball about the size of a cantaloupe sitting there in a brass, three-toed claw.

"Behold." Yelena tossed the cloth over her shoulder and gestured to the crystal ball. "The all-seeing eye. I know your present. I know your past. I can even tell you your future."

Glimpsing the TV listings in the newspaper on the shelf under the coffee table, Annja smiled. "Okay, I'll play. Tell me why I'm here."

That didn't stop the woman. "You *need* me. You seek the wisdom I have."

"No, tell me what I'm going to ask you."

Yelena hesitated and tried to recover. "You're going to tell me about the problem that has brought you to my door."

"Tell me who told me how to find you."

The old woman frowned. "Do not mock the dark powers, young woman. You do not realize what you are risking by doing so in such a cavalier manner. You try their patience."

"Dark powers?" Annja reached under the coffee table and brought up the TV listings. The newspaper was only a couple weeks old, and it carried a picture of Annja, showing an interview with her about being on *Chasing History's Monsters*. "I'm thinking maybe you read up on me."

Yelena grinned, showing perfect dentures, and leaned back more comfortably in her chair. "Okay, I'm busted, but I had you going for a minute, didn't I?" Her accent wasn't nearly so thick now and sounded more New York than Russian.

"It's a pretty good act." Annja put the TV listings back under the coffee table.

"I get away with it because I'm so tall. People aren't used to looking up at a woman. I intimidate them. I bet you understand that. Makes guys shorter than you uncomfortable, and makes women stay away."

Annja knew that was true.

The woman motioned toward the door. "At first I didn't know who you were. I heard Osip talking to you in the hall, telling you to look out for the witch. After I recognized you through the peephole, I thought I would have some fun. When you're the neighborhood witch, you don't get to crack a lot of jokes. Not if you want to keep your status." Yelena pulled her witch attitude back on and looked scary for a moment. "So maybe you miss out on some fun, but I get to hear all the gossip in the neighborhood. The women that come in here seek my *help* to find out if their husbands are cheating on them, to decide what to do about a job they are working or one they are considering taking, or to learn if they are in relationships that are going anywhere. They end up telling me much more than I tell them. They just don't realize it. Hearing everything like that helps me tell the *fortune* of most everyone else that wanders into here."

"Why do you do it?"

"For the money, of course. My mister, God rest him, was a stage performer up in the Catskills back when families liked entertainment like that. When that dried up, we started a telephone service, then we got into internet psychic stuff. I still do the internet stuff, but I keep up the witch shtick for the neighborhood because it makes me a few bucks and I enjoy it."

Annja smiled back at the woman. "I came here to talk to you about Maurice Benyovszky."

"Who said I knew anyone by that name?"

Annja pointed at the rogue taxidermist project. "Your catbat told me."

"Oh." Yelena reached out a hand and stroked the bat's head. "What does Fluffy have to do with anything?"

Fluffy? Seriously? "You got him from Benyovszky."

"How do you know that?" Most of the humor drained from Yelena's face.

"His nephews told me."

"Oh. Them." Yelena scoffed. "In the shape they're in, I'm surprised they can remember anything." She mimed smoking and being drunk and chuckled.

"You have to admit, that—" Annja looked at the bat-cat "—is hard to forget."

Yelena smiled and patted the stuffed animal again. "I think he's cute. If he existed, he would be thoughtful and wise."

"I want to talk about Benyovszky."

The levity and jokiness left Yelena's face then, and her features softened into a more somber attitude. "He was killed last night. Shot in his own home."

"I know."

"Of course you do. You're working with the police."

Annja lifted an eyebrow.

Yelena smiled and shook her head. "I watch the news on my computer in the bedroom. I saw the story. I didn't think you would ever end up here, though."

"I am working with the police. A friend of mine."

"Would you like to know about that relationship?" Yelena leaned over the crystal ball, waved one hand over it with practiced slowness and false drama, closed her eyes and put her other hand to her forehead. Her fingernails were painted black. "I'm sensing some feelings of attraction there."

"No, I don't want to know about that relationship." Annja and Bart had flirted over the years they had known each other, but they'd never crossed a line. They had also tabled that discussion a long time back, before Bart's engagement. Since that engagement had gone away, Annja wasn't quite sure where things were. She liked being Bart's friend. She liked him being her friend. She didn't like things in her home life changing much or being complicated, especially since the sword, Roux and Garin changed so much of everything else. "I want to know about Benyovszky."

Yelena dropped her hands to her lap and shrugged. "I bought Fluffy from Maurice."

"And?"

Yelena sighed. "And sometimes I hung out with him. A little. When you get old, that doesn't mean the passion completely drains out of a person. We were not in love. Our lives are—*were*—too much our own and we liked it that way. But sometimes Maurice and I would—"

Annja held up a hand. "Whoa. We're not going there."

A feral, mocking smile framed Yelena's red lipsticked lips. "Coward."

"I would just like to know what you know about Benyovszky that might help me find his murderer."

"I don't know who murdered him. If I did, I would have already gone to the authorities."

"I'm not looking for his murderer. That's the job of the police." Annja had been telling herself that since setting out on her own. She didn't want a conflict of interest with Bart, or to get enmeshed in the murder investigation. Those things took time, and time was something she had precious little of.

Yelena stared into Annja's eyes. "This relationship, it is with a policeman, yes? Do not disagree with me because I can see this in your face."

"We're not going there, either."

Yelena smiled and clapped her hands. "I knew it!"

Annja ignored her. "I'm especially interested in anyone who might have harbored ill feelings toward Benyovszky."

"No one harbored ill feelings toward Maurice." Yelena dismissed the idea immediately.

"Was anyone jealous of him?"

"Jealousy is a natural condition for people, don't you think? There is always someone who covets what another has. Can I think of anyone who would do such a thing to Maurice? No. Again, I would have been to the police."

"I was also told that Benyovszky kept company with known criminals."

At that, Yelena sat back and looked more serious than ever. "Who would tell you such a thing? Those nephews of Maurice? They are no-goodniks. You should know you cannot trust them."

"Maurice had a criminal history." Annja had seen it for herself. None of it had been more than robbery, and there hadn't been an incident in years. "Yegor and Demyan told me that Maurice sometimes hung with those people from the old days."

Still uneasy, Yelena ran a hand through her hair. "Some of those men are friends with Maurice, *da.* They would not have killed him."

Annja kept her voice steady. "Whoever killed Maurice was someone he knew, Yelena, and someone who would take someone else's life. If there were no personal reasons to kill Maurice, then his death had to be the result of theft. There is an article missing. Maybe more than one. We haven't been able to finish a proper inventory of his things yet." She paused. "Can you name someone Maurice knew who would do such a thing to him?"

"Of course not."

"Then I need to talk to someone who can name a person like that. Give me the name of someone I can talk to about Maurice who might know who killed him."

Yelena crossed her knees and leaned forward. She looked nervous as she smoothed her dress. "Perhaps you are right."

"I'm hoping I am."

"But you must understand, these men you are talking about, they are very dangerous men. Men who have killed. Men who would not hesitate to kill again."

"Do you think men like that will talk to the police?" Annja knew the answer before she even asked the question.

"No. Pride alone would keep them from communicating with the police. These men are still Russian, you understand? They may have lived in New York for thirty or forty years, but in their minds they are still Russian. They will trust no one." Yelena shook her head and shrugged. "Not all of them are immediately dangerous. Perhaps there are a few you may speak with."

"If I could get those names, I would appreciate it."

"You may wish to thank me after you meet them."

"I can take care of myself."

"Do not automatically believe this is true." Yelena hesitated a little longer and Annja waited her out. Talking to the Russian criminals might be a dead end, but she had nothing else to pursue at the moment. "Let me tell you about Leonid Klykov…"

11

At first glance to the casual observer who was passing through the neighborhood, the small neon sign over Buba's Bar looked like it had been misspelled, but Annja knew it was supposed to be Buba, which was the diminutive of "bubbala," or "bubeleh," and not Bubba's Bar. The Yiddish term was used to address older women with fondness. Originally it had referred to midwives and grandmothers in Slavic cultures. It was also used as a term of endearment.

Waiting for traffic on the street corner where the cab had let her out, Annja had to smile. *Grandmother's is a den of inequity. Who knew?*

The redbrick building stood four stories tall. The bar occupied a small space between a florist and a falafel shop. A faded green awning stuck out over the sidewalk, creating a narrow ribbon of shade in the noonday sun. The small windows offered only a peek inside the place, and much of that space was taken up by handmade signs advertising specials.

When the light changed, Annja hit the crosswalk. On the way over in the cab, she had pulled up a quick background of Leonid Klykov on her tablet. Back in the 1970s, Klykov had gotten arrested for a number of things, and finally took a nine-year fall for racketeering. According to the reporter who'd covered the case, business had gone on as usual for Klykov and his old life was waiting for him when he finished his sentence.

Annja knew Bart would not be happy if he found out what she was doing, but she felt certain she could get in under the radar on the visit.

When she stepped through the front door of Buba's, the warmth of the bar gusted over her, carrying the smells of beer and borscht and fresh bread. She stood there and just enjoyed the bread smell, realizing how hungry she was.

Small tables crowded the tiny floor space at the front of the bar. A few stools lined the bar, and a large-screen television, apparently the only modern convenience in the place, hung on the wall in one of the darkened corners. A horse race was in progress, the shrill ring of the starting gate opening echoed throughout the bar and the thunder of hoofbeats and the excited banter of the announcer followed it.

Several old men sat at the tables. A few younger men sat in the corners of the bar and watched with the hard eyes of wary bodyguards.

An old, bald bartender in a prim shirt and tie wiped his hands on his waist apron and came from behind the bar. He put on a nice smile and his heavy cologne arrived before he did.

"May I help you?" His English was good enough, but heavily accented.

"I'd like to speak with Leonid Klykov if I could, please."

The bartender hesitated, letting Annja know one of the old men was probably Klykov, but she hadn't a clue which one he would be. Yelena had offered very little in terms of a description, and the most recent photographs Annja had found of the man on the internet were from the 1980s. Klykov stayed out of the public eye.

One of the bodyguards stubbed out a short black cigarette in a tray at the bar and came over. He was almost six and a half feet tall, broad shouldered and wearing his black hair cut nearly to his scalp. Edges of tattoos showed above the collar of his turtleneck. He wore a shoulder holster with a semiautomatic snugged under his left arm.

"It's okay, Semyon. I got this." The newcomer's accent was mostly out of the Bronx with a hint of Slavic. His dark eyes were hard, and he smiled like a predatory beast as he ran his eyes over Annja.

Annja waited for his eyes to meet hers again. "You're not Leonid Klykov."

He smiled again and held out a hand. "Gimme your purse."

"I'm not carrying a purse."

That confused the guy for a minute, and it made a couple of the old fellas in the back crack up.

"That's right, Georgy. You get her straightened out."

Georgy waved with his free hand. "Gimme the backpack."

"Why?"

"Because I said." He lowered his voice and put more threat into his words.

"No."

Cursing, Georgy reached for Annja's backpack strap. Annja captured his arm, rotated it and pulled to get him to bend forward, then she spun sideways toward him and threw an elbow into his face. Georgy stumbled back and reached for his pistol, but Annja got there first and pulled the weapon free. He growled at her and tried to grab her. She backed away and kicked him in the crotch. When he stumbled, she spun to the side and slammed the pistol into the back of Georgy's head.

Already unconscious, the big man fell face-first toward the tiled floor. Before he hit, Annja held up the 9mm at chest level, pressed the magazine release and worked the slide to eject the bullet, then dropped them. Gun, magazine and bullets all hit the floor just a heartbeat after Georgy.

Several of the other bodyguards had weapons in their hands at that point, all of them aimed at her.

Annja kept her hands up at shoulder level. "I just came here looking for Leonid Klykov. I didn't come here to be manhandled."

A group of four old men in the back started laughing out loud and pointing at the bodyguard on the floor.

"Hey, Leonid," one of them hooted, "I think you are paying Georgy too much."

An old man with neatly cut gray hair and a short goatee frowned. He was short and had a small pot belly. His dark green eyes remained focused on Annja. He wore a light brown suit that didn't advertise wealth, but Annja knew from how the suit fit it had been tailored. He rolled a toothpick in his teeth.

"What do you want with Leonid Klykov?" the man asked.

Annja remained standing where she was but she put her hands down at her sides. "To talk."

"About what?"

"Maurice Benyovszky."

The man nodded. "That is a sad subject. Why would you want to talk about that poor man?"

"I'm trying to find out who killed him."

The man shrugged. "Why? Even if you find the killer, Maurice Benyovszky will still be just as dead."

"Something was stolen from him."

"Ah." The man nodded. "So this thing that was stolen belonged to you?"

"No."

"Then what is your interest in this endeavor?"

"If I find the thing that was stolen, then I'll probably find Benyovszky's killer."

"Again, Maurice will still be dead."

"But the property that was stolen can be returned to its rightful owner."

The old man lifted his eyebrows. "Someone hired you to do this thing?"

"No."

Lifting a hand to his face, the old man scratched at his goatee. "I do not see why you would trouble yourself in this matter."

"Can you help me, Mr. Klykov?"

Klykov picked up a glass of beer at his elbow and sipped. "Nor do I understand why you would trouble me."

"I was told you were Benyovszky's friend."

"That would be between me and Maurice, and no business of yours."

"Mr. Klykov, if you know anything about Benyovszky's murder, I would appreciate your help."

"You are police. I don't help police." Klykov turned his back to her and lifted his beer once more.

"I'm not the police." Annja started to take a step forward. Frustrated, she decided she wasn't going to take no for an answer. Unfortunately, the other bodyguards still had their weapons in hand and flipped off the safeties. She froze. "Please, Mr. Klykov. If you can help, I wish that you would."

One of the other men at the table leaned forward and whispered into Klykov's ear. The old Russian gangster listened, then reached under his jacket as he turned to face her.

Annja's heart sped up as she thought maybe Klykov was going to deal with her himself.

But the old man only pulled out a pair of glasses and slipped them on. He blinked at her, then smiled broadly. "You are Annja Creed! The chaser of monsters in history!"

Feeling somewhat relieved, but still not certain how everything was going to turn out, Annja smiled and nodded. "I am."

"Come! Come!" Klykov waved her over to his table. The other men shifted around to make room and one of the bodyguards brought over an extra chair after the old gangster ordered him to. The guns were also put away.

Annja slipped out of her backpack, placed it beside the seat and sat.

"I love your show." Klykov smiled hugely. "I save them all on my DVR and watch them."

"That's awesome." Annja felt awkward sitting there and didn't know what to do about it. "Did you know Benyovszky?"

"Maurice? Sure, sure. For a long time. He was one of us." Klykov motioned to the bartender. "Semyan. Get the lady something to drink."

Annja asked for a water with lemon. "Did you know about his business?"

"I did. Maurice was very industrious, very knowledgeable about old things."

Annja took her phone out, thanked Semyan for her drink when he placed it on the table and pulled up a picture of the elephant. "Can you tell me anything about this?"

Klykov adjusted his glasses and peered at the image. "It's an elephant?"

"Yes, it's an elephant." Annja felt her hopes dwindling.

"Then I can tell you it's an elephant."

"Maurice never mentioned it to you?"

"Maurice mentioned lots of things. He would talk all day, that one, if you let him."

One of the other men, a man with a smile made crooked by an old scar along his jaw that pulled his lips down, chimed in. "This is the elephant Maurice was talking about last week. The one he said was going to make him a lot of money."

Annja turned her attention to the speaker. "Do you remember anything else Maurice said about the elephant?"

The man gave the question some thought and stroked his scarred jaw. "He said it was an *old* elephant and he was gonna make bank on it." He shrugged. "That's all I got."

Stymied, Annja sipped her water and tried to think of her next course of action. All of her leads had dried up. She wondered if Bart had discovered anything new.

"Tell me something." Klykov ran a finger along his nose. "How was Maurice killed?"

"You don't know?"

Klykov burst out laughing and the other men joined him.

"This is trick, *da*?" the old gangster asked. "You try to entrap me?"

"No. I just thought you might have heard."

"No. Only Maurice, his killer and the police know how he was killed. That news has not reached the street or been on television."

Annja speculated if telling Klykov and his cronies that information would affect Bart's case.

"She is being careful, this one," the scarred man said. "She is very smart."

"Obviously she is smart," Klykov said. "She has a television show."

"Just because you have a television show doesn't mean you are smart," one of the other men said. "Look at some of those crazy reality shows. All my nieces and nephews watch them. They are not so smart on those shows, and they are not so smart in their lives."

"Well," Klykov said undaunted, "Annja Creed is smart." He flicked his gaze back at her. "Tell me how Maurice was killed."

After another, briefer, hesitation, Annja described the means by which Benyovszky was murdered.

"Ah." Klykov leaned back in his chair. "Someone Maurice knew. Someone who likes to use a hammer in his kills."

He pursed his lips. "Would you like to know who this male-factor is?"

"Yes." Excitement thrummed through Annja's body.

"Then we must work out a trade."

"A trade?" She thought for a moment that he was kidding her, but then she saw that he was deadly serious.

"Of course a trade. I am not going to do this thing for free. I have my reputation to think of."

"What do you want?"

12

Georgy took the box from the delivery guy who brought it into Buba's. The delivery guy stood there looking annoyed. Georgy wasn't in a good mood either. He'd woken up and discovered he was the butt of the other bodyguards' jokes, kind of like Rudolph at the reindeer games, as one of the bodyguards had put it.

"Georgy," Klykov called from the table. "Do not be a cheapskate. Pay the man for his troubles."

Frowning, or maybe grimacing because he still had a large bump on the back of his head that an icepack hadn't much helped, Georgy held the box in one hand and fished money from his pants pocket with the other. He gave the money to the deliveryman, who promptly made himself scarce.

"If you learn how to tip faster," one of the other bodyguards called out, "maybe you'll be in practice to pull your gun faster."

Georgy snarled an oath at the man while the other bodyguards cracked up. Annja tried to hide her own smile. She'd actually been having a great time listening to the bodyguards rag on Georgy, and soaking up the stories Klykov and the other gangsters told about their misadventures back in the day. All of the old men were good storytellers. As it turned out, crime was a lot funnier than she'd ever imagined. And strangely enough, she thought Roux and Garin would have fit right in with the old gangsters.

Annja shoved aside the remnants of her meal as Georgy placed the box on the table. Klykov had insisted on ordering from the falafel place next door after Annja had inquired about getting something to eat. He had paid for everything and the meal was good.

Taking out a knife, Georgy flicked the blade open with his thumb and slid it along the wrapping tape.

"Back, back," Klykov said, pushing the big man aside. "I've got this." He stood and reached into the box, hauling out *Chasing History's Monsters* T-shirts and Blu-ray collections. He parceled those around to his friends, grinning happily.

Annja still couldn't believe the old gangster had demanded television swag for his information. All of the items were easily attainable from the show's website. She waited till all of the items were distributed, including a T-shirt to Georgy, who actually seemed pleased but tried to hide it.

"All right," she told Klykov. "I've held up my end of the deal. Do you know who killed Maurice?"

"Sure, sure. I knew as soon as you told me about the hammer. Maurice knew only one man that would kill him like that. It was Pavel Onoprienko."

The name didn't mean anything to Annja, but she typed it into her tablet PC after she asked how to spell it. The scar-faced man, his name was Pitor Serov and he was a grandfather to four little girls whose pictures he loved to show off, leaned in and gave her the correct spelling. Klykov hadn't known.

"How do you know it was Onoprienko?" Annja got immediate hits on Pavel Onoprienko, known also by his sobriquet Pavel the Gavel. The reason for that followed almost directly.

"Because Onoprienko has a history of killing with hammers." Klykov frowned as though troubled. "He is a deeply disturbed man. Would you like me to take you to him?"

Annja quickly scanned through the information she'd gotten on the man. Onoprienko had a long history of violence. He'd only gotten out of prison a few weeks ago. If Klykov was correct in his assumption, and she felt that he was, Onoprienko would be headed back to prison.

"Do you know where Onoprienko is?"

Klykov shrugged. "I can make a few calls, if you would like."

Annja didn't hesitate. "Please." She only briefly considered calling Bart and telling him what she was doing, but she had the definite feeling that Klykov would not cooperate with the police no matter how much television swag was offered.

And there was a chance that Onoprienko was not guilty no matter what Klykov said. Calling Bart, until she knew for certain, would only deflect the ongoing investigation.

Klykov took out his cell phone and started punching in numbers.

SITTING IN A tiny cybercafe across the street from the bar he had tracked Annja Creed to, Rao sipped hot tea and waited. He had gotten lucky when he'd returned to the apartment building where Benyovszky had lived. If the archaeologist had not been there, he hadn't known what he was going to do. She was his closest lead to the elephant.

But she had been there, and he had tracked her to the building where the fortune-teller lived. Now she was across the street. Rao didn't know who she was talking to, but he knew the woman had not given up on finding the elephant. The fact built up his confidence at the same time as it filled him with trepidation. He needed to pick up the elephant's trail himself and find out if the legends about the Eye of Vishnu were correct.

Even if they weren't, even if the power of the eye wasn't real, there could still yet be so much recovered that had been thought lost.

"Hey, bro. You got any change you could donate to a worthy cause?"

Rao turned toward the three young men that approached him. He had marked the three of them when they'd entered the cybercafe and had known they could pose trouble. He'd made certain he never had eye contact with them, choosing to remain quiet and small.

The tactic hadn't worked primarily because there were so few people in the cybercafe. All of the other clientele were teenagers playing computer games.

There was no "worthy" cause. The men were there to rob him.

"I think I can help you." Rao reached into his pocket and

took out twenty-three dollars, all that he had left when a man had tried to mug him earlier. After he had knocked the would-be mugger out, Rao had taken the man's clothes as well, switching the unconscious man out with the orange jail jumpsuit. Rao placed the money on the table before him.

Money didn't concern Rao. Finances were the least of his worries with the temple behind him.

The tallest of the three men picked up the folded bills and flipped through them. As he totaled the amount, his lips moved. "Twenty-three bucks, that's it?" He didn't sound happy.

"It is all I have," Rao said truthfully. He hoped they would believe him and leave him in peace. He did not want to give up his observation post.

The man squinted at Rao doubtfully. "I don't think this money is all you have. You're holding out on us, man, and we don't like that."

"I have no more money. Please take that and go."

At the check-in counter, the clerk watched anxiously as he stood with his cell phone clutched in one hand. He was in his middle years, shaggy headed and wearing a heavy-metal T-shirt with the name of a band that Rao was familiar with from his days at university.

"Can't do it, " the tall gang member said. "This ain't enough to even get us some burgers."

"If I had more, I would give it to you."

"Let's see if that's true. Stand up and lemme see." The young man waved a hand at Rao.

Without a word, Rao stood. His clothing didn't fit him properly. The shirt and jacket were too big, and the pants were too short, ending a few inches above his ankles.

"Empty your pockets." The gang member waited as Rao did as ordered, turning up only a few coins.

"I ain't believing it," one of the other men said. "Guy's gotta be hanging on to something. Nobody walks around that broke that ain't got a credit card on them."

The leader nodded. "That's true. And why don't you have any ID?"

Not having ID was going to be a problem. Rao knew he would have to contact the temple to work that out. He intended to do that as soon as he pieced together what Annja Creed was doing.

"It was stolen," Rao replied. "This city is not a good place to live."

The men laughed at that.

The guy leading the group stepped forward and seized Rao's wrist. Rao let the man twist the arm behind him, but could not bear having the man put his dirty hands on him. Knowing precisely where the big man was by his stance and the way he held himself, Rao twisted out of the hold, caught a new one on the man's arm, then chopped the man in the throat.

The man staggered back, reaching for his throat and panicking because he couldn't breathe. The temporary throat paralysis would pass, but Rao didn't want to wait for that. He dropped to his hands and swept the man's legs out from under him with a foot. Then he rolled away and got to his feet in one lithe move.

His two companions tried to close ranks, slipping knives into their hands as they fell into striking stances. Rao dropped into a Crane stance, both his hands moving before him. The men hesitated, then rushed in.

Rao slapped the first man's knife hand away with the back of his wrist and slammed a palm strike to his opponent's chest. While the man struggled to catch his breath, Rao plucked the knife from his hand and spun behind the second man, who had overextended himself on his thrust.

Flicking the knife out, Rao fended off the man's second thrust with the blade. Metal screamed and hissed as the knives met. Holding the man's weapon at bay with his own, Rao lifted his left leg and drove his foot into the man's face, driving him backward into another table.

The man fell on top of the table and tried to get up. Rao reversed the knife and whipped it down. The point nicked the man's earlobe and nailed his hood to the table. Frightened, probably thinking he'd been stabbed, the man lay there and blinked rapidly.

Rao leaned over the man, invading his space. "Stay here."

The man nodded.

Calmly, Rao pulled up the hood of his own jacket, reclaimed his money from the first man, who was still struggling for his breath while lying on the floor, and left the cybercafe. The café manager was talking rapidly on his phone.

Outside the café, Rao searched for another position that would allow him to observe the Russian bar when he noticed Annja Creed leaving the building.

Two old men walked with her to a cab. A younger man, obviously not happy with the situation, followed them, but one of the old men waved him away. Like a sullen pup, the young man walked back to the door of the bar and stood there with his hands folded up under his arms.

Spotting another cab coming down the street, Rao flagged the driver. He opened the rear door and slid into the backseat.

"Where to?" the driver asked.

Rao rolled his window down a little to allow fresh air into the vehicle. He nodded at the cab just pulling away from the curb in front of the Russian bar. "Follow that car."

Without missing a beat, the cab driver reached over, flicked on the meter and eased into traffic.

"Do not lose them," Rao said.

13

The party aboard the yacht was winding down into drunken debauchery as Sequeira knew it would. These things always ended like this once enough alcohol had been poured into his guests. Most of them had already left, taking small transport boats back to the coast. Only a few would stay over on the boat. They would be witnesses if Sequeira ever needed them.

He sat out on the deck with a bottle of wine, a Cuban cigar and the old journal that had set him on to the trail of the elephant as the sun sank slowly into the sea to the west. He'd bought the journal three years ago from an online artifact dealer who had already had the original manuscript translated. Sequeira had a translation on the iPad that lay on the table next to the bottle of wine. He had been going back and forth between the two, smoking, drinking and dreaming of where it all might lead.

If he could only find the elephant.

Over the years, Sequeira had chased a few myths and legends. That had been how he had found the Spanish ship, and a few other caches of gold and gems in Europe and in West Africa. He lived for the excitement of finding more. There was no other drug like that of discovery.

His father had recognized that, too. While he'd only been in the beginning stages of his sickness, Sequeira had brought his father out to the shipwreck, had let him hold the treasure they had hauled up from the sea floor. His father had laughed and celebrated and gotten drunk. It had been the first time Sequeira had seen the old man act like a young man, and it had made him realize what he had missed in not truly getting to know his father.

Although he had the translation on his iPad, Sequeira preferred to turn the pages of the journal. The hardbound book felt old and smelled of smoke and spices and of the leather that covered the shaved wooden boards that bound it. Some of the pages were faded almost to the point that the ink had disappeared. Those pages had been chemically recovered, reconstituted and translated.

Mostly the journal was filled with boring, everyday things. The journal's author had been, according to his narrative, one of Catherine the Great's many lovers. He had also been an Austrian spy for the Ottoman Empire, which had battled Russian expansion many times and again in 1787 to 1791.

The author, Raimund Klimt, had presented himself as a scholar, a man of letters who intended to write a history of the great queen. Their love affair had been brief. Catherine had told Klimt that he wasn't very skilled, while Klimt argued that the queen was an insatiable beast. But she had set him up with an allowance and he had remained in Russia. Together with the stipend Klimt got for spying for the Turks, he did quite well for himself.

While in Catherine's courts, he had been there the day the elephant was brought to Russia from Japan.

Sequeira sipped his wine and flicked ash from his cigar as he studied the pages where Klimt had written about the elephant. Although he couldn't read the Austrian's handwriting, Sequeira knew what it said.

It was such a small gift, actually. No more than a trifle. I was, quite frankly underwhelmed by the cheapness of the gesture. After all, Queen Catherine had spared no expense to return those Japanese sailors to their homeland.

Over the years, Sequeira had learned of the ill-fated Japanese ship that had gone down in the Aleutians, and of their rescue—more or less—by Russian traders. Catherine the Great had spared no expense returning the Japanese survivors home because she'd hoped to open up trade to Japan, which had been closed off to the outer world at the time. In that, the infamous queen had been successful.

On the next page, Klimt had sketched a likeness of the elephant. There were several other sketches in the journal, most of them of the queen—including a few nudes that alone had driven up the price of the journal—and of the Russian court and the nobility.

Only one other entry had referred to the elephant. Klimt had gone drinking with the ship's captain that had brought the Japanese gifts back to the queen.

From what the fellow said, you would have thought the little elephant statue was legendary. Captain Musatov, himself a very intelligent man who spoke Mandarin, told me that the men who gave him the elephant insisted that it led to some forgotten past and was reputed to lead to a mystical legend involving a godlike power.

I asked him if he believed in such a thing. Captain Musatov laughed at me and told me that more than likely the pretty story the Japanese painted of the elephant was there only to serve as decoration for the piece, to give it value. There were many other items that the Japanese sent that intrigued Queen Catherine much more.

The next few pages included an inventory of those items as well as a few more sketches. They were mostly spices, robes, ornamental fans and furniture. The queen had been most taken with the robes, but only for a short time. She'd been in the middle of the second war with the Ottoman Empire, which she had won.

Sequeira stared at the image of the elephant. It was small, no more than five or six inches tall, and had been seemingly made of everyday stone. There had been no clues or ciphers described anywhere on it. Looking at it now made him want it even more.

One of the two burner phones on the table rang and the viewscreen showed a New York number. Sequeira had been waiting on the call for hours. One of his telecommunications companies manufactured the disposable phones and he always kept several of them on hand. He scooped up the device and answered.

"Yes?"

"It has been done." The lawyer on the other end of the phone was American, a man Sequeira had used before when negotiating legitimate business dealings in the United States. Most of the lawyer's work was in the realm of intellectual properties, but he had friends who were lawyers who worked in other fields. He did not use Sequeira's name. They never used names on the phone.

"They are free?"

"Yes. Only just. I doubt they cleared the building where they were being held before I called the other party."

"Good. Thank you." Sequeira broke the connection, took the phone apart and tossed the pieces over the side of the ship into the ocean.

The other party was quite possibly the most dangerous person Sequeira had ever known. Restrepo was only a few years younger than Sequeira. Born in Bogota, Restrepo had become an assassin for the cocaine cartels, and had left Colombia when the American DEA forces had closed in and shut down drug operations in that area. Better still, Restrepo had escaped before anyone could get a picture or fingerprints into any kind of tracking program.

The assassin was called *Brisa*, which translated into breeze, like a gust of wind. Brisa was called that because the assassin came and went with impunity, just like a breeze. Only when Brisa left a place, dead men littered the location.

Sequeira had found Brisa on the beach. Brisa had been living hand to mouth as a contract killer, working through an accountant in Lisbon who was a distant relative. The accountant also handled some of Sequeira's business. When a bit of business came up that couldn't be handled by cooking the books and it would be better if a witness disappeared, the accountant had recommended Brisa.

After that first kill, done so neatly and so quietly, Sequeira had put the assassin on his invisible payroll. Even Adrian Sequeira had been impressed by Brisa.

Sequeira closed the journal and placed it atop his iPad. He sipped his wine and smoked his cigar, dreaming of the time he would get his hands on the elephant. And he waited on Brisa's call. That would come in on the second burner phone, and Sequeira knew he wouldn't have to wait long.

Brisa was quick and efficient. Always.

TIRED AND NERVOUS, knowing that he had been fortunate to be released from the American police, Calapez hurried down the steps leading from the police station where he'd been kept. Since his arrest, he'd been moved twice to different places. He didn't know if that was to confuse him or to put anyone who tried to follow him off his trail.

"Can we get something to eat?" Pousao matched Calapez's stride.

"Later. The first thing we do is get out of this city." Calapez turned up his jacket collar against the chill.

"Why? The lawyer said we were free to go."

"This is America. We were arrested by New York City police officers. The next thing you know, we will be arrested by Homeland Security, and there is no getting away from them."

"If you have enough money, you can get away from anyone. The man we work for has plenty of money." Pousao was clever enough not to mention Sequeira's name in public.

Calapez made no reply. Pousao was young and did not know as much about the world as he wished to believe. The police could arrest them once more, that was true, but Calapez was more afraid of what Sequeira would do. Their employer did not like to brush up against the law and did not allow any ties to him regarding an illegal activity.

The man Calapez had killed was a definite liability. There was no statute of limitations on murder in the United States. If that murder was ever solved, the police could come after Sequeira as well as Calapez and Pousao. Sequeira might not know about the murder. Calapez hoped not. He chided himself for not simply tying the man up, but he had been angry that his assignment had turned difficult, and that anger had needed to be let out.

Walking with long strides, Calapez almost fled down the sidewalk through the thronging afternoon crowd. A street vendor offering hot dogs stood at the corner and called out his wares.

"Please. Something to eat." Pousao sounded pathetic, almost like a child. How he could be so professional on the job and be like this now, Calapez could not understand. "We can eat as we walk. Do you even know where you're—"

Startled by the abrupt cessation of Pousao's question, Calapez turned to look at the younger man.

Pousao stumbled backward, his face a mask of confusion. A single dot of blood wept from his forehead, then tracked down his face, between his eyes, and on the left side of his nose. Then he toppled over. His eyes were vacant.

Brisa! Calapez looked around as passersby started to skirt Pousao's corpse. A couple of women screamed in alarm. A teenager pulled out his phone and began taking video while he was talking to someone on an earpiece.

Everyone on the sidewalk was in motion. Calapez didn't know in which direction to run. He had never laid eyes on Brisa and didn't know anyone who had.

Calapez held his hands up in surrender. "Please! Please don't do this! I didn't say anything! I never said a—"

His words stopped when he felt a harsh pinch just behind his left ear. He felt dizzy and tried to take a step but discovered that he could not move. His legs no longer obeyed him, then they no longer held him up. He fell, knowing the impact against the sidewalk was going to hurt, but he was dead before he got there.

THE PHONE CHIRPED once and Sequeira picked it up. Anticipation made his heart accelerate. Maybe his goal would still be achieved. He read the simple text message.

THEY ARE BOTH DEAD.

The phone vibrated in Sequeira's hand. He glanced at the

viewscreen and saw the picture of Calapez and Pousao lying dead on a sidewalk in the center of a gawking crowd.

EXCELLENT WORK. THANK YOU.

NOW I WILL FIND THE ARCHAEOLOGIST.

Sequeira smiled. LET ME KNOW WHEN YOU DO. He reread the tests, thinking that he should have sent Brisa to get the elephant. He would have if Brisa hadn't been in Prague dealing with another situation that had gone badly. Calapez and Pousao had only been sent to New York to bring back the piece. Sequeira had fully intended to win the bidding war for the elephant.

Only that hadn't worked out.

But things were working out now. He tore the second burner phone to pieces and flung them over the side of the yacht, as well. Brisa would find Annja Creed and the elephant, then the hunt for whatever lay at the end of the legend would begin in earnest.

14

"Did you know that Onoprienko has killed three men?" Annja peered at her tablet PC as she rode in the backseat of the cab. She had been researching their quarry and putting feelers out about the elephant piece on the archaeology websites she regularly used for research. So far there hadn't been any pingbacks.

Klykov sat on the seat next to her and looked calm, not at all like they were on their way to visit a known murderer. He and Pitor Serov had both put on *Chasing History's Monsters* T-shirts and now wore them under their jackets. "Sure, sure. But that's only the number of men Onoprienko has been convicted of killing. He's killed many more. The police have suspected that for years. He is much better when he kills professionally."

In the front seat beside the driver, Serov nodded in agreement. "They haven't even found the bodies of some of those men. Onoprienko can be methodical and effective when he wishes."

"Meh." Klykov dismissed the praise. "I said only that Onoprienko was better. I didn't say he was someone you should go to."

In the pictures of Pavel Onoprienko that Annja had found online, the Russian appeared to be an average-looking guy. He could have been a plumber or a tire salesman. He wore a button-up shirt and slacks, and he looked to be in his late fifties or early sixties. His hair was a fading red and gray at the temples. Judging from the pictures, Onoprienko had a habit of squinting or had bad vision. Maybe that was why he killed with a hammer.

"What is he doing out of prison?" Annja asked.

"Because no one ever proved Onoprienko intended to kill those guys." Serov twisted around in his seat, causing the driver to shift aside a little. "The last conviction was for second-degree murder. That carries a mandatory five-year sentence, but since Onoprienko got five years for the first one, he received eleven years for the second. He had the bad luck to draw the same judge, and that man felt Onoprienko was too prone to violence, which is a fair assessment. Also, they made Onoprienko undergo counseling. I was told on good authority this did not help."

The driver ignored them, listening to a self-help on real estate over his ear buds. Pop music flowed from the radio, creating a soft undercurrent of sound that was incongruous to the conversation they were having.

"How did he manage to get second-degree murder charges *twice*?" Annja couldn't believe it.

"He had a good attorney," Serov said. "One that I have used in the past."

"And one that I have used. Maruska Deyneka's second boy, if I remember correctly."

Annja couldn't believe the two old gangsters were chatting so casually. She shook her head.

"I thought Oleg was her third boy," Serov said.

"Whatever." Klykov rummaged inside his jacket and took out a business card. He offered it to Annja. "Here. For if you ever need him. And if you do, tell him I sent you. He is very good with murder charges."

Although she never planned on needing the lawyer's services, Annja took the card and stuck it into her backpack to be polite. "What is Onoprienko doing these days?"

"Obviously he's still killing people. Look at poor Maurice."

"When he's not killing people. Legitimate employment."

"You mean what is he doing as a job?" Klykov asked.

"Yes."

Klykov looked thoughtful, tilting his head to one side. "He works as a bouncer at a club, right, Pitor? Someplace where the music is bad and it is too loud?"

Serov disagreed. "Pavel's working as a stocker at a discount liquor place these days. The club didn't work out after he put a couple people in the hospital. They were cutting in line. Pavel told them not to. They didn't listen. I heard they had to wait even longer at the emergency room." He smiled at Annja as if he'd told a joke.

Though the humor didn't quite suit, Annja smiled in return.

Klykov smirked. "Those people are lucky Onoprienko didn't have a hammer."

"Pavel complained to the club owner, Karl Braz, and the police. Said he didn't start the fight, he just finished it. Exactly what he thought he was supposed to do. He claimed he was doing his job and shouldn't have been fired or arrested. You ask me, Braz got the worst of it. Pavel got arrested and released after Oleg Deyneka used video in front of the club to show that Pavel warned the people repeatedly. They didn't listen, but they listened to the personal-claims shyster they retained."

"So Braz got sued."

"Of course. Cost him a fat bundle."

"Why would Braz hire Onoprienko in the first place?"

"Says he got him cheap. Thought Onoprienko could just stand in the corner and scare people. Pavel can look very intimidating when he wishes to."

Annja looked at the image of the man on her tablet PC. Upon closer inspection, she spotted the deadness in his eyes.

"Onoprienko complained to Braz?" Klykov asked as the cab driver took a right-hand turn and honked impatiently at the car ahead of him.

"Yes. Pavel said he was treated unfairly, and he even tried to sue Braz himself. That didn't go so well."

"How did Pavel get the job at the discount liquor?"

"His mother. She begged the owner, who was the son of her best friend, to give Onoprienko the job. Onoprienko said he wasn't to blame for the problem at the club, so his mother went to bat for him." Serov chuckled. "This guy is a real chump. No matter what he does, it is always someone else's fault."

"His *mother* got him the job?" Annja asked in disbelief.

"Sure, sure. His mother, God bless her, loves her son very much even though he believes the rules of the world do not apply to him."

Annja tried to comprehend that. "She knows Onoprienko's a killer?"

"Sure, sure. She was always at his trials. She got thrown out of most of them. She's a very demonstrative woman."

Serov nodded. "I think she is where Onoprienko gets all of his passion." He paused. "The job at the club should have been a good fit for him. Pavel just doesn't have much tolerance, you know. Especially not for authority."

"A guy like Pavel? The club owner should have known better. You can't put him in a corner and expect him to stay there," Klykov said.

"Before we get all *Dirty Dancing*," Annja said, "maybe we should talk about how to handle Onoprienko."

"Dirty dancing?" Klykov asked in confusion.

"Sure," Serov said. "You remember. The film with Patrick Swayze. We've seen it."

"Ah. The corner and no for *Baby*. Good movie." Klykov nodded with a small smile and focused on Annja. "Never you mind about Onoprienko. Pitor and I will handle him. You just be prepared to ask him about the elephant. You'll soon learn what Onoprienko did with it."

Annja didn't feel too certain of that, but before she could ask any more questions, her phone rang. She checked the screen and saw that the caller was Doug Morrell, her producer. She considered blowing off the call, but he had come through with the swag delivery for Klykov and his cronies.

She answered and put the phone to her ear. "Hey, Doug."

"Look, I know you're helping the police solve that murder and everything, but I tell you, we gotta come up with something for the show before long. Production wants to get something cooking. *I* want to get something cooking." Doug was ambitious and always looking for the next big thing in television.

"I've sent you three lists." Annja drew a breath, willing to bet that Doug hadn't even looked at the subjects she'd suggested. He seldom did until he was truly desperate, and he wasn't there yet. She could tell by the tone in his voice.

"Yeah, yeah, but we need something sexy. Not just that history junk."

Annja bristled at his casual disregard of her chosen field of study. If it hadn't been for her successes, *Chasing History's Monsters* might not have lasted a season. Of course, the whole monsters concept had been Doug's idea.

"Kristie is working on a volcano god story," Doug said. "She got herself scheduled to become a sacrifice in Hawaii. Grass skirt, hula hoops, the whole enchilada. Of course, she's not going to become a real sacrifice, but it sounds pretty intense. There'll be lava, tiki gods, some kind of evil worshippers. I can't wait to see it."

Kristie Chatham was the other star of *Chasing History's Monsters*. She definitely was not an archaeologist or historian. She played on sensationalism and generally had wardrobe malfunctions in every episode. Her popularity among the teens and European market was a little higher than Annja's own popularity, but the hardcore fan base of the show tuned in to see Annja. Generally she didn't feel the competition, but occasionally she got irritated.

"A sacrifice to a volcano god? Seriously? Doug, Christie just wants to go to Hawaii."

"Maybe so, but if she can pull off something worth filming—"

Or some article of clothing, Annja couldn't help thinking.

"—then we're locked and loaded. That's all I'm asking for, Annja. Something that will satisfy the fans. That's all any of us really want."

No, some of us would like to present a solid documentary. Annja sighed and tried to think of what to say. In a few days, Doug would be desperate and the tension would start to mount. Another call beeped in and the viewscreen showed Bart's name. He wouldn't call unless it was important because he thought she'd gone home and gone to bed.

"I have to take this call, Doug. It's the police. There could have been a break in the case." That possibility deflated Annja somewhat. Solving murders was Bart's job, but she felt like the elephant was much more than evidence in a homicide investigation. Once the police got their hands on the elephant, it would be impounded and she wouldn't have access to it.

"We need a show, Annja." Doug sounded whiny and desperate, but it was put on, certainly not his best effort.

"I'll get back to you as soon as I can. And thanks again for the swag." Annja broke the connection and answered Bart's call.

"A volcano god?" Twisted around in his seat, Serov nodded with bright interest. "Now that is something I would like to see. The other girl is not so good as you in my opinion, and she's *gorda.* A little heavy. She needs to go to the gym more."

Klykov snorted. "You're one to talk about gyms, you who have never been inside one."

"I used to box." Serov held up his hands and bobbed his head. The driver swayed away from the old gangster and looked concerned for a moment, then, when he realized the fists were just part of the conversation, he returned his attention to his driving and the real estate audio. "So why have we never gone to Hawaii?"

"Too much water." Klykov dismissed the question. "I don't want to end up fighting sharks."

"Annja?" Bart said. "Are you there?"

"Hi." Annja turned away from Klykov and Serov. They got the hint and started shushing each other, sounding like leaky tires. "Yeah, I'm here."

Bart hesitated. "We had to let those two guys who shot up the diner go free. Someone, we don't know who yet, hired one of Manhattan's top criminal lawyers to force us to cut them loose."

"They didn't pay for their own lawyer?"

"No. They never even called anyone. Judging from the little background we've got on these guys, neither one of them had the money to hire the attorney they got. But that's not the real problem. I take it you haven't been near a television."

The television above the bar had on a Russian-language channel. "No."

"As soon as those guys left the precinct, they were shot dead, killed right on the street. Whoever did it was a pro, put a .22 round in each of their heads in the open and got away with it clean. We're going over the videos of the security cams, but nobody's seen anything."

"Why would anyone kill those two?" It didn't make sense to Annja.

"I think the hunt for your elephant is still on." Bart didn't sound happy. "Whoever hired those guys to look for it decided to clean up the mess they left behind."

"That means they knew whoever had them killed."

"Yeah, so we're digging into their backgrounds, looking for anything that will lead us to anyone interested in stuff like that elephant."

"Antiquities."

"Yeah. Those. Just a second." Bart was silent for a moment, but a voice spoke up in the background. "Look, I gotta go, Annja. I just wanted to call and make sure you were okay. I didn't see these murders coming, and it made me worry about you."

"I'm fine, but now I'm worried about you. You're still looking for the person behind this."

"I'm with the NYPD. I'm not going to be alone. I just didn't want you out there doing anything stupid."

"Just a little shopping."

"Get it done and get home. Put your security on at your loft. Stay inside. That guy Nguyen? He's in the wind, too. He escaped the cruiser that was transporting him to lockup, and a few minutes ago I got a report that a guy matching his description got into a fight with some Russian thugs only a few blocks from the Benyovszky murder scene."

"Where was this?"

"A cybercafe." Bart read off the address and Annja realized it was on the same street as Buba's. Just across the street, in fact. "Does that mean anything to you?"

"No." Annja hated lying to Bart, didn't do it as a general rule because she respected him too much and their friendship was one of the things she valued the most, but she wanted to keep him out of her investigation, at least for now.

"Then why did you ask?" Bart was suspicious. He had good instincts.

"Just curious, that's all. If Nguyen is still in that area, maybe the elephant is, too."

"Exactly what Joe and I were thinking." The voice sounded in the background again, more insistent this time. "I have to go. I just want you to make sure you take care of yourself."

"I always do."

Bart said goodbye and hung up.

If the elephant led to Benyovszky's murderer, Annja told herself she would hand the artifact over. Reluctantly. She told herself the only reason she wasn't blowing the whistle on Onoprienko was because she wasn't yet as convinced of the man's guilt as Klykov and Serov were.

The cab glided to a curb in front of a dumpy apartment building.

"We're here," Klykov announced. He handed the driver a hundred dollar bill. "Stay here. We'll be down in a few minutes."

"Okay, but the meter's gonna be ticking."

After Klykov opened the door and got out, Annja slid over and followed him. She grabbed her backpack and pulled it on.

"I could carry that for you," Serov offered.

Annja shook her head. "Thanks, that's very kind of you, but this backpack goes everywhere I do."

Serov shrugged, then followed Klykov into the building.

15

"You're sure Onoprienko lives here?" Annja trailed after Klykov, who was taking his time with the stairs.

"Yeah. Fifth floor." Klykov looked at Serov and frowned. "You didn't say this was a walkup."

"You should have known. It would be easier to name the buildings with elevators in this neighborhood." Serov walked to one side of Klykov, both of them in front of Annja.

"You could have told me Onoprienko lived on the fifth floor."

"I did."

"Guys," Annja said as they neared the third-floor landing. The anticipation of getting to Onoprienko, and to the elephant, was making her impatient, and the familiar bickering between the two old gangsters was getting on her nerves a little. It also reminded her of how Garin and Roux acted sometimes. She assumed it had to do with people who had spent so much of their lives together.

They stopped and looked at her, breathing a little harder than they had been due to the strenuous climb.

"I can go up and see Onoprienko on my own."

"No," they said together.

"Onoprienko is a dangerous man." Klykov started up the next flight with a look of determination. "We're already half-way there anyway."

"A girl like you," Serov added, "he would kill you in an instant. That thing you did with Georgy? That was a fun thing to watch. But Onoprienko? He is no Georgy. He is a much different kind of man."

Annja continued, not having any choice because although she knew Onoprienko lived on the fifth floor, she didn't know which apartment the man lived in.

"You do realize there's a chance Onoprienko's not even there? I mean, if you're right, he did kill Benyovszky last night." Annja thought maybe if she suggested this was a waste of time she might talk them out of accompanying her any farther.

"He'd better be there," Klykov growled. "If I go all this way, and on my bum knee, and he isn't there, I may shoot him myself the next time I lay eyes on him."

Annja thought Klykov was kidding. She hoped he was kidding.

"Maybe we should have called first?" Serov suggested. "You know, to make certain Onoprienko is at home."

"Would you take a call after you'd just killed a man and knew the police might be looking for you?" Klykov asked.

"I never have. I always wait a few days. Let things cool down."

"Exactly. So Onoprienko is up in that apartment because he has nowhere else to go."

Annja followed, always glancing up to make sure Onoprienko didn't bump into them on his way out of the building. "Onoprienko doesn't still live with his mom, does he?"

Klykov and Serov reached the fifth-floor landing and stood there for a moment to catch their breath.

"No," Klykov said.

"She wouldn't let him," Serov added.

Klykov shrugged. "Onoprienko, he has a thing for the ladies. His mother, who should be a saint for all the trouble that son of hers has caused her, would never allow such a thing in her home. Getting to have girls come to his house is probably the only reason Onoprienko moved out of his mother's place."

"What about a roommate?" Annja glanced down the hallway.

"He lives on his own," Klykov said.

"No one would live with the likes of him." Serov nodded at Klykov. "I am ready."

Together, the two men walked down the hallway and stopped in front of number six.

Klykov removed his hat, then leaned in and pressed his

ear to the door. After a minute, he pulled back. "All I hear is the television. A game show, I think." He tried the doorknob slowly, then shook his head. "Locked."

"It won't be for long." Serov took a flat case out of his pocket and opened it, revealing an impressive assortment of lock picks. He knelt down and set to work on the door.

"You're sure this is the right apartment?" Annja glanced along the hallway, thinking that if a neighbor happened on them this would be hard to explain. Breaking into an innocent person's home would be hard to explain, too.

"Sure, sure." Klykov nodded. "Don't you worry, Annja. Me and Pitor got this. This is easy-shmeezy for us. You just stay back so you don't get hurt."

"Right." Annja leaned against the wall beside Klykov and thought about the mysterious assassin who had killed Calapez and Pousao, if those were really their names, in front of the police precinct. She hated thinking something might happen to Klykov and Serov, and if it did, it would be her fault.

Serov got to his feet, put his lock picks away and hauled out a massive revolver that Annja had not even realized he had. It had a long barrel and looked like it was capable of bringing down a charging rhino. "Okay, we can do this now."

"You've got a gun?" Annja asked.

Serov looked at the weapon. "Well, yeah. I'm not gonna go after Pavel Onoprienko with a hammer. Do you want a pistol? I have an extra."

Of course he did. Annja felt the situation was sliding out of control. "No. I'm good. Thanks."

"Pitor likes those big guns," Klykov said. "Like something those guys out in the Old West would carry. I go for something a little more sophisticated." He pulled out a sleek Beretta, then took out another one. "Maybe you'll find it more to your liking."

"No, but thanks."

Klykov shrugged. "I didn't know if you had one in your backpack."

"No."

Klykov nodded at Serov, who reached for the doorknob, turned it, then pushed and followed the door inside.

PAVEL ONOPRIENKO ALREADY had guests. He sat in a straight-backed chair in the middle of a small living room that evidently spent part of its time as a trash bin. Empty pizza boxes and Chinese takeout containers covered most flat surfaces. The temperature inside the room was cooler than outside, and a breeze blew over Annja that felt like air-conditioning.

Dressed in boxers with red hearts on them, his skin sallow and sagging a little, Onoprienko sat nervously with his elbows on his knees. Hair hung down into his face, partially covering a swelling purple bruise on the side of his face that also threatened to close his right eye. Angry red spots on his chest, stomach and arms showed he'd been hit several times.

Four other men occupied the room. All of them were young and hard looking, dressed in jeans and pullovers. One of them sat in the open window. Another sat backwards in a chair with his arms folded. Another rested against the doorway that probably led to a bedroom. The fourth man stood in front of Onoprienko while holding a pistol to the captive's head and a phone to his ear.

Wheel of Fortune played on the large-screen television against one wall. The players were clapping their hands and the audience was cheering a letter selection.

Klykov and Serov brandished their weapons. The four young men looked back at the two old gangsters in disbelief.

"You boys just sit tight," Klykov said in a flat voice, "and we'll all get out of this alive."

The guy holding the pistol to Onoprienko's head looked nervous. "Back on out of here, old man, or you're gonna get hurt. Got me some business to take care of and I don't need no distractions. Or witnesses."

"Who's he calling *old*?" Klykov asked, but he didn't take his eyes off the men. "He must have been talking to you, Pitor."

"He wasn't talking to me. Punk like that knows I'd kneecap him for talking fresh like that."

"You, tough guy," Klykov said, waving toward the guy with the gun pointed at Onoprienko's head. "You want to listen to me."

"No, I don't." The young man sneered. "I got a lot of extra bullets, old man. Mess with us and you're gonna get one of 'em."

Klykov ignored the threat. "What are you doing with Onoprienko?"

The young man cursed at Klykov.

"You know who this is, Leonid?" Serov asked his friend.

"Just some punk getting too big for his britches."

"That there is Johnny Kaneev. He works for Mikhail Guro."

"Guro? The loan shark?"

Serov nodded. "The very one. Kaneev here enforces for Guro. People get behind on their payments, Guro sends Kaneev and his creeps to bust heads."

Klykov glanced at Onoprienko. "Is that true, Pavel? Do you owe the loan shark?"

"*Da*." Onoprienko nodded and blood spilled out between his cracked teeth and poured down his chin. "I keep finding slow horses."

"Guro is a bad man to owe money to. How much are you into him?"

"Seventy-three thousand and change." Onoprienko shrugged and spat blood on the floor.

Serov gave a low whistle. "That's a lot of money, Pavel."

"I've been working it off with Guro, a nickel here, a dime there. I just can't catch a break and nobody wants to hire me for a real job that pays." Onoprienko nodded in disgust at the young man who held him. "Mostly I have been doing this pig's work. Getting people to pay Guro. I should get a bonus for that. Payment has never been so good as when I am working for Guro. Then, after I am about to finally get free of debt to Guro, he sends around this one to take my good fortune."

The knowledge of what that *job* was sent a chill down Anja's spine. She kept her hand to her side, already feeling the sword in the *otherwhere*. She wanted to say something, to do something, that would get them all past the moment, but she was afraid the next moment would be filled with the stench of spent gunpowder.

"What good fortune?" Klykov asked.

"Just a little something I chanced upon."

Understanding dawned in Annja. "Do you have the elephant Benyovszky was auctioning off?"

"Enough questions!" Suddenly concerned, the young guy with the gun peered at Annja, but he asked his question of Klykov. He took a fresh grip and kept the pistol steady. "Who is she?"

"A friend. A television-star friend." Klykov tapped his *Chasing History's Monsters* T-shirt with one of his weapons but kept the other pointed at the man. "She wants to talk to Onoprienko."

Kaneev shook his head. "Uh-uh. Onoprienko ain't gonna talk to nobody but Mr. Guro. That's how this goes down. Wassily, what are you waiting for?"

The man in the window moved so fast that the pistol just seemed to appear in his hands as if he were a magician. As fast as he was, though, Serov already had his weapon out and didn't hesitate to use it. The big revolver bucked and spat fire, and a large-caliber bullet slammed into Wassily's chest, blowing him back through the open window. He vanished without a sound.

Annja moved away from Klykov, trying to find a good battleground as detonations filled the air. The sword felt calm and sure in her hand, but she didn't pull the weapon from the *otherwhere* because there was no room to use it. Bullets slapped into the wall only a couple feet from her and tore at Klykov's jacket, taking his hat off. Klykov never batted an eye, just lifted his pistols and fired.

Kaneev pulled his pistol from Onoprienko's head and pointed it at Klykov. Before he could fire the weapon, though, Klykov shot him three times. Slack in death, Kaneev fell to the floor.

The man sitting in the chair managed to get up, but bullets from Serov's or Klykov's pistols, or maybe from both, struck him in the chest and drove him backward.

Onoprienko leaned sideways in his chair and managed to land on the ground hard enough to break the chair. Semifreed, he started pulling the ropes up over his head and shoulders. He managed to get free, and reached for the dead man's pistol.

Moving more swiftly than either of her companions could, Annja grabbed the pistol and stepped back from Onoprienko as voices filled the room, coming from the bedroom. The man lounging in the door stood on both of his feet and brought up an elegant-looking machine pistol. Behind him, two more men with fully automatic weapons appeared in the doorway.

Klykov or Serov shot the man, but he managed to trigger a burst that chopped the wall beside Serov. The men in the bedroom opened fire, but they'd fired in a hurry and didn't manage to hit the old Russian gangsters.

Racing back toward the apartment entrance, Annja caught up with Klykov and Serov. Something tugged at Annja's backpack, then she was through the door.

"The walls are thin!" Klykov roared as he dove to the hallway floor. "Get down!" He dropped one of his pistols and grabbed her wrist, taking her down with him.

16

Annja went to the hallway floor readily. She'd already thought of the thinness of the walls and how they would provide no real protection. She had been concerned about the old men and was about to warn them of the same thing. Covering her head with her arms, she watched as bullets smashed through the apartment and tore into the hall. She hoped that the neighbors there weren't home or the bullets didn't penetrate. The sharp reports of the machine pistols ricocheted through the hallway.

Lying on his back, Klykov fired both pistols into the wall, keeping his aim low. A startled cry of pain came from within, and Annja hoped that it didn't belong to Onoprienko. She was certain now that the killer's "good fortune" had been in murdering Benyovszky and taking the elephant.

She dropped the magazine from the weapon she'd taken, found it fully loaded, then checked the action and saw a bullet in the chamber.

A shaggy-haired man appeared in the doorway of Onoprienko's apartment. He stepped out farther and tried to bring the machine pistol he carried into play. He started firing prematurely, stitching an uneven line across the tile toward Annja and her companions.

Coolly, lifting one arm to take aim, Serov shot the man in the face twice and continued lying on his back in the middle of the hallway. He swung the cylinder of one of the revolvers open, dumped the brass and replenished it with a Speedloader.

"Reminds you of old days in Russia, *nyet*?" Serov smiled at Klykov.

"Reminds me more of East Germany when we were thwarting the Stasi." Klykov smiled, animated and excited. Their English had regressed during the excitement. "Look at you with your grandfather's gun. Already having to reload. You should have one of these." He shook his Beretta proudly. "Would be better to have two."

"Is better to only have six rounds. Counting so many as in your guns, I sometimes forget." Serov snapped the cylinder closed with a flick of his wrist. "Is not good to forget count and run out of bullets at wrong time."

"They say math keeps the mind sharp."

"Until it is blown out of your head."

Annja started to get up, but Klykov restrained her. In the next moment, another wave of gunfire tore through the apartment wall.

"I wish I had grenade," Serov said in a low voice. "Grenade would make this so much simpler."

"Grenade would mean Annja could not question Onoprienko about the elephant," Klykov countered.

"Grenade also much harder to conceal in suit, you know? And as for Onoprienko, he is probably already dead."

Klykov nodded. "Let's go." With surprising agility, the old gangster rolled to his feet. "I think maybe they are getting away. We must not let that happen. Others may get the wrong impression, would make us look weak."

Look weak? Annja didn't even have a response to that. They'd already killed a handful of men and somehow dodged hundreds of bullets. She rolled to her feet as well and stayed low with both hands locked on the pistol.

"Where do you think the extra men came from?" Klykov asked.

"From bedroom."

"That was a lot of men to bring to face Onoprienko."

"Maybe Guro is scared of him. If Onoprienko wanted me dead, I would be scared." Serov peered cautiously around the doorway. "Is good. All clear."

Annja didn't risk the doorway. She just peered through one of the big holes in the wall made by repeated bullets passing through. In addition to Guro's enforcers, Kaneev, his three men, and three other men lay on the floor, dead or dying. Including the man Serov had shot in the doorway of the apartment, so that made eight men.

It was a massacre, and Annja was in the middle of it.

Worse than that, Onoprienko was nowhere in sight.

"Where is Pavel's body?" Klykov asked as he stepped into the apartment after Serov. "It should be here somewhere."

"That one is lucky when it comes to sudden death," Serov said. "Not so much lucky with picking horses."

Annja stepped over the bodies and looked out the window. Five stories below, Onoprienko was running for his life wearing only his heart-covered Skivvies. She was just about to throw a leg over the window and take up pursuit when a loud, authoritative voice rang out behind her.

"NYPD! Drop the weapons!" A man in his thirties took cover beside the doorway and leveled a handgun at Klykov, Serov and Annja. "Do it now!"

Klykov looked at Serov. "You think he is a cop?"

"Probably," Serov said. "Only cops yell warning, and even they do not do it all the time." He lowered his weapons to the floor and laced his fingers behind his head while dropping to his knees. "We don't want any more trouble."

Klykov surrendered his weapons as well and took the same pose. "We will surrender, Mr. Policeman, but we did nothing wrong."

The police officer directed his attention. "You, too! Put down the weapon!"

Annja wanted to protest, to tell the police officer that Onoprienko was getting away, but she knew it would do no good. Even now, two armed men were pursuing him, and she didn't know where they had come from. Frustrated, she placed the gun on the ground and put her hands behind her head. Bart was *so* going to love this.

RAO FROZE AS the man clad only in his underwear and carrying a pistol in his fist bailed out of the fire escape from the building where Annja Creed had gone. The cab she'd arrived in had taken off shortly after the bullets started flying. Rao was across the street watching.

Two men with guns emerged from the fifth-floor window and pursued the underdressed man. Pedestrians had paused on the street and shopkeepers had come out of their businesses to investigate the source of the gunshots.

"Onoprienko!" one of the men roared as he vaulted down from the fire escape and pursued the man who wore only his underwear.

Rao assumed Onoprienko was the man's name, though he had never heard of him. Still there were many things Rao didn't know about concerning Maurice Benyovszky, and he hadn't had much time to learn them or even identify the things he didn't know.

Onoprienko ran down the sidewalk and the two younger men pursued him, waving their weapons and threatening passersby.

At first Rao had been confused because he certainly hadn't expected a war to break out in that building, but from the staccato reports that had blasted forth from the structure, that was exactly what it had sounded like. He worried about Annja Creed. From everything he had seen and heard, she was a good person. She was just in his way, one more person to go through to find the elephant

He didn't want anything to happen to her, though. When he saw her framed in the apartment window on the fifth floor from which the running man had climbed down, he felt relief. When she tracked the running man with her eyes and prepared to climb out onto the fire escape, Rao guessed that the man had something to do with the elephant.

In the next moment, he was surprised when Annja Creed did not take up pursuit of the man and halted her climb from the window. Instead, she pulled herself back into the apartment, raised her hands and turned to face someone. Rao assumed that she had been detained.

The man who had escaped the apartment kept running, moving with considerable haste now.

Rao ran, flowing through the pedestrians on the other side of the street where his quarry shoved through the crowd slightly ahead of him. Both of them achieved the same speed, though Rao left no one cursing in his wake as the other man did.

Police sirens screamed into life and came nearer.

Onoprienko ducked into a hair salon at the next corner and the two gunmen were only a few feet behind him, closing fast. Rao crossed the street, taking advantage of the stalled traffic, and drew closer to the men, as well.

One of the large plate glass windows suddenly shattered and the harsh drumbeat of gunshots rolled over Rao as he took cover. Three women dressed in salon capes and a man in a barber's apron ran from the building.

Inside the salon, Onoprienko had taken up a position behind a short wall festooned with potted plants. One of the potted plants erupted, throwing dark soil, ceramic shards and the ivy in all directions. Another bullet chipped a wedge from the top of the short wall only inches from Onoprienko's face.

Onoprienko swore and fired his pistol three times in quick succession. His shots struck a chair, ripped pages from a magazine atop a short glass table and smashed the wall of a large aquarium, flooding the tiled workspace with water and fish.

Moving quickly, Rao launched himself into the building, grabbed the coatrack that stood to one side of the door and slung the garments from it with a vicious shake. He charged into one of the two younger gunmen, flattening him from behind. Aware of the threat from a different quarter now, the other gunman tried to turn around, but he was too slow. Rao swung the coatrack and caught the man in the face, striking him solidly on the jaw. The man's eyes rolled back up into his head as he fell.

The first gunman recovered slightly and tried to bring his weapon to bear. As he moved, Onoprienko fired and bullets cut the air between Rao and his opponent.

Spinning the coatrack in his hands, Rao kicked the pistol from the man's hand, then drove the coatrack's base down on either side of the man's head. The support strut between the two legs of the coatrack slammed into the man's head, batting his skull against the tiled floor with a meaty *thunk.*

Onoprienko hesitated a moment, trying to identify Rao, then opened fire again. The bullets struck the coatrack, snapping it in two. Rao dove to one side, slapping the ground to absorb the shock, then getting to his feet when he heard Onoprienko's weapon fire dry.

By the time Rao got to the back of the salon, Onoprienko was already through the rear door. Rao followed, catching up the man quickly.

Fortune favored Onoprienko, though. A pizza delivery guy stood to one side of the alley behind the salon with a pizza in one hand. The guy was singing along with whatever was playing through his ear buds. Onoprienko threw himself into the car and slid behind the wheel.

"Hey!" the startled pizza delivery guy yelped, his attention snared by the sight of Onoprienko streaking past. He started forward, then backed away when Onoprienko pointed the empty pistol at him.

Rao had almost reached the vehicle when Onoprienko put the transmission in gear and floored the accelerator. The tires shrieked as they grabbed the pavement. Onoprienko oversteered and the front of the car smashed against a wall and he backed into a garbage bin. The clangor of the collision hammered Rao's hearing.

He almost had his hands on the car, realizing then that he had no means of stopping it. But Onoprienko pressed down harder on the accelerator and the garbage bin flew down the alley and out onto the street. Horns blared and rubber screamed as drivers tried to avoid colliding with the car.

Onoprienko slammed on the brakes and cranked over the steering wheel before flooring the accelerator again. Police cars were only then arriving at the building Annja Creed had flushed the man out of.

Unable to do anything, Rao watched as Onoprienko and whatever he represented sped away.

17

Annja sat at Detective Joe Broadhurst's desk in the homicide bull pen and worked on her tablet, searching through the archaeology websites she'd used in her search for the elephant. With all the carnage that had been found in Onoprienko's apartment, she, Klykov and Serov had been immediately taken into custody. Not arrested. At least, not yet, but judging from how upset Bart had been—as well as his bosses—that could happen soon.

She glanced around. Bart still hadn't come back from the investigation at the crime scene. He hadn't been happy. They'd started out with two murders that morning, or last night depending on perspective, and now they were going to be in double digits if a couple of guys died in the hospital as expected.

Annja wished she could help, but trying to help had brought them to this place. She needed to find that elephant and figure out what this was all about.

Onoprienko had apparently gotten away scot-free. *How can a man dressed in underwear covered in bright red hearts just disappear*? But this was New York and stranger things than that had happened.

She'd gotten a few hits on the elephant posting.

HEY ANNJA,
SAW YOUR ELEPHANT. LOOKS REALLY COOL. I'M SURE YOU'VE NOTICED THAT IT'S PROBABLY INDIAN IN ORIGIN. SMALL EARS? IF THIS IS AN ARTIFACT, AS YOU SEEM TO THINK, AND IT'S REALLY OLD, MAYBE IT HAS SOMETHING TO DO WITH PLINY THE ELDER'S QUOTE ABOUT THE ELEPHANT BEING THE ONLY ANIMAL NEARLY AS SMART AS A MAN. ALEXANDER WAS TRAINED BY THE GREEKS, AND HE CONQUERED A LOT OF TERRITORY WHERE INDIAN

ELEPHANTS WOULD APPEAR. MAYBE LOOK IN THOSE AREAS? OR AT ALEXANDER?
greekguy@greekguy.gre

Annja wrote a quick note of thanks, but knew the subject matter was too broad. She'd already thought of those possibilities. She needed something that would narrow down the hunt, give her more of a true target. She moved on through the list.

HEY, DID YOU EVER READ "THE TOWER OF THE ELEPHANT" BY ROBERT E. HOWARD? I DID. IT HAD AN ELEPHANT IN IT UNTIL (SPOILER ALERT) CONAN KILLED IT TO SAVE IT FROM BEING TRAPPED BECAUSE IT WAS A BEING FROM ANOTHER WORLD TRAPPED BY AN EVIL WIZARD. I ♥ YOUR SHOW! JUSTIN (AGE 10). ADDRESS WITHHELD.

HEY JUSTIN. I DID READ THAT STORY AND LIKED IT A LOT. THANKS FOR WRITING.

The missive wasn't helpful, but it did make Annja feel better. She'd done school visits to promote her books and the television show (something Kristie Chatham had done exactly once, a high school, and was blacklisted from doing so again) and enjoyed the curiosity kids exhibited without holding back. Curious minds were awesome to engage with.

The next entry was from buddhaboy@starrysky.worldsapaart

EVER HEARD OF GANESHA? THE GOD OF WISDOM IN THE HINDU PANTHEON? EVERYBODY LOVES THAT ELEPHANT. HE HAS A HUMAN BODY AND AN ELEPHANT HEAD.

ONE VERSION OF THE STORY GOES LIKE THIS. THE GUY WAS SUPPOSED TO HAVE BEEN CREATED BY PARVATI, THE CONSORT OF SIVA, WHEN SHE WAS LONELY. SHE WANTED A SON BUT SIVA DIDN'T WANNA BE NO BABY DADDY, SO SHE COVERED HERSELF IN OIL, ROLLED IN DIRT, THEN RUBBED THAT OFF AND SHAPED THE RESULTING MUD PIE INTO A KID. ONLY HE WAS FULL GROWN.

SHE TOLD THE KID/YOUNG GUY TO GUARD HER HOME. THEN SIVA CAME BACK AND THE KID WOULDN'T LET HIM IN HIS OWN HOUSE. SO SIVA WHIPPED OUT HIS SWORD AND LOPPED OFF THE GUY'S HEAD, NEVER KNOWING HIS WIFE MADE HIM.

WHEN PARVATI FOUND OUT WHAT HAPPENED, SHE GOT ALL UP IN SIVA'S GRILL AND TOLD HIM IF HE DIDN'T BRING THE GUY BACK TO LIFE, SHE WAS GONNA MAKE HIS LIFE MISERABLE. SO SIVA NEEDED A HEAD.

HIS SERVANTS WENT AND FOUND AN ELEPHANT, KILLED IT AND TOOK ITS HEAD. DON'T KNOW WHY SIVA JUST DIDN'T KILL ONE OF THE SERVANTS AND TAKE THEIR HEAD. THAT'S WHAT I WOULDA DONE.

ANYWAY, HE STICKS THIS ELEPHANT'S HEAD ON THE GUY AND BRINGS HIM BACK TO LIFE. AND THAT'S WHERE GANESH COMES FROM.

THANKS, BUDDHA. YEP, I'VE HEARD ABOUT THAT ONE. SADLY IT DOESN'T FIT WITH WHAT I'VE GOT GOING ON HERE.

Annja flicked her finger to move on to the next post.

HELLO ANNJA
PLEASED AM I TO BE MAKING YOUR ACQUAINTANCE! PERHAPS YOU COULD HELP ME. IN MY COUNTRY, BEFORE ARAB SPRING, I WAS A PRINCE. UNFORTUNATELY, I WAS DRIVEN OUT OF MY PALACE AND LEFT $2.3 MILLION EUROS IN THE BANK. NO ONE BUT ME CAN TOUCH THIS MONEY, THOUGH. I NEED ASSISTANCE IN RECOVERING THESE FUNDS AND I WOULD BE WILLING TO GIVE YOU A PERCENTAGE. COULD YOU HELP ME OUT? HUMBLY YOURS, PRINCE SEMMI.

Even though the posting was spam, it still made Annja smile.

She deleted the post and blocked the sender.

DID YOU KNOW THAT ELEPHANTS COMMUNICATE THROUGH ULTRASOUND? I DIDN'T UNTIL I STARTED LOOKING AROUND ELEPHANT STUFF. THEY KIND OF "FEEL" WORDS AT EACH OTHER. WOW! THAT'S REALLY AWESOME!
Turtlegirl9@iloveanimals.spq

PRETTY AMAZING, ISN'T IT, TURTLEGIRL? Annja kept reading but wasn't holding out much hope. The subject matter was too broad, and maybe elephants were too interesting, as well.

The next post was from ziggymoon@thesecretoflifeis42.cpr and addressed history.

COULD THAT ELEPHANT HAVE A TIE TO CHARLEMAGNE, THE KING OF THE FRANKS? MAYBE AN HEIRLOOM PASSED DOWN THROUGH A FRENCH FAMILY? SUPPOSEDLY HARUN AR-RASHID, THE FIFTH ARAB ABBASID CALIPH, GAVE AN ELEPHANT TO CHARLEMAGNE BACK IN THE NINTH CENTURY. THAT WAS A LONG TIME AGO THOUGH.

I'LL CHECK INTO THAT AND LET YOU KNOW, ZIGGY. RIGHT NOW I'M STILL IN THE FACT-GATHERING STAGE.

The next post took a tack that Annja hadn't thought about. It didn't help her solve the puzzle, but it was interesting nevertheless.

I DIDN'T KNOW THIS BEFORE I STARTED LOOKING, BUT THERE ARE A LOT OF PICTURES OF NOAH AND THE FLOOD THAT HAVE ELEPHANTS IN THEM. MAYBE ARTISTS JUST LIKED TO DRAW ELEPHANTS, BUT YOU KNOW THEY WERE DEFINITELY SHOWING SOME LOVE.
painterlad@thoseamazingheroes.bgr

THAT'S INTERESTING, PAINTERLAD. YOU'VE OPENED UP A WHOLE NEW LINE OF POSSIBILITIES. *SIGH* THANKS FOR THE HELP!

COULD THE ELEPHANT BE PART OF A SET? THE FIRST THING THAT CAME TO MIND WHEN I SAW THE ELEPHANT WAS THAT IT MUST BE A PART OF SOMETHING ELSE.

I KNOW YOU'VE PROBABLY HEARD OF THE COSMIC EGG THAT HATCHED AND CREATED THE SUN, BUT THE STORY GOES ON TO SAY THAT THE GOD BRAHMA TOOK THE SHELLS AND CHANTED UP AIRIVATA, THE ELEPHANT SHIVA WOULD RIDE INTO BATTLE.
gamerghuy@flagitandtagit.brb

THE POSSIBILITY OF A SET EXISTS, BUT I DON'T KNOW YET. THANKS!

Annja wanted to believe there was only the one piece, but she had to admit that it was certainly possible there were more. She'd seen Indian chess sets that featured elephants as rooks, but never this particular style of elephant.

The next letter caught her attention and pumped up her hope even though she knew it was a long shot. She would take a long shot now, though, because she didn't have anything else.

Unless Onoprienko turned up somewhere.

HI ANNJA. I THOUGHT ABOUT NOT WRITING, BUT THAT LOOKS A LOT LIKE AN ELEPHANT I REMEMBER SEEING AT THE HOUSE OF A FRIEND OF MINE. I WAS JUST A KID THEN, AND WE'RE NOT REALLY FRIENDS ANYMORE BECAUSE STUFF HAPPENS AND YOU MOVE ON. SHE SAID THAT HER GREAT-GREAT-GRANDFATHER OR SOMETHING CAME FROM RUSSIA. ACCORDING TO HER, HER GREAT-GREAT-GRANDFATHER STOLE IT FROM CATHERINE THE GREAT.

WE WERE LIVING IN BRIGHTON AT THE TIME, SO MAYBE THAT'S SOMETHING. MY DAD GOT A JOB IN SEATTLE A FEW YEARS AFTER THE PICTURE WAS TAKEN, AND THAT'S BEEN NINE YEARS AGO.

IT'S PROBABLY NOT THE SAME STATUE, BUT I ATTACHED A PICTURE OF US AND YOU CAN SEE THAT THE ELEPHANT IN MY PICTURE LOOKS A LOT LIKE YOURS.

GOOD LUCK!

Annja studied the attached jpeg and had to agree that the elephant in the photo looked a lot like the one she'd seen on Benyovszky's computer. The jpeg was small and she couldn't blow it up much, but she wanted to.

In the picture, two girls that might have been eleven or twelve stood at a desk where an old man sat. Several other presumably made Russian things—coins, paper money, pewter replicas of buildings with spires and onion domes—were spread over the table. The girls held the elephant, displaying it proudly.

Excitement stirred in Annja as it nearly always did when she started getting closer to a goal.

Annja wrote back to hiddenheroine@fieldofpoppies.ssl.

HEY RACHEL,

YOUR ELEPHANT CERTAINLY DOES RESEMBLE MINE. CAN YOU GIVE ME MORE INFORMATION ABOUT THE FAMILY THAT HAD THE ELEPHANT? AND PERHAPS SEND ME A LARGER JPEG? I'D LIKE TO BLOW UP THE IMAGE.

BEST,

ANNJA

She saved the file to her hard drive and the Cloud in folders she'd created for gathering news stories, pictures and anything else she came across in her search.

Annja kept reading, but most of the next entries were repetitive. No one out there seemed to know anything more about the elephant than she did.

The results could have been discouraging. Annja chose to remain focused on what she was doing.

An hour later, Bart returned and he looked even more stressed than before. He walked over to Annja and shook his head.

"What are you doing at Joe's desk?"

Annja chose to ignore the combative tone. She understood how frustrated Bart felt. She was frustrated, too.

"Detective Broadhurst said I could use his desk while the two of you were gone."

"You were taken into custody. You should be in a cell with your gunslinging buddies."

Annja made herself be calm. This wasn't Bart talking. This was frustration and lack of sleep. "Do you want to lock me up?"

The question, asked so casually, stopped Bart in his tracks. He tried to speak, couldn't, then ran a hand over his face and let out a sigh. Everyone in the detective bull pen was watching with avid interest.

"We're not going to do this here," Bart said. "Come with me." He turned and started off.

Annja thought about ignoring the command and sitting, but she didn't because she knew that wouldn't get her any closer to getting out of the police station and back on the hunt.

Provided she could pick up the trail again. She packed her computer away in her backpack, slung it over her shoulder and followed Bart.

18

"What were you thinking, Annja?" Bart stood on the other side of the room with his arms folded across his chest. He looked tired and frazzled.

"What was I thinking about going to Onoprienko's?" Annja tried to concentrate on the fact that Bart was her friend and not take offense at his confrontational manner. But it was difficult.

"Yes."

"I was thinking maybe I could help you find Benyovszky's killer."

Bart took in a breath and let it out. "If you had a lead, you should have come to me."

"I didn't know if Onoprienko murdered Benyovszky. Leonid Klykov is the one who thought that. And I still don't know if Onoprienko killed anyone. Other than the guys I read about him killing."

"And you just took Klykov's word and went after Onoprienko?"

"I didn't have anything else to follow up on. Klykov sounded convincing."

"You asked Klykov to go with you?"

"No. Going with me was part of the deal he made with me for his help. He wouldn't give me the address. I think he was trying to look out for me. Onoprienko just got out of prison a few weeks ago after serving a second-degree murder sentence." Annja thought Bart should go easier on her and be more focused on the real criminal.

"I know that. I'm a cop. You should have called me as soon as you had Onoprienko's name."

Annja shot Bart a look. "I should have called you?"

"Yes! You should have called me."

"Take a minute. Think about how that would have gone

over with Klykov. Asking him about Benyovszky was one thing, but he'd have drawn the line at inviting the police along."

"If we'd had the name, Klykov wouldn't have gone."

Annja looked at Bart, wondering if he was even listening to himself. "That wouldn't have worked."

"Ruffling Klykov's feathers isn't my problem. If you'd called me, Joe and I could have picked up Onoprienko for questioning."

"On what grounds?"

"Onoprienko is a convicted felon. Once a guy's in the system like that, I have a lot of latitude in how I deal with them. I don't need a reason to check up on Onoprienko. I could have pulled him in anytime I wanted to. That's the law. He gave up a lot of rights when he killed those two guys. And Joe and I think Onoprienko is responsible for some other open unsolved cases we have. Getting a search warrant for that apartment, getting to look at evidence before it was compromised, might have helped with some of the other cases Onoprienko is connected to. If I'd known Onoprienko knew Benyovszky, I would have already had him in here for questioning. So, I repeat, why didn't you call me?"

"I thought about it," Annja admitted. "I chose not to."

"Why?"

"Because you'd have cut me out of this."

"You bet I would have." Bart was more angry than Annja had ever seen him. "I started out with one body last night. We picked up another one that may be related to the first murder. And somebody killed the two guys we thought had killed Benyovszky and that guy across the street. We were looking at four homicides. That shoot-out the Trigger Twins pulled has put nine more bodies in the morgue we have to work. And it's not the work I'm concerned with. It's the fact that you were hanging out with those two killers."

"Leonid and Pitor were only defending themselves. And me."

"Now you're on a first-name basis with these guys?"

"Bart, I could tell you I'm sorry I didn't tell you about Onoprienko when I learned about him, and I am, but that's not going to undo this."

"No, it's not." Bart ran a hand through his hair.

"Then this is where we start."

Bart rolled his neck on his shoulders.

"Have you found Onoprienko?" Annja asked, hoping to change the direction of the conversation.

Bart's eyes narrowed. She felt like most of his anger wasn't directed at her. She just happened to be the one he could get to at the moment. Klykov and Serov had already lawyered up.

"Annja, this is not your case."

Stung, Annja clamped down on her frustration. In all the years she had known Bart, they'd never gone head-to-head over something. They'd had disagreements and tension occasionally, but that was more from external situations rather than something directly between them.

This was different, and she wondered if their friendship would weather the storm. She didn't want to lose it, and she didn't want it permanently damaged. Bart was an important person in her life.

"You invited me into this," Annja said in a neutral tone.

"Not to team up with guys like Klykov and Serov. Do you realize how lucky you are that you're not one of those bodies cooling in the morgue?"

"That's the thing, though. I'm not. I'm fine."

"I'm aware that I got you involved in this, but this investigation wasn't supposed to get all crazy like it has. You were supposed to come in, look at a few things, give us some insight and go home."

"I couldn't just stop with so many questions unanswered. You know me. And you know that about me."

Bart shifted, loosening up a little. "I know. I see how you get when you're chasing one of those artifacts that take you away so often. I should have known that you'd do the same thing with this."

"If Nguyen Rao hadn't shown up at the diner, I might have walked away. But when Nguyen did, and he was asking about the elephant, I knew that something weird was going on. I don't walk away from stuff like that."

"I get it. I do." Bart paused. "I just saw you almost get killed this morning at the diner, then I hear about this shoot-out in Onoprienko's apartment, and I go over there to have a look, and I honestly don't know how you got out of there alive. That apartment and hallway looked like a war zone."

"I did get out of there, Bart. That's the important part. I did get out of there alive. Leonid and Pitor helped. I could have taken care of myself. And to be honest, I've been in tighter scrapes than that while I've been out of the country."

For a moment the silence stretched between them. On the other side of the closed door, detectives talked to each other and made phone calls, a drunken woman had a screaming fit and had to be taken away and footsteps passed by.

Annja spoke first, hoping to dodge the personal issue between them. Bart felt responsible for her safety, and he felt like she'd betrayed him by joining forces with Klykov and Serov. She knew she probably would have felt the same if she'd been in his shoes. But he wasn't responsible for her and she wasn't going to let him be. She also wasn't going to be ordered around.

"Did Onoprienko murder Benyovszky?" she asked.

Stubbornly, Bart didn't answer.

After waiting for a full minute, Annja picked up her backpack and started for the door.

"You can't just walk out of here," Bart protested.

"Yes, I can." Annja turned to look at Bart. "Unless you plan on arresting me."

"I could." The challenge hung heavy in his words.

"Okay, that's what you'll have to do." Annja knew she couldn't back down. If she did, she might evade the argument now, but their relationship would never be the same. They had to each stand on their own and go the distance.

"No." Bart straightened. "That's not what I want to do."

Annja waited.

"Onoprienko is still in the wind." Bart's tone turned softer and he sounded more tired. "We don't know where he's gone.

We found a hammer at his house that the ME's office says might be a fit for the weapon that killed Benyovszky. We'll know more when we get the report back from forensics. One of the assistants in the ME's office has already confirmed that Benyovszky's blood was on the weapon. Onoprienko tried to wash it off, but you can never completely get rid of blood."

"Then he's your killer. You can close the case on Benyovszky's murder." Annja knew she couldn't rest until she'd tracked down the elephant or believed the piece was unrecoverable.

Calapez and Nguyen Rao were chasing after the elephant; it had to mean something, and if they knew what it was, Annja felt confident that she could learn what was going on, as well.

"Maybe we can close that investigation. We still have to be able to prove that hammer is the weapon that was used to kill Benyovszky and then put that hammer in Onoprienko's hand doing that. The same way you verify that an artifact is what you say it is, that it was made in a certain place at a certain time by a certain person."

"Certificate of authenticity."

"Right. That. We still have that to do. But Joe and I are pretty confident Onoprienko's the murderer. We just have to find him. You don't suppose Klykov has any more ideas about where Onoprienko is, do you?"

"You'd have to ask him. He didn't mention anywhere else to me on the ride over, and we haven't exactly had time to talk since everything occurred."

Bart grinned crookedly. "Asking him questions isn't going to be possible. *I* am not one of Klykov's favorite people right now."

"Is he still here?"

"Yeah. I haven't cut him loose yet, but I'm going to have to. His lawyer got here thirty minutes after we brought you guys in. They're playing the quiet game, waiting to see what we have and what we're going to do. Even charging him with shooting those men in the apartment is off the table for the moment until we get all the evidence sorted.

"Or if we didn't have your statement saying he and Serov shot back in self-defense."

"They did act in self-defense. Their own and mine."

"They didn't have to be so good at shooting back."

"He was just defending himself. And if we hadn't gotten there, Guro's men might have killed Onoprienko."

"You *know* Guro's people?"

Annja shrugged. "I don't really know them. I only met them tonight, and that was only for about a minute before they started trying to kill us."

"You got really lucky there. Although nobody's talking, and most of those guys aren't even alive *to* talk now, the way Joe and I read it is Guro's head enforcer—"

"Kaneev."

Bart frowned. "Yeah. Kaneev. We think he was there to kill Onoprienko, but he was also doing a bit of gun smuggling on the side. I guess he figured Onoprienko's apartment was safe to do it in. So while Kaneev was getting ready to blow Onoprienko's brains out, he was making a little extra side money selling weapons. One of the buyers gave us that."

Picturing the scene in her mind again, Annja shook her head. "If Kaneev was there to kill Onoprienko, Onoprienko would have been dead. They wanted something out of him."

"Had to be money. Guro is a loan shark."

"Onoprienko had something they were trying to get. Otherwise they wouldn't have tortured him. The only thing I can think of is the elephant that Benyovszky had."

"Onoprienko was tortured?"

"He'd been hit a lot. His face was busted up pretty good."

"Doesn't that bother you?"

"What?"

"That a guy was tortured? That people got dead real fast tonight?"

Annja considered that. She was bothered, but there was nothing she could do about it. There were things a person could fix, and things that could not be fixed. To get through life sane, a person had to figure out what went on each list. A kind sister had taught Annja that back in the New Orleans orphanage she'd grown up in. The same sister had also helped

Annja start martial arts because knowing herself better would help her separate those lists.

"Yes, it bothers me. Probably on the same level that it bothers you."

"I see a lot of this in my job."

"I'm sure you do, but have you ever seen children dying of malnutrition and disease while lying in their mother's arms only a short distance from a medical facility they're not allowed to go to? Those trips I go on, Bart, it's not all about digging a hole in the ground and trying to find a treasure. I see people at their lowest. And to be honest, there are a lot worse things happening in a number of countries than happen here. Tonight was bad, but no innocents were killed. You need to be thankful for that."

Bart just stared at her for a moment. "You know, I've never stopped and thought about that. What you see, I mean."

A knock sounded on the door.

"Come in," Bart said.

The door opened and an older plainclothes detective stuck his head in. "Sorry to interrupt, Bart, but Creed's attorney is here."

Bart glanced at Annja and she saw the flush of anger in his face. "You called a lawyer?"

"No."

"Excuse me, detective," a new voice interrupted. "Perhaps it would be better if I explained."

19

The plainclothes detective backed out of the doorway, and a heavy-set man entered and glanced around the room. His dark blue suit was fashionable and tailored. The round face was pale and undefined, and his dark brown hair was going thin on top but still showed rebellious curls. He carried a slimline briefcase in one hand and a stylish fedora in the other.

"Actually, the detective got it wrong." The man gave a small smile that was more serviceable than filled with kindness. "I'm not Miss Creed's attorney yet, Detective McGillis." He fixed his gaze on Annja. "But I will be, Miss Creed, if you so choose to invoke your rights to an attorney in this matter. My name is Oleg Deyneka."

Bart's expression soured and Annja guessed his and the attorney's paths had crossed before.

"We're finished here," Bart said.

Deyneka beamed. "Splendid. Mr. Klykov was becoming concerned on how long you were keeping the professor. He thought I should inquire after her situation."

"Professor Creed did her civic duty, so we can't impose on her any longer."

"I'd hoped that would be the case," Deyneka said. "Especially in light of the fact that you originally called her in to assist with this investigation. I understand then, that she's free to leave now?"

"Yes. I will want her available for further questioning if that becomes necessary."

Before Annja could agree to that, the attorney said, "Miss Creed, Mr. Klykov would like to make certain you are well represented in this matter—since it involves him."

"All right." Annja felt she owed Klykov that. The old gangster was in more danger of being prosecuted than she was.

"Splendid." Deyneka smiled again. "What about Mr. Klykov and Mr. Serov? Are they free to go, as well? They've been here several hours answering all the questions you and your department have had for them."

"They didn't answer all of them," Bart said.

Deyneka never batted an eye. "They answered as many as they felt they needed to. Now...are they free to go? Charge them or release them."

"Sure." Bart folded his arms. "They're free to go."

Deyneka turned to Annja. "Mr. Klykov has extended a dinner invitation to you. Given the shocking events this afternoon that you've been witness to, he feels it is the least he can do."

"He doesn't have to do that," Annja said.

"Perhaps you'd like to tell Mr. Klykov that yourself, Professor."

"I will." Annja turned back to Bart. "I'll let you know anything I find out."

Bart nodded. "Just be careful, Annja."

She left him standing there, feeling as if things were still unresolved between them, and headed off.

Klykov and Serov stood near the exit to the bull pen and looked completely out of place in their *Chasing History's Monsters* T-shirts under their jackets. Most of the detectives were watching them.

"Annja." Klykov smiled and nodded as Annja joined him. "I hope Oleg didn't interrupt anything important."

"No. Detective McGilley and I are old friends. He was just voicing his...*concerns*."

Bart stood nearby and looked like the protective and disapproving older brother Annja had never had. The threat he offered was etched in the straight lines of his body and the curved frown.

Klykov nodded. "I didn't know you were on such good terms with the police."

"Not with the police. With Bart. When I first met him, I didn't know he was a detective. He didn't tell me that until later."

"Well, some of the best people are police. Oleg told you about dinner?"

"He did, but it's been a long day—"

"I totally understand. I wasn't sure you'd want to continue chasing Onoprienko after everything that happened today."

That caught Annja's attention immediately. "You know where he is?"

"I know where he's going to be."

Annja struggled with her desire to find the elephant piece and not wanting to disappoint Bart again. "Does he have the elephant?"

"He does indeed. Does dinner sound more interesting now?"

"Yes, but I don't want to cut Bart out of the investigation again. He needs to find Onoprienko."

"Unless your friend has jurisdiction in Ukraine, that's going to be a problem."

"ONOPRIENKO KILLED BENYOVSZKY for the elephant to pay off his debt to Guro." Seated at one of the back tables in a well-known Russian restaurant on 2nd Street, Klykov talked as he ate.

"Leonid." Serov glanced at the other man reproachfully. "I must protest."

"What?" Klykov's knife and fork hovered over an order of meat dumplings called pelmeni. The folded shells contained beef and pork seasoned to what Annja felt was perfection. She'd eaten at this restaurant a lot when she was in town.

"This hardly seems to be an appropriate topic of conversation to have with a young lady over a meal."

"Faugh." Klykov continued chewing. "The only reason Annja is here with two old men is because she wishes to know what I have learned about this matter."

"Not completely true." Annja sipped her wine. "It's mostly true for tonight, but the company is good. On another night I would have come without being bribed."

"You see?" Klykov made shooing motions with his hand. "She is fine with this topic."

Serov glanced at Annja in mock despair. "I have tried hard to elevate his social graces, but I fear it is hopeless."

Annja laughed. Watching the two old gangsters play off of each other was fun. The average person probably wouldn't have thought so if dealing with them, but Annja was enjoying herself. She also realized Bart wouldn't have thought so either, and that took a little of the fun out of it.

"At any rate, as I was saying, Onoprienko learned from Benyovszky that he was about to get a windfall and he decided to take advantage of it to save himself. Benyovszky was only celebrating his good fortune, had too much to drink and told Onoprienko of the auction that was doing so well."

Annja took another bite of her own dumplings served with sour cream and delighted in the flavors. She hadn't realized how hungry she'd been, and eating at the restaurant had sounded a whole lot better than going home to fix a meal.

"So Onoprienko goes over to Benyovszky's apartment, bashes in his head and takes the elephant," Klykov said.

Serov shook his head sorrowfully. "Leonid, we're eating."

Annja wiped her mouth with her napkin. "Don't worry. I'm fine. I've had dinner down in burial pits while we were exhuming graves. Some of the bodies were fresh enough that they still had flesh on them. This doesn't bother me."

Klykov grinned. "You see, Pitor? You worry too much. Annja is not a typical woman. You should have realized that earlier today when all the shooting was taking place."

"Fine. I will mind my own business." Serov turned his attention back to his meal.

"Where is the elephant?" Annja asked.

"Onoprienko has it. He didn't keep it at his apartment."

"You can't keep anything in that building," Serov said. "It's filled with thieves."

"And one police officer," Annja pointed out.

Serov laughed. "That's a funny story, actually. The police officer did not live there. He was only there in the building to make a buy from a drug dealer. That is why the police arrived so quickly."

Bart hadn't mentioned that. "How did you find that out?"

"The same way Leonid knows so much. While we were wasting time at the police station, time that we won't get back, Leonid and I had people out talking to people. We only remained at the station to make certain you were released and in no trouble."

"Oh."

"Please," Klykov said to Serov, "may I tell my story? It is, after all, my story and I am buying dinner."

"Of course. I was only answering Annja's question."

"As Pitor said, I asked a few people who know people to go out and ask about people. It was not so much to do. After the shooting in Onoprienko's apartment, everyone was talking. My people only had to listen and report back to me. What I learned is that Onoprienko stole the elephant in order to pay off his debts to Guro. Onoprienko told Guro about the elephant. Guro didn't trust Onoprienko, so he sent Kaneev and his men to get the elephant and to kill Onoprienko. Guro wanted the elephant to settle the debt, if it was worth that much, and he also wanted Onoprienko dead as a statement to his other clients."

"Bart said there was a group of people there buying weapons from Kaneev."

Klykov grinned. "Guro wasn't aware of that. If Kaneev had lived—"

"And he might have if Leonid did not shoot so straight," Serov put in.

Klykov performed a small mock bow. "Had Kaneev lived, Guro would probably have killed him for his betrayal. As it is, Guro now owes me a favor for exposing his enforcer as a weak link."

"A weak link?"

"Sure, sure. Think about it. If Kaneev had gotten caught doing business on the side, and he would have, then he could have spilled everything to the police and claimed Guro was behind it all. It was genius, actually. Kaneev had his own insurance policy in place in the event of his apprehension. The police would have wanted a larger fish than Kaneev, and he is the kind of person who would sell out his employer. Make a deal and be gone, all the while his illicit profits would be waiting for him."

"Guro didn't know that?"

"Not until today. And now he has Kaneev's stashed money, which Guro is also thankful for. He owes me a *big* favor."

Annja realized that she was getting sidetracked. "Okay, so we're certain that Onoprienko has the elephant."

"He does."

"How do you know?"

"Because Onoprienko doesn't have a buyer here." Klykov smiled. "But he does have one in Odessa."

"Who is it?"

"That I am not certain of. Yet. But I have people asking questions. Once questions start getting asked, once a thing is almost known, soon the answers come."

"Is Onoprienko still in New York?"

"No. He flew to Canada with a man who regularly travels between New York and Saint John, New Brunswick. That man does some smuggling business and taking Onoprienko was easily arranged because they have worked together before."

Annja stopped eating as her appetite all but disappeared. "So the elephant is already gone."

"I did not say that." Klykov sliced into a dumpling. "You have passport, *da*?"

"Yes."

"Then we will go to Odessa and continue tracking Onoprienko. My travel agent has booked us seats on a flight out of LaGuardia at seven o'clock in the morning. Can you be ready by this time?"

"I can be." Annja looked at Klykov. "Why are you doing this?"

He smiled at her. "Because it has been a long time since I have been on an adventure with a beautiful woman. And do not worry that this is some kind of romantic overture. This is done because I respect you. If I had ever had a daughter, I would have wanted her to grow up like you. Fierce and independent."

Appetite returned, Annja dug into her meal with renewed gusto. There was nothing like a fresh clue to revitalize flagging enthusiasm. The hunt was still on.

20

“You’re in Odessa?” Bart sounded half-asleep. “But you were there in Brighton all day yesterday.”

Annja walked through LaGuardia at 4:30 a.m., not feeling exactly at the top of her game either. After finishing dinner with Klykov and Serov, she had returned to her loft, packed, and made everything as ready for being away for a few days as she could.

“Not Little Odessa. Odessa as in Odessa in Ukraine.” Annja paused and looked around the terminal for Klykov and didn’t see him. Her e-ticket had been waiting for her online and she only had to swipe a credit card to claim it. Since the booking had been at the last minute, she had been treated to extra scrutiny that had left her feeling just short of violated.

“You’re leaving New York?” Bart sounded more awake now.

“To get to Ukraine, you must leave New York, so yes, I’m leaving New York.”

“Why?”

“Because that’s where Onoprienko is headed.”

“Wait. Slow down. How do you know this?”

“I don’t know it, but that’s what I’ve been told.”

“By Klykov.” Bart made that sound more like an accusation than a statement of fact.

“Yes. By Klykov.”

“You could have told me this last night.”

“And then you would have spent the night asking me questions I don’t have the answers to. That wouldn’t have been good for either of us. I’m telling you now so you’ll know. The answers, if I’m lucky, are in Ukraine.” Annja didn’t like feeling she had to report to anyone, let alone Bart, but the search for the elephant was part of his murder investigation.

"Where's Onoprienko now?"

"On his way to Odessa."

"Who is Onoprienko meeting there?"

"I have no idea."

"Is Klykov holding out on you?"

"I don't think so."

Bart sighed grumpily. "You're trusting that old guy too much, Annja."

"We'll see. In the meantime, I'm going to grab breakfast and get ready for the flight. I just wanted you to know where I was and that maybe you'll get a break on the case. If the ME and forensics people tie Onoprienko to the murder of Benyovszky, you should be able to get extradition, right?"

"Maybe."

"Then let's hope it works out like that."

"I appreciate it, but that's not going to stop me from worrying about you."

"I worry about you, too, but you still have a job to do and I do, too. We can't let worry stop us. We both love what we do, so we deal with it."

"I know, but this is kind of crazy."

"So is chasing killers through New York City and you do that every day."

"I don't think of you doing something like this. I usually picture you in some quaint little restaurant eating the local fare and drinking wine after a long day playing in a sandbox digging up bones and trinkets somewhere."

Annja checked an immediate attack on his casual dismissal of her vocation. "That's not what this job is."

"I'm getting that. You know I didn't mean it like it sounded. It's early. I'm not at my best. Call me when you can?"

"I will." Annja said goodbye and went looking for breakfast. Despite her fatigue, she felt energized. It was always good to be moving toward a goal.

"GOOD MORNING, ANNJA."

Glancing up from her tablet, Annja spotted Klykov standing only a few feet away from her table in the terminal's lower food court. He was dressed in another neatly pressed suit and pulled a carry-on bag behind him. He held his fedora in the other hand.

She smiled at him. "Good morning."

He pointed with the hat to the seat across the small table from her. "May I sit?"

"Of course." Annja took her tablet off the table and pulled her breakfast toward her to make room for him.

Klykov sat and hung his fedora on the extended handles of his carry-on. "Sleep well?"

"I got a couple hours' sleep." Even those had not been restful. Yesterday's argument with Bart kept replaying in her head in spite of the polite conversation they'd had only a short time ago. And the violence in Onoprienko's apartment thundered around in her brain, as well. Normally she didn't think too much about events like those because once something was done there wasn't much she could do about it, but she knew most of the feelings now were because the situation had involved Bart. "And you?"

"I slept well enough. I have to admit, I'm excited about going on this trip. I mean, it's one thing to watch you do what you do on your show, but it's really something to be part of it."

"There's usually not as much gunplay." *At least, not that ended up in the shows.* Annja kept as much of that out of those stories as she could.

Klykov grinned. "That is nothing. I have seen years of that in this country and in Russia. The chase to learn the secret of the elephant is so different."

"It is."

"You lead a remarkable life, Annja."

"I can go get you breakfast," Annja offered.

"No, thank you. I had breakfast before I left the house this morning. I would have invited you to meet somewhere, but I guessed that you were a lot like my wife and probably liked to have time to yourself when you had to get everything together. Meeting you here seemed less invasive."

"Thank you. I didn't know that you're married."

"Was married. For forty-two great years." A shadow

dimmed the lights in Klykov's eyes. "I lost her to cancer three years ago."

"I'm sorry."

"Life is what it is, Annja. We had forty-two years and we loved each other very much. I still love her." Klykov shook his head. "I don't talk to many people about her."

"Then I feel privileged."

Klykov chuckled. "You would have liked her. She would have liked you. Your spunk. Your zest. Those are qualities Katia respected in people."

"She sounds like a great lady."

"She was." Klykov looked at the rest of the food court bustling with travelers around them, but she knew he wasn't seeing them. He was somewhere else.

"Can I get you some coffee then?"

"No." Klykov shook his head. "I'm fine. Thank you. I did find out who Onoprienko hopes to sell the elephant to in Odessa. More information came in last night. There is a… woman Onoprienko likes to talk to. When he has the money. He mentioned his scheme to her the night before he killed Maurice Benyovszky."

"Who?"

"A fence named Viktor Fedotov. An honorable man as far as thieves go. I talked with him this morning. He has agreed to stall Onoprienko in the event he arrives in Odessa before we do."

The PA announced the initial boarding call to their Aeroflot flight to Odessa. There was one layover in Moscow. They were going to be in the air and in Moscow for almost fifteen hours before they reached Odessa. Thankfully Klykov had reserved two first-class seats.

ON THE OTHER side of the terminal, Rao watched Annja Creed talking to the old Russian. Having had precious little sleep the night before because he'd been camped outside the woman's apartment, Rao looked forward to the long flight. He still didn't know why the archaeologist was leaving New York City. As far as Rao could tell, she had not found the elephant.

Rao felt troubled as he sat there. He had followed her from her apartment that morning, and had nearly panicked when he realized her destination was LaGuardia.

He had purchased a ticket that had gotten him inside the terminal, spied on her while she worked on her computer, and saw her e-ticket printout just long enough to confirm she was going to Odessa in Ukraine.

That had puzzled him. He had wondered then if Annja Creed had given up pursuing the elephant. That didn't seem like something she would do. In the end, he knew he simply had nowhere else to go. Onoprienko had not turned up and the police in New York City were searching for the man. Rao knew he could not find Onoprienko before the police did.

If the police got their hands on the elephant, there was a possibility that the temple could file diplomatic claims and get the elephant returned. That would take time, and there was a risk that information might come to light that would slow down that return.

It would be better if Rao was able to get the elephant himself.

The trip to Odessa could be something Annja Creed had already scheduled. Rao was cognizant of that. If that were the case, all he could do was turn around and begin the search for the elephant anew.

When the old Russian showed up and took a seat with Annja Creed, Rao felt more certain he was on the right track. He sat, hidden in plain sight, clad in American street clothes and expensive sunglasses.

When the boarding call came, Rao picked up his carry-on and headed to check in.

SHE IS HEADED TO ODESSA, UKRAINE. DOES THIS MEAN ANYTHING TO YOU?

Sequeira sat on the edge of his pool and watched Joana swimming laps. He enjoyed the smooth play of her muscles as she moved through the water.

Then he returned his attention to the cell phone text from

Brisa. The assassin had included a picture of Annja Creed walking through the airport terminal. The woman was very beautiful.

WHY IS SHE GOING TO ODESSA? Even as he asked that question, Sequeira thought of the history of the elephant piece and how it had passed through Russia. Ukraine was not so far from Russia.

I HAVE NOT BEEN ABLE TO FIND OUT. IF I WAS ALLOWED TO ENGAGE HER, I WOULD HAVE AN ANSWER.

And Annja Creed would also be dead. Despite the tension that filled him, and the fear that he was going to lose the elephant, Sequeira smiled at that. Brisa was not always calm and cool. The assassin preferred to know a target, identify it, and eliminate it.

ANNJA CREED IS OUR ONLY LEAD TO THE ELEPHANT AT THIS POINT. I WANT HER ALIVE FOR NOW.

ALIVE IS HARDER.

YOU'RE GETTING A BONUS FOR BRINGING THIS IN.

I CAN'T SPEND A BONUS IF I'M DEAD OR IN JAIL.

GETTING NERVOUS?

NO, BUT AN OPERATION HAS TO RUN CLEANLY IF IT IS TO BE SUCCESSFUL. THERE ARE TOO MANY MOVING PARTS IN THIS ONE.

WAIT A LITTLE LONGER.

IS THE MONK NECESSARY? I COULD KILL HIM.

LEAVE HIM IN PLACE FOR THE MOMENT, AS WELL. IN CASE ANNJA CREED DOESN'T WORK OUT. Sequeira sat there in the early afternoon sunlight feeling content and excited. Authorities had noticed Melicio was missing, but the tide had not brought the body back into the coast yet. Perhaps it wouldn't show up at all. He returned his attention to the phone, to the picture of Annja Creed. I AM COMING TO ODESSA.

IT WOULD BE BETTER IF YOU STAYED OUT OF THIS.

I WILL NOT INTERFERE WITH YOUR WORK. I JUST WANT TO BE THERE WHEN YOU GET THE ELEPHANT.

THE POLICE HAVE ALREADY TIED YOU TO CALAPEZ.

"POSSIBLY" TIED ME. That information had come from the attorney Sequeira had hired in New York. NOW THAT CALAPEZ IS DEAD, THERE ARE NO MORE TIES TO ME. I'M COMING TO ODESSA. IF YOU HAVE THE ELEPHANT BEFORE I ARRIVE, ALL THE BETTER.

There was no response. Sequeira didn't expect one. He usually agreed with whatever Brisa said. But in this instance he couldn't.

"Fernando, you are not paying attention." Joana pulled at her bikini bottom as she walked up the steps out of the pool. She showed him a mock pout. "You need to stop doing business and swim. Get your cardio in. Spend time with me."

Sequeira smiled up at her. "I'm afraid I'm going to have to go."

"Why?"

"Business."

"Where will you go?"

"To Odessa."

Joana stood before him, radiant and beautiful, and he knew from the tight corners of her eyes that she was thinking he was planning on a rendezvous with another woman.

Sequeira stood and kissed her hard enough to bruise her lips. "Do not worry. I will think of you every minute I am gone."

"How long will you be away?"

"I don't know yet."

"Then take me with you."

"I can't."

Quietly, with a small frown, Joana accepted that. She had known when she'd taken up with him that his loyalties were divided. Some days he could be wholly hers, and other days he would be all business, and some of that business dealt with things she would never know about. Sequeira had made certain she understood how things must be when he had taken her into his household.

"What am I to do while you are gone?" she asked.

"Do what you always do. Shop."

She hugged him. "When do you have to go?"

"Soon."

"Then enjoy the pool with me for a little while." She put her arms around his neck and kissed him, pulling him toward the water.

Sequeira destroyed the cell phone and scattered the pieces behind him as he let her guide him into the water. He owned a private jet. He could leave as soon as he wished.

21

"Annja?"

"Yes." Answering the vibrating phone had brought Annja out of a dead sleep. The phone had been lying across her chest, hooked into a charging station in the wall next to her seat. First class was awesome that way. She blinked her eyes and glanced at the compartment around her.

Most of the other passengers were engaged in quiet conversations, read, watched the onboard movie or slept. Beside her, Klykov snored slightly. His fedora rested on his chest and rose and fell with his breaths.

"Where are you?" This time Annja recognized Doug Morrell's voice.

"I'm on a plane."

"Going where?"

"To Odessa."

"Brighton? Why would you go there?"

"Not Brighton. Odessa in Ukraine. On the Black Sea."

"You know we need to get an idea for the next episode. We've only got so much of a window for these things."

"I'm doing background research for a possible show."

"In Odessa?"

"Yes."

"What is it?" Doug sounded suspicious. He knew she stayed torn between doing the television show and following up on whatever artifact had seized her attention.

"Have you heard of a *upiors*?"

"Not really."

Annja coughed to clear her throat. "It's a Slavic vampire. In fact, many etymologists believe that the English word *vampire* was derived from the original *upior* legend."

"*You're* going to do a piece on vampires?" Doug's voice

held absolute delight. He loved the whole idea of vampires. Only instead of blood-sucking fiends, he preferred the sexy near-god version of them that was currently popular.

Annja preferred her vampires, if she had to have them. "Polish ones. They have barbed tongues. They're supposed to bathe in blood."

"Like Countess Bathory? Amazing!"

"When you stake them, they're supposed to explode."

"Even more amazing. Annja, this is a great idea!"

Annja knew that Doug would think so, and she felt bad that she wasn't going to be able to deliver an actual *upior* for the show, but she thought she could do some background for a piece on the vampire while she was in Odessa.

"Good. I'm glad you like it."

"Can you send me anything? Some local stuff? Legends?"

"As soon as I get to Odessa in a few more hours."

"Amazing. Let me tell the powers-that-be and we'll get cranking on things at this end."

"I'll leave you to that." Annja ended the call and closed her eyes again.

"A *upior*?" Klykov asked from beside her.

"I didn't mean to wake you."

"Is okay. I can go back to sleep, but maybe I will have nightmares now."

"Sorry."

Klykov smiled without opening his eyes. "I have seen many things worse than *upiors*, Annja. I have never seen a *upior*."

"Neither have I, but there should be enough of a history of them in Odessa and nearby environs for me to put a show together."

"You should use caution when you are in Odessa, though. There are many people who believe *upiors* exist. I am just not one of them."

Unable to go back to sleep immediately, Annja reached into her backpack and took out her tablet and her mini–satellite receiver. She hooked the devices together and booted up the tablet. Her first stop was her usual archaeology website.

Rachel, who was hiddenheroine@fieldofpoppies.ssl, had written back about the picture of the elephant she had sent.

HEY ANNJA!
SO COOL TO BE PART OF THIS. I GOT HOLD OF TANECHKA AND WE HAD A LONG TALK. I'VE MISSED CHATTING TO HER, SO THIS WAS A GOOD EXCUSE TO RECONNECT. LIFE SOOOO GETS IN THE WAY OF LIVING SOMETIMES!

ANYWAY, TANECHKA TOLD ME HER GRANDFATHER'S NAME WAS ASAF CHISLOVA. HE WAS HER MOTHER'S FATHER, WHICH IS WHY I COULDN'T REMEMBER THE NAME.

TANECHKA SAID THE STORY ABOUT THE ELEPHANT WAS THAT HER GRANDFATHER'S GRANDFATHER, OR SOMEWHERE BACK DOWN THE LINE, GOT THE ELEPHANT BECAUSE HE WAS A COMMANDER IN THE CRIMEAN WAR. I HAD TO LOOK UP CRIMEAN WAR. I DIDN'T KNOW WHAT IT WAS. AND THEN I LEARNED THAT WAS WHERE FLORENCE NIGHTINGALE WAS! I'D ALWAYS THOUGHT SHE WAS A BRIT! AND SHE WAS! BUT SHE GOT FAMOUS WHILE NURSING IN RUSSIA! WHO KNEW?

WELL, YOU PROBABLY DID. ☺

HISTORY! YOU GOTTA LOVE IT!

ANYWAY, ABOUT TANECHKA'S GRANDFATHER, THE SAD THING WAS THAT NOBODY KNEW ABOUT HIS STORAGE LOCKER UNTIL IT HAD ALREADY BEEN SOLD OFF AND EMPTIED. HER GRANDFATHER WAS IN A NURSING HOME AFTER A MAJOR STROKE. SHE WENT TO SEE HIM, BUT HE COULDN'T TALK AND NO ONE KNEW WHERE HIS STUFF WAS. I FEEL BAD FOR HER. L

ANYWAY, I HOPE THIS HELPS.
BYE!

Annja opened an email and sent a response.

RACHEL,
THANKS FOR ALL THE EFFORT. THE INFORMATION DOES HELP. I FEEL BAD FOR YOUR FRIEND, TOO. I'LL SEE IF

SOMETHING CAN BE SALVAGED FROM THAT STORAGE UNIT.

Picking up her phone, Annja put a call through to Bart. She knew he would be awake and working by now.

"McGilley."

"Bart, it's Annja. I've got a favor to ask."

"Okay, ask in a minute. I got some news I'm not happy about. Since Fernando Sequeira's name came up in this murder investigation, I've had a couple Interpol contacts keep tabs on him. I just got off the phone with them. Sequeira's private pilot filed flight plans for Odessa, Ukraine. The jet took off only minutes ago. What is going on over there?"

"I don't know." Annja considered the situation. "Leonid and I have negotiated with the fence Onoprienko is going to use to sell the elephant. Leonid got the name from a mutual acquaintance. The fence is going to hold Onoprienko up till we get there."

"You do realize you're getting deeper and deeper into the criminal element, right?" Bart sounded more worried than angry. Annja counted that as a win.

"When you're dealing with artifacts and national treasures, you sometimes deal with criminals. Every archaeologist I know has come across tomb raiders and grave robbers. This isn't the first time I've had to work with people like this."

"You know, I'm beginning to think that the more I know about what you do, the less I like what you do."

"I love what I do."

"Look out for Sequeira. He's bad news. He's supposed to have someone who's good at making people disappear. It's possible that's the person who whacked Calapez and Pousao in front of the precinct. Until we get the middle guy, it's going to be hard to connect Sequeira to those murders. But we think we have a lock on Calapez and Pousao for the murder of the neighbor across the street. Having a homicide on the sheets changes the game and I can now go after Sequeira harder if I'm somehow able to put him with Calapez and Pousao. As you'll recall, though, they're not talking."

Annja heard the annoyance in Bart's voice and sympathized. "Before I ask for that favor, let me see if I can do one for you. Would your Interpol buddies have a working relationship with the police in Odessa?"

"They might."

"If I can get hold of Onoprienko, maybe I can hand him off to local authorities who will get him to you."

"No. Do not do that. Onoprienko is a killer. You've seen some of his work firsthand. Forensics confirmed that the blunt object used to kill Maurice Benyovszky was the hammer we found in Onoprienko's apartment. Do *not* get around this guy."

"If he has the elephant, that's going to happen. If I get the chance to capture him—"

"Do *not*!"

"—I was thinking it would be good to have someone to hand him off to." Annja paused. "Unless you'd rather I just let him go."

Bart sighed. "I'll see what I can do. You said you needed a favor?"

"Yes. The storage unit the elephant came from belonged to a man named Asaf—"

"Chislova. Yeah, we know, Annja. Sometimes we're pretty good at doing our jobs, too."

"I can put you in touch with the granddaughter."

"We've got her name, too."

"Well, then here's the favor. The granddaughter didn't know about the storage unit, or that it was lost. All she knew is that a lot of her grandfather's things disappeared. She'd like to have a few of them as keepsakes."

"Sure, I can arrange that. Benyovszky still had some of that stuff in the storage unit he was using as a warehouse for the goods he was selling on the internet."

"Thanks. And if you can work out something in Odessa, let me know who I should call."

"What you should do is turn around and come back to New York."

Annja smiled, enjoying the fact that Bart cared, but she

had her own calling to tend to. "That's not going to happen. I'll be in touch when I can."

RAO WOKE AND had the distinct feeling someone was watching him. Without moving, he scanned the economy-class section of the plane, but there were no faces familiar to him that he could see. He sat up a little straighter and looked in the back section.

Most of the passengers had nodded off, giving in to the long flight. Only a few people remained awake. The adults worked on computers, probably preparing presentations or crunching numbers for a project. The kids played video games with rapt attention.

Unbuckling his seat belt, Rao walked back to the bathroom to get a better look at everyone. No one seemed to have any undue interest in him, but the feeling that he was being watched persisted.

Although he couldn't pinpoint the watcher, Rao was certain that he and Annja Creed were not alone on the flight.

22

As the passenger jet began its approach to Odessa, Annja peered out the window and watched the large city grow closer. Odessa had always been an important port city on the Black Sea and in the surrounding region. It was one of the few warm-water ports in the area, and it had been a point of territorial aggression for hundreds of years.

Residential and business areas occupied neat blocks and geometric shapes marked off by tree-lined streets. The verdant growth was so robust that it looked like the commercial structures had sprouted trees, or that the trees were threatening to climb over the buildings. Nature and industry warred over space, and in that Annja saw a reflection of Odessa's restless past.

Along the coast, docks thrust out into the harbor. Massive cranes moved like giant robotic arms to clutch cargo containers from the decks of ships and carry them to the docks where stevedores waited to move the goods where they belonged. A few boats sailed the water out beyond the commercial area marked off by buoys.

"Tell me what you see, Annja."

Annja glanced over her shoulder at Klykov. He'd woken up shortly before the jet had begun its descent. "I thought you'd been to Odessa before."

Klykov smiled. "I have. Many times. But I'm not talking about what you see below. Everybody sees that. That look I saw in your eyes in the reflection in the glass tells me you are looking at more than what is out there. Tell me what you see."

"Odessa was settled by the Greeks. Some of the artifacts that have been found in the eastern Mediterranean are from the same time period as those found here. So I can see the Greeks here, flourishing with fields of olives and beautiful buildings."

"Then where are these buildings?"

"They would have been destroyed by the Pechenegs and Cumans, the ancestors of the Ottoman Empire that fought so hard to reclaim Odessa. They won it back for a time, then lost it again to Catherine the Great. Sometime before Catherine's armies took this place, the Mongols were led by Batu Khan, who was the grandson of Temujin, who became the greatest threat the civilized world had ever known at that time."

"I do not know this person."

"Temujin was known by another name. Genghis Khan."

Klykov nodded. "That name I do know."

"Batu Khan formed the Ulus of Jochi, and they were also known as the Golden Horde."

"Because they came to rob the gold?"

"No. Because of the color of their tents." Annja could almost see the Mongol campsites that had littered the hills. She could imagine the burning villages along the coast, the survivors huddling in fear at the savagery the invaders had displayed. "The Mongol language translates their name literally into Golden Horde, which some people think was due to the color of their tents, but for Mongols it probably simply meant 'central camp.' But legends grow up around such things. After the Mongols, the Ottoman Empire claimed the area."

"Why?"

"For the same reason Odessa is so important today. It's a warm-water port this far north. Trade can get through. The military can get in. Back before planes changed the geography of war, the lines were drawn by accessibility. You can't march an army into enemy territory without a supply line. Once you get into Ukraine, you can go east into Russia, or west into Europe. The country has been in the center of some particularly nasty military operations, and many of them were staged here."

The seat-belt sign flashed on, followed by the captain's orders to buckle them.

Annja secured her seat belt, still lost in the history of the place, aware that Klykov was listening intently. "For a while, the Ottoman Empire took control of the city, but they couldn't hold it against the Russians. Catherine the Great named the city Odessa because they believed it was the site of the Greek city Odessos. Later, historians found out that probably wasn't accurate. Odessos was more likely over in Bulgaria, near Varna. Catherine built the city on the bones of Khadzhibey, the prior Turkish town. The Ottoman Empire and Catherine the Great fought over Odessa for a while, but Catherine's forces held the city."

The plane banked and began a sharper descent. Below, the surface of the Black Sea grew close enough to see the chop of the waves.

"You know many things, and it is interesting to hear them." Klykov's eyes twinkled and his smile was broad. "You have a remarkable mind, young lady."

Annja shook her head. "What's remarkable is history. Anyone who studies it can open up whole worlds, each different and exciting. They can be as small as an Englishwoman trying to make a living after the Napoleonic War when the men returned from the army, or as large as the World War II campaigns. I can take someone from now and put them in the shoes of someone who lived thousands of years ago, show them that the daily concerns and needs and fears are pretty much the same. Despite the fact that hundreds or thousands of years separate a person of today from someone in the past, if I do it right, they can feel what it's like to live that person's life. That's why I love what I do."

"It is always good to have passion. I have always said this. Life without passion is nothing." Klykov looked through the window once again. The jet sailed on toward the airport, and the runway was only a few feet below them. "Soon we will have that elephant you are searching for, and then you will find more stories to tell, *da*?"

"I hope so." The jet's tires hit the runway and Annja resisted the forward momentum the reduced airspeed caused.

WHILE WAITING AT the car rental agency, Klykov called his contact, Fedotov the fence, and talked quickly in Russian. Annja couldn't pick up enough of what was said to know for certain what was going on. She tried not to let herself become anxious, but that was difficult. There was no way to know if Onoprienko was going to actually show up at the place, or if Fedotov could keep Onoprienko there.

There was also the possibility that Fedotov would tell Onoprienko that people were there looking for him so that he could renegotiate the amount he'd agreed to pay for the elephant. The fence was a thief, after all.

While she stood a short distance away, a Hispanic woman approached her with a travel book in one hand and a hopeful expression on her face. She was in her midthirties, dressed conservatively and wore little makeup. She didn't need it. She was a pretty woman without it. She wore her hair cropped short and stood almost as tall as Annja.

"Pardon me," she said in English with a definite Western accent. "Have you been to Odessa before?"

"I have."

"It's my first time and I feel pretty lost."

"Where are you trying to go?"

"I'm supposed to meet some friends at a restaurant called Ode to Odessa?"

Annja nodded. "I've been there. It's a good place to eat. It's located just a short distance off Deribasovskaya Street."

"That's one of the main streets?"

"Yes. It's in the center of the city."

Annja found the restaurant on the map easily and pointed to it. "Here. Are you taking a cab or a rental?"

"I was thinking of renting a car."

"Okay, in that case you'll need to plan your parking. Deribasovskaya Street is purely pedestrian traffic."

"All right. Thank you."

"If you've got time later, I'd advise a sightseeing trip to the park." Annja shifted her finger to another place on the map. "The park was built at the turn of the nineteenth century. There are a lot of monuments to document the city's history, including a sculpture of a lion and lioness with cubs."

"For *The Twelve Chairs*, right? The story about the hidden jewelry?"

"You know your literature."

The woman laughed. "I teach at San Antonio, Texas', English Department. Emphasis on foreign literature. I read the book on the plane during the flight. I'm here for a conference on Russian lit."

Annja nodded. "Well, I hope you enjoy your stay."

"Thank you. And you do the same." She smiled and walked away, merging with the foot traffic leaving the terminal. Thinking about the park and the restaurant, Annja wished she was there on a less stressful agenda. She'd enjoyed her time in Odessa, and there was still so much of the city she hadn't seen.

Finally, Klykov hung up and turned to Annja with a smile. "You are tour guide, *da*?"

"I don't mean to be, but I like this city."

"Maybe we will take a day or two after we get the elephant for you. A celebration."

"Only if we have something to celebrate."

"Fedotov says Onoprienko has been in touch with him. Onoprienko is in the country now. He has been for a couple of hours. So far Fedotov has been able to keep Onoprienko waiting."

"Is Onoprienko there with your friend?"

"Annja." Klykov's face turned grim. "Something you must keep in mind. Fedotov is no friend of mine. He is an acquaintance. A man who does business, who keeps his eye on the bottom line at all times. You understand this, *da*?"

Annja nodded.

"I am sure Fedotov will not betray us or I would never endanger you by taking you there. Fedotov has no real honor, but he does have a very strong self-preservation instinct. He likes to live and he likes to eat. He knows that if he tries to betray me, I will have him killed." Klykov didn't try to put a polite face on things. That should have bothered Annja more than it did, but these were dangerous men. "Even if I do not live through his betrayal, Fedotov's death would come as surely as winter in Russia."

"I understand, Leonid. Don't worry about me so much. I

can take care of myself." Annja thrust her hands in the long coat that hung to midcalf. The weather was a little warmer here than in New York, but that was only while they were in the city. If they traveled far from the coast, the temperature would drop.

"It is my job to worry about you when I bring you here," Klykov said. "I do not think this policeman friend of yours would allow me to get you hurt and not take umbrage with me."

"Probably not." Admitting that made Annja feel good.

The car rental clerk handed a set of keys to Klykov and they spoke in Russian while the clerk pointed them in the right direction. Klykov nodded and then handed the keys to Annja.

"You will drive. I have always liked being the passenger in a car. I can sightsee."

23

The keys belonged to a silver BMW X3 SUV that sat out in the rental lot of the Odessa International Airport. Annja hesitated when she saw the vehicle, then looked at Klykov. "That's an expensive car."

"Then it should be a good one, *da*?"

"The guy at the counter stiffed you, Leonid. We should get a more economical car. You don't need to spend this much money. I'm going to go in halves on this rental." They'd already argued over the airplane tickets, Annja insisting on paying for her fare. Klykov had won that round, but Annja was determined to keep herself on equal footing with the old man.

Klykov just kept walking, pulling his carry-on behind him. The wheels groaned and rattled across the pavement. He wore a thick coat against the winter chill that gusted across the parking lot. "It is okay. I asked for this one. The clerk showed me a picture and I said this one. I wish to have the leg room. You are tall. You will appreciate the leg room, too. And I like that the car sits up tall so that I can see everything on the street. This will be a good vehicle for us. Come. You are wasting time that Onoprienko may not be so generous to give us."

Annja gave in and used the key fob to open the rear door. They stowed their luggage in the rear and got in.

Behind the steering wheel, Annja adjusted the seat and the rearview mirror as the engine warmed. "Where are we going?"

"Have you been to the Seventh-Kilometer Market?"

"No. I've seen it a few times as I've driven by, but I've never gotten to stop there." The few times Annja had been to Odessa and landed at the airport instead of coming in by ship, she had been in a hurry and hadn't been able to visit the place.

The Seventh-Kilometer Market lay between the Odessa

International Airport and the city itself. The marketplace got its name from the fact that it was seven kilometers outside of Odessa.

"We will be going there today," Klykov said. "That is where Fedotov is. But first we must make a small stop."

"Where?"

Klykov waved forward. "Along the highway away from the airport. I will tell you."

Annja opened the map navigator on the console and punched in the address for the Seventh-Kilometer Market when Klykov gave it to her. The software only took a moment to locate the destination and plan the route.

"Along this way?" she asked.

Klykov nodded. "This way will be fine."

Annja put the transmission in gear, watched the traffic and put her foot on the accelerator. Klykov took out a cell phone he had purchased inside the terminal, made a call and spoke in rapid-fire Russian. A few minutes later, she'd pulled onto the Odessa-Ovidiopol Highway that would take them to their destination.

CONFIDENT THAT HE wouldn't lose Annja Creed or the old man getting out of the airport, Rao sat in his rental car and watched them leave. He'd already arranged for a car and his check-in time had been short, allowing him plenty of opportunity to shadow his quarry.

While he'd done that, he'd searched for anyone else that might be following them. No one had acted overly concerned about losing sight of Annja and her companion.

Then he realized that if anyone had been following them on the flight, they could just as easily have had someone waiting at the airport. An overlap of observation would be easy to arrange. His anxiety grew; even though he wanted the elephant, he didn't want Annja Creed harmed.

He put the car in gear and rolled out of the parking lot toward the access road that would take him toward Odessa. He was tired of always being concerned and in unfamiliar foreign territories. He longed to be back in the museum cataloguing artifacts.

"OVER HERE." KLYKOV pointed at the side of the highway.

According to the tripometer, they had only gone three miles from the airport. Annja looked at the small bronze sedan parked on the side of the highway as she turned on the signal and stepped lightly on the brake.

"We're meeting someone?" she asked. The idea of a clandestine meeting by the road didn't appeal to her. They were too exposed.

"*Da.* A friend. Have no worries, Annja." Klykov smiled toward the sedan. "Pull in behind him and be at ease."

Annja did as she was told regarding the parking, kept enough room between the two vehicles to pull away quickly if she needed to, but she did not feel at ease. She left the transmission engaged and her door locked.

Two young men with hard faces opened the sedan doors and got out on either side. One of them was smoking a black cigarette and gray smoke curled from his mouth. Annja spotted the tattoos that showed on their necks and knew they were Russian mafia.

"These are the two people you're meeting?" she asked.

"*Da.*"

"You know them?"

"No, but they are known to men who know me. A friend of a friend, you might say."

"What do they want?"

"They want nothing. This is about what I want. Is okay, Annja. Please do not worry. I will be back in a minute." Klykov opened the door and got out. He called out to the two men and they nodded to him. Neither of them looked overly friendly.

One of them looked at Annja suspiciously, then returned his attention to Klykov.

Cars whipped by on the highway and the wind buffeted the SUV, rocking it on its tires. Annja kept her eyes on Klykov.

RAO HADN'T BEEN prepared for Annja Creed to stop alongside the highway. He knew he could not pull off the road and wait behind her because that would have alerted her to his presence. Thankfully a petrol station lay just a mile and a half ahead or so and the ground was level enough that he could see the SUV from there.

He drove into the petrol station and parked near the outside curb, trusting that if Annja Creed had noticed him that she would only think he was a person who needed to check a map or make a phone call. Then he waited and watched.

No other cars seemed overly concerned that Annja had stopped.

Rao wondered about the feeling of being watched aboard the jet. Perhaps that had merely been an effect of not enough sleep and rising tension regarding his involvement with the chase for the elephant. He hoped that was so, but he still felt strongly that his initial instincts were correct. They usually were.

ANNJA'S PHONE RANG and she answered it, spotting Bart's name in the viewscreen. "Hello?"

"You should be on the ground by now, right?" Bart sounded grim and professional.

"I am."

"I've got some more interesting news for you. You remember the guy who approached us in the diner?"

"Nguyen Rao."

"That's him. As it turns out, he also took a flight out of New York yesterday about the same time you did. I just confirmed that. He's traveling under another name, but he popped up on facial recognition when I asked my buddies at Interpol to run him." Bart gave her the flight number.

"That's the plane Leonid and I flew in on."

"You didn't see Nguyen?"

"Leonid put us in first class. We boarded later and I worked on my computer until takeoff." Annja thought back, trying to remember seeing Nguyen Rao. She couldn't place the man, though. "If he was there, I missed him."

"He was there. My friend at Interpol confirmed Nguyen's arrival in Odessa less than an hour ago. He's around somewhere, Annja."

"I'll watch for him."

"I've also turned up more news on him."

"Nguyen has a criminal record?" That didn't jibe with Annja's immediate assessment of the man. Nguyen Rao had reacted quickly, and he had been trained how to take care of himself, but he hadn't struck her as a violent person. He had approached them to talk, not with a weapon.

"Not a criminal record, but he has been a person of interest in a couple of incidents involving artifacts. Evidently he crossed paths with a guy named Gerald Cleary. Have you heard of that guy?"

"Cleary is from Belgrade. He's a professional grave robber. The last I heard, he was working in Iraq, taking antiquities from there during the confusion."

"You know Cleary?"

"I've met him. Archaeology can be a small world, depending on what you're looking for. Cleary usually finds a client who wants something, sets up a buy, then goes after a piece or a collection of pieces."

"That's what Interpol says about him." Bart sounded a little nonplussed. "We have really got to talk more about what you do. Why haven't you ever told me this before?"

"Because you're not interested in history unless it pertains to one of your cases."

"That may be true..."

"It is."

"...but you should mention someone like Cleary."

"And have you worry more? Do you tell me about every dangerous felon you're chasing? Do I ask?"

Bart remained silent.

"Exactly," Annja said. "We do our jobs, Bart. That's what we're supposed to do. We do friend things together, and I like the ability to step away from the job for a while every now and again with you. I'm sure you appreciate the break, too. That's why we don't discuss your caseload."

"Yeah." The admittance was grudging, but honest.

"Is Cleary a part of this?" Annja so did not need another group involved in the elephant hunt.

"Not as far as I know. The report says Nguyen had an altercation with Cleary over in Kosambi, India. I've never heard of the place."

"Kosambi is a district in the Uttar Pradesh state. India isn't just India."

"Geography, too? I don't know how your head doesn't explode with all the stuff you have packed in there."

Annja grinned, glad that they were back to an easier, more relaxed relationship. "It's all stuff I enjoy. So what happened between Nguyen and Cleary?"

"They were after the same artifact. Things got violent. Cleary ended up with a broken arm and a broken leg, and Nguyen got the artifact."

"Do you know what it was?"

"Something to do with the Buddha. That's all I know."

Annja tapped her fingers on the steering wheel, watching Klykov continue to talk to the two men, and putting her thoughts in order. Piecing the puzzle together was a welcome diversion to thinking about what was going on with Klykov. "Maybe Nguyen is after religious artifacts." That added a whole new dimension to why the man might be after the elephant.

"That could be, because one of the things that was in the report I got through Interpol is that Nguyen isn't just a professor and a curator. He's also a monk for a temple in Phnom Penh that I can't even pronounce."

Annja thought about that. An old-school temple monk would be trained in martial arts, the defense systems were taught as a means for a monk to gain control over his body and his mind. But what would make the elephant so important?

"Annja?" Bart asked.

"I'm still here. Considering scenarios."

"I know this isn't really my field, but if you ask me, this is all getting weird."

"Interestingly enough, the weirder it gets, the more finite

it gets. Once the weirdness passes the point of no return, it kind of isolates everything that's going on and makes things easier to sort out."

"What do you think you're after?"

"At this point, an elephant. I'll know more when I find it."

Klykov finished his talk and one of the men handed him a thick box that he tucked under his arm. The old gangster thanked the men, shook hands with both and came back toward the SUV.

"I have to go," Annja said. "We're getting back on the road."

"To where?"

"To the world's biggest flea market. I'll pick you up a souvenir if I find something really cool. I'll talk to you when I can." Annja said goodbye and pocketed the phone.

24

Klykov opened the door and hoisted himself inside the SUV. Holding the box in his lap, he opened it and took out a pistol that looked almost like a sleek slab of black metal.

"What is that?" Annja asked.

"This is an OTs-33 Pernach. It is a very good pistol. Military grade. The designers created it to replace the Stechkin APS, another very good pistol, but it was chambered in 7.62mm, not the more attainable 9mm. The Stechkin also had a problem with recoil. With such a powerful cartridge, that was to be expected. In the hands of an expert, that was manageable. I am such an expert." Klykov chortled. "I bet you did not know this."

"No, but I can't say that I'm surprised."

"Munitions are a very big business." Klykov shrugged. "I have interest. I dabble." He slapped one of the dozen or so magazines into the butt of the weapon and racked the slide to chamber a round. "I think if we get into trouble, perhaps we need superior firepower."

"I'd rather we didn't get into any trouble."

"As would I. Unfortunately, given the situations we have encountered up to this point, and how violent a man like Onoprienko can be, we may not have that luxury. I will not suffer to see you hurt." Klykov pulled his coat off, then took a shoulder holster from the box and pulled it on, fitting it around his arm almost as easily as pulling on a sock. Two pouches on the other side of the shoulder holster provided spaces for extra magazines. He filled those, then dumped still more into his coat pockets. "Those men told me that Kaneev has family in the area and they have learned of our arrival, and sworn a vendetta against us for killing Kaneev." He glanced at Annja.

"Their unwanted attentions may complicate our efforts to get your prize."

Annja just stared at him for a moment, trying to comprehend it all. Possibly Fernando Sequeira and an unknown assassin, for certain Nguyen Rao a Buddhist monk, and Onoprienko were all involved in searching for the elephant. And now there was a contingent of Russian mafia looking for her and Klykov?

"I didn't kill Kaneev."

Klykov shrugged. "It is what it is, Annja. These people blame who they want and kill who they can." He paused. "We can turn around if you would like. Leave the elephant to whoever gets it. That would be much safer, perhaps."

That possibility didn't linger in Annja's mind. The mystery of the elephant had grown stronger and she felt she was getting closer. She wasn't about to willingly give up the pursuit. Even if the elephant led nowhere, Onoprienko needed to pay for killing Benyovszky. "No. We're not doing that."

"Good." Klykov smiled. "I would hate to walk away from what could be my last adventure."

"Your last?"

He shrugged an acceptance. "I'm an old man. There are only so many adventures allotted to men. I am grateful for the ones I have had, and I am grateful for this one."

"This isn't going to be your last adventure," Annja said. "We're going to be careful." She checked the highway traffic and pulled back onto the road.

"I thought about getting you a pistol as well, but I did not think you would wish for one."

"I don't like to carry guns. But I do know how to use them." Annja pressed harder on the accelerator, feeling the pressure winding up inside her.

SEVENTH-KILOMETER MARKET was a collection of long aisles created by cargo containers stacked two deep. Many of those cargo containers were painted bright colors, even hot pink. The market looked like someone had been turned loose with an inexhaustible supply of toy blocks and told to create intricate mazes.

Annja drove slowly, following Klykov's directions while feeling she was getting more and more lost. There was so much visual spectacle that she was almost overcome. White lines marked parking areas and pedestrians were everywhere. Signage was mostly in Russian, but here and there other subsets of signs were in English and French and German for tourists. Many of them also featured Chinese and Japanese translations.

In the 1960s, the market had opened for business as an outdoor shopping area. Early entrepreneurs had purchased cargo containers and had them delivered to the site. They'd operated right out of those containers, and only refurbished them into something more stylish in appearance after they'd become successful. Only open on Sundays in the beginning, the booming trade inspired still more budding capitalists to step into the business of knockoff clothing, jewelry, accessories, electronics and everything else that could be manufactured that was currently in vogue.

"You are not speaking," Klykov said.

"I'm trying to take it all in."

Klykov laughed. "So perhaps you have not become a jaded traveler after all."

"No."

"Then let me teach you. I am sure you know of the history of this place, probably more than I do. But let me tell you what you are truly looking at. This is free trade, Annja. The merchants here wheel and deal to make a profit. Give and take, buyer and seller. It is one of the oldest stories there is, no?"

"It's a…bazaar. A *huge* bazaar."

"Exactly. And the people who really make the money are the container owners."

"Those places are rented out?" Annja nodded toward the long lines of cargo containers that made up the market and the expansive perimeter.

"Yes. The real estate here, as you would guess, is quite

expensive. Seventh-Kilometer Market will never leave this place. People will always come here to trade."

Annja slowed to allow a man carrying a boxed flat-screen television to cross the street. His two children tagged along excitedly after him. On either side of her, groups of women, couples and families wandered along rows of container businesses. Vendors accosted them in a variety of languages, always smiling, but always pressuring them to come see their wares. Most of the cargo containers had large display windows cut into them as well as doorways. The fronts of many of them also shared similar designs, giving them an appearance of belonging to the same company.

"Some people believe that almost twenty million dollars' worth of merchandise is sold here every day," Klykov said.

Every. Day. Annja couldn't believe that amount, but she knew Klykov had no reason to lie to her.

"There are free health clinics, modern toilets, a fire department and a security staff that are provided for by profits taken from these businesses. It's a small city. This place is the area's largest provider of jobs. Over sixteen thousand merchants flock here to do business, and they have to have a staff of over twelve hundred people to operate the shops. I am told that over one hundred and fifty thousand people come here daily."

"You seem to know a lot about this place."

"I should. I own six of these containers myself. These are legitimate businesses. More or less." Klykov pointed. "Park up there. Fedotov's shop is not far from here."

Annja found a spot and parked. She cut off the engine and pocketed the keys. "Are you sure we're not going to get arrested because you're carrying a concealed weapon?"

"I am positive. I have brought money to take care of any *inconveniences*. Some policemen prefer to be paid in cash. As long as I don't try to hurt the patrons of this place no one else cares. Come along."

Annja got out of the vehicle, opened the rear door to get to her backpack and shrugged into it. Then she followed after Klykov, stepping into the dizzying world of the marketplace.

Rao drove past Annja Creed and the old man, but he kept them in view in his side mirrors. He was lucky that the market was so busy because it made him easier to blend in.

He pulled into a parking spot and watched in the rearview mirror as Annja walked past his position. Then he got out and locked the car behind him. The chill air was bracing. He pulled his long coat more tightly around him and took a woolen cap from his pocket to cover his head. The cap helped keep him warm and provided some disguise. He put on a pair of sunglasses to further change his features and followed Annja and the old man.

He also kept an eye out for anyone else who might be interested in him. That feeling of being watched again scratched at his shoulder blades.

A man stepped out of a nearby cargo container and grabbed Rao's arm. Instinctively, Rao gripped the man's arm in return, pulled him a step forward, and locked the arm in a painful hold that wouldn't have taken much to snap.

The man groaned in pain, then spoke in a flurry of languages, finally getting to English. "Please! Please no hurt me! I mean no offense!"

Rao quickly released the man. "I'm sorry. You startled me."

"No, no. Is okay." The man massaged his arm and grimaced slightly, but he was unwilling to forego a potential sale. "Only try to get attention. Show you many things. Many wonderful things." He waved toward the cargo container of pop culture T-shirts featuring television shows and superheroes. "Do you want buy shirt? Make you look cool."

Some of the shirts were for *Chasing History's Monsters*. That would have brought a smile to Rao's lips had things not been so serious.

In the end, in part because he felt badly about unintentionally hurting the man and because carrying a package would add another layer to his disguise, Rao purchased a T-shirt and continued on his way, bag in hand.

Then he realized he had lost Annja Creed.

25

"Leonid, my old friend! It is so good to see you again!" Viktor Fedotov greeted Klykov exuberantly and wrapped him in an immense bear hug. Big as a bear himself, Fedotov lifted the smaller man from his feet and kissed him roughly on both cheeks, laughing joyously the whole time. Shaggy gray hair fell to the fence's broad shoulders and his beard hung to his chest. He wore round-lensed granny glasses, a faded red sweatshirt and blue sweatpants. He also wore pink bunny slippers that had drooping ears and googly eyes.

Fedotov continued speaking in rapid Russian as he returned Klykov to the ground. Two young women stood behind counters on either side of the shop. Both of them were dressed in skinny jeans, blouses opened to a provocative degree and way too much eyeliner. They stared at Fedotov's display of affection with bemused interest.

The tough guy at the back of the shop cast a more prurient eye on the proceedings. His hand never strayed far from the pistol on his right hip almost out of sight under a blue windbreaker.

Annja's Russian was good enough to follow the introductory burst of enthusiastic welcome, but she couldn't grasp the rest of the dialogue. Given the fact that Klykov had volunteered information that he and Fedotov were not good friends, the effusive display of affection was surprising. Then she reconsidered. Both men were on the verge of doing business together. Everyone wore a happy face till they got to the bottom line.

"Viktor," Klykov protested as he rearranged his coat. "English, please. Out of respect for my friend, Annja, who does not speak our language so well."

"*Da*, of course, of course." Fedotov turned to Annja and

lumbered toward her. "Annja Creed, star of *Chasing History's Monsters, da.* You I know, and never did I think I would ever see such as you in my shop." He picked her up in a bone-crushing embrace, then set her carefully down. "I am so honored by your presence in my humble business."

The shop was anything but humble. Annja had been expecting a small place on the order of a pawn shop, something shadowy and mysterious tucked in an out-of-the-way spot. She'd had in mind a business with dim lighting that featured a smorgasbord of worthless items out front for show while the illicit sales were done out of the back room.

Instead, the Mad Russian's Emporium of Nice Things was a gala affair in a prominent place in the market and was filled with flashing lights, including a string of bright red jalapeno peppers that were incongruous in present surroundings. Spinner racks held paperback books in a dozen different languages. Electronics, statues and ceramics from many different cultures, Russian icons in a half-dozen different sizes, ships in bottles that ranged from Clipper ships to nuclear submarines and rifles and shotguns occupied locked display cases. Festive helium balloons announcing "specials" wafted on the breeze. A hidden PA system blared songs by the Beatles.

"Tanya." Fedotov addressed the red-haired young woman manning the counter that displayed jewelry and expensive watches. He spoke quickly and she ducked behind the counter for a moment, then reappeared with a gray-and-silver bottle of vodka. The young woman set up six shot glasses and poured out drinks in a long stream as quick as an LA bartender on a Friday night.

"Come, come." Fedotov motioned to Annja and Klykov, then to the other young woman and his obvious security guard. "Galina. Emil. Come. Join me in a toast to my old friend, Leonid Klykov."

They drank and Klykov and Fedotov slammed their shot glasses back on the counter almost at the same time. Annja finished up shortly after them and the vodka burned all the way down.

Tanya resupplied the glasses without being told to do so.

"And now," Fedotov said, "a toast to my new friend, Annja Creed. Drink!" He hammered the second shot down.

This time the vodka brought tears to Annja's eyes and she choked back a ragged cough. A momentary disconnect flashed through her senses, then quickly faded, but she'd had warning enough. The vodka was not something she wanted to mess around with.

"And now a drink to the business we are about to do," Fedotov announced, and pointed to Tanya to pour yet another drink.

"I surrender," Annja said, holding her hands up and laughing. "Two is my limit."

"Ah, you Americans." Fedotov grinned broadly at her, exposing a lot of gold dental work. "So weak when it comes to drinking. You lack the true sadness that lurks in the Russian soul."

Annja didn't argue. She watched as the others slammed back another shot and didn't appear to be any worse for wear.

"And now," Fedotov announced, "we should get down to business, *da*?"

"*Da*," Klykov agreed.

"I will call our friend Onoprienko and tell him I am ready to make a deal for his bauble, that I have his money. He should arrive here in a short while. I have sensed he is both greedy and in a hurry. In the meantime, my new friend Annja, perhaps you could do me a small favor."

"If I can," Annja replied.

Fedotov walked to the back of the shop and took up a box from the floor, then carried it over to her. Inside were stacks of *Chasing History's Monsters* DVDs.

"If you could autograph these, I would be thankful."

Annja did a quick estimate of discs in the case. There had to be over a hundred copies. "Sure. What would you like me to put on them?"

"I would like you to put, 'Special bargain from the Mad Russian Emporium of Nice Things,' but we do not have time for such niceties. Onoprienko is very desperate for cash. He will be here in short order and I call him. Unless you wish to wait so you can do proper job."

"No. No waiting."

Fedotov nodded in understanding and handed her a black Sharpie. "So just put, 'With love, Annja Creed.'"

"All right."

Fedotov took her to a back room office on the second-floor cargo container and sat her at a messy desk. Framed posters of science fiction movies hung on the walls. He escorted her to the executive chair behind the desk. The interior of the area had been refinished with Sheetrock and painted bright blue.

"Please be comfortable. There is security camera to show front of shop." Fedotov indicated the CCTV screen hanging on the wall near the door. "There is facilities." He pointed to a small cubicle in the corner of the cargo container near a set of circular stairs that led up to the second floor.

Annja was amazed at how homey the cargo containers had turned out.

Klykov sat in the chair on the other side of the desk while Fedotov called Onoprienko. Annja grew anxious when the call was not immediately answered, but then she could hear Onoprienko's gravelly voice come on the line.

The conversation between Fedotov and Onoprienko was short and to the point. Fedotov had the money, Onoprienko was on his way.

Finished, Fedotov returned his phone to his sweatpants pocket. "He will be here soon. Then we will have him."

"STOP HERE," FERNANDO SEQUEIRA ordered his driver.

The luxury sedan glided to a halt next to the narrow aisle of containers. Only a hundred feet away, the Mad Russian's Emporium of Nice Things stood out from the other shops around it. Lines of multicolored triangular flags snapped in the breeze.

There was no sign of Annja Creed or the Russian who was supposed to have the elephant.

Sequeira texted Brisa for an update. I AM HERE. WHERE IS ANNJA CREED?

SHE IS INSIDE THE SHOP, Brisa responded.

YOU SAW HER?

THE TRACKING DEVICE I PUT ON HER AT THE AIRPORT SHOWS THAT SHE IS THERE.

Sequeira relaxed a little. He would relax more when the elephant was in his hands, and be a happy man when he knew for certain what he was dealing with.

IS THE ELEPHANT INSIDE?

NO. THEY ARE WAITING ON THE RUSSIAN.

Impatience chafed at Sequeira. WHERE IS THE RUSSIAN?

THAT I DO NOT KNOW. WE TRACKED ANNJA CREED, NOT THE RUSSIAN. HAVE PATIENCE. SHE IS NOT GOING TO WAIT AROUND HERE FOR NOTHING. THIS IS WHERE THE ELEPHANT WILL BE.

Time passed and finally Sequeira's phone screen lit up again.

THE RUSSIAN IS HERE.

Staring out the windshield, Sequeira spotted the lanky Russian walking along the line of shops toward the Mad Russian's Emporium of Nice Things. Some of the bruising still showed on Onoprienko's thin face. Sequeira had heard about the beating the man had taken. Onoprienko wore sunglasses to disguise some of the damage. A long coat covered his cheap suit.

There was nothing else, no sign of a box or a bag.

Frantic, Sequeira tapped out a message on the phone. HE IS NOT CARRYING A PACKAGE!

HE IS A CAREFUL MAN. WAIT A LITTLE LONGER. THE MAN HE IS DEALING WITH WILL NOT GIVE HIM THE MONEY

HE WANTS UNTIL HE HAS THE ELEPHANT. NEITHER OF THESE MEN ARE TRUSTING PEOPLE. THE ELEPHANT WILL BE HERE SOON.

Sequeira glanced at the two mercenaries he had in the car with him, then over his shoulder at the five in the car behind him. He pushed an earpiece into his ear and opened the radio channel they would be using.

"All right, when this goes down, remember that I want the elephant. *Unbroken and in one piece*! I don't care how many other people you have to kill to get it, but I do not wish to lose that statue."

Monitoring the front of the shop, Sequeira hated the fact that he had to rely somewhat on the mercenaries he'd hired. He trusted Brisa implicitly.

ANNJA HAD BARELY finished autographing the box of DVDs when the red-haired woman, Tanya, stepped into the room and announced, "The man you are waiting for is here. Viktor will bring him back to you once he is certain the man has what you seek."

"Thank you." Annja put the last DVD in the box beside the desk. She got up and walked around the desk, seeing immediately that there was a problem.

Onoprienko hadn't come alone. Two burly men trailed after him a few minutes post his arrival. Both of the newcomers looked like they had handled plenty of trouble in their lives.

On the CCTV screen, Fedotov waited behind the counter where the red-haired girl had been. A hidden microphone picked up the conversation and broadcast it into the office.

Nervously, Onoprienko glanced around, then focused on Fedotov and spoke. Klykov provided a running translation because they spoke in Russian.

"Do you have the money?" Onoprienko asked.

"Of course." Fedotov spread his hands. "I am a businessman. My word is the only thing I have to sell. If I started breaking trust, I would be out of business overnight."

"Where is the money?"

Fedotov's face turned to stone and he leaned over the counter a little, threatening Onoprienko's private space. "Where is the elephant?"

"It will be here."

"Then bring it and let us conclude our business. I am not here for tomfoolery." That last word was actually delivered in English. It must have been one of Fedotov's pet words.

Onoprienko hesitated. "I want to renegotiate our deal. I want more money."

A tremor of uncertainty shivered through Annja as she realized that she might not have the elephant after all. She tried to console herself with Onoprienko. At least they would have him. If Bart's friends had made it possible to extradite Onoprienko, Benyovszky's murder would be resolved.

"Then," Fedotov said in an icy voice, "I suggest you peddle your elephant elsewhere. I have it on good authority that you are wanted for murder back in New York City, from which you just fled, and that this thing you offer to sell me is something that law enforcement agencies will know. If I get caught with it, I will be tied to that murder. That makes it very unattractive to me now. You understand this?"

"I gave you a list of names you could sell that piece to," Onoprienko argued. "You do not have to hang on to this thing so very long."

"Bah!" Fedotov spat. "Names I can get. People who look for something like this, they can be found. Selling an object that is linked to a murder doesn't allow me to move the piece quite so much in the open. I have to take care that I am not caught up in your problems."

"Do not think it is so simple."

"I don't! In fact, I have to wonder how many of those people on the list that you gave me will still want the elephant now that it is a known stolen item. You may have undercut my opportunities to sell the thing, and I have no wish to own the elephant."

"It is a very important thing."

"In what way?"

Onoprienko held his gaze steady for a time, then cursed. "I have not had time to ascertain that."

"Then you see my point."

Onoprienko cursed again and walked back toward the door.

Annja started to go after him, afraid that Onoprienko was going to leave and she'd never see him again, much less find the elephant.

Klykov caught her arm, his eyes still on the screen. "Give the situation a moment to develop, Annja. Please. If Fedotov had not started haggling with Onoprienko over the price, the man might have gotten suspicious. There are not many places Onoprienko can go to get the price he is asking. And he wants to move quickly. He will not pass up on Fedotov's deal. He knows Fedotov is good for cash and carry. Wait and see."

Annja remained stationary, but it was difficult doing nothing when it seemed like everything was about to go wrong.

At the doorway to the shop, Onoprienko hesitated. Then, with an angry look, he turned back to Fedotov. "You will give me the price I asked for?"

Fedotov crossed his arms and nodded. "Against my better judgment, and only then because I myself have been in bad situations before, I will. I trust you will not tell others of my generosity toward you."

"Then we have deal."

"Not till I see the elephant."

Onoprienko took a phone from his pocket and spoke briefly. "It will be here in short order." He gazed around the shelves, taking in the stock. He pointed to a Bluetooth watch and phone set. "I want that."

"It is a bargain at twice the price." Fedotov picked up the set and laid it on the counter.

"Add it to the amount you are giving me. I was most generous when I agreed to sell the elephant to you."

Fedotov looked like he was going to argue, and the foreboding of that action swelled within Annja. Then Fedotov shrugged. "All right. But only because you are on the run."

Five minutes passed and another man joined Onoprienko and the original two men in the shop. Like the others, this man was armed. He also carried a messenger bag, which he stripped off and handed to Onoprienko.

Annja felt her pulse beat at her temples. She wanted to be in that room.

Onoprienko opened the messenger bag and took out the contents. The plastic baggie looked like all it contained was shredded paper, but after Onoprienko rummaged around in it for a few seconds, he displayed the elephant in the palm of his hand.

26

"Do you know what this is?" Fedotov stared at the elephant sitting on the counter between Onoprienko and him.

"Is something many people want. You will get good price for it, and count the day you did business with me as the day fortune shined upon you." Onoprienko rubbed the back of his neck impatiently. "Give me my money so that I may take my leave."

Annja stared at the scene revealed on the CCTV screen.

In the office, Klykov unlimbered the pistol he'd purchased. "There will be trouble. Fedotov will not allow Onoprienko to have the money for the elephant now that he knows he will not be able to sell what he is buying."

Annja nodded her understanding of the situation and the tension inside her wound tighter.

"I truly wish you had taken a gun," Klykov said. "I did not expect Onoprienko to show up here with hangers-on."

Annja ignored that. She didn't want to get into the habit of reaching for a gun. But it was getting awfully easy to reach for the sword. "What do you want to do?"

"Wait till Fedotov makes his move."

"His man is outnumbered by the hired muscle Onoprienko brought."

"Emil is a dangerous man and will not desert Fedotov in his hour of need. Onoprienko's guards may be dangerous men, but Emil is trained. He is quick to kill when the need arises. He will surprise you. There are several people he surprised the last time."

Nodding her acceptance, Annja sat impatiently on the corner of the desk and felt the sword almost within her grip.

"I hope you are right about people wanting this," Fedotov said, "otherwise I have made a very bad bargain." He closed a hand over the elephant. "But I must regret that I can no longer pay you what we agreed on."

"You cannot renege on the deal we made!" Onoprienko's face flushed red in anger.

"We made the deal before you decided to become a murderer. I did not know you were going to kill a man for this elephant you wish to sell me."

"Deals have been made. You will give me money." Onoprienko reached under his jacket.

Fedotov pulled a sawed-off double-barreled shotgun from under the counter and aimed it at Onoprienko. "I promise you, such a mistake will be the last you ever make should you choose to make it." The big Russian sounded unfazed.

Onoprienko gave up taking the pistol from his coat pocket and raised his hands. He cursed bitterly.

One of the men behind him pulled his weapon anyway. Fedotov shifted the shotgun slightly and fired at the man, filling the shop with deafening thunder. The man staggered back under the impact and fired twice into the shelves over Fedotov's head.

Annja threw herself into motion then, but she was already a stride behind Klykov. The old guy moved fast when he put his mind to it. She closed her hand on the sword and pulled it into the shop with her. As she stepped outside the office, Emil had his pistol up and firing at the two other bodyguards. He was fast and his bullets shattered the heads of the two men a split-second apart.

Dead or dying, the two men slumped to the floor.

Onoprienko went for his pistol again, but a barked command from Fedotov and spotting Klykov coming with his weapon at the ready held the man in place. Emil relieved Onoprienko of his weapon.

Annja released the sword and no one seemed to be the wiser.

Fedotov handed Annja the elephant, then he took a plastic band from under the counter and walked around behind Onoprienko. After pulling the man's hands together, Fedotov secured the band around Onoprienko's wrists and pulled it tight.

Sirens sounded outside, and a few of the shopkeepers from nearby businesses peered around the corner of the front door.

"Viktor," Klykov said. "Annja and I must go. We apologize, but getting caught up in a police matter will only delay us and things could become very complicated."

Fedotov pushed Onoprienko toward Klykov. "Is okay. Is how we agreed, *da*?"

"Will there be any trouble for you?" Klykov took Onoprienko by the arm and pulled him toward the exit.

"It will be nothing I have not handled before. The right money in the right pockets, this will be no problem." Fedotov smiled at Annja. "It has been most good to meet you, Annja Creed."

"Likewise," Annja replied. "I'll have to visit again, when things aren't so hectic."

Fedotov smiled broadly. "Let me know. I will set up signing. You have many fans here."

Annja started out the door and spotted the group of men walking deliberately toward her. They were dark and swarthy, not Russian looking at all. She turned back to Klykov and Fedotov. "We have a problem."

SEQUEIRA ACCOMPANIED the mercenaries he'd hired for the recovery. He carried pistols in both of his jacket pockets. The screaming police sirens rattled in his ears, but he felt certain that he could be in and out of the Mad Russian's Emporium in minutes.

In the doorway, Annja Creed retreated inside. She had seen them. Sequeira didn't believe that mattered. There was nowhere for her to run. His mercenaries surrounded the cargo container in the back as well, and there didn't appear to be another door.

His team advanced on the container with their weapons pointing at the ground, then they raised them as they entered the shop.

"No one's here, sir," the lead mercenary said.

"What do you mean?" Sequeira advanced up to the man and peered over his shoulder.

The inside of the shop was empty of people. Three dead men lay on the bloody floor.

Sequeira pushed the transmit button on the comm headset he wore. "Does anyone have eyes on Annja Creed?"

A chorus of nos answered.

Sequeira stared hard at the mercenary leader. "Get in there and find her. She can't have gone anywhere."

Before he could move, bullets hammered the top of the second floor of the shop. Following the mercenary's line of vision, Sequeira spotted Annja Creed sprinting across the top of the cargo container. The rapid bursts of autofire nipped at her heels, chopping into the metal edge of the shop and ripping triangular flags from the lines.

Sequeira pointed a pistol in the mercenary's face. "Shoot again and I will put a bullet through your head."

Reluctantly, the man stood down. "She's getting away."

Sequeira didn't move his pistol. "I don't want that artifact harmed. It may not be any good to me damaged."

The man nodded and looked away.

Turning to the rest of the men, Sequeira pointed to the shop's rooftop. Bent over, taking shelter along the rooftop from the angle of fire, Annja Creed was still running deeper into the market.

"Get up there," Sequeira ordered. "Get her."

In less than a minute, five men pursued the fleeing archaeologist across the container rooftops. She reached the end of one container and jumped ten feet to land on the next.

Sequeira turned and trotted back to his car, intending to pursue her from the ground. He could see her plainly. As long as he could see her, he could follow her. He opened the door and slid in beside the driver while some of the mercenaries piled into the rear seat.

"Go!" Sequeira commanded. "What are you waiting for?"

The driver put his foot down hard on the accelerator and the big sedan lurched into motion. Several shoppers and merchants had cautiously entered the street to see what was going on.

Sequeira rolled down his window and fired a half-dozen shots into the air. Everyone scattered.

Gazing through the window, Sequeira watched as Annja Creed ran, then remembered that she was alone. He glanced back at the car following him and keyed his comm, only realizing then that she might not have taken the elephant. "She is alone. Find out what happened to Onoprienko and the man who was with her. They didn't just disappear."

Sequeira was torn over what to do. It was possible that Annja Creed had left the elephant with someone and merely ran to be a decoy. Then he dissuaded himself of that idea. She was like him. She liked the hunt.

She would have the elephant.

He shouted at the driver. "Faster! Go *faster*!"

"I FEAR FOR ANNJA," Fedotov said as he shifted slightly. He stood with one foot resting in the middle of Onoprienko's back while they all hid in the secret room at the back of his shop. "No one can outrun a bullet, and those men are not hesitating about shooting."

Klykov nodded glumly. Over the past couple of days, he had come to like Annja Creed very much. She was courageous and brave, and now he was afraid that she would be dead in the next few minutes.

Of course, that might happen to them all. Klykov tightened his grip on his pistol and waited.

"To be honest," Fedotov said, "I fear for us, as well. Soon those men will realize Annja left this building on her own and they will wonder what has become of us."

Klykov stood in the darkness of the small hideaway Fedotov had created for contraband he did not keep on the public shelves. The space was barely large enough for the two girls, Onoprienko lying on the floor, Emil, Fedotov, and Klykov. Emil had armed himself with a machine pistol and Fedotov had reloaded the shotgun.

Footsteps sounded outside the fake wall. The hiding space was cleverly hidden, so it would take time to find. Klykov, however, did not wish to wait to be found. He leaned into the fisheye peephole Fedotov had equipped the secret room with to watch anyone who might be outside.

Three men searched Fedotov's office, quickly spotting the spiral staircase that led to the second floor. One of them started up the staircase, which was within arm's reach of the door of the secret room.

Klykov watched, telling himself to remain calm. He took regular breaths.

Onoprienko, from his position on the floor, raised his foot and started kicking the wall.

Knowing they were dead if he did not move fast enough, Klykov pushed open the door and came out firing on the fly. He targeted the man standing in the office, stitching a three-round burst from the man's chest to his head. Perhaps the man's body armor stopped the first round, but the next two ripped into his throat and face. The man went down.

Swiveling, not even bothering to try to take cover, Klykov raised the pistol and fired at the two men who were almost close enough to reach out and touch. Both of them fired their weapons in an effort to kill Klykov, but none of them hit their target. Some of the bullets got deflected by the spiral stairs, and others cleared Klykov's head. One of them hit him in the left shoulder, causing the arm to go numb.

One of the men was wounded but not out of commission. Klykov struggled to lift his pistol again but knew he was not going to be able to manage that in time.

Fedotov strode through the doorway on Klykov's heels and finished the man off with a shotgun blast. Even as the man fell, Fedotov broke open the shotgun's action, popped the spent shells out and pushed in fresh ones.

Glancing back at Fedotov and the others, Klykov waved them forward. "Come. The way is safe for the moment."

Fedotov reached back into the hidden room and yanked Onoprienko out. Onoprienko stumbled and then bounced off the wall when Fedotov slammed the shotgun into his face. Onoprienko staggered and nearly fell, blood leaking from a ragged split over his right eye.

"No, no, no," Fedotov growled. "You will walk out of this place. Annja Creed wished for you to live to face a trial in her country, so you will live. But if you do not walk, I will break your legs and drag you out of this place. Understand?"

Dazed but comprehending, Onoprienko nodded.

Taking the lead, Klykov guided them out of the building and looked out the front door. Many people were interested in what was going on in the shop, but none of them were brave enough to come ask or even to venture close.

"Let's go." Klykov was first to the rental vehicle he'd claimed at the airport. No more armed men showed interest in them.

Klykov managed to get the keys from his pocket with his wounded arm and unlock the SUV's rear hatch. Fedotov opened the hatch, hoisted Onoprienko inside and took a moment longer to strap a plastic band around the man's ankles to secure him.

"Is nice car," Fedotov said as he came around to the front with Klykov. "Too bad now will have blood in it."

"Is okay," Klykov said as he opened the driver's side door. "Is rented and I bought the insurance."

"Can you manage Onoprienko by yourself, my friend? I could send Emil."

"I am good. Thank you. You will have to answer for shooting those men in your shop. It will be better if Emil is there to offer testimony. Which reminds me." Klykov handed over the pistol he'd been using. "You will need to wipe this down and put your fingerprints on it so you can explain how you shot those men in your office."

Fedotov nodded and took the pistol. "You will need another weapon to replace this one." He reached under his jacket and took out a Russian Tokarev. "Not so fine a gun as the one you give me, but lethal nonetheless. Until you arrange to have another."

"Thank you, Viktor. I will owe you."

"And I will collect. We will drink vodka." Fedotov slapped a big hand against the SUV. "Now go. You must see if Annja Creed yet lives, and give her assistance if she needs it. She must come back and sign more DVDs."

Klykov nodded and pulled away, glancing along the rooftops. Annja's plan had been sketchy at best, but if she managed to escape her pursuers, she was going to double back around to the market's entrance. Klykov hoped that the young woman yet lived.

27

Annja ran to the end of the latest cargo container she was on and threw herself across a fifteen-foot wide space between that shop and the next. She landed hard and rolled, hoping that the distance was enough to give pause to the men following at her heels like hounds on a scent. She protected the elephant in her cupped right hand and rolled on her left shoulder, coming dangerously close to the two-story drop. The fall wouldn't have killed her, but if she'd landed wrong she could have broken something.

Including the elephant.

She came to her feet as bullets drummed the metal roof of the cargo container next to her. Her backpack jerked and made it hard to get her rhythm back.

"Stop!" someone shouted. "Stop and we will not kill you!"

Annja already knew they weren't going to kill her. They weren't shooting their weapons enough to be taken seriously, and when they did fire them, the shots went wide enough that Annja knew they weren't trying to hit her. If she'd thought they were still gunning for her, she would have dived from the shop rooftops and taken her chances on the ground. The only reason she hadn't done that was because she didn't want to put the shoppers at risk.

She ran and leaped again, noticing that the group running along the ground trying to keep up with her had fallen behind, mostly due to portable tables that had been placed out to expand some of the shops' visible inventory.

The men atop of the roofs had fallen behind, too, but they weren't giving up the chase.

When the current container car she was running along stopped and other container cars branched off in ninety-degree angles to both sides, she stayed to the right. Her backpack thumped against her and cut down on her speed, but in case she got separated from Klykov, she wanted her tools with her. Working quickly, she stowed the elephant in her backpack, tucking it into a T-shirt she had tucked away in there.

Glancing over her shoulder, she spotted the sedan that had been keeping pace with her suddenly swerve off to the side and speed up, obviously intending to get around the line of shops in front of it. That car had been one of the reasons she had chosen to go to the right.

Another salvo of bullets cut the air around Annja just as another alley between shops opened up. Instead of leaping to the next shop, she turned to the right again, let her feet go out from under her and slid toward the roof's edge. She pressed her palms against the metal just hard enough to create friction to keep from skidding out of control over the side.

She dangled for just a second on the roof's edge, hanging full length from her extended arms, then dropped to the ground. Bending her knees, she absorbed the shock and glanced around as the guys on the ground closed in on her. It was a chance she'd had to take if she was going to still have time to turn back and reach the front of the market where Klykov was hopefully waiting for her.

She pushed herself up and ran, exploding through a group of tables with barely any room to spare. The men on the ground charged after her, knocking over tables, shopkeepers and shoppers. The physical contact barely slowed them.

Annja got her bearings and angled away from them. She sprinted past three shops and almost saw the man lurking behind the fourth one in time to avoid him, but her speed kept her from moving away fast enough.

The man reached out and caught her around the throat before she had a chance to defend herself. Her momentum tore the man from his hiding place, but he kept his grip locked around her throat, shutting off her air supply and very nearly her blood flow.

Thrown off balance, Annja became tangled with the man when they hit the ground. The man was fast, and the backpack made her awkward. He thrust the muzzle of a gun up under her jaw and spoke in English.

"Stop struggling and I will not hurt you."

Two other men jockeyed for positions to try to help the first man secure her. Annja lashed out with a foot and caught one of them in the groin, causing him to double over and hobble away. She slapped the first man's pistol away with her hand and the weapon went off, missing her by inches but close enough to singe flesh.

Following up the slap, taking advantage of the man's closeness, Annja kept driving her arm forward, bent it, then slammed her elbow into the man's jaw.

He grunted in pain and sagged to the side. Annja rolled and pushed herself up, grimly aware that the third man had his weapon pointed at her.

"Stop!" he ordered. She understood him even though the command was in Portuguese. His knuckles whitened on the pistol.

Lunging forward, Annja reached into the *otherwhere* and brought out the sword. She swept it forward quickly and hammered the pistol in a side stroke that knocked it from the man's hand. While he stood there gaping at her, she swung the sword again and caught him with the flat of the blade against his head. He dropped to the ground.

Before Annja could get clear of the area, her pursuers from the chase across the cargo container rooftops joined the battle. Annja stood there and gathered her courage. She was outnumbered and definitely outgunned. She held the sword in both hands, weighing her chances and not liking any of them.

A shadow stepped from a nearby alley between two of the container cars. Dressed in street casual, Annja didn't recognize Nguyen Rao until the man slammed his staff into the back of the nearest man's head. Reversing the staff, he took a two-handed grip on it and swung, connecting with the forehead of the man to the left of the first man he'd felled. The gunman's eyes glazed and he fell backward, out on his feet.

Rao's arrival threw the capture team off guard and they tried to set themselves to address the new threat. He whirled the staff, spinning it in his hands, then knocked one man's front foot from under him, reversed the staff again and smashed him in the face. Nose broken and streaming blood, the man slumped backward, unconscious before he hit the ground.

Annja now worried for the museum curator, despite his amazing martial arts skills, as her attackers turned to face Rao.

She swung the sword to disarm the men first, not wanting to kill unless that was forced on her, unfortunately, bullets thudded into the unconscious man's body and sprayed over the nearby shops, knocking a woman to the ground.

Knowing that hesitation on her part was going to get more people killed and she was not going to surrender either the elephant or herself, Annja stepped forward. As the man with the machine pistol spun toward her, Annja thrust with the sword and pierced his heart.

The man froze, eyes wide, and the pistol quivered there in his hands but didn't fire.

Annja yanked her blade free and shifted her attention to two other men as they swiveled toward her with their weapons. Lifting the sword, she sliced through one man's leg, then spun again as bullets ripped into the ground near her. One-handed, she threw the sword into the second man's chest, taking him just under the throat and driving him backward.

Willing the sword to return to the *otherwhere*, Annja drew the weapon again on the run and took it in both hands, cutting deeply into a man as he fired his weapon indiscriminately. Blood flew and he slid into pieces.

In the rhythm of the close-quarters battle now, Annja let instinct and training take over. She cut another man's hand, taking off a couple of fingers, but causing him to release his stuttering weapon. Moving forward, she drove the sword hilt against the man's forehead, putting him out of his misery, then slashed another man in the side, shearing through his ribs. Dropping his weapon, screaming in fear and pain, the man fell, and yet tried to get up. He failed.

Only Nguyen Rao stood in front of her. Blood leaked down

into one of the monk's eyes as he held his staff ready to swing. His breathing was elevated, but Annja's was, too. Frustration filled her from the deaths and injuries she had caused, but there had been no choice if she was going to save herself and the innocents standing around her.

"What have you done?" Rao looked horrified as he took in the carnage Annja had wrought.

"I've saved my life," Annja replied, telling herself that as much as she was telling him. "Probably saved yours, too."

"Killing is not good."

"Getting killed is worse."

The police sirens seemed closer.

Rao focused on her. "Give me the elephant."

"Why?"

"You do not need to know."

"I want to know."

"This is not your concern, Miss Creed."

"I've had people trying to kill me for days," Annja replied. "I've had to kill people. It *is* my concern now."

Rao lashed out with the staff with blinding speed. If Annja had been any slower, the weapon would have caught her in the face. As Rao set himself and tried to pull the weapon back to him, probably for another attempt, Annja slashed with the blade and hacked the staff in half only inches in front of Rao's hand.

The sliced-off section of staff dropped to the ground between them. Rao started to dart forward anyway, but Annja kept the sword between them.

"Don't," she ordered, holding the blade level as she pointed it at him.

Rao quivered for just a second, then he stepped back and bowed his head in surrender.

Annja ran toward the front of the market, unable to keep Rao from following her. People ahead of her drew out of her way, ducking back into their shops or the alleys between them. One man held an assault rifle in a doorway. For a moment Annja thought she was going to have to fight for her life again, but the man only nodded at her and never raised his weapon.

Klykov was waiting in the SUV where he'd said he would be, near the first shops in the market and on a patch of grass just off the road. The window was rolled down and he extended a pistol out.

Annja glanced over her shoulder and saw only Rao trailing after her.

"Don't shoot him!" Annja shouted.

Klykov gave no indication of hearing her and fired two rounds.

Annja stumbled as she spun around, expecting to see Rao falling dead. Instead, the museum curator had taken shelter behind a shop. Rao hadn't been hit, and she didn't think Klykov would have missed at that distance.

She ran around the SUV, willing the sword back to the *otherwhere*, and slinging her backpack off in one hand. She opened the door and heaved herself in as Klykov got the vehicle rolling. Storing the backpack between the seats, Annja looked back at the market and saw Rao emerging from hiding with a look of disgust.

"Get down!" Klykov warned as he cut his gaze over at Annja.

Leaning back in her seat, bracing her feet against the floorboard, Annja spotted a long sedan hurtling at them. Klykov fired five times in rapid succession. The bullets shattered the window, but they also ripped the sedan's front left tire to shreds. The driver lost control of the vehicle as it slewed to the side. Another sedan that had been following the first one too close smashed into the lead car.

Klykov pulled the SUV back out onto the main highway just as gray coupes with blue and yellow stripes and police insignia made the turn into the market. Their sirens were loud and filled the SUV's interior, but Annja couldn't hear over the thick cottony ringing in her ears from Klykov's pistol.

His foot heavy on the accelerator, Klykov watched the road. "You are well, Annja?"

"I am. Thank you."

"Who is man you had me not shoot?"

"I'm not sure exactly." Annja sat up and pulled her seat belt on. "He was in New York, too."

"He is trailing the elephant?"

"I think so."

"Because he had to have some way to find you here."

"Maybe he followed Onoprienko."

"Why did you not let me shoot him?"

"Because I'm not sure how he fits into all of this yet."

Klykov grunted and shook his head. "Is problem, that is what he is. If he was in New York, then again here, he is not one to give up."

"I know. I got that impression, too."

"I should have killed him anyway. You are too tender-hearted for your own good. That kindness will one day get you killed."

"Really?" Now that the action was over, Annja felt the aftereffects of the adrenalin rush and was winding down tiredly. "As I recall, you offered to help me—out of kindness—and have nearly gotten killed twice."

"You should do as I say, not as I do." Klykov shrugged. "Besides, I have lived long, full life."

"You've got some years left."

"True, but I do not wish for them to be boring years."

"Do we have Onoprienko?"

"In the back."

"Good, then let's see if we can rendezvous with Bart's go-betweens and get him off our hands." Annja took her satellite phone from her backpack, looked up the number and placed the call.

28

"Stanislav mentioned that someplace called the Seventh-Kilometer Market experienced a violent shoot-out today." Bart sounded peeved.

Annja looked at the small sedan and the two Interpol agents currently securing Onoprienko in the back of the vehicle. She decided Stanislav, the taller, young agent of the two, was a blabbermouth. "There was an incident."

"The story's gone viral, Annja. I keep waiting for your name to crop up."

"Let's hope it doesn't."

Bart sighed unhappily. "They tell me you got Onoprienko."

"We did. Klykov and me." Annja wanted to make certain credit was given where credit was due.

Klykov sat in the SUV and kept his distance from the international law enforcement people. He tapped his fingers against the steering wheel impatiently while he listened to the radio.

"The old guy's still hanging in there, huh?"

"Yes."

"I gotta admit, I'm impressed."

"He's an impressive guy. If he hadn't been with me today, you wouldn't be getting Onoprienko."

"I'm glad of that at least. What about you? Where are you off to next?"

"Moscow. I've been in touch with Tanechka Chislova, the granddaughter of Asaf Chislova, the man who'd been renting the storage unit. She put me in touch with a cousin of hers who lives in Moscow and knows more of the elephant's history."

"She couldn't tell you what the elephant was over the phone?"

"She doesn't know. All she knows is that it belonged to her grandfather." That lack of knowledge had disappointed Annja, but at least she'd introduced her to Nadia Silaevae, who was more than happy to reveal the story of the elephant as far as she knew it. She even had documents to prove the authenticity of the piece and the story, which she was willing to share with Annja, and explained why Annja was en route to Moscow as soon as she and Klykov could get moving.

"If Nadia Silaevae doesn't know what the elephant is, why bother to talk to her?"

"Because she has information about where the elephant has been, documents that came from around the same time the elephant was first brought into her family. When you work a case, you depend on witnesses and informants. My job demands that I resource the same kind of people. Although, a lot of it is just boring and repetitious."

"Like police work. Ninety-nine percent boredom, one percent fear."

"I'd say that sums it up. Only you can replace fear with excitement of discovery. This is just…different. At any rate, you should be seeing Onoprienko again in a couple days when Interpol hands him off, and I've got to be going."

"All right. Take care of yourself, Annja." There was enough of a hesitation in his response that she knew he didn't want to just hang up and let her go. That came out of his feelings of responsibility, though, and maybe just a little protectiveness. Bart had become a policeman, and then a detective, to help people. That was hardwired into his DNA.

"Definitely. You do the same." Annja broke the connection and slipped the phone into her coat pocket as Stanislav walked over to her.

"We are ready to transport prisoner. Bart wanted me to ask you one more time if you wanted us to bring you back home."

"No," Annja replied. "I don't let anyone *bring* me anywhere. That's never going to happen unless it's at gunpoint. And you told Bart about the shooting in the Seventh-Kilomenter Market."

Stanislav lifted his eyebrows. "You *were* involved in that, correct?"

Annja shook her head at the man. "Ratting me out to Bart.

That's bad, Stan." She turned and left him standing there, her thoughts were already turned to Moscow.

SEQUEIRA SPIELED A simple story, and he told it more than once. He knew he was going to get out of dealing with any real trouble. He'd brought bribe money for just that occasion. Except that now, after he'd started spreading that cash around, the Odessa police were attempting to hang onto him longer.

YOU PAID TOO QUICKLY AND TOO MUCH, Brisa texted.

Seated in the back of the police car, Sequeira watched the world around him. Being in the back of a police vehicle was a new experience for him. That hadn't happened since he'd been a teenager, and he'd gloried in it then because his arrests had irritated his father so much.

Now he was in a hurry to get back after Annja Creed. Thankfully the locator was still pinging its GPS coordinates to Brisa's tracking device. In addition to the police, other emergency vehicles had joined in to take care of the wounded. There were a lot of those, and they were proving to be more costly than Sequeira had suspected.

I WAS TRYING TO GET OUT OF THERE, Sequeira texted back. I SUCCEEDED IN NOT BEING ARRESTED IMMEDIATELY, BUT I AM BEING DETAINED.

YOU'LL HAVE TO PAY THEM MORE MONEY OR THREATEN TO GET THE PORTUGAL EMBASSY INVOLVED.

WHICH COURSE OF ACTION WOULD BE BEST?

BRIBE ONE OF THE SENIOR OFFICIALS ONSITE. PAY HIM DIRECTLY THROUGH AN ELECTRONIC FUND TRANSFER. IT WILL COST YOU MORE MONEY THAN YOU HAVE ON YOU, BECAUSE THE WAY THEY'RE LOOKING AT IT, THEY ALREADY HAVE THAT MONEY. THE SENIOR OFFICIAL ALSO KNOWS THAT MONEY HAS TO BE SPLIT WITH THE OTHERS. PAY HIM AND HE WILL GET YOU OUT OF THERE.

YOU ARE STILL FOLLOWING ANNJA CREED?

OF COURSE. SHE'S HEADED BACK TO THE AIRPORT.

WHY?

I WOULD THINK TO TAKE A PLANE.

Sequeira cursed quietly. WHERE IS SHE GOING?

I AM NOT A MIND READER. THAT'S WHY I PUT THE TRACKING DEVICE ON HER. WE WILL FIND HER. DO NOT WORRY.

Sequeira was worried, though. Brisa didn't know any of the stories about the elephant or what it might lead to. That knowledge was Sequeira's alone. He put the phone in his pocket and opened the car door to get out.

"Sir." The policeman assigned to the vehicle put a hand on the door to restrain Sequeira. "You must remain in the vehicle." He spoke English with a heavy accent.

"Let me speak to the man in charge of this operation." Sequeira remained outside the vehicle.

"Get back in the car."

"If I don't talk to your commanding officer now, there'll be no more money. I will call the embassy and things will go very bad for him, and for you. And I believe that if the commanding officer finds out you refused to let me speak with him he will be upset, and he will direct that at you."

The man frowned, but he obviously understood the ramifications of both threats. "Wait here."

Sequeira shrugged.

The policeman walked toward a police car parked in the middle of the road to the market and spoke to someone through the window. After a moment, he stepped back and the door opened.

A tall man in a pristine uniform emerged from the vehicle. He paused to tug at his gloves, then reached back into the car and retrieved his hat. His face seemed more bone than flesh, but didn't look emaciated, just hard. The dark eyes looked intelligent. He walked over to join Sequeira.

"I am Captain Savenko. There is a problem?" he asked.

"Yes, there is a problem. I do not want to be held here any longer. I have many things to do, and you and your men are keeping me from them."

"You and your men were involved in several shootings."

"Only to protect ourselves."

Savenko smiled thinly, and his almost lipless mouth drained the expression of any warmth. "A funny thing, that. According to the interviews my men have conducted, and are conducting, most people in the market remember you and your group as being the attackers."

Keeping a straight face, Sequeira said, "Obviously they are mistaken. Witnesses, as you know, can be horribly unreliable."

"It has been my experience, *da*. This is why I always do a thorough investigation. So my superiors do not question my ability to do my job."

Sequeira understood then. Savenko didn't want to release him and his men too early because his superiors would know he had been paid off handsomely.

"Then let me pay you again. Privately." Sequeira took out his phone. "Give me a bank account you wish to receive the money in and I will put twenty thousand euros there in minutes. Your superiors can only guess at that money."

Savenko didn't go for the deal immediately.

"Otherwise, I will contact the Portuguese Embassy and ask that they intercede on my behalf," Sequeira said. "I assure you, captain, they will intercede." Bribery was an international commerce. Favors and cash greased wheels everywhere. "Then things will become even more messy for your superiors."

The captain smiled again and tilted his head. "Of course. Are you ready?"

"Yes." Sequeira accessed his bank account through his phone and then moved money around. He'd already paid thousands of dollars to smooth the situation over. Money like that was only a drop in the bucket to what he had and how much money he had coming in from his various legitimate and illegitimate businesses. He could even have managed millions easily.

Savenko checked his own phone and accounts, confirming the transfer. "I will have you and your men released within minutes, Mr. Sequeira. Obviously you were a target of a kidnapping attempt gone very wrong."

"Obviously. There is one more thing you can do for me, captain. Now that I have been so generous."

Savenko didn't reply.

"A small thing that will require you only making a phone call."

"What?"

"I need to know where Annja Creed is flying."

"Who is Annja Creed?"

"An American. She was here at the market today, and she was involved in this." Sequeira pointed at his wrecked sedan. "She was the one who shot my car."

Savenko's face grew harder than Sequeira would have believed possible. "Why am I only now hearing of this person?"

Sequeira ignored the question. "Can you help me or not?"

Without a word, Savenko took out his phone and began dialing.

"Would it be possible to have Annja Creed held at the airport?" Sequeira asked.

The captain shook his head. "Not without a proper warrant."

"She was part of the situation here."

"If I have her held at the airport, then I must hold you now. Someone must testify against her."

Sequeira reconsidered his options. If Annja Creed were taken into custody, and if she had the elephant on her, it would be held as evidence. Getting the piece away from Odessan police impound might be difficult, and that choice would definitely delay his efforts to resolve the mystery the elephant posed.

"On second thought, if you can, Captain, just find out where she's going. A bonus could be arranged for your trouble."

29

Deplaning passengers crowded Sheremetyevo International Airport and, after passing through the security checkpoints, Annja and Klykov flowed into the crowd and walked down to claim their baggage. She checked for Nguyen Rao and anyone else who might be following them but spotted no one.

"This has gotten a lot more dangerous than I thought it would be," Annja said as she watched for her carry-on at the baggage carousel. She'd hung on to her backpack, but the carry-on had had to be stowed.

"Are you thinking of turning back?" Klykov stood beside her and tapped the prepaid cell phone he'd picked up at a communications kiosk. He entered letters with a lot more dexterity than she'd thought he was capable of.

"No, but I was thinking it might be a good place for you to turn back. This isn't your problem."

Klykov grinned and didn't pause in his texting. "Have you suddenly learned to speak Russian fluently?"

Annja didn't answer him because he already knew the answer. She was also curious about who Klykov was in contact with.

"This woman we seek, Nadia Silaevae, I can assure you she will be reluctant to talk to you even after this granddaughter called her to tell her you were coming. She will be wary of tricks, and be suspicious of anyone who is not family. Many people still living in this country, they are not so far from the old days."

"Do you think she'll trust you?"

Klykov smiled broadly as he tucked his prepaid phone in his coat pocket. "I am handsome Russian man. What is not to trust?"

Annja couldn't argue with that either. Klykov was smooth.

He'd gotten them out of Odessa with no fuss, although she still didn't know how much he'd paid to accomplish that feat. Her bag came by and she grabbed it. Klykov snared his, dropped it to the floor and extended the handle to pull the bag along after him.

"Come," Klykov directed. "We must make a stop before we go to Nadia Silaevae's home."

"For a gun?" Klykov had been forced to get rid of his pistol before they'd reached the airport in Odessa.

"No, no. I have already taken care of weapon."

Feeling suddenly anxious, Annja looked around as they headed for the exit. "You've already got a gun?"

"Don't be silly, Annja. This is airport. Very hard to get weapon in airport." Klykov shrugged thoughtfully. "Not impossible, but very difficult. And no real need with so many waiting in streets."

"Then why are we stopping?"

"To get gift for Nadia Silaevae. I will not go calling on this woman's house, especially since we are strangers, without something for her. It is not proper."

As they stepped out into the bracing chill, Annja pulled her coat tighter, hoping to maintain some of the airport's warmth. She gazed around, taking in the taxis, the buses and the crowds waiting for each.

No one seemed overly interested in them.

"They are not here, Annja. Do not worry. I would know. I am watching for them now." Klykov touched his nose in a knowing way.

Annja didn't point out that Klykov wasn't going to be there forever, or the fact that she'd been used to taking care of herself long before he showed up. He was just demonstrating the male mindset, the same way Bart had been doing by trying to protect her, she supposed. She didn't mind because they were good men—as long as that attitude didn't slow her down. "They surprised us at the market."

"Here we are ahead of them." Klykov paused at the curb. "For now."

Just before she could ask him what he was waiting on, a

dark sedan slid to a stop in front of them. A big man with a sad, seamed face and iron-gray hair got out from behind the steering wheel and walked around to the rear of the car to open the door.

When the burly man waved her in, Annja slid across the backseat to make room for Klykov. The chauffeur put their bags in the trunk then took his seat behind the steering wheel. He spoke in Russian.

"English, please, Vladi," Klykov said, nodding to Annja. "Out of respect."

"You have address?" Vladi's English was a trifle stilted. He put the car in gear and eased into traffic.

Annja gave the address. Nadia Silaevae lived in the Kitai Gorod neighborhood, not far from the old KBG building on Lubyanka Square. Annja was faintly aware of the area being part of Moscow's old city, and a quick perusal of the neighborhood via the internet hadn't broadened her familiarity with the locale appreciably.

Once they were on the highway, Vladi reached under the seat and brought out a shoe box, which he passed back to Klykov.

"Is good," Vladi said. "Is one I have used, but never on business."

"Thank you, Vladi." Klykov opened the box and took out a pistol. "Very nice."

"I have included three extra magazines since you have had trouble in Odessa. And there is a silencer for when you wish to be quiet. Very good silencer. Easy on, easy off."

"Thank you, my friend." Klykov tested the weight of the weapon, then put it in his right coat pocket. He dropped the spare magazines and the silencer in his left pocket.

Annja silently hoped that they wouldn't need them. She didn't wish to bring trouble to Nadia Silaevae's door.

DEEP IN THE Kitai Gorod neighborhood, Klykov had Vladi pull the sedan to the curb in front of a small grocer's. Klykov got out of the car and Annja followed.

She loved the small shop because it felt casually comforting in its sameness even though the products were all listed in Russian. It still felt a little like the bodega down the block from her apartment. She couldn't help thinking that there wasn't a metropolitan area, anywhere in the world, where someone wouldn't be able to find quaint neighborhood shops or markets. Cities were like home everywhere.

A handful of children in school uniforms under their jackets stood in front of the candy section. Klykov walked over to them, talked briefly and got them all to laugh. Then he pressed coins into their hands. For a moment, he looked like any Russian grandfather doling out allowances, but Annja couldn't forget how heavily his coat pockets hung with the pistol and extra magazines.

He picked up a large shopping basket, walked to the back of the shop where the bread was kept and picked out three large loaves. He added a dozen small *pirozhkis*, which were pies filled with fish, cheese, cabbage or jam. He added *klyukva s sakharom*, which were sugar frosted cranberries, cans of sardines, a jar of pickles and packets of tea.

"Not just tea," Klykov told Annja when she asked about it. "This is black tea meant to be served with cardamom and lemon or cream. If you have not had it, you will enjoy it. Very robust." He picked up the condiments for the tea, as well.

"I didn't know we were going on a picnic."

Klykov smiled at her. "At her age, Nadia Silaevae is probably a woman alone. Even if she is not, she will appreciate not having to make a meal or two for her husband and herself after we have gone. She is doing us a favor. She should not be doing this for nothing."

Annja couldn't argue with that logic.

After the purchases were made, they returned to the car and Vladi drove on.

NADIA SILAEVAE LIVED on the first floor of a six-story apartment building that looked as if it had survived most of the era since the time of the Bolsheviks. Scars decorated the bricks, and the mortar needed replacing in several areas. A few children lounged around the steps and the small yards, eyeing Annja and Klykov with open and wary speculation.

Arms loaded with food, Annja and Klykov stood outside the unit that Klykov said had the woman's surname on it. Annja couldn't read the Cyrillic alphabet, but Klykov verified the address. He knocked on the door.

The peephole inset in the door darkened for a second, then a woman's voice spoke in Russian.

Klykov quickly replied and Annja recognized her own name. Then he smiled and looked at Annja. "Nadia Silaevae is afraid we are door-to-door salesmen trying to sell her something."

A short round woman appeared in a dark dress and scarf. She held a heavy cast-iron frying pan in one hand. Quietly, she and Klykov talked for a few moments, then Nadia Silaevae stepped back from the open door and directed them in. As they passed, she inspected the grocery bags with keen interest. Annja suspected the groceries had done more to gain entrance to the home than anything Klykov said or Tanechka Chislova had told her.

The living room was small and it led to the kitchen. At Nadia's instruction, Klykov and Annja carried the bags to the small, modestly dressed dining table where white-petaled chamomile blossoms stood proudly on spindly stalks in a leaden glass vase. The faint scent of apples from the fragrant blossoms lingered in the kitchen.

Once the bags were on the table, Nadia chased Klykov and Annja from the kitchen to the living room and began to put the food away. Klykov guided Annja to the small green sofa and he sat beside her. Across a low coffee table, a matching love seat sat with a knitting basket beside it. Judging from the way the knitting project laid on top of the basket, they had interrupted Nadia's work.

Klykov and Nadia spoke back and forth intermittently. Annja felt left out of the conversation and satisfied herself with looking around the room. Guessing from the number of knickknacks on shelves and a small shadowbox on the wall, Nadia had lived in the apartment for a long time.

There was a shelf of books that made her curious. Closer inspection of those revealed that some of the titles were in English and that they were spy novels by British and American authors. None of them were recent editions, so she supposed Nadia's husband had been the reader.

No sign of the husband, other than pictures of a couple with a much younger Nadia featured in them. The absence was circumspect, but Annja felt sad for the old woman.

"I am sorry, Annja," Klykov said. "I could translate my communication with Nadia Silaevae, but there is nothing of consequence we are discussing. Merely pleasantries and some catching up on events and people in Moscow."

"I heard my name come up a few times."

Klykov smiled. "Nadia Silaevae is very curious about you. She asked if you were my granddaughter, and I told her that you were an American television star, that I was merely your guide."

Annja stopped herself from pointing out that she was an archaeologist first and foremost, then she decided making the argument wasn't justified.

"Nadia Silaevae is most impressed. She has never had a television star of any kind in her home, let alone one from America. She feels very honored."

"Please tell her thank you for me, and mention that she has a lovely home."

Klykov nodded and spoke to the old woman again. They had a brief exchange and Klykov turned to Annja again. "Nadia Silaevae would like to know how you will take your tea."

"Lemon, please."

The choice was relayed. A few more minutes passed, and then Nadia Silaevae carried a tea service to the living room. She spoke to Klykov and he nodded and began pouring tea while she returned to the kitchen. When she reappeared, she carried another tray, this one covered with bread and jam and a few of the *pirozhkis*. She passed out small plates, sat in her chair and gestured to the food with a smile.

Annja accepted her tea from Klykov, selected one of the

pies stuffed with fish because she suddenly realized she was hungry and added a couple of pickles.

Nadia Silaevae spoke to Klykov, who immediately translated for Annja. "She would like to see the elephant."

"Oh, sure." Annja reached into her backpack beside the sofa and brought out the piece. While at Odessa International Airport, she'd found a curio shop that featured small keepsakes that came in boxes with foam padding. She'd bought the keepsake, which she hadn't kept, and tucked the elephant safely inside.

She took the piece out and handed it to Nadia Silaevae, who smiled in recognition and talked in an excited voice. She handed the elephant back to Annja and left her seat to walk to a small closet.

"She has never before seen the elephant," Klykov explained, "but she has seen pictures of it. Her family was very proud of it."

"What does she know about it?"

Klykov shrugged. "We will see."

Nadia Silaevae returned to her seat and opened the thick photo album she had brought back with her. Growing more animated, she flipped through the album and stopped a few pages in. She pointed proudly.

Six black-and-white photographs on the page were of a gray-bearded old man who looked wrinkled as a prune. He was grinning widely in most of the pictures, and he was holding the piece in his hand, posing with it on his biceps and holding it again in his cupped hands.

"May I?" Annja pointed at the photo album.

"*Da. Puzhalsta.*"

Yes and *please* were two of the words Annja knew in Russian. In fact, she knew *yes*, *no*, *please*, *thank you*, and *where can I find food* in most languages. "*Spasiba.*" Thank you.

"*Puzhalsta*," Nadia Silaevae repeated, only this time it meant, "not at all."

Annja surveyed the photographs, then turned the page and saw still more paragraphs of different family members showing off the elephant. Evidently the piece had become something of a treasured heirloom.

"This is wonderful," Annja said, listening to Klykov translating beside her. Evidently he had experience in playing the go-between. "What can you tell me about the elephant? Where did it come from?"

30

"The elephant was given to Queen Catherine by the Japanese sailors who were rescued from America," Nadia Silaevae explained, and Klykov translated only a few seconds behind her words. The old woman spoke slowly so that Klykov had no problem keeping up. "It was among the gifts delivered to the queen in return for the safe passage for the men to their homes in Japan."

Annja interrupted for a moment, apologized and asked about the Japanese sailors.

"They were part of a trading business sent to America." Nadia Silaevae held up a gnarled finger, then got up and went to the bookshelves. She returned with a geography book that looked ancient. The book was in Russian and contained many maps. When she opened the book, it fell open to a familiar place.

The map was of the western border of the United States. Her finger traced the Aleutian Islands.

"My father was brother to Asaf Chislova," Nadia Silaevae went on, "great-uncle to Rachel Chislova, with whom you have spoken. My father was younger brother, so their father left the elephant to Asaf. But my father was a sailor in World War II. He was on a ship that patrolled the islands where the Japanese sailors were rescued so many years before. The Russian ships were there to help protect America from the Japanese after the attack on Pearl Harbor. They were quickly recalled though, because the United States and Canada did not trust them so much in those days. My father said it was his wish to visit that island where the Japanese had been, but that was never to happen."

Annja had her journal out and was taking notes. The battles in the Aleutians were sometimes called the "Forgotten War" because so much focus had been on what later developed into the Battle of Midway. For a time the Japanese had occupied a couple of islands before they were taken back by Allied forces.

"My father was more interested in the elephant than his brother."

Annja gestured toward the pictures. "Are those pictures of your father?"

"No, those are of my grandfather. My father's father." Nadia Silaevae sipped her tea. "My father was forever worrying at the story of the elephant. Always a curious man. He was the one who discovered among my grandfather's things how the elephant came to be in our family's hands. You know of Queen Catherine, *nyet*? Also called Catherine the Great?"

"I do."

"It is said she took hundreds of lovers while she was in power." Nadia Silaevae looked somewhat embarrassed by her words, but a hint of merriment danced in her eyes. "I would not speak ill of the dead, but the woman took excesses."

Annja grinned. "Yes, she did. It is well documented, so you are not speaking ill of her."

"One of the men in her life was Captain Leon Argunov." Nadia Silaevae pronounced the name carefully and spelled it, which Klykov had to guess at for the translation. "He was one of the queen's lovers, but only for a short time. He was supposed to be related to Grigory Grigoryevich Orlov. He was an important man. Do you know this name?"

"Yes." Annja nodded. "Orlov helped Catherine overthrow her husband, the Grand Duke Peter, and take the throne. She didn't marry Orlov because he wasn't a very good strategist, and she needed someone who could help her with political arrangements."

"A very practical woman," Nadia Silaevae stated with a small smile. "Very Russian."

"She knew what she wanted and would settle for nothing less."

"*Da.* As I said, Argunov was a lover only for a short time. He made a name for himself during the second war with the Turks."

Annja jotted that down as well, fixing the time frame in her mind. Time was so important in her line of work, and when an artifact had been around for centuries like the elephant had, figuring out a time line became exceedingly important. The Second Russo-Turkish War had taken place in the late 1780s to the early 1790s.

"When did the Japanese deliver the elephant to Queen Catherine?" she asked.

Nadia Silaevae shook her head and looked troubled. "Sometime after the war, but I cannot say when for certain."

Annja made a note to check on the Japanese story. That seemed too big to not have been mentioned somewhere. "That's fine. You said Argunov took the elephant?"

"Yes. Usually Queen Catherine gave a—" Nadia Silaevae hesitated, obviously searching for the correct word even in her native language.

Annja grinned. She'd already known of the queen's habit of giving her lovers something, which included positions of power and palaces, depending on how much they could do for Catherine once she'd dismissed them from her bed. Almost always she had put them in places that had benefited her, either by shoring up her rule or getting them out of her way.

"In Captain Argunov's case, no such arrangement was made," Nadia Silaevae continued. "Or, if an arrangement was made, he considered that arrangement too small. So he took the elephant before he left Queen Catherine's palace."

"Why did he choose the elephant?"

The old woman shrugged, and her answer made Klykov laugh before he was able to translate. "Who knows what goes through a man's mind? Over fifty years I was married to my husband, and still I never knew exactly what he was thinking."

Annja grinned again.

"I have been told he took the elephant because he believed it would lead him to great wealth."

"What wealth?"

Nadia Silaevae frowned. "These are old stories, handed down and handed down yet again, over and over. Who is to say what was then and what is now? I cannot."

"Was Captain Argunov part of your family?"

"No."

"Then how did the elephant end up with your family?"

"Captain Argunov remained with the Russian army after his separation from Catherine. The person I have been talking to regarding this matter—I will give you her name and an introduction when we are finished here—believes that Captain Argunov hoped to discover the secret of the elephant. Instead he ended up dying during the march into India when Emperor Paul decided to join forces with Napoleon against the British."

"How did Argunov die exactly?"

"Captain Argunov perished from sickness. One of those things men get when they are out chasing wars. I do not know the precise cause. While he was there in India, and he knew he was going to die, he gave the elephant to my ancestor, who was also a soldier and carried the elephant home with him when the Russian army turned back from India. It had been with our family ever since, here in this country, till Asaf Chislova brought it to the United States." Nadia Silaevae smiled and looked at the elephant there on the coffee table between them. "And now you have it."

"Once I am finished with it, I'll return the elephant to your family," Annja promised.

"No, no. My family has carried the elephant long enough, and it was never ours to begin with. It would be better if you discovered who it truly belongs to and gave it back to those people."

"If I can. If not, I'm sure there is a museum that would love to have this piece if I can successfully document its history."

"As you wish. You know more about such things than I do."

Annja looked down at her notes. "You said there was someone else who might be able to give me more information about the elephant?"

"Yes. Her name is Sophie Ezria. She is descendant of Argunov. She is also ballerina here in Moscow. We met through my husband, who had always been in love with the story of the elephant. He and Sophie Ezria searched some of the same histories and discovered each other. Their interests made them friends, and I became friends, too. She is lovely girl. But, even though they worked together, they could not find answers to mystery of elephant. My husband always wished he could solve the puzzle." Nadia Silaevae smiled sadly. "Is always way of Russian men, you know, to fall in love with things they can never possess."

Klykov leaned toward the woman, spoke softly and patted her on the shoulder. Nadia Silaevae smiled at the old gangster, and for a moment Annja got a glimpse of what the woman must have been like as a young woman.

"My husband always wished my father had gotten the elephant from his father instead of my uncle receiving it. Asaf Chislova never cared so much to have the elephant, only that he possessed it and my father did not. There was jealousy between them. Brothers, you know. Either they get along or they fight. Sometimes both. My husband, like my father, treasured old things. They were forever taking me to markets to look at old junk."

Annja felt a kinship because of that. She always trolled the markets and bazaars wherever she was because artifacts still turned up in curio shops. So much history had been lost, and still continued to be lost.

"My father and husband only bought a few things while my father still yet lived," Nadia Silaevae continued. "Most of our finances were used to raise our children. Things were very hard then, but we made do, as people always must." She shifted forward and touched the elephant gently. "I am so glad you came my way, Annja Creed, and I am so glad I finally got to see the elephant that has been so much a part of my family."

It was almost dark by the time Annja and Klykov left Nadia Silaevae's home. The old woman had insisted on feeding them supper, and she had offered them the use of her home to stay in. Klykov had politely turned her down and thanked her again for her time.

Vladi still waited for them in the sedan out front, and Annja realized guiltily she had forgotten about the man in the excitement of getting the story. As they approached the car, Vladi got out and opened the rear door so Annja and Klykov could get inside. It was already running, and the interior was warm, taking away the bite of the cool night breeze.

"Did you get something to eat, Vladi?" Klykov asked as the big man slid behind the wheel.

"*Da*. I hire boys to bring me dinner from restaurant." Vladi put the car in gear. "Where you want to go?"

"A hotel. Somewhere nice."

"Sure." Vladi nodded and pulled onto the street.

Annja's phone rang. She didn't recognize the number but saw that it was from Moscow. "Hello."

"Annja Creed?"

"Yes."

"I am Sophie Argunov. We have a friend in common, yes? Nadia Silaevae?" The young woman spoke good English with only a hint of an accent.

"We're just leaving her house now."

"I know. She just told me you would like to talk to me. Would you have time to meet this evening?"

"Definitely, but I don't want to inconvenience you."

Sophie laughed pleasantly. "I am dancer in Russia. My life off the dance floor is an inconvenience to my trainer. I am just now out of dance school, out of practice for so long, so I can meet if you wish. I must admit I am very curious. Nadia Silaevae told me this is all very exciting and that you have the elephant."

Exciting? Annja and Klykov hadn't even mentioned the murders and the close calls they'd had while searching for the story behind the elephant. "I'd love to meet with you if you have time this evening."

"Good! I was hoping this would be no imposition to you. We are preparing for big competition and time is very scarce. Since you are in Moscow, is all convenience, yes?"

"Yes. Maybe we could meet somewhere for drinks?"

"Good. Where do you stay?"

Annja asked Vladi where they were heading and relayed the answer on to Sophie.

"Fabulous. Is not far. I can meet you there in an hour?"

"An hour?" Annja looked at Klykov, who nodded. "An hour will be fine."

"Also, I took liberty of contacting my boyfriend, Peter Kargaltsev, and asking him to join us. He is a historian and, as a favor to me and Nadia Silaevae, was working on deciphering the origins of the elephant Captain Leon Argunov stole from Queen Catherine. I thought perhaps you and he could speak. Did Nadia Silaevae tell you about the night the elephant was nearly taken from the Winter Palace by Japanese thieves only a few weeks after its arrival there?"

"No."

"Well, I believe you will find this a most enjoyable story. Peter found out about the attempted robbery when he was doing research on the elephant."

"I'm looking forward to it." Annja said goodbye and pocketed her phone.

"What is on your mind?" Klykov asked.

"According to Nadia Silaevae, the Japanese gave the elephant to Catherine the Great, but Sophie says her boyfriend discovered that Japanese thieves tried to steal it back a short time afterward."

"That's interesting. Perhaps this will help explain this young man's interest in the elephant. Nguyen Rao, *nyet*?"

"Yes, but he's not Japanese. He's Cambodian. And if the elephant is Cambodian, how did the Japanese get their hands on it?"

31

"The thieves who broke into the Winter Palace were not Japanese." Peter Kargaltsev sat across the table from Annja in the lounge around the corner from the main desk at the hotel Vladi had delivered them to. Peter was tall and blond and blue-eyed, a charmer who was very confident of his language and his subject matter. He kept himself in shape and looked nice in his dark blue suit. "Sophie got that part wrong." He flashed a grin at the beautiful, elfin woman seated next to him. "Sometimes when I talk, she does not listen as closely as she thinks she is."

Dark haired and dark-eyed, her skin the color of milk, Sophie Argunov swatted playfully at her significant other. "He never shuts up, this one. Always with dates and wars and things. Some days I can think of nothing else from listening to it all. I do not know how he remembers so much. Thankfully he is beautiful man, so when I am not listening, I can still look at him."

Smiling, obviously in love with the young woman, Peter shrugged. "Perhaps I do talk about my job too much."

"Tonight we are here to talk about your job, so talk and I will listen," Sophie said. She wore a little black dress and the two of them together made Annja feel underdressed in her khaki pants and pullover. Klykov didn't help because he had evidently packed a nice suit in his bags, and the hotel was more upscale than Annja had expected.

Peter spread his hands and looked at Annja. "Where would you like me to begin?"

"How did you get involved looking for the elephant?" Annja asked.

"Sophie mentioned the elephant to me and showed me pictures of it, copies she had gotten from Nadia Silaevae. I met

Nadia and her husband a few times. He was a wonderful old man, and Nadia's charms you have seen for yourself."

"Boris Silaevae and I met on a genealogy site," Sophie said. "He had contacted my mother a few years ago and started talking. Then, because I was interested in elephant, I talked. I got to know Nadia Silaevae, as well." She glanced at Peter. "I met this one at university two years ago and wanted to get to know him better. Since I knew he liked historical things, I decided to find something mysterious in my past to catch his interest."

"*Nyet*!" Peter laughed, picked up her hand and kissed it tenderly. "This one had my heart from the moment I laid eyes on her. The mystery of the elephant was only a gift. A bonus, I believe you Americans would call it."

"We would." Annja smiled.

"Finding information about the elephant and Captain Argunov was not easy. And I was sidetracked often by her." Peter grinned at Sophie. "But, thankfully, her dancing is demanding and I have time to deal with trifles such as work and elephants and historical mysteries." He reached into a briefcase at his side and pulled out a sheaf of papers. "I took the liberty of printing these off."

Annja accepted the papers and began leafing through them. All of them were in Russian, which disappointed her.

"If you don't have someone who can do the translations, I will be happy to provide them," Peter offered. "I had not thought to transcribe them in English, but I thought you might like the copies."

"Yes, thank you. I have someone who could do it, but if you have time, that would be wonderful."

"Absolutely." He nodded. "As to the story, it is a small enough tale, but very enigmatic. Perhaps even a bit sinister. Only a few weeks after Catherine the Great received the elephant, an attempt was made to steal it back from the Winter Palace where she was staying. Captain Argunov was there, possibly thinking even then of stealing something from the queen. Evidently the attempt made by the bandits convinced him as to what he should take."

Annja made notes diligently on her tablet, but her attention never wavered from the young historian. He had a speaker's natural voice and used it to enhance his tale.

"Captain Daikokuya Kodayu commanded the few surviving Japanese sailors that had sailed from Amchitka in the Rat Islands. His return home was not direct. He landed in Russia in 1784, but it was not until his audience with Catherine the Great in 1791 that he was returned home. And that audience was, strangely enough, made possible through the efforts of a Finnish-Swedish clergyman named Erik Gustavovich Laxmann. In addition to serving in the church, he was also a scientist and an explorer. Men wore many hats in those days."

The details of the story dovetailed with what Annja had learned from the internet while awaiting Sophie and Peter. "It took Captain Kodayu a long time to get back home."

"I think the Japanese captain had a bit of wanderlust in him, as well. It was a time when the world was new and there were so many things you simply had to see for yourself. There was no *Discovery Channel* after all." Peter grinned. "I envy you all the places that you go and the things that you see."

"Sometimes I miss the time to devote to studying," Annja replied. "Traveling eats up a lot of hours, and you can spend weeks or months at a dig and not learn much."

"The elephant," Sophie reminded. "You two can talk like old women later."

Klykov grinned and winked at the pretty ballerina.

Peter toyed with his empty wine glass. "The decision to return Captain Kodayu and his men to Japan was not entirely an act of humanitarian kindness. Queen Catherine chose to do so in hopes of opening trade with Japan. She hoped it would be an opening gambit in a new trade empire."

"At that time, all of Asia was pretty much closed to the rest of the world," Annja said.

"Things didn't turn out as well as Catherine had hoped, but she did manage to establish trade relations of a sort."

"A trading post on Dejima." Annja had looked into the Japanese end of the trade voyages, too.

"Exactly." Peter nodded happily. "Dejima has a fascinating history, as well. Since the Tokugawa shogunate forbade foreigners to enter Japan, and Japanese merchants wanted foreign trade, the locals dug a canal through the peninsula at Nagasaki and created an island to carry out their exchange of goods. Even then, the shogunate imposed strict rules about who came and went on the island."

"It's always about trade," Annja said. "The quest for profits built roads, railways, shipping lanes and in this case, an island."

"Yes. Catherine sent Captain Adam Laxmann, Erik Laxmann's son, to take the Japanese crew back to Nagasaki. Meager trade was allowed in time, but it was never what Catherine had hoped it would be. Captain Laxmann brought back the elephant as part of the gifts given by the shogunate for the safe return of Captain Kodayu and his crew. Then, only weeks after Captain Laxmann's return to Russia, bandits broke into the palace and attempted to take the elephant."

Peter pulled out one of the papers that had a copy of a pencil drawing and placed it in front of Annja. She studied the image of robed figures armed with swords that dueled with Russian guardsmen in a great hall.

"This page was taken from Captain Argunov's journal," Peter said. "Captain Argunov was visiting the palace at the time, though his affair with Catherine was over—he was even involved in the fight."

"The bandits were never identified?" Annja asked.

"No. Captain Argunov at first thought they were Japanese, but investigation into the matter revealed that they were monks from Cambodia."

"How did he find that out?"

"As men do, Captain Argunov was telling the story over drinks in a tavern. One of the captain's acquaintances, a Portuguese merchant named Joao Clemente, had a look at the drawings of the men and their personal effects, and identified them as Cambodian."

"How did a Portuguese merchant know about Cambodians?" Sophie asked. Evidently parts of this story were new to her.

"Because, dear one, the Portuguese had, in their day, been ambitious traders. They had traded with Longvek and other cities of the Cambodian kingdom. The trade was given up in light of the wars between the Siamese and the second Le Dynasty, though. People often forget that Asia has been swallowed up in one war after another, which is why Japan and China remain so standoffish these days. They've had trouble enough inside their continent without seeking more elsewhere."

Sipping her wine, Annja thought about the connections, turning them over in her mind, trying to fit the pieces together. Russia had been an interesting connection to make, but the thought of feudal Asia with all its various dynasties and kingdoms was even more so.

"Captain Argunov was never able to find out where the elephant came from?" Klykov asked.

Peter shook his head. "Nor have I been able to, though I have spent many days investigating. However, I may have had a breakthrough." He glanced at Annja. "I have followed the story of the elephant of late, tracking back through the various news stories that have surfaced concerning it. I hope I did not offend, but I did want to give Sophie and Nadia Silaevae answers if I was able."

"Certainly," Annja replied.

"Given what I knew, and of the high profile that elephant has gotten in the United States recently, I managed to get in touch with Professor Ishii in Nagasaki in hopes that the history of the elephant might be better investigated there. I have inquired at the history department of the University of Tokyo several times before, but no one was interested." Peter smiled ruefully. "Perhaps I would not have gotten an answer this time, but I dropped your name, Annja. Professor Ishii replied only minutes before we met here. He is open to meeting with you, and he believes he has information about the elephant."

"He couldn't just give you the information?"

"He would like to meet with you." Peter reached inside his jacket and took out a sheet of paper. Professor Hamada Ishii's name, phone number and email were all written neatly in English. "He says if you cannot come, he might be able to make arrangements."

"What do you know about Professor Ishii?" Klykov asked.

Peter shrugged. "Only what I have read about him on the university website and in papers he has written. He appears to be very erudite and quite knowledgeable about Asian history, particularly Cambodian and Vietnamese." He paused. "If the elephant did, indeed, come from one of those areas, he might very well know where it came from."

Annja hoped it wasn't that easy. She loved the chase. When things were just handed to her, a lot of the excitement was lost.

She took the paper, folded it and stored it in her tablet cover. "I'll give him a call in the morning and see if we can work something out."

"Perhaps," Klykov said, "this Professor Ishii will also know why Nguyen Rao pursues the elephant so rigorously, as well. You have so many mysteries, and so few answers."

32

"You cannot keep pursuing Annja Creed, Nguyen Rao. We barely managed to get you into Moscow."

"I am trying to catch her, Venerable Father, but the path she takes is unknown to me, and Sequeira and his minions make the task more difficult." Rao spoke quietly on the cell phone as he rode in the backseat of the Russian cab. "I know part of the path she must yet take if she discovers the nature of the elephant, but we do not know where it will lead in the end."

The old man was silent for a time. "We know this as well, and we have been thinking upon your suggestion to join forces with Annja Creed. You have risked your life on several occasions, and we constrain you by insisting that you continue to operate independently of her."

Some of the tension inside Rao relaxed. Finally the elders were starting to see that they had asked him to engage on a battlefield on two fronts. Even though Annja Creed was not an enemy the way Sequeira was, she still thwarted his attempts to recover the elephant and divine the secrets that it hid.

"You feel that you can trust her?"

"I do, Venerable Father. I think Annja Creed would only wish to know what we believe the elephant holds secret. She does not intend to take that which is not hers."

"In that we have reached agreement. Contact Annja Creed, and tell her what you know of the elephant. Perhaps together you will discover the rest of its story."

"Thank you, Venerable Father." Rao peered out at Moscow's colorful nightscape. In the distance the lighted skyscrapers towered over the Volga River that snaked through the heart of the city. "Unfortunately, though I have arrived in Moscow, I do not know where Annja Creed is at this moment."

"We have found her."

"How?" Though he had been raised around the temple all of his life, the methods of the monks remained mysterious to Rao.

"Some of the younger members hacked into Fernando Sequeira's computer network."

Rao grinned at that and felt foolish. Sometimes he forgot that the temple was wired into the modern world, as well. The elders kept the doctrine and the teachings, but they availed themselves of younger acolytes that knew about the internet and electronic communications. After all, they had recruited him to follow the elephant and Annja Creed because he had his own skill set.

But another problem troubled him.

"Sequeira knows where Annja Creed is?"

"He does. He is going there now." The monk gave Rao the name of the hotel, which Rao relayed to the cab driver.

"How far away is Sequeira?" Rao asked.

"We do not know."

The anxiousness that had lifted returned with a vengeance. Judging from the violence Sequeira had unleashed at the Seventh-Kilometer Market, Sequeira was no longer interested in taking Annja Creed alive. The Portuguese crime lord only wanted the elephant, and no one knew for certain how much he knew about its history or where it would lead.

"We do know Sequeira is getting his information from someone named Brisa."

"I have never heard this name."

"Nor have we, but we will continue searching for information. Until then, be safe."

Rao thanked the monk and thought furiously for a moment. Annja Creed was in immediate danger; in fact, he might already be too late to help her. Still, he wondered what he could do to warn her.

Then he thought of the police detective, Bart McGilley, and he realized there might be a way after all.

SEQUEIRA GLANCED UP at the impressive hotel as he strolled along the street. The downtown area was quiet in the early morning hours after the nightlife finally gave way to impending daybreak and responsibility. If Sequeira were not so pressed for time, he might have been tempted to stop at some of the clubs he had seen to enjoy the festivities.

Unfortunately, he was pressed for time, and he had his prey almost in his crosshairs. Annja Creed had arrived in Moscow hours ahead of him and had enjoyed a temporary lead, but the distance had now closed. He was upon her and she didn't know it.

He anticipated that victory, and he wished he was leading the team inside the hotel. That wasn't possible, though. Language was a barrier, as well as knowledge of the premises. In order to achieve the results he'd wanted, he'd had to rely on others.

Brisa had set up the liaison with a local mafia enforcer named Mikhail Kramskoi. The man trafficked in arms, and it was possible he and Brisa had met while involved in that business. Sequeira didn't know everything that Brisa did, though he promised himself that one day he would.

A nondescript black cargo van sat across from the hotel in front of a parking garage and government building. The early hour guaranteed that no government interference would occur, and the parking-garage attendant had been paid off.

The back door of the van opened as Sequeira approached, revealing three men and one woman seated inside at a built-in computer desk. Bald and heavily tattooed on his face, neck and exposed forearms, Mikhail Kramskoi looked like the photograph Brisa had sent Sequeira over his phone.

Dressed in a black V-neck pullover with the sleeves pulled up almost to his elbows and black slacks, Kramskoi was all muscle. He stood loose and ready, a half smile on his twisted lips. Stubble lined his hard chin.

"Mr. Sequeira." Kramskoi's voice was a deep, pleasant baritone. His Russian accent was almost undetectable.

"Mr. Kramskoi."

Kramskoi's grin widened. "You may call me Mikhail. Brisa spoke very highly of you."

"Brisa also spoke highly of you."

"You wish to see the capture?"

"I do."

"It would be better if you stayed away from this operation entirely. I am sure Brisa told you this."

"Do you intend to get caught?"

"No."

"Then I am just as safe here."

Kramskoi grinned again. "As you wish. After all, you are paying for this." He extended a big hand and effortlessly pulled Sequeira into the van, closing the cargo door immediately afterward.

The van was roomier than Sequeira had anticipated. He stood beside Kramskoi and they stood behind the woman operating the computer. The other two men evidently stood by as security and watched video feeds of the street coming from outside the vehicle.

The computer station had six feeds coming into the large 42-inch monitor. The views were divided into a three-by-two template and moved constantly, letting Sequeira know they were coming from cameras mounted on men inside the hotel.

"You have six men inside?" Sequeira asked.

"I have twelve men inside," Kramskoi replied. "Only six of them are wired for video feed. Brisa said you wanted to make sure you intercepted the woman."

"She's proven elusive. Do not underestimate her."

"I won't. The people I have sent are very good at what they do."

"You know which room she is in?"

"Yes, her and the old man. One of the night clerks has done work with me before. It was all easily arranged."

"You were also told about the piece she is carrying?"

"They have their orders. Take the woman alive if possible, but kill her if necessary. And no harm is to come to the elephant."

Feeling tense, Sequeira watched the video feeds as Kramskoi's warriors crept through the hotel.

THE VIBRATION OF her sat phone woke Annja from a sound sleep. She hadn't realized how tired she'd really been till she'd hit the bed last night. After her bath, which she'd luxuriated in, she'd taken her tablet to bed with her, thinking she would catch up on email, other leads she was pursuing and maybe even download a television show. The tablet lay nearby and she hadn't even unpacked her backpack.

Feeling a little groggy, not as refreshed as she'd expected to be since she and Klykov had agreed to brunch instead of breakfast, she reached for the phone. She'd planned to connect with Professor Ishii and set up a meeting time.

A glance at the viewscreen showed Bart's photograph. She thought about letting the call go to voice mail, then felt guilty. Then she realized Moscow time was 4:30 a.m., and Bart would have known that.

So this wasn't just a social call.

Curious, she answered. "Bart?"

"Annja, you've got to get out of the hotel. Sequeira knows you're there. He's closing in on you as we speak. Don't ask questions. Don't think. Just *go.*"

Already moving, Annja left the football jersey she slept in on, then pulled on her khakis and stepped into her boots. She shoved the sat phone into the thigh pocket of her khakis, grabbed her tablet and dumped it into her backpack, then slung the backpack over her shoulder. She sprinted for the door, not bothering with any of the rest of her things.

She barreled into the hallway, surprising a maid who was already making the rounds. She tried to remember the layout of the hotel. Klykov was on the same floor as her. She raced to that door and banged on it.

"Leonid!"

"Annja?" Klykov opened the door, looking very concerned. "Is something wrong?" To her surprise, he was already dressed for the day.

"Sequeira's found us. We need to get out of here now."

Klykov didn't ask any questions. He retreated for just a moment to get his coat, then returned and joined her in the hallway. His right hand was buried in his coat pocket.

Annja led the way to the elevators in the center of the floor.

"They will be watching elevators," Klykov objected.

"We're seven stories up," Annja countered. "If we use the stairwell, they'll box us in. If we get down to the lobby, I don't think they will try anything there. We should be safe till we reach the street."

Klykov smiled. "Very good, Annja. Still, is chancy proposition."

"I know." Annja's pulse crept up as she stood waiting for one of the six elevators to arrive.

"Who told you Sequeira has found us." Klykov fished his phone from his pocket with his left hand and hit a button on speed dial.

"Bart."

"Your policeman friend, *da*?"

"Yes."

"He is in New York. Someone must have told him."

"He didn't say. When we get somewhere safe, I'll ask."

"This is most troubling." Klykov spoke rapidly into the phone and put it away. "Vladi stayed in hotel down the block. He will get car and meet us outside."

That was news to Annja. She had assumed the driver had gone home.

"I thought it best if Vladi remained available while we were in Moscow," Klykov said. "In light of events in Odessa."

The elevator on the other side of the waiting area and on the right dinged as it arrived. Annja nodded and headed for it as three young men stepped out of the cage. She watched them for any sign of trouble, but they appeared caught up in their conversation. As they approached, she smelled cigarette smoke and alcohol fumes that clung to their clothing.

At the same time, two men emerged from farther down the hallway. One of them glanced at the elevators and spotted Annja. He called to his companion and pulled a silencer-equipped pistol out of his pocket.

The three young men tried to scatter, but the gunman's bullets slammed into them before they could get away.

Annja darted into the elevator and pulled the sword from

the *otherwhere* as Klykov joined her. One of the gunmen darted in front of the elevator before the doors could close. He had his pistol up and firing. Bullets thudded against the back of the elevator cage.

33

Standing to one side of the elevator doors, taking advantage of the meager cover offered there, Klykov fired his weapon from the hip. At least two of his three rounds struck the gunman standing in the hallway while the other went wide of the target. Then a fourth round smashed into the man's forehead and he dropped back against the opposite wall as an elevator there opened to reveal two more young men.

The recent arrivals in that cage dodged away from the falling dead man, hesitated for just a second as he dropped among them and brought out weapons, as well. The elevator Annja and Klykov were in started to close its doors, then a hand wrapped around one of the panels and stopped them.

With a quick flick of the sword, Annja severed the restraining fingers and punched the button to close the doors. The doors swept closed just ahead of the fusillade of rounds that cored through the doors, scattering laminate veneer and metal splinters. Annja and Klykov sheltered behind the extra thickness of the sides of the cage and that protected them.

Calmly, Klykov replaced his partially expended magazine for a fresh one. He nodded at Annja's sword. "Where did you get that?"

"Found it in the elevator." Annja felt only a little guilty and hoped that Klykov did not press her about it. Of course, they had other distractions taking place, as well.

"This is a most strange place to leave sword."

"I'm just glad to have it."

"You are very lucky to be finding swords so easily."

"We seem to be finding gunmen even easier."

Klykov smiled and shrugged. "This is unfortunately true." He glanced up at the digital readout as the numbers decreased. "They will have a team waiting in lobby."

"Yes, but we're not taking the elevator to the lobby." Annja hit the button for the second floor and the elevator began slowing at once. When the doors opened, she checked for gunmen, found the hallway empty except for a few obvious hotel guests and stepped out with the sword still in hand. "We'll take the stairwell to the lobby."

"That is a good plan." Klykov trailed her toward the end of the hall on that floor. His phone rang, he answered, spoke quickly and put it away. "That was Vladi. He will meet us in alley around back of hotel."

"He moves quickly."

"That is why he is good driver, and one of the reasons I hired him to chauffeur us."

In the stairwell, Annja checked to see if the way was clear, then, not spotting anyone, she started down. She reached the door without incident, but something whipped through her hair and tore into the wall beside her head. She ducked and spun to warn Klykov.

The old man had already stepped out to put himself between her and the next bullet. He pointed his pistol and fired four times at the gunman leaning over the railing three floors up. At least one of the bullets struck the gunman in the face because blood obscured his features and the man fell back out of sight.

"Go!" Klykov waved Annja to keep running.

She pushed through the door and entered the main lobby. She held the sword down at her thigh to hide it from the handful of people occupying the chairs and sofas in the center of the room. None of them appeared to be threats, but four suspicious-looking men stood near the bank of elevators.

The side emergency door leading out to the street was only a few feet away near a matched pair of potted plants with large leaves. Annja headed toward the door.

At the elevators, the men turned suddenly toward the stairwell and spotted Annja and Klykov. Without warning, they lifted their weapons and opened fire. Bullets tore into the plants, ripping through the leaves and stems and shattered the massive pots, spilling earth onto the tiled floor.

Annja hit the door's crash bar, setting off the security alarm, and passed through, almost running over the two armed men waiting on the other side. Astonished by how quickly the gunmen had responded to her location, realizing then that someone somewhere was controlling their movements, Annja threw herself forward, following the line of the sword.

Even though the blade was made more for slashing attacks, the point crashed through the man's chest, through his heart and out his back. Annja released the sword as she shoved the dead man backward and willed the weapon into the *otherwhere*. By the time the surviving gunman recovered and took aim, Annja had pulled the sword back from the *otherwhere* and swung the blade across his midsection under his outstretched hands.

Seeing the grievous wound leaking blood, the man dropped his weapon, wrapped his arms around himself as he cried out in pain and fell to his knees. He died before he took his next breath, going slack and tumbling to the ground.

Traffic stopped out on the street as onlookers stared.

Annja didn't know how many street cams Moscow had these days, but she hoped she hadn't been caught by one. Klykov followed her out, took in the dead men at a glance and kept moving to the right.

"Quickly, Annja. We must keep moving."

Sparing less than a minute to pick up one of the dropped pistols, Annja ran after Klykov, surprised by his speed but catching him easily.

Klykov shouted a warning in Russian and waved his pistol in the air, emphasizing the immediacy of the threat.

Early morning pedestrians got the message then and ducked away from Klykov and Annja.

Klykov instantly shifted direction and took up a stance behind a car parked at the curb. He raised his weapon and aimed at approaching gunmen who fired a volley of bullets that shattered the vehicle's windshield. Klykov's coat collar jerked and his fedora leaped from his head, but the old gangster never wavered. He squeezed the pistol's trigger and one of the men dropped back, bleeding from a face or head wound.

Annja stopped behind the next car down and let the sword return to the *otherwhere.* She steadied the pistol, took aim, and fired at another of the men, catching him center mass with two shots in rapid succession. He stumbled back but didn't go down. He didn't appear interested in continuing the battle as he swayed drunkenly on his feet.

Glancing over her shoulder at the alley, Annja wondered where Vladi and the car were. Then two more gunmen ran from the alley and she realized the building had been surrounded.

"Leonid!" she called out in warning.

Klykov turned, but Annja knew they were both caught in a bad place. Then a long black sedan wheeled from the street and drove into the two men, knocking them away before they could open fire. The car rocked to a stop and Vladi got out with a pistol in each hand. He shouted at Annja and Klykov to get inside the big car.

Racing to the sedan, Annja opened the rear door and clambered in, followed almost at once by Klykov as scattered shots slammed into the vehicle but did not penetrate the interior.

Vladi slid behind the wheel again, tossed his pistols into the passenger seat beside him and pulled the transmission into Drive. He roared forward along the alley. He glanced into the rearview mirror and shook his head in apology.

"Sorry. Traffic this morning was terrible."

Annja reached forward and patted the chauffer on the shoulder. "Thank you, Vladi."

He shrugged. "Is no problem. Now where you want to go?"

IN DISBELIEF, SEQUEIRA watched the black car race along the alley, carrying Annja Creed and the elephant away from him. He glared at Kramskoi. "These were your best people?"

"Other than myself, *da.*" The man didn't look any too happy either. "This is Moscow. She cannot go anywhere I will not find her. I will be in touch when I locate her again." He opened the cargo door. "There is no payment till I settle this matter."

Sequeira nodded and stepped out of the van. He texted Brisa. SHE GOT AWAY.

I KNOW.

ARE YOU STILL TRACKING HER?

OF COURSE.

Sequeira took a deep breath and felt only a little relieved. He could hardly wait to put a bullet through Annja Creed's heart.

LOOKING AT ALL the debris and the Moscow law enforcement surrounding the streets where the violence in the hotel had spilled over, Rao was again surprised at Annja Creed's propensity to survive in life or death situations. He stood in front of the parking garage across the street from the hotel. Wind tugged at his jacket and ran cold fingers along his exposed flesh. Judging from the violence that had taken place, she should have died a dozen times over.

His phone rang and he answered.

"This is Bart McGilley." The detective did not sound pleased.

"She got away, Detective McGilley," Rao replied.

McGilley let out a relieved breath. "I haven't heard from her. Is she okay?"

"I believe so, although several of her assailants are not." Rao watched an emergency medical team remove yet another body on a stretcher while a crowd stood by to observe.

"Sequeira's people?"

"No, these appear to be local criminals, judging from the few conversations around me I have been able to understand. Perhaps Sequeira hired them to apprehend Annja Creed. I cannot see any other reason these men would have gone after her."

"Her work has turned out to be a lot more involved than I had known."

"Yes."

"Look, you called me and I was able to alert her, so I owe you, but I need to know how you fit into this."

"I want the elephant, Detective. That is all I have wanted from the beginning."

"Why?"

"That I may not tell you. There are some secrets I must keep."

McGilley cursed.

Rao turned from the scene. "I would earn your continued support in this matter if I may, Detective. I give you my promise that I wish no harm to Annja Creed. I have acted to save her when I have been able."

"I know Annja. She's not going to give up that piece until she figures it out or she has no choice."

"The people I serve have come to realize this and they have allowed me permission to share with her the information I have. If she will permit that."

"She doesn't trust you. And I don't know that I do either."

"Then we are at an impasse. You wish Annja Creed to have protection while she investigates the elephant, and I am limited in what I can do to aid her if she continues to view me as a threat."

McGilley hesitated. "I'll talk to her, but I can't guarantee that she will listen. She tends to have her own mind about things. Which is one of the reasons I like her. But I promise you now, if you're lying to me and you hurt her or get her hurt, I will find you and there will be a reckoning." He hung up.

Replacing the phone in his coat, Rao couldn't help feeling that he and Annja Creed were both in small boats on a treacherous sea with no safe harbor in sight.

"PROFESSOR ISHII?" ANNJA walked into Domodedovo International Airport, thinking that using Moscow's other large airport might be a good idea. Sequeira was somehow trailing her so easily. She hadn't yet returned Bart's phone calls because she'd been busy watching her back and trying to get in touch with the history professor.

She felt a little safer inside the terminal with all of the security around them, though she knew Klykov wasn't so happy without a weapon close to hand. He'd had to abandon his. *Again*, he'd pointed out. There had been no sign of Sequeira, but Annja knew that the man and his enforcers were out there somewhere.

"*Hai*, this is Professor Ishii." The man's voice sounded strong and authoritative. "To whom am I speaking?"

"Annja Creed. You had left word you wanted to speak to me, and I would like very much to speak to you."

"Ah, this is good, Creed. We are in agreement regarding our need to meet. You have the elephant in your possession, yes?"

"I do." As she admitted that, Annja couldn't help glancing around to see who might be listening.

"I had heard you have had some trouble keeping it."

"I have."

"I see. Are you safe now?"

"I believe so."

"Can you come to Tokyo?" Ishii's voice remained level and unchanged, but Annja detected the keen interest in his words more because he sounded so calm.

"I can be there tomorrow. I haven't yet secured tickets, but most likely I can get there by the morning. If that's acceptable."

"But of course. I will clear my schedule for this day and the day after. And, if need be, for longer, as well."

Annja thought, all things considered, the offer was being overly generous, and she wanted to know why. "What do you know about the elephant, Professor Ishii?"

"Enough that I look forward to seeing you, Creed. Unfortunately, there is much about that elephant, if it is the one I believe it to be, that I do not know, but I have stories to share with you. And perhaps a path you may follow that will lead you to the rest of the history."

"Maybe you could give me a preview."

"And spoil the surprise?" Ishii laughed good-naturedly. "You will find what you are looking for in Nagasaki, Creed, not the final answer you seek, but enough to put you onto the last trail you will need to follow. I promise."

Despite her wariness, Ishii's words made Annja tingle in anticipation. "All right."

"Email me the details of your flight and I will happily meet you at Haneda Airport."

Annja promised she would and hung up.

"DO YOU GROW weary of my companionship, Annja?" Klykov gazed at her guilelessly. He knew perfectly well that he was trying to guilt her. "Is that why you're suggesting I remain behind now?"

"No. I just think that you're not going to fit into Japan as well as you do Brooklyn, Ukraine and Moscow." Annja sat across a small table at one of the restaurants in the terminal. They had dined on a Russian menu that was far better than she had expected, then followed it with *Kissel a la Russe* made with raspberries and cream.

"I will fit in where I need to fit in," Klykov declared. "You should not be alone."

"I've often been alone. I work better that way. I mean no disrespect, and you have been very helpful."

"Then tell me I am holding you back and I will be gone."

Gazing at the old man, Annja knew her suggestion, made as politely as she could, had stung Klykov's pride. She tried to harden her heart and let him know that she didn't intend for him to risk his life on her behalf anymore, but that was difficult. Klykov had helped her throughout Ukraine and Russia. In fact, she figured things might have gone much differently in those places had he not been along.

"I can't tell you that because it wouldn't be true."

"Good." Klykov smoothed his coat. "I am not some old man to be put on a shelf and left to wither away." His eyes twinkled. "Well, perhaps I am old, but I prefer a life of adventure. Tell me truly, Annja, were you my age, would you not want to chase after adventure if it came your way?"

Annja made no reply, but she knew Klykov knew what her answer would be.

"Then allow me the same privilege. This undertaking has been exhilarating. Do not seek to push me away when we are so close to the goal that you seek." Klykov looked humbled. "Would you break an old man's heart so willfully?"

Unable to stop herself, Annja burst out laughing loud enough to attract the attention of nearby diners.

"What?" Klykov demanded, and he even managed a look of indignation.

"That," Annja said, "is the biggest con job I've heard in a long time."

Klykov tried to hold his stern face, but a few seconds later, he was laughing, too. "So," he said when they regained themselves, "I am allowed to come?"

"What if I said no?"

"I would come anyway."

"That much was obvious."

"I am not a man to be denied without concentrated effort. Possibly even physical restraint." Klykov shrugged. "You already have several people following you. Doubtless I would be lost in the crowd, but at least I would be on your side when those others are not. My presence could be very useful."

Uneasily, Annja realized that might just be true. No matter how hard she tried, she could not grow eyes in the back of her head.

Klykov evidently read her apprehension. "You may not need someone with you, Annja, but I would like the chance to help. And, though your young detective would be loath to admit it, I think he expects me to watch over you."

She smiled at him, knowing Bart would agree. "If you're going to be following along, I want you where I can keep an eye out for you."

34

"You trust Rao?" Annja frowned in disbelief as she held her sat phone to her ear and considered what Bart McGilley had just told her. Seated in the gate area, awaiting her flight, she kept watch over the arriving passengers. "And when did you two get on a first-name basis?"

She and Bart had been missing calls from each other for the past few hours. Annja had been busy making arrangements for the flight to Tokyo and purchasing some necessary clothing to replace the things she'd been forced to leave behind at the hotel. Airport fashion wasn't exactly chic, but she managed to get the essentials she needed.

Bart had been fielding a homicide that involved a politician and someone who had not been his wife. That investigation promised to be controversial for the homicide division because it was already blowing up in the media.

"It's not a matter of trusting him," Bart replied tiredly. "I don't trust many people when it comes to looking out for you. Even fewer people since I've gotten a better firsthand look at what you do. It's a matter of the lesser of two evils. Out of everyone else chasing after you, Nguyen Rao hasn't tried to kill you."

"Yet."

Bart ignored that, but Annja knew the thought rested uncomfortably in her friend's mind. "Rao is also the reason you and that old gangster didn't end up captured—or maybe killed—at the hotel this morning."

"I like to think that Leonid and I had quite a bit to do with our escaping."

"I know, but if Rao hadn't called me so I could get in touch with you, things might have worked out differently. And the state department is going to be busy squaring your involvement in this. Luckily, the hotel had security cameras that showed those men were trying to kill you."

Annja knew that was true.

"You're going to need friends," Bart continued. "And, like you said, the elephant is leading you back into Asia. Klykov has had the Russian connections you've needed. Nguyen Rao knows the Asian beat, and he's a historian, familiar with the past you'll be digging into over there, too, so he'll be another pair of eyes and hands. Maybe if you guys join forces, you can figure out why that elephant is so important. The sooner that happens, the sooner you're safe and the sooner I stop worrying."

Annja glanced at Klykov, who was talking to an older Russian couple only a short distance away. They appeared animated and engaged. She couldn't help wondering if they'd brought Klykov a weapon, then she thought maybe she was being too paranoid. Maybe. "I've already taken on a partner."

"Klykov is making the jump with you?"

"He is."

"Good." Bart actually sounded content.

Feeling surprised and happy, Annja grinned. "I'm sort of shocked to hear you say that."

"Yeah, well, I gotta give the old guy credit. He stays the distance and he can handle himself. *And* I'd rather you *not* tell him that."

"I won't. For a while."

"Terrific." Bart's tone held mock despair.

"Where is Nguyen Rao?"

"On his way to you. That's all I know."

Annja glanced at the clock on the wall over the check-in desk. "We start boarding in ten minutes."

"Not sure if he'll be there by then. Getting through the mess you guys left at the hotel has probably held him up."

"Not exactly our mess."

"Noted."

"I can't wait for him, Bart. The next flight to Tokyo won't land until hours after this one. I've already got a meeting set up."

Bart sighed. "Fine. But will you at least relay the details of your flight and meeting to Rao? He can rendezvous with you when he can."

Annja promised that she would, then they said goodbye. The boarding call went out only a few minutes later. She stood and pulled her backpack over her shoulder while Klykov bade his new acquaintances farewell. Together, they headed toward the check-in.

BE PATIENT, FERNANDO. IF YOU TRY TO TAKE ANNJA CREED HERE YOU WILL LIKELY LOSE HER. THERE IS NO WAY TO SPIRIT HER AWAY FROM THE AIRPORT WITHOUT GETTING THE AUTHORITIES INVOLVED.

Sequeira glared at the text on his sat phone, not liking the truth of Brisa's words. But they were the truth. It frustrated him that Annja Creed was only a short distance away, so accessible, yet off-limits. From his seat in a small bar, he caught occasional glimpses of her as she shuffled through the boarding line.

I KNOW, he responded. It was already too late to try to kidnap her. Any resistance on her part, and he knew she would resist, would summon airport security. The situation would become sticky immediately.

SHE HAS A DESTINATION AND A PLAN. REMEMBER THAT WE CAN FIND HER ANYTIME WE WANT TO. EVEN IF SHE FOUND THE TRACER I PUT ON HER, OR IF IT SIMPLY STOPPED FUNCTIONING, YOU KNOW WHERE SHE IS GOING. THERE CAN BE ONLY ONE PLACE.

Sequeira finished his glass of wine and ordered another as he watched Annja Creed disappear into the yawning mouth of the tunnel leading to her flight.

She was going to Dejima Island. There could be no other place in Japan that she would go if she was staying on the trail of the elephant. According to the journal that had found its way into his hands, the true secret of the elephant began there. Annja Creed would have to solve that puzzle before she could go any farther.

The problem was that there were others who would also be interested in the elephant now that it had surfaced. The monks had been searching for the elephant and the secret it guarded for centuries.

"ANNJA CREED?"

Propelled by the crowd that had deplaned at Tokyo International Airport, Annja kept moving forward but searched for the man who'd called her name. Klykov kept pace at her side.

"Annja Creed!"

The voice was more strident this time, and Annja had no problem spotting the thin, middle-aged Asian man standing at the front of the crowd waiting to greet the arrivals. He wore a dark blue suit, wore black-framed glasses and had shoulder-length graying hair that he obviously took pride in. He held up a sign with her name on it.

Klykov swept the crowd with his gaze, as Annja did, then she followed Klykov through the arrivals because they gave way naturally before him.

"I am Professor Hamada Ishii." The man bowed carefully. "It is an honor to meet you, Creed-Chan."

"The pleasure is all mine. Thank you for meeting us so quickly." Annja took Klykov by the arm and introduced him to the professor. "Leonid Klykov, Professor Ishii."

Klykov nodded and Ishii bowed again. The professor started walking toward the baggage claim and spoke over the noise of the other bystanders.

"Will you need hotel reservations?" Ishii asked.

"They have already been made," Klykov replied. "But thank you."

Ishii spoke quickly to one of the uniformed men standing at the baggage carousel. He handed him a folded sheaf of yen, and then turned back to Annja and Klykov as the man walked along the line of suitcases and carry-ons. "He will gather your bags and bring them to us. Perhaps you would like a cup of tea while we wait." He coaxed them along.

Annja went because getting out of the press of the crowd sounded fantastic. The flight had been long and her mind had been busy. It felt good to be moving instead of sitting and standing around.

THEY TOOK THEIR tea at a small noodle shop not far from the baggage-claim area and sat at a round table. Ishii assured them that the man could find them with their luggage.

The professor was effusive and fastidious. "Do you have the elephant?"

"Yes," Annja answered.

"May I see it?"

"Of course." Annja swung her backpack up and took the elephant from inside its protective case. She placed the elephant gently on the table. Analyzing it there, the tiny statue looked like a cheap souvenir, a child's toy with the warriors riding in the basket on the great beast's back.

"May I touch it?" Ishii gestured to the elephant.

Annja nodded. "As long as it stays on the table."

Ishii looked up at her in surprise.

"After the trouble I've gone through for it, I'm not letting it out of my sight."

"I understand. I would be protective of it, too. In fact, I already feel that way." Slowly, Ishii picked up the elephant and examined it closely. He shook his head. "I see nothing special about it."

"Neither do I, but several people seem to think it's worth killing over."

Ishii placed the elephant back on the table. "Do you know any of the legends of the Elephant of Ishana?"

"No." Curiosity filled Annja because she'd never before encountered the name. "*Ishana*, as in the Hindu god Shiva?"

Ishii pushed his glasses farther up his nose. "The very same. There is a legend that Ishana, as an aspect of Shiva, created a hiding place for a lost temple during the war between Le Thanh Tong and P'an-Lo T'ou-Ts'iuan during the fifteenth century. That was back when the Vietnamese were building their empires at the expense of the Khmers. Do you know these names?"

"Vaguely." Annja took notes in her journal. "Thanh Tong was the emperor of Vietnam."

"*Hai*." Ishii's eyes gleamed. "You are well versed in the histories of these lands. As you may recall, wars over territory have been prevalent throughout Asia. Empires have risen and fallen, and the blood of warriors has long soaked into the ground where those empires once stood."

"Thanh Tong believed that the country should be ruled by men of noble character, not just nobility through family names." It seemed that many nations had their version of this notion during those times. She'd done some writing about it—that as civilizations grew larger, the people tried to figure out ways to work together.

"To achieve this," Ishii said, "Thanh Tong took power away from those ruling families and gave it to the scholars. He ordered places be built throughout the provinces, places where all the classic works of Confucius could be found. As a result of this, Thanh Tong also halted the building of any new Buddhist and Taoist temples."

"The war between Thanh Tong and P'an-Lo T'ou-Ts'iuan wasn't based on religion as I recall."

"No." Ishii shook his head. "That war had to do with P'an-Lo T'ou-Ts'iuan's raid into southern Vietnam while Thanh Tong was engaged fighting with pirates to the north and a mountain tribe to the west that was skirmishing along the borders. P'an-Lo T'ou-Ts'iuan, known as Tra-Toan in Vietnam, hoped to seize more territory for the Champa Kingdom, the empire he ruled. Thanh Tong wasted no time in addressing the attack. Besieged by the Vietnamese, P'an-Lo T'ou-Ts'iuan appealed to the Khmers, who lived in what we now recognize as Cambodia. The Khmers refused because they had an unpleasant history with the Champa Kingdom."

The details tumbled through Annja's mind in freefall. Sometimes the connections were like that, pieces that fit together that she didn't even remember. History was a mosaic.

She gazed at the elephant with renewed excitement. "They had a history of hostility."

"Exactly. Not only that, Thanh Tong had made Vietnam strong and the Khmers did not want to stand against him because they feared him."

Klykov tapped the table. "The elephant," he reminded. "Where does it come in?"

"It is said the Elephant of Ishana hides the location of the Temple of the Dreaming Rumdul."

Annja picked up the elephant and took her camera from her backpack, snapped a picture of the flower on the elephant's head, then magnified the view. As the details sharpened, she took out her tablet and pulled up a photo of a rumdul plant.

The long leaves and balled blossom amid the three petals was a close enough match. Of course, there were a lot of other flowers and plants she wasn't familiar with, too, but the three petals clustered around the ball of fruit looked a lot like the rumdul.

"You see?" Ishii asked animatedly. "It is a rumdul plant, *hai*?"

"Perhaps."

Ishii's eyes shone as his excitement grew. "According to the histories I have read, long thought to be legends, the Temple of the Dreaming Rumdul was one of the first temples of Angkor Wat, but it was lost during the wars with the Champa Kingdom." He paused and swept a hand through his hair. "According to legend, monks hid the treasures of the Temple of the Dreaming Rundul somewhere in what is now Cambodia when the Champas attacked them."

As Annja sipped her tea, she imagined all those years of history rolling by. So many things happened during the passage of time, it was a wonder that lost things ever showed up again.

Yet she had the elephant. Sometimes it happened, and those instances were glorious.

"The elephant was made to show the way to the temple's hiding place, and only the monks of the Dreaming Rundul are supposed to know how to decipher the clues. If you believe the stories, the monks have searched for it since it was lost shortly after the fall of Angkor Wat to the Vietnamese. They did not know what had become of it till after Thanh Tong seized Champa. For a brief time, it is said, the monks of the hidden temple chased stories of the elephant though they never got their hands on it."

"But it eventually ended up in Japanese hands," Annja said.

"Yes." Ishii toyed with his tea cup. "There came a time of unrest again in Thanh Tong's reign. Chinese merchants began illegally trading with the Vietnamese. Thanh Tong took dire steps to prevent this, turning those guilty of the practice into eunuchs that served at the palace."

Klykov grimaced.

"Somewhere in there, though, the elephant was lost to thieves." Ishii shrugged. "The Tokugawa shogunate did not know what they had lost till they captured a group of monks attempting to steal the elephant back. By that time, the elephant—thought to be only a mild oddity that might please Queen Catherine—was already in Russia. The Tokugawa Emperor chose not to pursue the Elephant of Ishana because he did not believe in the stories."

"And Japan didn't want to open its borders for any reason."

"Exactly. There was a tale that the monks of the Dreaming Rumdul Temple ventured to Queen Catherine's palace in an attempt to retrieve the elephant. Have you heard of this?"

"Yes. According to Russian records, an attempt was made by what was then believed to be Japanese thieves. Later an investigation revealed them to be Cambodian monks, but the proper royal records were never corrected."

"Interesting. They obviously did not get the elephant?"

"No, but one of Catherine the Great's disgruntled lovers chose to steal the elephant later, and that was how it ended up in New York."

Ishii smiled. "History is often so very fascinating, and the further back you go, the harder it becomes to separate fact from fanciful tales. Until recently, I had not believed in the Elephant of Ishana, yet here you are with it. This is very exhilarating."

Annja silently agreed, but she held herself in check. So much remained to be seen, and she still didn't know where she was supposed to go with the information she had.

"The statue could also," Klykov spoke up, "be a fake. A totem created to play on the myth of the Temple of the Dreaming Rumdul. Just a curiosity that someone constructed to satisfy a whim."

Clearly unhappy with that line of thought, Ishii frowned irritably and leaned back. "Perhaps. But there is a way to find out."

"How?"

"The myth goes on to say that documents regarding the Elephant of Ishana were taken from the monks that arrived there. They are kept in a small museum on Dejima. I have arranged permission to go there today and look over them." Ishii spread his hands. "Unless you'd prefer to go by your hotel rooms first?"

Annja looked at Klykov.

"If you do not mind," Klykov said, "there is one stop I would like to make first. It will not take but a moment. I would like to check in with an old friend."

35

"You are familiar with the history of Dejima Island?" Professor Ishii asked as he peered over the backseat of the rented car he'd arranged. He had also rented a driver to pilot the vehicle, a hard-faced man who remained quiet and drove with aggressive authority along the packed streets of Nagasaki leading down to the harbor.

"Yes." Annja peered past the professor at the coastline. She had reviewed the history of Dejima Island while en route from Russia and what she saw now only slightly fit with what she had expected. "In response to Japanese merchants wanting to trade with the Portuguese, part of Nagasaki's coastline was cut off from the mainland."

"*Hai.* That maneuver was to satisfy the emperor's desire to keep Japan isolated from the rest of the world. *Sakoku*, the emperor's law, promised death to any foreigner who landed on Japanese soil, and death to any native who sought to leave Japan. The original island has been classified as a national historic site."

If she looked hard, Annja could still see the vague outlines of the fan-shaped island that had been created by the trenching effort back in the seventeenth century. However, as the centuries had passed, Nagasaki had reclaimed its wayward creation, linking it with elevated highways.

The driver slowed at an intersection. He conversed quickly with the professor, then made a left-hand turn.

Annja glanced at Klykov, trying to get some measure of the man's mindset. He had been mostly quiet since they'd gotten into the car, and there were times he had stared at the driver in the rearview mirror.

"Are you feeling all right?" Annja asked Klykov while Ishii gave more directions to the driver.

Klykov shrugged. "We are far from home, Annja. Far from people who may help us if we need it. This is something that concerns me."

"It concerns me, too."

"I do not like trusting people I do not know."

She smiled at him. "I know, but I went looking for you a few days ago and that seems to have turned out all right."

He gave her a ghost of a grin that revealed some of the tension that he was feeling. "Yes, but you were fortunate in that instance. You chose to trust me."

She reached over and patted his hand. "Everything went well with the meeting with your friend?" She assumed the transaction for a weapon had gone off without a problem.

"Yes."

"Then you should be feeling better."

Klykov shrugged again. "Some better."

A few minutes later, the driver pulled into the private parking area of a small gray two-story brick building. There was no advertising, no signage of any kind except warnings of security and NO TRESPASSING in a handful of languages.

The driver opened the door and Annja got out, surveying the building. She glanced at Ishii. "This is a museum?"

"A private museum," Ishii said. "It is owned by a businessman I know who is interested in archaeology and history. The tale of the Elephant of Ishana is something he has been acutely fascinated by." The professor led her to the front doors, which were opened by a young man in a dark suit.

Annja settled her backpack over her shoulders and entered the building. She couldn't help noticing the way Klykov and the driver gave each other space like two aggressive male dogs.

THE INTERIOR OF the museum was quiet and the climate was perfectly controlled, slightly cooler than the outside temperature. A number of exhibits occupied the main room, which stretched two stories tall, but it was the almost complete skeleton of an allosaurus that claimed center stage.

The assembled skeleton stood on a three-foot-high pedestal and towered almost seventeen feet above that. Most of the bones were true fossils, but one leg, parts of the tail, a few of the ribs and part of the skull plate had been created out of resins. The copies were expensively made because it took a second look to see that they weren't real.

"Impressive, isn't it Creed-Chan?"

Turning to her right, Annja took in the slim man in an elegant suit who stepped from the hallway there. Handsome and cruel looking, the man held himself with easy confidence. It was hard to place his age. He could have been anywhere from thirty to sixty, depending on whether the coal-black hair was natural or dyed.

"It is impressive," Annja admitted.

The man advanced across the tiled floor and stopped just out of arm's reach. Two younger men that looked an awful lot like the driver Ishii had hired flanked him.

"I would have preferred a Tyrannosaurus Rex, but those are hard to get. Still, a full-grown allosaurus is quite a specimen." The man gazed at the dinosaur with obvious pride. "I got this one from Thailand, from the Muang district of Nakhon Ratchasima Province. It cost me a lot of money, but it is worth it. So far it has been the centerpiece of my museum."

Annja didn't say anything. Dinosaur-fossil trafficking remained a booming business. The man's casual mention of the price automatically let her know he was used to dealing in criminal matters. Some of Klykov's unease seeped into her and she realized how far from home and help they presently were.

"Not everyone can have a Tyrannosaurus Rex," the man stated good-naturedly. "And not everyone has an allosaurus." His eyes gleamed. "I do. I am quite fascinated by monsters, the giants that used to walk the earth. Have you ever been on a dinosaur dig?"

"A few times," Annja admitted. "I prefer more current history. Shifting fossilized dinosaur poop isn't work I enjoy. I'd rather learn about people, who they were and how they lived."

"I understand. You are here on another matter. The Elephant of Ishana."

"We haven't confirmed that's what I'm looking for."

The easy grin returned. "Professor Ishii tells me he believes you are looking for that very thing."

"Professor Ishii may be easier to convince than I am." From the corner of her eye, Annja watched as Klykov took a slow step to her left and remained facing the man and his two companions. The tension was thick enough to cut with a knife.

"All the more reason to put the professor's theories to the test." The man gestured to the rear of the museum. "I have the documents related to the elephant laid out in a study. Shall we adjourn there?"

"Maybe we should have an introduction first," Annja replied.

The man smiled. "I am just an ardent supporter of historical things, Creed-Chan. No one you need trouble yourself over."

"His name is Yoichi Shirasaki," Klykov said. "He is *yakuza*. A criminal."

The unease that had been coiling through Annja solidified into a stronger warning. She checked for exits in the building and noticed that other men had joined them in the main room now, all standing in the shadows.

The man's eyebrows rose slightly. He looked angry, surprised and troubled all at the same time. "Do I know you, old man?"

Klykov shook his head. "No."

Shirasaki turned to Ishii and spoke rapidly in Japanese. The question was evident from the anger in Shirasaki's tone.

Klykov spoke before Ishii could reply. "I am Leonid Klykov. I have done business on occasion with Kano Kenzen."

The smile flickered across Shirasaki's lips again, but it quickly died. "Kenzen is no longer involved in this business."

"I had heard that. Kenzen's son holds you responsible for his father's death." Klykov's words were flat, uninflected.

"Is that going to be a problem?" Shirasaki asked.

"Not as long as you deal with us in good faith. Kenzen and I did business only occasionally."

The driver started to step forward but Shirasaki held the man up with a look, then focused his gaze on Klykov. "Careful, old man. You would do well not to insult me."

"It's not an insult," Klykov replied. "Just something that needs to be addressed."

"We are all interested parties in this endeavor," Shirasaki said.

"Annja and I came here looking for answers, not partners," Klykov said.

Shirasaki's eyes narrowed and his voice turned harder. "The information I have grants me an interest in the outcome of this treasure hunt."

The words burrowed into Annja's mind and she regretted accepting Ishii's offer of help so quickly. She should have vetted the man more completely before jumping in. But time, ironically, wasn't always on an archaeologist's side when pursuing an artifact or a story.

Klykov said nothing.

"Maybe I could look at those documents now," Annja suggested.

Shirasaki smiled again, once more the host, but the cold ruthlessness never left his eyes. "This way, please."

THE WORKROOM WAS twelve-foot square, an eight-tatami room, and it seemed cramped with the long table that held the documents Shirasaki had laid out for Annja's inspection. The inclusion of Klykov, Professor Ishii, Shirasaki and five of the bodyguards made the room seem even smaller.

The documents were kept in a thick, oversize, leather-bound book and dated back hundreds of years. Unfortunately, that also meant they were in Hanyu logograms, graphemes that represented words or morphemes, which were helper words and didn't exist on their own.

Annja didn't read Hanyu. She gazed at the pages in silent frustration.

"If you will permit me, Creed-Chan." Ishii acted contrite and polite as he stepped closer to Annja. "I will provide the translations."

In a calm, steady voice, Ishii read from the documents, more or less relating the story he had already told Annja.

Judging from the bored and impatient look on Shirasaki's features, the Japanese crime lord had heard the story before.

Only as Ishii finished up this time, there was an added layer to the story.

"It wasn't until the Elephant of Ishana was sent as a gift to the Queen of Russia that the Emperor's advisors realized they had made a mistake about the worth of the statue," Ishii continued. "When monks from the Temple of the Dreaming Rumdul came to Dejima Island pursuing the Elephant, they were captured and tortured. Gradually, the story of the Elephant and the Maze came out."

The Maze? Annja leaned over the page Ishii slowly moved his finger along. In addition to the Hanyu logograms, this page also featured a drawing of a box. Markings outside this box might have listed the dimensions, but Annja didn't know how big the construction was.

"In addition to the information of the Elephant and the lost temple," Ishii continued, "the monks also carried with them the Maze, which is the second part of the map to the Temple of the Dreaming Rumdul."

Annja moved to the other side of the table and peered at the drawing of the Maze. Even though the image was upside down, she made out the three-dimensional representation of what had to be a map. Rivers ran between broken countryside and trails cut through the jungle. Bridges spanned the river, paths throughout.

"Do you know where this is?" Annja blurted out, consumed with the new piece of the mystery.

"We have not been able to narrow it down." Ishii peered at her through his glasses. "The temple was lost hundreds of years ago. Rivers change their courses."

"Mountains don't move," Annja countered. "Have you searched for this location using satellite imaging?"

"Yes." Shirasaki stepped toward the table and peered down at the book. "No expense has been spared. I have searched for the Elephant of Ishana for eight years, since I learned of it. Until the Elephant turned up in New York, I had thought it destroyed or lost forever."

"It might still be a tall tale," Klykov said, "and you've wasted your time and money for nothing more than a fabrication."

Shirasaki shot Klykov a withering glare, then snapped his fingers. One of his men came forward carrying a small protective case. Without a word, the man opened the box and poured out pieces of carved teak inlaid with ivory. Age had darkened the wood and yellowed the ivory, but the carved images on the wood remained beautiful works of art.

Quietly, the man began assembling the pieces, clicking the wooden sections together with obvious familiarity. They fit together so well the seams vanished, making it seem like the entire thing had been carved from one piece of wood. Within minutes, the Maze sat on the table, covering a two-foot square. Sections created the mountains and the river and the bridges. Other sections created clumps of trees and valleys.

"Part of the legend of the lost temple refers to the Elephant's memory," Shirasaki said. "The monks believed that the Elephant would always know its way home."

Annja leaned over the wooden construction and ran her fingers along the smooth grain and the ivory. "This is beautiful."

"It is a map." Shirasaki's grating response betrayed his irritation. "One that we have not been able to read. Now, Creed-Chan, let us see the Elephant. Let us see if it does remember the way home."

Annja was intrigued, but hesitant about revealing the location of the temple to Shirasaki. Not only because she felt certain the man would no longer need her or Klykov, but because she didn't want to allow whatever had been left behind to be picked over by a grave robber.

"Now," Shirasaki demanded. "I have waited for this moment for a very long time."

Before Annja could reach into her backpack, assault rifles opened fire out in the main lobby of the museum. Then a section of the back wall blew out in a fist-sized chunk. One of the guards beside Annja suddenly dropped and rolled, revealing that from the nose up, nothing remained of the man's head except crimson ruin and shattered bone.

36

Standing outside the museum on Dejima Island, Fernando Sequeira held the AK-47 rifle and took cover beside the door. He wore a protective vest and helmet with a bullet-resistant faceplate.

Three of his men had charged into the room and the gunfire had started immediately.

Brisa had provided information about the man who owned the museum. Judging from Shirasaki's criminal background and his interest in history, Sequeira had known immediately that the *Yakuza* warlord wouldn't have been interested in any kind of a deal.

That had left only force as a means of acquiring the elephant. Sequeira had planned on ambushing Shirasaki and his people when they came out of the building. Then this mysterious *Maze* had been brought up. Sequeira hadn't expected that, and he didn't want anyone else to know where the temple lay. That prize belonged to him and he intended to claim it.

When the shooting slowed, Sequeira risked a glance around the door frame. All three of his men walked forward in crouches. Two Japanese guards lay prone on the floor amid a shambles of dinosaur bones. Shattered glass from display cases lay strewn across the tiles.

"Espallargas, where is Annja Creed?" Sequeira demanded. Espallargas was the sniper Brisa had assigned to the team after the debacles at Seventh-Kilometer Market and in Moscow. The Portuguese mercenary had a reputation and he'd come at once when Brisa had called.

"She is still in the back room." Espallargas's response was quiet and controlled.

The distinct sound of the .50-caliber sniper rifle carried over the comm.

"Two of Shirasaki's people are no longer a threat." Another rifle shot punctuated the response.

"No one escapes," Sequeira stated.

"Understood."

Sequeira plunged into the building, leading the second wave of mercenaries.

NO SOONER HAD the dead man hit the floor than Klykov pulled his pistol and fired at the driver, who had already drawn his weapon and took aim at the Russian. Both men started firing at what seemed to be the same time. The driver got off two shots. Klykov staggered back a moment but never stopped shooting. Annja believed all of Klykov's rounds struck the driver in the chest, and at least one of the bullets hit the man in the face, snapping his head back.

Another heavy-caliber round punched through the wall, creating another fist-size hole, then caught another of Shirasaki's guards in the chest.

The man who had assembled the Maze hurriedly worked to take the artifact apart. Annja went to him, placing the pieces into the protective case, like they were engaged in some macabre board game.

Ishii turned to run, but another round from the heavy-caliber weapon blasted through the rear wall of the building and caught him in midstride. He dropped, his forward momentum slowed but unchecked.

Shirasaki fired at Klykov as he retreated from the room through the doorway. The other guard tried to follow him, but Klykov cut him down. Gunfire from the outer room drove Shirasaki into hiding amid displays of samurai armor, reducing all the artifacts to ruin in seconds.

When the final piece of the Maze was in the protective case and the latches were snapped closed, the man went for the pistol holstered at his hip. Annja placed both hands on the table and vaulted across, swinging her leg around in a roundhouse kick that caught the man on the jaw. He staggered and tried to recover, but Annja landed on her feet, swept his pistol from his grip with one hand, and snap-kicked him in the face hard enough to bounce him off the nearest wall.

He shook his head and pushed himself at her as blood streamed down his face. Annja raised the pistol to back him down, then another heavy-caliber round exploded through the wall and smashed into him, sprawling him dead before her.

Grabbing the case containing the pieces of the Maze, Annja ducked, knowing that wherever the sniper was, he could somehow see into the room. They weren't safe there, and the bullets exchanged outside the back room let her know they weren't safe out there either.

Desperate, Annja glanced at the walls, realizing then that three of the walls were prefabricated. She looked over to Klykov, who had dropped down into a crouch in the corner.

Staying low, Annja slipped a multi-tool knife from her backpack. She slashed a large *X* across the wall, slicing deeply into the Sheetrock to score it. Balancing on one foot and her hands, she kicked the wall, shattering it. On her knees, she battered the broken surface and yanked the pieces away, exposing the studs and the opposite wall.

The cratered opening let out into another room, this one an office with a window.

The wall studs were sixteen inches apart. Annja shimmied out of her backpack and shoved it into the office, following it quickly with the case that held the Maze. She slipped through, then turned back for Klykov.

"Come on."

Klykov looked at the wall studs doubtfully, but took off his coat and tossed it through. Then he followed, getting stuck only for an instant.

"Smart," he said as the din of gunfire echoed around them.

"Lucky," Annja replied. "But unless we find a way out of here, we've just gone from one mousetrap to another."

Klykov took up a position beside the hole. Blood leaked from his left shoulder.

"How badly are you wounded?" Annja asked.

"A scratch. Find a way out of here while I keep watch."

Knowing that Klykov's wound didn't matter if they didn't

find a way out, Annja scanned the office. Her immediate thought was that this was Shirasaki's personal space. A large desk with an executive chair in back, two smaller chairs in front and several shelves filled with small artifacts.

The only door led into the main museum, but there was a window on the side. Annja rose up and looked outside at the narrow alley that separated the museum from the building next door.

"There's an alley. Maybe fifteen feet across. It's made of stone and should provide some cover from the sniper."

Klykov nodded. "Then we go. We cannot stay here. Shirasaki and whoever is fighting out there both want us dead."

Annja stood and picked up one of the chairs in front of the desk. "We go fast."

"Of course." Klykov stood and pulled his hat on tightly.

Twisting her hips, Annja threw the chair through the window. A shower of broken glass spun out over the alley. Grabbing the small area rug from the center of the room, she heaved it over the windowsill to provide protection from the glass shards.

She pulled her backpack over her shoulder and picked up the case in one hand. Heaving herself through the window, she landed on her feet on the other side and immediately sprinted for the building, hoping that the sniper hadn't yet spotted them making their escape.

Klykov came through the window immediately after her. He landed wrong, though, and fell, scrambling at once to get to his feet. As he shoved himself up, a large-caliber bullet hit the alley pavement and left a cracked crater where his head had been only a moment before.

At the corner of the building, Annja spotted the rooftop sniper a hundred yards away, well beyond a reasonably accurate pistol shot. Klykov reached the building, but a bullet chewed a chunk off its corner.

"The other men the sniper is working with will know we have escaped." Klykov searched the area. "They will come after us."

Annja knew they couldn't outrun the gunmen if pursued

on foot. She was too burdened and Klykov was wounded. She pointed to the closest of the three SUVs parked in front of the museum.

"There."

"A driver may have been left behind."

"I know." Annja freed her captured pistol and, carrying the case in one hand, sprinted for the vehicle. She hoped that the keys had been left in the SUV. Hot-wiring on the fly wasn't anything new to her, but they had absolutely no time for that.

The driver stood on the other side of the vehicle with a pistol in his hand. His attention was divided between the front of the museum and the street. He heard Annja and Klykov running toward him and turned, swinging the pistol around.

Annja didn't know if she fired first or Klykov did. The gunshots, several of them, cracked in quick syncopation. The driver went down. Annja passed her pistol to Klykov, then reached for the door, yanking it open and breathing a sigh of relief when she saw the keys in the ignition. She pulled herself up into the seat as Klykov opened the door behind her and clambered in.

Tossing her backpack and the case onto the floorboard in front of the passenger seat, Annja started the engine and yanked the transmission into Drive as a handful of gunmen bolted from the entrance to the museum.

"Hang on."

"Drive," Klykov responded. He had both guns up and was firing methodically, hitting the gunmen but not doing much damage because they were wearing vests. Bullets raked the SUV's side, knocked out the windows, but didn't penetrate the body.

One of the SUVs suddenly exploded, turning into a fireball. Shrapnel and the concussive wave slammed into the gunmen, knocking them down and ending the lethal spray of bullets.

Amazed, Annja glanced in her rearview mirror as she passed, and spotted Nguyen Rao running after their SUV. At the street's edge, she tapped on the brake and slowed the vehicle so Rao could catch up.

Klykov was already tracking Rao with his weapons.

"Don't shoot him," Annja said. "He's on our side. I think."

Klykov nodded grimly and held his fire. Rao reached the other side of the SUV and opened the door, sliding in beside Klykov. Annja accelerated into traffic, leaving the museum behind and trying to think of where she could ditch the SUV and where they were going to hide.

"You turned their vehicle into a bomb?" Klykov said to Rao.

Rao nodded. "I knew the two of you were trapped in the building. I thought I would create a distraction, perhaps split their forces, and that somehow I could find you in the confusion. Before I could do that, I saw you run across the alley. I put a rag in the gas tank of one of the SUVs, thinking I would put that vehicle out of commission and maybe injure some of them. Then you stole this vehicle." He nodded. "You work very fast."

"Sequeira and his people work very fast, too," Annja said as she negotiated a lane exchange in heavy traffic. "We need a place to go to ground."

"I have a place."

37

"This is your *place*?" Annja stared at the small temple ahead of them. Traditional naga heads stood out in bold relief on either side of the double doors covered in red lacquer. Brightly colored Shiva lingams brandished swords and snarling faces. The style of the temple was more Khmer than Japanese Shinto. After ditching the SUV in Nagasaki a short distance from Shirasaki's private museum, certain they hadn't been followed, Annja, Rao and Klykov walked a few blocks, then caught a taxi. They'd changed taxis three more times as they'd driven to Kitakyushu in Fukuoka Prefecture, spending hours to complete the relatively short drive.

Rao had been adamant that they not bring trouble to their final destination.

"This is the Temple of Small Streams," Rao said. "We will be welcome here. Wait, please."

Annja studied Klykov as he took up a post beside her. He looked a little grayer than he normally did, but he was standing on his own two feet and was alert. She had dressed his wound and bought him a fresh shirt while walking through a market. The damage wasn't life threatening, but she knew he was in pain.

"How are you doing?" she asked.

"I am fine, Annja. Thank you for your concern, but you needn't worry. It will take more than a scratch to kill me."

"Are you still happy about coming along?"

Klykov grinned at her. "I would not have missed this. I will have many stories to tell my comrades when I return. They will all be envious of me. And do not worry. I will continue."

Although she knew he was pushing himself and exhausting his reserves, Annja didn't bother trying to argue with him.

Being near the end of a particularly twisty pursuit of archaeological lore filled everyone involved with nervous excitement.

"Do you trust this man?" Klykov nodded slightly toward Rao, who was still conversing with the monks.

Annja thought seriously about that, then she nodded. "Bart does, and I'm pretty sure I do, too."

"Why?"

"The same reasons I feel like I can trust you."

Klykov scowled. "You trust too easily. So does your friend."

Amused, Annja smiled. "Bart told me he trusts you, too."

"Well," Klykov said, "the detective is at least fifty percent correct."

INSIDE THE TEMPLE, the monks showed Annja, Rao and Klykov to a tiny room where Rao said they could stay until they made other arrangements. Although the monks displayed keen interest in what had brought the group there, no one asked questions. They did, however, bring food, all of it Cambodian cuisine featuring fish paste, mixed with pork and served with cucumbers, squash soup and sticky rice.

As they ate at a low table and sat cross-legged on the floor, Annja reassembled the Maze and brought Rao up to date on what they had learned from Ishii and Shirasaki. Rao sat quietly and listened, his eyes watchful as the Maze took shape. For the first time, Annja noticed how some of the wooden pieces seemed attracted to each other while others didn't fit together so easily. She ignored that for now and concentrated instead on the assembly.

"I cannot believe I am seeing this." Rao stared at the completed construction. "The elders in the temple had believed the Maze lost or destroyed. It disappeared before the Elephant of Ishana vanished."

"Speaking of the Elephant, what if it's not the genuine article?" Klykov was picking up where he had left off earlier.

Rao's lips twitched. "Rumors suggested that many copies of the Elephant had been made to throw off anyone who came looking for it."

"Replicas?" The possibility gave Annja pause. "I haven't heard anything about replicas of the Elephant."

"I have never seen a replica," Rao replied.

"There's only one way to find out if this statue is the real Elephant." Annja reached for her backpack and took the case from within. "Ishii didn't get to the part about how the Elephant is supposed to find its home."

"According to the legends that were handed down to my temple elders," Rao said, "the Elephant was crafted from rock embued by a gift from Shiva. After receiving this gift, it is said that it would always know its home when it was within the Maze." The golden light from the candles the monks had supplied to light the room played gently over the planes of his face.

"How is it supposed to do that?" Annja tapped the assembled Maze with her forefinger. "There isn't a groove or any method to attach the Elephant."

"Once the two are together, the story recounts that the divine will of Shiva will drive the Elephant to the location of the Temple of the Dreaming Rumdul."

Gently, Annja placed the Elephant in the center of the Maze along one of the trails represented there.

The Elephant sat and did not move for a moment, then the statue quivered and slowly began sliding across the Maze. Not believing what she was seeing, Annja had to resist plucking the Elephant up from the Maze. Tensely, she watched it continue across the terrain, winding through hills and valleys, through the jungle—though it actually slid through or over the representative pieces, and began to climb one of the mountains.

Halfway up the mountain, the Elephant came to a stop. It stood tilted slightly sideways.

Staring at the statue, Annja felt certain it had gotten stuck. She attempted to remove the Elephant from the Maze and discovered that some force held it to the wooden construction. Gingerly, she pulled it free, then ran the Elephant over the surface slowly. She felt the attraction then, but the farther she got away from the mountain, the attraction grew steadily less.

Understanding then, Annja grinned in amused appreciation.

"What is happening?" Klykov asked.

"The whole Maze has lodestone built into it. Probably beads of it worked into the wood, with increasing density in the layers to pull the Elephant along till it reaches the strongest magnetic point on the board." Annja placed the statue back on the lacquered wooden surface at a different starting point and the Elephant shivered and once more began its trek across the Maze.

"Magnets?" Klykov watched the Elephant with bright interest.

"Not magnets," Annja said. "Magnets as we think of them are artificially created with electricity, usually pieces of steel or iron, something that can be given a permanent magnet charge. Lodestone, on the other hand, is a naturally occurring magnetic substance that also retains a permanent magnetic charge. The strongest of those is a mineral called magnetite. Judging from the strength of the magnetic field, what's embedded in the wood of this Maze has got to be magnetite."

The Elephant reached the mountain again and stopped once more, seemingly defying gravity because it should have tipped over.

"Some of the current thinking is that lodestones are charged by magnetic fields that occur from lightning-bolt strikes."

"Lightning strikes cause the magnetite to become magnetic?" Rao asked.

Annja nodded. "Some scientists think so. Not just magnetic for a little while, but magnetic permanently. Lodestones, not magnets, were originally used in compasses. Lodestone in Middle English means *leading stone*, which is where the name came from, because they led compass users home."

"The men who put this board together were very clever," Klykov said with a note of appreciation.

"Definitely." Annja stared at the Maze. "If we can find this location, if we can find this mountain, chances are good that we can find the hidden temple."

"It should not be too difficult," Rao said.

"Shirasaki couldn't find it, and he was using satellite imagery."

"Several hundred years have passed since the temple was hidden." Rao rested his hands on his knees while he sat in a full lotus position with ease. "The land has changed."

"That's the problem."

"However," Rao went on, "the monks I am working with have maps that go back to those days. They will show the land as it was then. We have access to those." He nodded at the Maze. "Now that we have this, we can find this valley… and hopefully that mountain."

One of the young monks entered the small room and addressed Rao. They spoke quickly, then Rao got to his feet. "We need to go. The brothers tell me that men who, judging from their description, are men serving Sequeira are searching the neighborhood for us."

Dissatisfied with the amount of time they'd had to devote to understanding the board and the statue, Annja dissembled the Maze and packed the pieces away, then got to her feet, slung her backpack over her shoulder and picked up the case. "How are they finding us so quickly?"

"That is a question we'll have to address later." Rao pointed toward the door. "For now we must once more escape. There is a back way out of the temple."

SEQUEIRA STRODE INTO the temple and looked around the dim rooms. His men had secured the small structure and stood conspicuously with drawn weapons.

"Who's in charge here?" Sequeira demanded.

One of the old men stepped forward. His face was weathered and blotchy from age. A large birthmark marred his forehead over his right eyebrow. "I am most senior among our brethren."

"Where is Annja Creed?" Sequeira moved menacingly next to the man.

The old man shook his head. "I know no one by that name."

"Nguyen Rao brought a woman and an old man here with him," Sequeira stated. "Don't bother lying to me. This is true."

"It is true. Brother Nguyen brought visitors to the temple."

"Where are they?"

"They have gone."

"Where did they go?"

The old man shook his head. "Several minutes ago they left the temple. That is the last I have seen of them."

Sequeira cursed and lifted his pistol, pointing it at the birthmark. For a moment, he held that position. The old monk never batted an eye and waited calmly to see if he would live or die.

Finally, Sequeira realized killing the old man might bring down even more trouble for him here in Nagasaki. Shirasaki wouldn't be helpful with the local police.

Sequeira lowered his pistol and put it away. Turning, he walked out of the temple and fished his sat phone from his pocket. He texted Brisa.

CREED'S GONE. DO YOU STILL HAVE A FIX ON HER?

YES. SHE'S A HUNDRED AND TWENTY-SIX METERS FROM YOUR PRESENT POSITION. SHE'S STAYING PUT.

SEND ME THE LOCATION. Excited again, thinking that Annja Creed and her companions believed themselves hidden, Sequeira called his team together and they climbed back into their vehicles.

FRANTICALLY, ANNJA SEARCHED her backpack, knowing a tracking device had to be there somewhere. That was the only idea she could think of to explain Sequeira's ability to know her location. Klykov and Rao had instantly agreed.

She'd changed her clothing and she had already checked her coat. Even though she hadn't found the device on her coat, she'd decided not to take the chance that two tracking devices weren't being used. She'd hung the coat in a noodle shop they'd passed, then kept walking, searching the backpack.

"It's got to be here." She ran her hands along the outside of the backpack, feeling for any irregularity. With as much rough handling as the backpack had been victim to over the years, the surface was also intimately familiar to her and the idea of losing it pained her. She liked old things, and her backpack was one of those.

Klykov held her elbow and guided her along the street, avoiding collisions with pedestrians. Rao kept watch for Sequeira and his stormtroopers, who had to be closing in on them. The thought that they were only seconds away was unnerving.

"Perhaps you should abandon the backpack," Klykov suggested.

"Not until I have to."

"It's a backpack, Annja. It can be replaced."

"This backpack and I have been through a lot together. Plus, I'm not going to be able to find another one that holds everything I carry the way this one does. It was handmade for me."

"Would you forfeit your life—*our* lives—for a vanity?"

"No." Annja strengthened her resolve, knowing she would lose the backpack before she let anything happen to Klykov or Rao. "If I don't find it in the next— *ah*!" Her fingers quickly dug out what looked like a straight needle with a crystalline bead about the size of a stylus point at one end. A trace of circuitry gleamed in the stem.

She stopped and looked at the device. "I've never seen anything like this."

Klykov glanced at it, then tugged on her sleeve and got her moving again. "It is indeed a tracking device. It has a GPS locater. A very clever gadget."

"You've seen these before?"

"*Da.* A few times. In the business I do, I find myself sometimes involved in situations where you have to know about such things."

Annja stared at the tracking device. "When was this put on my backpack?" The past several days had been so busy that she couldn't remember. There had been plenty of opportunities at the Seventh-Kilometer Market when she'd come into contact with Sequeira's enforcers.

But then she had to wonder how they had found her there in the first place. The mystery was maddening.

She dismissed the question, knowing that she wouldn't figure that out anytime soon. And that wasn't the most intriguing conundrum facing her. The Temple of the Dreaming Rumdul was in Cambodia awaiting discovery.

Focusing on that, she tossed the tracking device into the gutter and kept going.

WALKING QUICKLY ALONG the sidewalk, shoving through pedestrians that didn't get out of his way fast enough, Sequeira scanned the street where Brisa said Annja Creed was located. Brisa had insisted the American woman was there, surely within view.

"Does anyone have eyes on Creed?" he barked over the comm.

There was no answer.

Incensed, Sequeira stood in the middle of the sidewalk. "She's here! Find her!"

His men spread out, moving quickly along both sides of the street. Their vehicles waited at either end of the block. They had already started to draw attention. Sequeira knew it wouldn't be long before police officials came to inquire as to what their business was.

"Sir? I've found something."

Sequeira spotted one of his men kneeling in the street. The man picked up a small object and held it out. He was too far away for Sequeira to see the object clearly, but Sequeira felt certain he knew what it was.

"She found the tracking device. She's in the wind."

Cursing, driving away pedestrians through the sole strength of his anger, Sequeira spun and searched helplessly for any sign of Annja Creed. Many people walked along the shop-lined street. None of them were Annja Creed or her companions. Sequeira felt helpless.

He'd lost. She had the Elephant, the Maze and her freedom.

His phone buzzed for attention. He peered at the screen, seeing the text from Brisa.

THORN HAS BREACHED THE MONKS' COMPUTERS IN PHNOM PENH. WHEN NGUYEN TALKS TO THEM AGAIIN, AND HE WILL, WE CAN TRACK HIM. WE CAN STILL FIND THEM.

Sequeira smiled, and the deep hunger to kill ignited within him again. The hunt was back on.

38

Behind the wheel of the Land Rover, Annja followed the tenuous, seldom-traveled trail through the verdant growth atop the Damrei Mountains. The range ran along the western shoreline of Cambodia. Annja and Klykov had traveled to Phnom Penh with Rao and been greeted by the monks of the temple Rao served.

While they had stayed there, the monks had been kind, giving their guests rooms to stay in and delicious meals to eat. Discovering the region where the temple was believed to be located had taken three days. Three days of hard searching through hundreds of maps by nearly forty monks and the hunt had become more tense.

Annja had guessed that Rao was forced to make a case for herself and Klykov to continue pursuing the temple because the elder monks hadn't wanted them to be allowed involvement. Rao had reluctantly affirmed that when they had talked the night before they had left.

"They do not fault you, Annja," Rao had told her. "They recognize your efforts and your cooperation with us, but the elders do not trust many people."

Annja couldn't blame the monks, either, but she had been happily relieved to know they were allowing her to participate in the rest of the search.

Rao had grinned at her then. "They also know that you will not simply walk away at this point, and that you would search for the temple on your own if you had no other choice. They would rather you were somewhere they could watch over you."

"*Somewhere* being with you?"

"That was my suggestion."

As suggestions went, being with Rao was a good one. Of course, there was the matter of the nine other monks that had accompanied them from Phnom Penh. Two of the monks rode with Annja, Rao and Klykov—who had refused to be left behind or go home, and who was proving to have an indomitable constitution.

The other seven monks rode in two more Land Rovers with the camping gear and supplies. They had come fully equipped and armed with ancient as well as modern weapons. As it turned out, Rao's temple beliefs revered life, but they had no problems fiercely protecting their own when threatened.

Steadily, the caravan rolled into the dank heart of the mountains. So close to the coastline, the climate remained temperate and muggy.

Annja drove because she was more skilled with the Land Rover than Rao, and she led the expedition because she was a better judge of the terrain. The monk drivers had reluctantly learned that lesson when both of them had gotten their vehicles stuck while attempting to lead, causing the expedition delays that had added hours on to the trip.

As the grade grew steeper, Annja downshifted and the transmission groaned in protest. Even with four-wheel-drive, the tires occasionally grabbed hold of loose ground and spun out, throwing dirt and rock in vicious sprays. Klykov clung to his seat belt with white knuckles but didn't speak. With wide eyes, he stared out over the broken countryside that plunged on the western side of the mountain ridge. Farther west, the Gulf of Siam gleamed in the afternoon sunlight.

Finally, after several instances of churning tires and grinding gears, Annja coaxed the Land Rover to the summit and pulled ahead to allow the other two vehicles to slide in behind them. She let the engine idle for a moment as she reached for the water canteen between the seats next to her backpack. The hot tropical climate drained moisture from them like a sauna. She drank deeply and searched the surrounding jungle for the landmarks they'd found in the Maze.

The histories kept by the monks were amazingly complete. Still, finding the right maps had taken prodigious effort. Matching them up against satellite imagery hadn't taken quite as long to accomplish, but that had required a different skill set and they'd been aided by computer programs. The monks proved surprisingly proficient with technology.

Annja felt confident they were in the right area.

After she finished drinking her fill, she capped the canteen and put it back between the seats. Then she picked up the binoculars from her backpack and started searching out the next route.

"I think I see the mountain." Rao sat in the passenger seat with another pair of binoculars.

"Where?" Annja asked.

Rao pointed and Annja followed his direction, spotting a familiar-looking mountain peak perhaps three miles away. The land looked much different than the Maze had portrayed it, but the tall precipice appeared pretty much as it had been depicted on the Maze model.

But the distance between looked almost impossible to cross, like landscape from another world. The jungle was an impenetrable wall of overflowing growth. Miles away in the distance, Phnom Bokor, the tallest mountain of the Damrei range, stood above the other spires.

"Is this the mountain we are searching for?" Klykov asked as he bent foward between the seats.

"I think so." Annja pulled her hair back from her face and banded it into a ponytail. She put the Land Rover in gear again. "We'll know soon enough."

WHAT THEY HAD been calling a *road* played out over a mile from the mountain, growing steadily less apparent till at times Annja hadn't been certain she was actually following it. But her navigation had been good and they'd picked up remnants of it short distances later on till it finally just became nonexistent. The going had been made harder by intermittent streams and muddy ground that remained almost invisible till they'd arrived in the middle of them.

Annja got out and saw to her gear and Klykov's, while Rao and the monks divvied out what they considered to be necessary supplies. What they couldn't carry, they left with the Land Rovers. In addition to her backpack, Annja carried a small bedroll and two-man tent, a chest pack with a week's rations, water canteens, a medical kit and water purification tablets.

Klykov carried his own bedroll and supplies. He also packed two pistols and a Dragunov sniper rifle, a Russian weapon he swore he put faith in. He hadn't had a munitions contact in Phnom Penh, but he'd had a friend of a friend who had.

Annja carried a 9mm Sig-Sauer and AK-47 because Klykov had gotten the weapons for her and insisted she carry them. She'd hesitated until Klykov had reminded her how dangerous Sequeira had been so far, and that the country they were in sometimes had bandit trouble.

Rao and his temple brothers hadn't hesitated about carrying weapons either, though Rao didn't seem as comfortable being armed. He was obviously competent with the rifle and pistol he was given, just not relaxed. The pith helmet he wore looked somewhat ridiculous, but it provided shade and a modicum of comfort.

Once everyone was set, they marched into the jungle with Annja in the lead.

SEQUEIRA LOUNGED IN short-tempered impatience in the air-conditioned comfort of the Eurocopter Super Puma. On the laptop he watched footage of the jungle expedition winding through the Damrei Mountains only a few miles away. The Super Puma was one of three that Sequeira had hired for transport to the site when he was certain Annja Creed had discovered the lost temple.

Each of Sequeira's leased helicopters carried two pilots and twelve men, giving him a small army of gunmen ready to venture into the jungle to claim whatever lay in the lost temple. The drones used to watch over Annja Creed's progress had been easy to procure, as well. Brisa continued to have amazing connections.

The hardest part for Sequeira was the waiting. The helicopter sat in a clearing near the Bokor Hill Station. The French had built the Bokor Palace Hotel & Casino on the site, flanked it with a small town to provide a necessary labor pool, then abandoned the whole lot during the First Indochina War in the 1940s, then left the site permanently when the Khmer Rouge took control of the area in 1972.

Had the casino still been operational, the waiting might have been tolerable, but the cramped space aboard the helicopter was claustrophobic. And the anger Sequeira felt over the way Annja Creed had managed to escape him time and time again churned through his guts.

Not this time, he promised himself. *This time there will be no escape.*

All they needed was the exact location of the temple.

He drank a chilled glass of champagne, never completely giving up the creature comforts he insisted on, and watched Annja Creed closing in on the mountain that appeared to be her destination.

Her final destination. Sequeira intended to carve that on Annja Creed's headstone and kick dirt over her body. Her death and the location of her grave would be one of those mysteries her viewers fawned over.

THE STEEP AND treacherous grade of the mountain prevented a straightforward ascent. Annja followed the ridges carved into the face by wind and water, zig-zagging back and forth. She also insisted that they use ropes to keep the climb safe.

The monks were sure-footed, but not used to vertical ascents. Strangely, Klykov seemed to have less difficulty than the younger men because he made no assumption about the worthiness of a prospective step without first testing it.

Drenched in sweat, Annja worked steadily, pausing to hydrate and watch over the monks and Klykov, who all trailed in her wake. She checked the time on her sat phone against the approaching sunset.

"We only have a couple hours of light left," she told Klykov and Rao. "We'll travel another hour, then set up camp."

Both men nodded in agreement.

Annja went back to the climb, searching for any signs of

the hidden temple, but it looked as if no one had come by here in a long time. She chose to view that as a positive thing.

THREE HOURS LATER, they sat in groups at the campsite around fires that burned low in the darkness. Protected behind brush and boulders situated to hide the glow of the flames, Annja sat with Klykov and Rao. The monks gathered in two groups around other fires and talked among themselves in voices that sounded more like songs than conversation. Annja envied them their language. She was good at languages, but she hadn't learned much of the Cambodian dialects.

Although they had brought MREs in their packs, the monks had foraged as they'd walked to the jungle. The result was a nice collection of wild vegetables they'd used to make a hearty soup, also flavored with spices they'd taken from the local flora. Klykov had taken the soup, but he had wanted meat, as well. Annja had reminded him that the MREs weren't known for their tasty choices and pointed out that the soup was fresh and hot. He'd eaten his fill.

Finished with her second helping, Annja scrubbed her bowl and spoon clean with a towelette and set them aside to dry. She cleaned Klykov's and Rao's bowls and silverware as well, then burned the towelettes in the fire.

With her back against a rock, Annja positioned herself so the glow coming from the fire played over her journal. She detailed the trip through the jungle in shorthand she'd learned and created for herself over the years.

"What are you writing?" Klykov asked. He capped the ibuprophen bottle he'd just taken capsules from.

"Notes, mainly."

"About what?"

"Our trip. What I've seen of the mountain."

"You've also been sketching." Klykov extended a hand. "May I see?"

Reluctantly, Annja handed the journal over. She didn't let many people look at her private thoughts, but Klykov had come a long way with her and been through a lot to be with her.

Klykov flipped slowly through the pages, taking his time with the ones that had images. "Why do you draw things if you carry a camera?"

"Because when I draw something, I feel it more than I do when I simply take a picture. Drawing is more…intimate." That was the best she could explain it. She also liked to have two different views of important sites and artifacts.

"That is a very good likeness of you," Rao said, nodding at a sketch of Klykov standing at the Seventh-Kilometer Market. The other page had a drawing of Fedotov. The man appeared even more bear-like in the image she'd drawn.

"I look old." Klykov frowned for a moment, then he smiled up at Annja. "I am joking. I know I am old." He laughed. "This is a very good picture of Fedotov. You should send him a copy."

"When this is over, maybe I will."

"*Da.* He would be very proud of such a thing." Klykov returned the journal and lay back with his hands behind his head. His latest pistol lay beside him on a towel.

Annja worked for a little while longer on her journal, letting her mind wander. Even though it was dark, it was still early for her. Apparently it wasn't too early for Klykov, though. The man was asleep within minutes and softly snoring.

Rao smiled. "He is tired."

"We've been on the run since New York." Annja put her journal away. "I suppose you have been, too."

"Yes."

"Are the monks posting guards?"

"Throughout the night, yes. We do not wish to be… surprised."

"I've had enough surprises."

"Sequeira is not a man to give up on something he wants. If we have not lost him, he will be here." Rao fed small sticks to the fire.

"I think so, too. I can help with the guard detail."

Rao shook his head. "The monks will not allow it. You are to be watched."

"They're still having trust issues?" Annja grinned to show she had no hard feelings.

"If you watch, you do not have to trust." Rao folded his arms around his knees and looked relaxed. "This temple is important to them."

"And to you?"

"Yes, but not as important as it is to them. They have been looking for it much longer than I have. I only hope that we are fortunate enough to find it."

"We'll find it," Annja replied. "It's out here."

"How do you know?"

Annja paused, trying to think of the best way to put her thoughts into words. "I just feel it, Rao. I don't know what else to say."

"Then I hope in the morning you will feel your way to where the temple lies. The longer we take, the more time Sequeira or someone like him has to catch up to us."

"I know. There's something else that's bothering me, though."

Rao looked at her inquisitively. "Yes?"

"The monks that hid the temple went to a lot of trouble to move it here. They wouldn't have left it here without defenses."

"No, I don't think they did either." Rao fed a few more sticks to the fire. "We will be careful when we find it."

39

By midmorning, Annja was covered in sweat despite the chill that clung to the mountain. The grade had increased and the going was more difficult. Even the monks, seemingly as nimble as mountain goats, struggled with the climb. What Klykov lacked in finesse and youthful vigor, he made up for in determination and managed to keep pace. From the brightness in his eyes, Annja knew the thrill of discovery was pushing him on, as well.

Even though she'd been looking, Annja hadn't noticed the stone that potentially marked the temple's hiding spot until she'd climbed above it. Standing on a small ridge to sip water and rest for just a moment, she'd gazed down over the jungle hundreds of feet below and spotted the marker.

Catching it in that moment, in the right light, from the right angle, and looking for *something*, anything really, she saw it.

"Annja?" Klykov's voice held a note of concern. "Are you all right?"

"I am." Annja smiled as the adrenaline surged through her with the promise of secrets yet to be revealed. "We found it."

"We did?" Klykov looked around.

Annja pointed down at the outcrop. "There. What do you see?"

Hesitantly, not liking the sharp edges of the mountain so much, Klykov peered over the edge. "Rocks. Trees. Brush."

"Exactly. The rocks." Annja fished in her backpack and took out her camera. She snapped a picture, certain that the magnified digitized image would better reveal what was so cleverly hidden from the human eye—yet was there once a person saw it.

She showed the captured image to Klykov, then to Rao, who had come over to join them.

"What do you see now?"

Klykov's face lost some of the tiredness that framed it when he realized what he was looking at. "It looks like the top of an elephant's head." He shook his own head. "But surely that is just a trick of the light. Or our imaginations."

Annja put the camera away and took out a metal stake. She looked for a good, stable place to hammer the stake into the rock. "That's not a trick of the light. That's the back of an elephant's head. Look at how the ears are flared out. And it's an Indian elephant, not African. The ears are small. This is it."

She hammered the stake into the rock as the word spread to the rest of the monks, who immediately ringed the cliff's edge. Rao helped her tie a rope onto the stake, then helped her rig her harness for the climb down the mountain.

Excitement swept through Annja as she positioned herself at the edge of the drop. She kept her body perpendicular to the steep rock face as she walked backwards down the mountainside, paying out the rope as she needed to. The elephant's head, not neatly carved at all but showing tool marks now that she was almost to it, was only slightly larger than she was. The tool marks were revealed in sharper relief on the underside of the rock where hundreds of years of rain and direct exposure to the elements hadn't worn them away.

Pausing beside the elephant, which she now saw was fully eight feet tall, Annja took pictures with her camera, then tucked it back into her backpack and began inspecting the elephant head. She was certain of the carving, and feeling the edges beneath her fingertips, she grew even more convinced of her find.

However, there was no immediate clue about what she was supposed to do next.

She looked up at the monks, Klykov and Rao clustered together, all anxiously awaiting whatever news she had to give. "Rao, can you lower the tool bag?"

Rao secured the bag fast to a rope and lowered it to her, tying it on at the appropriate length so it would hang beside her.

She reached inside the bag and took out brushes and cleaning tools to work on the elephant, hoping there would be further clues about how to proceed on the carving.

"I am coming down," Rao called out.

"Come ahead."

Rao dropped a line on the other side of the elephant head and made the descent quickly and carefully. In a couple minutes, he hung beside her in his harness.

"May I help?" Rao offered.

Annja handed over another tool and brush. They worked together, hanging on the side of the mountain as the wind pried at them with chill fingers and the sun made them sweat inside their jackets.

Her efforts revealed the eye and the tusk that lay alongside the trunk, which was curled under the massive head. As the details became cleaner, she couldn't help but think of the sculptor who had worked with the existing rock. Whoever that had been had clung to the rock much as she was doing. Now that the head was more revealed, she saw that it had been cut out of what had been a much wider outcrop.

"Whoever did this spent a lot of time getting this right." Annja brushed at the eye, getting more dirt out of the recessed area.

"Do you know what the Damrei Mountains are known colloquially as?"

Annja answered without hesitation. "The Elephant Mountains."

Rao smiled and nodded. "At first I thought that the elephant statue was a random choice, or one dedicated to Shiva."

"Or Ganesha," Annja said.

"Perhaps. Then, finding this, I wonder if the elephant was made for the mountains or the mountains were named for the legend about the elephant."

"Maybe we'll find out once we locate the temple."

They worked in silence for a few more minutes. Only the scraping of the tools and the brushes interrupted the near-silence of the wind. Small debris continued to fall down the mountain and the wind carried the dust away.

"Annja," Rao called. "Look at this."

Carefully, Annja paid out more line so that she could scramble under the elephant head and join Rao. Clinging to the line and to the elephant's chin, she peered up at four small holes along the elephant's jaw behind its ear. The holes were so small that even her pinky would not fit. None of the holes was equidistant, and she knew what Rao was going to ask for next.

"You have the elephant?"

Annja dug the statue out of her backpack and held on to it tightly, knowing that if she lost it they might look for days before they found it in the jungle below.

If the fall didn't destroy it.

"I tested these holes." Rao inserted a narrow scraping tool that barely fit. "I detected movement in all of them. Something is in there."

Gingerly, Annja grasped the elephant and turned it so that its feet pointed out from her hand. For the first time she realized the elephant was shaped so that none of the legs were the same length. The rounded stomach threw off the lengths.

"There is an old saying about the Temple of the Dreaming Rumdul," Rao said in a quiet voice. "The legend goes that you must whisper into the elephant's ear to find the temple."

"Elephant whisperer, then." Slowly, Annja eased the elephant's legs into the holes. She leaned in closely and listened as thin scrapes echoed from within the rock. The tone of the scraping led her to believe that somewhere within the massive rock carving there was a hollow spot, and that made her excitement grow.

She moved the elephant several times, and was beginning to think that whatever was supposed to happen within the rock had gotten too old to ever work again. She hated to think about resorting to explosives, and hadn't even thought about finding any, still she was betting that Klykov could have worked out something.

A series of clicks suddenly came in rapid syncopation. The elephant head no longer simply resonated with the clicks, now it vibrated.

"Watch out." Annja readied herself to kick away, thinking the elephant head might fall away from the side of the cliff.

Instead, a section of the cliff below the elephant head recessed and revealed an opening nearly six feet square.

"The gateway to the Temple of the Dreaming Rumdul can be found in the shadow of the Elephant of Ishana," Rao said.

Annja grinned at him. "Might have helped if you had mentioned that earlier."

Still astonished, Rao shook his head. "The shadow could have been anywhere, or meant anything."

"Evidently it meant exactly what it said." Annja let out more line and dropped down to the opening. Sunlight penetrated the darkness for only a few feet, but enough illumination got inside to show a long tunnel lay on the other side of the entrance.

CAPTIVATED BY WHAT was taking place on the computer screen, Sequeira stared as Annja Creed clambered inside the opening beneath the rock outcrop where she had been dangling. Within minutes, she had made her line fast and the people with her started climbing down after her, bringing with them packs of equipment.

Sequeira called his second-in-command. "Nicolau."

"Yes, sir."

"Get the men ready to move out. Annja Creed has found what we are looking for."

"Yes, sir."

It would not take them long to fly to the mountainside, and they could easily be lowered to the cliff by the helicopters. However, Sequeira resented the fact that Annja Creed was the first person to enter the lost temple after he had been looking for it for so long.

Whatever was there, though, he would have. He told himself that was all that mattered.

HOLDING THE MAGLITE LED flashlight in front of her, Annja followed the severe incline leading into the heart of the mountain. The bright light pushed back the darkness, but the remaining shadows made the steep steps cut into the stone difficult to judge. They walked in single file, Rao after her and Klykov after the monk. The others followed the Russian.

The cold air held a thick, dusty musk and came up from whatever lay ahead. The opening acted as a chimney flue, drawing out the stale air. Annja just hoped there weren't any surprises lying in wait. In the narrow tunnel, the small space would be a problem.

Nearly a hundred and fifty feet into the mountain, the tunnel ended, opening into a large cavern. Six feet from the tunnel's mouth, a sudden drop-off offered a long fall, the bottom invisible in the darkness.

"Here," Rao called. He tracked his flashlight beam to the right to reveal steps cut into the wall. He flicked his light over the wall to illuminate the figures carved into the stone.

The mythic figures celebrated stories from the Hindu tales of the gods. Annja recognized Palden Lhamo, the goddess, and the only female of the Eight Guardians of the Law. The carving had been tinted to replicate her more fully. Her skin was deep blue and her hair was as red as freshly spilled blood. She rode a white mule and carried a scepter that drew down lightning from the sky above. In her other hand, she carried a human skull as a drinking cup filled with blood. Her three eyes were fierce and uncompromising.

"These people worshipped demons?" Klykov asked.

"Palden Lhamo isn't a demon," Annja said. "She is one of the Eight Guardians, or wrathful deities. They're the flip side of the *bodhisattva*, the enlightened version of the same being. They look demonic because they're supposed to influence mankind to make proper decisions."

"And nightmares," Klykov commented.

Annja took a picture with her camera. The flash eliminated the darkness for a moment and they all paused till their vision recovered.

She headed down the steps and noted the figures on the wall-carved-in bas-relief.

Annja kept walking, spotting more of the Tibetan influence on the images as well as nagas and other creatures.

Senses spinning, listening to the shuffling of their feet and their voices echoing within the vast chamber, Annja tried to take in all the art but found it too overwhelming. She only remembered bits and pieces of it as she reached the cavern floor.

On solid ground now, she took a glow stick from her backpack and placed it at the foot of the steps leading back to the opening at least a hundred feet above them. They were still somewhere in the heart of the mountain.

The monks started speaking quickly, alerting Annja to the fact they had seen something she had not. When she turned around, she saw that their flashlights had focused on a path created by cut stone and laid together to form a walkway.

Annja stepped forward, drawn by the mystery of what lay ahead. The cavern was huge and the walkway seemed to go on forever. But it stopped when her flashlight beam revealed the outer wall of the hidden temple.

40

Excitement thrummed through Annja as she surveyed the Temple of the Dreaming Rumdul. She knew at once the structure could be no other. It stood at least forty feet tall at its center, but the outer walls stood over twenty feet high.

The center dome structure reflected the beehive appearance most observers thought it was most like, but it was really meant to resemble a mountaintop. The walkway became a bridge a short distance from the temple, and the bridge spanned a moat twenty feet across. Judging from the cut edges that showed along the moat, the waterway was a manmade construction.

Annja couldn't fathom the years or the number of people it had taken to build this shrine.

"I don't know what I expected," Klykov said beside her, "but I didn't expect this. I thought the people who moved the temple here were in a hurry. I guessed that they had merely found a place to dump everything they wanted to hide from invaders."

"It might have started out like that," Annja said, "but they didn't leave it as such." She shined her light down into the dark water and saw darting forms. "There are fish, so the water's probably coming from an artesian well, something that will support life. There's a passage into and out of the mountain. At least underwater."

Annja crossed the bridge, listening to the hollow click of her boot heels as she went.

Statues decorated the ground in front of the temple on the other side of the moat. There were even stone palm trees. The monks who had built the temple hadn't been able to import the vegetation that grew outside, but they'd replicated it instead.

"How did so many people lose a place like this?" Klykov asked.

"The legend says that even though the Temple of the Dreaming Rumdul was hidden away, jealous kings searched for it," Rao said as he walked with them. "The armies came too close to finding it. In order to protect their secret, they chose to die."

"They killed themselves?"

"You must remember that the men who built this place and lived here were ordained monks who had achieved Nirvana. They did not fear death because for them death only represented a metamorphosis, a transition from one thing to another. They themselves were protected in death, but they could not protect this place. So, as the legend says, they starved themselves."

On the other side of the bridge, Annja caught a shimmer of something in the water. She redirected her flashlight and shined it down into the depths. She didn't know how deep the moat was, but the ivory reflection of a skull shone from four or five feet down.

"My god," Klykov said softly. He added his light to Annja's and Rao did the same.

Some of the monks joined them and continued the underwater exploration.

Annja removed another glow stick from her backpack, taped a stone to it with duct tape, cracked the stick to life and eased it into the water. The blue light stood out against the darkness as the stick and stone dropped into the depths. As it went down, it illuminated the skeletons that lay piled on top of each other.

The monks commented excitedly as others made the same discovery.

"They drowned themselves?" Klykov asked.

"No," Annja said quietly, "this is where those who survived the longest brought the bodies of those who died first."

AFTER THE DISCOVERY of the dead lying in the moat, the expedition's mood turned somber. Walking through the presence of death had that tendency. Annja had seen the reaction set in many times, and the more death that was present, the more somber the people became.

Still, she felt the thrill of excitement course through her as she helped open one of the huge gates at the entrance to the temple. The iron hinges squealed in protest, and one of them shattered after centuries of disuse.

She paused at the entrance, taking in the layout. Even though the central dome was ahead of her, there was an inner wall set back thirty feet. One of the young monks strode forward, drawn by the need to see more, faster. Annja recognized the same feelings inside herself, but she was able to rein them in.

The young monk stepped on a section of the flooring a few feet from her and the stone quivered just long enough to warn Annja about what was going to happen.

"Get back!" she yelled even as she hurled herself forward toward the monk.

Klykov, Rao and the others stepped back at once, aware of the shifting floor only a short distance away.

When the stones gave way beneath the monk, he dropped with a cry of surprise.

Annja threw herself flat on the stone floor at the edge of the gaping hole that had opened up and managed to grab the monk's pack in her left hand. She hoped that the pack harness was on tight and would hold.

The pack proved to be too loose. As the monk fell and she pulled on the pack, he slid out of the straps. Thankfully he was quick enough to grab one of them as he dropped. Annja shimmied to the edge of the hole before she was able to properly brace herself and keep from being pulled in after him. Her shoulder screamed in agony and burned like fire, but she held on stubbornly, refusing to let the monk fall.

Then Rao was beside her, throwing himself on the ground and reaching down after the monk. The man caught Rao's hand, and together, Annja and Rao pulled him back to solid ground.

After the man was safe, Annja picked up her dropped flashlight and shined it down into the hole. At the bottom twenty feet down, sharpened stakes set in rows awaited the unwary.

The monk thanked Annja fervently.

"Okay," Annja said as she got to her feet, "we pay attention to that warning. From now on, we go slowly and in single file. Understood?"

Everyone acknowledged her.

"I can take point," she said with a small smile, "but if any of you would rather lead, let me know."

There were no takers.

ANNJA USED A wooden staff she'd found just inside the gates to probe suspicious areas and set off traps. The temple builders had been inventive, and they hadn't intended for uninformed interlopers to survive. In addition to the pit area at the entrance, they'd found two other places where the floor broke away, and six areas that had an assortment of sharp blades that would have pierced or slashed those who weren't careful.

Shoving the staff against the third stone in the narrow walkway where she felt certain another trap lay in wait, Annja hopped away sharply as a section of the wall spun around to reveal sharp disk-shaped blades protruding from the stone. If she'd made the mistake of walking there herself, she would have been disemboweled. As it was, displaced air danced over her.

Finally, though, they found the entrance to the inner courtyard. The huge doors showed scenes of a veritable paradise lying in wait, a mountaintop overlooking a peaceful jungle where birds flew in a cloudless sky.

Annja tapped all around the gates, on the floor and on the walls. Nothing seemed amiss. She used the staff to press against the door, then dodged back out of the way as sharpened sticks thrust through the door, narrowly avoiding them.

Gently, she pushed on the door and had to put her weight behind it to get it to open. She shined her flashlight inside and found the main building towered only a few feet away. Given the distance and the darkness, it was hard to see how big the structure was.

She took glow sticks from her backpack and tossed them into the courtyard, watching as the blue pools of light did the trick. The front of the temple was nearly a hundred feet across. Judging from the structure of the dome that capped the building, the temple was a square.

Before the main temple, walkways covered the area between smaller buildings along the inner wall that flanked the courtyard. Small pebble gardens broke up the flat, lifeless landscape that had been created from the natural cavern.

Cautiously, Annja ventured inside the courtyard, testing the ground with the staff as the glow sticks provided a pool of light around her. Her footsteps echoed inside the immediate vicinity, making the temple sound hollow and empty.

The feeling that had overtaken her was unmistakable. The thrill of discovery was a drug that never got old even though she'd been through this so many times before.

The temple and this cavern were a point in history that had been frozen and forgotten except for legend and myth. Now, since it had been found, it was once more part of the world, and all the secrets it contained, all of the history, would be ready for generations to come.

She looked back over her shoulder. "Ready to go inside the temple?"

"I am. If you think it's safe."

Annja grinned at the monk. "We're not going to know that until we get there." She stepped forward and Rao followed her. Klykov matched the young monk step for step.

ALTHOUGH THE WINDS from the hovering helicopter buffeted him as he dangled from the rappelling rope, Sequeira didn't like the heights or the fact that the landing area was so small. Still, he reminded himself to focus instead on the prize that lay waiting for him.

Annja Creed and the monks had been inside the mountain for almost an hour. They were far ahead of him, but Sequeira knew that whatever was inside also remained within, and he would soon have it.

Nicolau de Figueiredo and his handpicked team were finishing up checking the climbing ropes left by Annja Creed and her party.

Two men steadied Sequeira as he touched down. He tried not to show how fearful he was of falling and looked at de Figueiredo as the mercenary approached.

De Figueiredo was lean and swarthy, and known for his cruelty, yet he always behaved in a taciturn, professional manner.

Sequeira had approved of him immediately.

He even wore sunglasses and a helmet that was a duplicate of the one Sequeira wore.

"The ropes are all in good shape, Mr. Sequeira. We will be able to use them to get access to the tunnel as soon as we have everyone gathered. I'll leave a team here to safeguard our back."

Sequeira nodded, totally preoccupied with getting inside the mountain, imagining what riches lay buried there. He glanced up and saw that Brisa's helo was descending. His heart hammered inside his chest, but he knew it was eagerness, not fear, that drove him now.

AFTER PASSING THROUGH two antechambers without encountering any more traps, Annja started to hope that no more deadly devices awaited them. Either they'd found them all or the temple builders had felt that anyone who had made it this far meant no harm.

Or they've got one extremely nasty surprise still left for us. Annja told herself not to dwell on that.

She tossed the last of her glow sticks onto the floor of the central chamber. Reflected in the soft light of the room's interior were pots containing diamonds and gold. Others held silver, coins and gems. Still more contained jewelry and bars of precious metals. Statues constructed of gold and ivory, all of them of the Buddha and the various Hindu gods, stood mixed in.

Rao spoke in his native tongue, as did Klykov, and though Annja didn't understand the words, she knew she had the gist of it. What lay before them was unbelievable.

"I thought these people took vows of poverty," Klykov said.

"We do," Rao said, "but it takes money to build a temple, to feed and clothe monks, and to help those who need assistance. The Temple of the Dreaming Rumdul was highly successful in its day. The monks left this treasure here so that the work they had started could be continued." He paused. "You have to remember, the monks who lived here gave their lives so this—their legacy—would be protected from the invading Vietnamese."

"This isn't all they left." Annja strode across the chamber to a wall of scrolls. She shined her light over them, not daring to touch them till she was certain they would survive the handling. "These are texts, probably of the temple's history, the life stories of the monks who live here, and some of them might even be discourses made by the Buddha himself." Annja smiled at the thought. Her excitement disappeared when she heard gunshots punctuate the near silence that filled the cavern.

Klykov drew his sidearm only a second or two before Annja did the same. Rao, armed now himself with a machine pistol and looking fairly adept with it, ran back through the other chambers to reach the main temple's entrance.

At the doorway, barely revealed by the flashlights in the hands of the monks that held them, Annja spotted muzzle flashes of fully automatic weapons sparking in the darkness.

A nearby monk jerked sideways and his flashlight shattered, the light extinguishing immediately as bullets ripped through it. The monk went down, then scrabbled on all fours for another position as more bullets tracked him.

"Turn off the flashlights!" Even as she yelled the order, Annja flicked off her own flashlight, followed almost immediately by Rao and Klykov.

Bullets hammered into the temple door frame beside Annja's head. Stone splinters stung her face as she took cover.

"The shooters have night-vision capability," Klykov warned. On the other side of the doorway, he rummaged in his chest pack and took out a flare pistol. He loaded the pistol and fired it into the open space above the temple.

The flare streaked upward like a shooting star, then exploded into a bright nimbus of light. The effort showed the mercenaries poring through the outer gate. All of them started stripping the NVGs they were wearing.

Klykov passed Annja the flare gun and a bag of extra flares. "Keep the flares over them. Do not allow them to use their night vision again."

Annja holstered her pistol, then reloaded the flare gun.

Klykov slid the Dragunov from his shoulder and readied the weapon. As Annja fired the flare gun into the open space again, Klykov fired his massive rifle three times, shifting the sniper weapon slightly each time.

A hundred feet away, three of the mercenaries went down as the large-caliber bullets found their targets.

The second flare joined the first, adding to the brightness. The bodies of four monks lay sprawled on the floor in spreading pools of blood. They had never stood a chance.

Pushing aside her anger and fear, Annja concentrated on fighting back. She hung the pouch of flares from her belt, thrust the reloaded flare gun into her belt as well, and unlimbered the AK-47. She sighted in on one of the mercenaries coming into the courtyard and squeezed the trigger, watching as the bullets caught the man and knocked him down.

Klykov put down two more mercenaries before Rao grabbed him and yanked him back from the doorway, then shouted a warning to Annja. "Rocket launcher!"

Annja had already seen the man with the weapon on his shoulder, had fired two shots at him and might even have hit him, before seeing the contrail spit out behind the launched grenade. She dodged back and hoped the temple walls were thick enough to withstand the coming blast.

41

The grenade detonated against the temple wall only a few feet from the door. Annja wasn't sure if the mercenary had deliberately aimed for that area or if her shots had caused him to miss his actual target.

Deafened by the blast, knocked off her feet by the concussive wave and the flying stone shrapnel that thudded against her, Annja fell and sprawled and rolled till she was able to get to her feet. She knew Sequeira's mercenaries would be on the move.

Senses reeling, Annja picked up her weapon and returned to the door just as Klykov once more set up and started firing. Two more men went down under his bullets before return fire drove him once more to shelter. Blood wept from two places on his left cheek. Annja didn't know when those wounds had happened or what had caused them.

She looked around wildly and spotted the stairs on one side of the room. They had ignored them earlier, thinking to explore them later. She darted across the doorway and joined Klykov and Rao. Knowing they couldn't hear her if she spoke because she couldn't even hear herself, she tapped them on the shoulders and pointed up the stairs.

They nodded and she took the lead, picking up her flashlight and using it to light the way. Thankfully there were no traps along the stairs.

Gaining the second floor, Annja oriented herself to the layout of the building and dashed to the rooms that overlooked the main entrance. The first two flares were dying down, their lights dimming in the open windows along the wall.

Quickly, Annja drew the flare gun and fired toward the cavern room, which they still hadn't hit, then reloaded, aimed for a different section and fired again. The bright balls of fire hung in the air and showered the temple battleground.

Annja reloaded the flare gun and watched as a group of the mercenaries streaked toward the temple entrance. Klykov managed to get two of them, but the other five disappeared from Annja's point of view.

Knowing she couldn't let the men get behind them, she tapped Klykov on the shoulder again to get his attention. Even though he couldn't hear her, she spoke to him, hoping he could read her lips.

"Stay here and shoot them."

Klykov nodded. "Where are you going?"

"Downstairs."

The old man shook his head. "That is too dangerous."

"It's just as dangerous to let them come up behind us. Stay and keep shooting."

Reluctantly, Klykov nodded and wheeled back to the window, managing to pick off yet another mercenary almost immediately.

Annja ran for the stairs, joined by Rao. She shook her head at him and pointed back toward Klykov. Rao ignored her and ran faster. They arrived at the stairs at the same time, just as the first of the mercenaries reached the top step.

Unable to get the AK-47 ready in time, Annja let go of the assault rifle and reached into the *otherwhere* for the sword. She closed her hand around the hilt and began swinging it instantly. The sword slicked through the air and through the mercenary's neck just as he fired a stream of bullets that blew heat over the side of Annja's face.

Astonished by the blood pouring from him, the mercenary stood transfixed till Annja put a foot in the center of his chest and kicked him back down the stairs. The mercenary flew backward, taking out two of his comrades and sending them all tumbling down the steps.

The other two flattened to either side of the stairs and brought their weapons up. Rao planted himself and fired his pistol at one of the men, catching him in the face and driving him backward.

Annja drew the sword back quickly as the second man fired and missed her by inches. She threw the sword like a spear and the heavy blade pierced the mercenary's chest.

Afraid their position would get run over otherwise, Annja sprinted forward as the two men who'd been knocked back by the first dead man started to regroup at the bottom of the steps. She ran to the side of the stairwell, bent to put her hands on the stone railing and pushed off as she went over, spinning in the air as bullets hammered the spot where she'd been.

She arched her body and came down on her feet, willing the sword into her hand. The mercenary closest to her lunged for her with his weapon. Fortunately, she had time to swing the sword and connect with his ribcage, slicing through his body. Leaving the sword embedded, she shoved the dead man back against the other mercenary, pinning both against the wall. The man struggled to reach over his dead partner but Rao shot the man while coming down the stairs.

Yanking the sword free of the dead man, Annja turned to face the next wave of attackers. The three mercenaries hadn't expected to be so suddenly in the midst of a battle after following the others inside, and the close quarters threw them off.

Stepping into the first man, Annja swung the sword, cutting through both of his arms as he held his assault rifle. Before the man had time to register surprise or pain, Annja slashed with the sword again, killing him. She kicked him back into the mercenary behind him and turned her attention to the man on her right.

Annja spun the dead man around and stepped behind him to take cover. His body armor stopped the bullets his companion fired, striking him in the chest while Annja held him still. She drew her pistol and fired from under her makeshift shield's arm, putting three rounds into the other mercenary's head.

As the man fell, Annja released the dying man, summoned the sword back to her hand and advanced on the remaining mercenary. He fired at her, but she ducked to the side, planted her feet and swung the sword, taking off the man's head.

Without wasting a minute, Annja returned the sword to

the *otherwhere* and pulled the flare pistol out once more as she closed on the doorway. Nine dead men lay behind her and several others, brought down by Klykov's marksmanship as well as Annja's and Rao's bullets, lay in the courtyard.

The monks had settled themselves in the courtyard now and used their familiarity with temple grounds to counter the superior firepower and numbers of the mercenaries. Klykov's sniper rifle boomed, punctuating the din of noise again and again. Annja didn't see what the old gangster was shooting, but she didn't doubt that he was finding his targets.

Rao took up a position on the other side of the doorway as Annja pointed the flare gun up at the cavern roof and pulled the trigger. The flare rocketed up as she reloaded the pistol and put it away, and then the flare ignited, throwing a fresh wave of red light over the courtyard.

The Dragunov blasted again, and on the opposite side of the square a mercenary toppled from the wall, spilling onto the hard stones. In the fresh light, making everything look like it was lit by hell itself, Annja scanned the impromptu battlefield. So many were dead, but most of them were the mercenaries.

Sequeira, if he was the one who had brought them here, couldn't have been expecting that.

But where was he?

A startled cry of pain pierced the deafening sounds that filled Annja's hearing.

Whirling, bringing her assault rifle up to her shoulder, Annja gazed back up the stairs and spotted Klykov standing there. The Russian gangster's head was bleeding profusely and his arms had been wrenched painfully behind him. A knife at his throat kept him still.

"Annja Creed," a woman's voice called out. In the dimming glow of the dying flares, the woman's face stood out briefly as a pallid oval behind Klykov's shoulder. "You will put down your weapons and surrender, or I will kill the old man."

"Do not do it," Klykov protested. "She will kill me anyway."

The knife flicked across Klykov's throat and drew a line of blood.

Annja feared that the woman had sliced Klykov's throat and that he was dying as she watched helplessly. But Klykov remained on his feet and grimaced in pain.

"Put down your weapons," the woman ordered in a calm voice. "Otherwise I will not cut shallowly again."

Annja dropped the AK-47, then added the pistol and the flare gun. She nodded at Rao, who reluctantly put down his weapons, as well.

"Step away from the weapons." A little more confident now, the woman let herself be better seen.

In the uncertain shadows, Annja recognized the woman as the tourist she had met in Odessa. Right then she knew how the tracking device had been put on her backpack.

"Step away from the weapons," the woman repeated.

Annja did, moving away from the weapons, stepping over the bodies she'd left from her earlier attack.

Out in the courtyard, the remaining mercenaries regrouped and drove the monks back with massive firepower, full-auto and grenades. The unforgiving detonations signaled the damage being done to the inner courtyard and Annja hated her inability to do something.

Less than a minute later, Sequeira stood in the chamber room with them. Three mercenaries had survived the sprint with him. He grinned up at the woman. "Ah, Brisa. I see that you found your way inside."

"I did," the woman replied. She shook Klykov. "I had to resist killing this old fool, but I thought he might serve us better as collateral to use against this woman." She guided Klykov down the steps.

Klykov's eyes burned brightly and Annja knew the old man was thinking of trying to break free or sacrifice himself so they he couldn't be used.

"Don't, Leonid," Annja said. "Please. I want all of us to get out of this alive if there's a way. And there's a way."

"You're not getting out of this," Sequeira said. "You've cost me too much money to allow such a thing." He paused and smiled. "Brisa, cut the old man's throat."

With a harsh cry, Annja ran toward Klykov, keeping her hands in sight above her head.

"Do not kill Creed yet," Sequeira ordered. "We can use her to—"

Whatever Sequeira had been about to say was lost. Brisa smiled at Annja over Klykov's shoulder, certain of herself. Thankfully, she waited and did not kill Klykov immediately.

Annja thrust forward, reaching into the *otherwhere*, and surprising Brisa because the woman expected to easily dodge a punch that was coming too soon. The woman was even more surprised when steel glinted in Annja's hands and a razor-sharp blade slashed her head, killing her instantly.

The knife dropped from Brisa's nerveless fingers and bounced off Klykov's chest. The old gangster was already in motion, diving for the nearest assault rifle left lying on the floor.

Whirling, hoping she was ahead of the bullets that she knew had to be coming at her, Annja flung the sword. The blade sped across the distance to the nearest mercenary. The tip pierced the man's chest, killing him in less than a heartbeat and sinking into the man behind him, as well.

Klykov blasted the other remaining mercenary, but Sequeira shot him, then chased Rao into hiding. As Klykov fell, Annja charged toward Sequeira and pulled the sword from the *otherwhere* once more. She stared at Sequeira across the muzzle of his weapon, seeing the troubled look on his face, then she swung the sword and took the gun and Sequeira's face away.

The dead man toppled backward as the mercenary who had been pierced by the sword but not killed brought up his weapon. Annja heard the gunshots and waited to feel the pain. Then she noticed the bullet hole in the man's head as he fell back.

Only a few feet away, Rao lay on the floor with a captured pistol in one hand. He kept the weapon pointed at the mercenary.

Remembering Klykov, Annja returned to the old man's

side, fearing that he was dead. Instead, he had been shot in the same shoulder that had already been wounded.

"It is bad luck to be shot in the same arm twice," Klykov said.

"It's better *not* to get shot," Annja pointed out.

Klykov shrugged, then regretted it with a grimace. "I will keep that in mind." He looked at her, then glanced at the sword in her hand. "You always seem to find these things."

Annja smiled at him. "I think it's better that I do."

"*Da*. So do I."

Epilogue

Three weeks after her return from Cambodia, Annja sat across from Bart McGilley at a table in Maria's, one of their favorite restaurants. The first few days she had been back, Annja had caught up on her life—as much as she was able, and made apologies to Doug Morrell for the *upior* vampire story that she hadn't been able to deliver.

She was currently in a time crunch for the next segment on *Chasing History's Monsters*, but she knew from experience that something would work out. Things always did.

There had been some tension between her and Bart at first, and getting an agreement to have dinner had taken some careful planning. Both of them were busy.

"So the elephant Benyovszky found in the storage rental led to an actual treasure?" Bart shook his head in disbelief.

"It did." Annja dipped a chip in queso and ate it.

"How much treasure are you talking about?"

Annja reached into her backpack and took out her tablet. She booted it up and opened the folder that had pictures of the temple treasure with her standing in front of it. It looked, she had to admit, like quite the haul.

"How much do you think it's worth?" Bart asked.

"Millions."

He grinned, nonplussed. "You say that like it's nothing."

"You're talking about material worth. That's not what I'm interested in. The texts we found document a whole period of history that we don't know much about."

"You are aware how many people will care about that?" Bart lifted an eyebrow.

Annja didn't reply because she didn't like the answer.

"Definitely not millions," Bart said.

"Doesn't matter," Annja replied. "*I* care. Rao and the

monks care. Other historians and anthropologists will care. They'll care a lot." She narrowed her eyes and frowned. "Are you still upset with me?"

Bart looked shocked. "Why? Because you ran off into danger with a known Russian criminal?"

"If you were upset, maybe we shouldn't have agreed to do dinner."

Bart chuckled. "No, I'm not upset. Maybe still a little worried about you because I know you'll do this sort of thing again."

"It's kind of what I do."

"*I know.* I think I liked it better when I didn't know so much."

"That's not going to happen."

"Yeah, I get that. I also get how important this is to you."

Annja looked at him.

"Benyovszky didn't have a lot of connections outside of his neighborhood, and most of those people didn't know him. You saw what his nephews were like. They didn't care about his death."

Annja saw where he was going now. "But you did."

Bart nodded. "I did. I still do. You've asked me a couple times why I would be a homicide detective. Always getting there too late to save whoever turned up dead. Always dealing with grieving families. I do it because it makes a difference to those families. And I do it because I'm good at what I do. You, at least, have a television show that turns you into a celebrity. Granted, those fans would rather see you chasing after imaginary monsters—"

"So not what I do," Annja interrupted.

"—like the other woman on that show does."

Annja raised her eyebrow. "You've seen Kristie's work?"

Bart shrugged. "A few of the guys around the office are fans of hers."

Annja thought about saying something regarding the other detectives' taste in television, but she settled for another chip instead.

"We both work in fields that we love and respect," Bart

said. "That's all I'm getting at. And I wanted to apologize for not realizing exactly what it is that you do."

"Don't worry about it." Annja smiled his apology away.

"It matters."

"It does, but the friendship we have doesn't rely on what we do. We're friends because we share a lot of other interests—and we make each other laugh." Annja smiled at him again. "You can go a lot of places, meet a lot of people, but there are only a few places and a few people that feel like home." She put her hand on his. "That's what we have, and I wouldn't trade that for anything."

"Me neither."

Annja took her hand back and picked up another chip.

"Tell me something else," Bart said.

"What?"

"Do you get any part of those millions you found? Because I don't remember us discussing that. Maybe some kind of finder's fee?"

"Do you get a bonus for catching a killer?"

"No, but it feels really good."

"Then why would you want anything else?"

Bart picked up a tortilla, rolled it, dipped it in salsa and ate it. "You seriously don't get anything for helping find all that bling?"

Annja grinned. "Well, maybe I get a little of it. A percentage when—and *if*—the temple sells any of it. And I got a keepsake, as well."

"What?"

Annja reached into her backpack and took out the protective case that contained the elephant. She removed the small statue and set it on the table.

"You wanted that?" Bart sounded like he couldn't believe it.

"I did."

A shrewd look spread across his face. "You realize that elephant is a piece of evidence in a murder investigation, right?"

"Benyovszky's murder isn't being investigated anymore. I helped solve the murder, and I even made sure you got the guy who did it. I *delivered* him to you."

"Sure, but—" Bart leveled a forefinger at the elephant, "—that's still evidence."

"I'm paying for dinner tonight," Annja said. "That should buy me some lenience."

"I don't know." Bart pursed his lips.

"I'll throw in dessert."

"Better be a big dessert."

"All the gelato you can eat at Leçce Lecce's in Hawthorne." Hawthorne, New Jersey, was almost an hour away, but the dessert shop was a favorite of theirs, as well.

Bart considered the offer, then finally nodded. "Fine. But not tonight. I'm not going to eat Mexican and then fill up on Italian ice cream. I'll end up hurting myself."

Annja laughed at him, knowing this was what her relationship with him was all about. As someone who grew up in a state home with time out for foster care, friends were important to Annja. Bart was part of her earliest days in New York after she'd made the move from New Orleans. She didn't ever want to lose that.

* * * * *